The Book of Remedies

P.D. NELSON

"When one door of happiness closes, another opens; but often we look so long at the closed door that we do not see the one which has been opened for us."

-Helen Keller

"A successful man is one who can lay a firm foundation with the bricks others have thrown at him."

-David Brinkley

Part I

abre os olnos

"open your eyes"

Chapter-1

...On the morning of September 10, 1629...

DAYBREAK BROKE over the eastern horizon with the wind from the south-west still blowing at a steady 12-18 knots across the starboard quarter of the *Sardam*. The one-hundred-thirty-foot-long square-rigger had now logged fifty-four consecutive days at sea, and still, there was no sign of those wretched islands.

On this morning, Commander Francisco Pelsaert stood tall on the fo'c's'le with both eyes fixed on the ocean haze that formed the shifting horizon. The archipelago of low-lying coral atolls that makes up the agglomeration known as the Houtman Abrolhos Islands due west of *het Zuidland* had caused Pelsaert to become overwhelmingly frustrated at the lingering navigational difficulties he was experiencing in these godforsaken, windswept waters. His 2,600-kilometre return journey from Djarkata, to rescue the three hundred sixteen shipwrecked souls, had been hampered daily.

There were no charts available for the Brouwer route to the Dutch East Indies, and the *Batavia*'s one and now *only* captain, Skipper Ariaen Jacobsz, with his own carefully recorded latitude points of reference, were now obviously proving to be less than accurate. Pelsaert allowed his thoughts to drift with worrying images filling the recesses of his disturbed mind regarding the welfare of the stranded women and children he'd been forced to leave behind over fourteen weeks ago now. He also needed to consider his own personal future. After the loss of the *Batavia* and more than likely the majority of its valuable cargo, notwithstanding the expected loss of life, the burden of responsibility weighed heavily on his guilt-ridden conscience. He thought about his incompetent captain, whose responsibilities certainly did *not* include ramming the ship's hull into a coral reef in the dead of night. His incarceration back in Batavia was a small price to pay for his gross incompetence.

The flagship of the fleet, the *Batavia*'s main hold, was filled with what represented one-fifth of the total wealth of the *Vereenigde Oost-Indische Compagnie* or widely referred to as just the VOC. The twelve chests of gold and silver coins plus countless other valuables were now going to prove pivotal in determining Pelsaert's future with the all-conquering company. He took the time to contemplate the other priceless items he'd been meticulous in concealing from prying eyes. The four bags of jewels and the thousand-year-old, 4th-century Eastern Roman Empire Cameo celebrating Constantine the Great's coronation, and the fact that somehow they were both miraculously able to be saved and brought ashore with the first rescue of one hundred seventy survivors the very next morning after running aground. The other gift destined for the 5th Mughal Emperor of India and a way to gain back the favour of the Mughal Court was more than likely scattered about on the seabed and lost to mankind for eternity.

...September 12...

Cornelis Janszoon had already decided to escape the island, now referred to as Batavia's Graveyard. The crazed *onderkoopman* and second in command to Pelsaert, Jeronimus Cornelisz was each night exercising his self-appointment as *kapitein-generaal,* ordering his fellow mutineers to carry on with their premeditated plan to cull the remaining survivors to just forty hungry mouths to feed. Tonight it would be the sick and the young that would feel the well-honed edges of their orchestrated bloodlust. They were of no use to Jeronimus. Next, it would be the remaining able-bodied men who refused to commit murder and willingly participate in the premeditated raping of the hand-picked women to perform whoring duties like a revolving door. All he needed was enough cutlass-wielding mutineers to prepare and ready themselves to seize the rescuing yacht from Batavia, if at all, any rescue attempt would one day be forthcoming. That now simply rested with Commander Pelsaert's resolve and ability to survive the trip to Djarkata with forty-eight souls on board a single, over-crowded longboat.

Cornelis Janszoon was one of the *Batavia*'s many carpenters, and since the wreck had broken up, he'd been unrelenting in retrieving enough of the floating planks of wood to repair a holed yawl washed up on the rocks on nearby Traitors Island. He already had in his possession the basic tools and some boxes of nails and corking to prepare the yawl to cross the stretch of water separating the mutineers and the soldiers, led by the trustworthy, Wiebbe Hayes. Since Cornelisz had ordered the soldiers to search for food and water in his successful plan to separate them from his own debauched marauders, it was painfully obvious to Janszoon that they had indeed found both.

Anneken Hardens sat huddled in a state of terrifying fear on Seals' Island. She was nursing her sick and wailing six-year-old daughter, singing a whispered hymn she could recite word-for-word from her days attending church in Amsterdam with her God-fearing mother. The smell of stewing seal blubber wafted through the make-shift-shelter made from a yardarm with a length of the ship's sail still attached, stretched between two hastily built pancake-shaped coral walls. She was still coming to grips with the father of her only child, her very own husband, and his decision to join the mutineers in a feeble attempt to first save his own skin and hopefully secure the wellbeing of his family. It made no sense to Anneken for him to leave his wife and child alone and to their own limited devices.

This was to be Janszoon's second trip to Hayes Island, since dusk had fallen that lay about ten kilometres to the west. The previous trip had successfully resulted in his dearest friend, a bulbous man known to all as the Fat Trumpeter and five others, arriving safely into the fold of Wiebbe Hayes and his unarmed soldiers. Apart from the assured safety of the abandoned Harden woman and her child, Cornelis also wanted to gather a small wooden and brass chest full with coins salvaged from the dying wreck and an unusually shaped polished wooden ball with a handle attached that he found rolling around the floor of the commander's private cabin. If anything, it certainly sparked Janszoon's interest as a carpenter and a man that had whittled and worked his mastery on a variety of different types of timber from all over Europe. This was different from anything he'd seen previously, and the sheer weight of the object was perplexing and beckoned further scrutiny.

Cornelis Janszoon allowed the wind to push the bow of his small yawl onto the broken coral and soft sand. He then strode purposefully without breaking into a stride that might attract the attention of the three men he could see leaving the *kapitein-generaal's* grand tent that was almost a replica of the Great Cabin, previously occupied by Captain Ariaen Jacobsz, on board the *Batavia*. He opened the rear flap of Anneken's makeshift camp and motioned for her to listen but remain silent with a finger to his dried and cracked lips.

"Gather just your most precious and essential belongings, Mrs Hardens, and prepare to meet me at the small bay I showed you previously. Please, for both you and your child's sake, you must move like a ghost, for there are men on their way that mean you harm and quieten your sick daughter once and for all." Janszoon's tone and raw honesty caused Anneken to harbour her own feelings of heightened anxiety.

David Zevanck, Lenart van Os, Hans Jacobsz and Jan Hendricxsz were eager to please Jeronimus as they shared wine from what they proudly called the 'killing cup', which had become a prerequisite to an ensuing murderous foray. The sounds of coral shifting-underfoot from their wooden *klompens* could be heard heading towards Anneken's scant shelter. She dipped her finger into a mixture of wine and ditto bread, then eased it into her daughter's mouth. The sound of her child quietly suckling was no louder than the breeze that swept over the baron coral landscape. Anneken lifted the rear flap and silently melted into the black void of the moonless night to her prearranged rendezvous point.

Cornelis Janszoon was about to start his own game of Russian roulette that might very easily cost him his life. He headed in the exact opposite direction, towards the water's edge. The four men eyed their defenceless prey with a fixated lust in their warped sense of duty to please their bloodthirsty leader, Jeronimus. Jan Hendricxsz slowed and sliced a vertical hole in the billowing canvas sail with his razor-sharp sword. He peered inside and was angered not to be met by a cowering mother with her crying child cradled in her arms. And he knew exactly why.

"That snivelling Janszoon is as weak as piss," he cursed out loud, before joining in the continuing hunt.

The four men soon had successfully corralled their first victim into the knee-deep water, and Zevanck was first to raise his sword high into the air to land the first lusty blow. His blunted steel failed to pierce the skin along the top of Janszoon's right shoulder blade. His time of late had been predominately occupied with the freely available sex-on-demand now available all day—every day.

Cornelis inched backwards with eyes straining to identify his attacker's next move. His first instincts were beckoning for him to head for deeper water, but like so many other sailors—he could not swim. Hendricxsz gripped the handle of his sword and clubbed the butt into the side of their defenceless victim's head, forcing Cornelis to drop below the waterline. Cornelis Janszoon clawed his way with open hands along the uneven coral bottom, ignoring the painful scrapes and cuts. Zevanck swung blindly again and again into the shallow water. Time after time his blade came back clean as the injured Janszoon remained in a motionless, frozen thaw under the water with his lungs filled with air—and waited.

The sound of fifteen cabin boys running to the opposite end of Seals' Island combined with the screams of the many other fleeing women and children was a disturbing but life-saving distraction. The four men slowly turned and refocused their attention on the job at hand. The in-discriminative culling at will, without mercy, in ridding themselves of the unnecessary extra mouths to feed.

Cornelis had survived, and under cover of a pitch-black night, he moved his legs in a slow crawl, careful not to break the surface of the water and draw attention to himself from the escaping boys. It was now a matter of survival for the quick thinking with the strength of a man's resolve his only weapon to see out this terror-filled night.

He recited under a hushed breath, "God, please have mercy on those poor children's souls," while he fingered the holy cross that hung across his chest, all the while continuing to set a steady pace.

Anneken was pushed up hard against the blind-side of the beached yawl when Cornelis limped around the last rocky point. He helped the mother place her child inside the bow section, then asked for her help to push the wooden hull through the small shore slop. They needed to negotiate a long narrow channel before rounding the northern end of Seals' Island and then head west towards Little Pigeon Island to pick up his stashed booty.

The wind was from the south-west, allowing Cornelis to set a full sail as he headed a few points east of north. His tack to port was soon followed by another as the sails began luffing, slowing the boat until the sound of coral scraping on the hull was his call to action. Cornelis tied off the halyard. Then he dared to light his lantern before he eased his body over the side.

He tapped his passenger on the shoulder. Anneken turned to face him. "Mrs Hardens, the water is only shallow. I ask you to join me and hold tight to the anchor rope to keep the boat in a steady position. I shouldn't be more than a few minutes."

Anneken slid from the bench seat over the gunwale and watched Cornelis fade into the darkness towards a rising rocky outcrop with a steep vertical crag away in the distance with the anchor rope held firmly in her grasp. The wind was now blowing over 20 knots, and the tops of the lapping waves were starting to break, leaving an inquisitive trailing phosphorous wake. Anneken was struggling to hold steady the pitching yawl, and her daughter was again in the throes of another misery-filled cry for the basic necessities of life . . . Food and water.

Cornelis returned with his two prized possessions, which represented to him at least the one and perhaps his only chance of a decent life, be it somewhat slender if they were ever to make it off these abominable islands, alive. He stowed his cargo for'ard and prepared his two passengers for what he knew might be an impossible task, with the strength of the south-westerly winds gaining in strength as each minute passed.

The young girl was hastily shifted inside the safety of a small nook located at the bow to offer scant protection from the elements with the aid of a piece of thick canvas. He steered the yawl into a broad reach and allowed the jib, main and mizzen sails to fill. The strengthening gusts were testing the strength of each halyard with creaking groans, and he knew he needed to reduce his sail before his next tack to port to navigate his way past another lump of exposed coral. It was a choice between the devil and the deep dark sea, each enticing them to the same perilous destination.

Anneken was still attempting to subdue her child when Cornelis shifted his position to reach out and then prepare to unleash the boom safety rope from the cleat located on the mainmast. It was out of his reach. Cornelis considered asking Mrs Hardens to assist, but thought better of it.

That was when he made a fatal sailing error.

Cornelis let go of the rudder, leaned forward and unhitched the lifeline. The aft mizzen filled with clean air, and the yawl suddenly, and without warning, slewed sideways. The mainsail billowed, causing the boom halyard to slip through his fingers. He gripped tightly as the rope burn caused his palm to pang with a scorching affliction of intense heat. He was forced to let go, causing the boom to swing violently from port to starboard. The splintering sound of wood and skull bone coming together was followed by a guttural moan. Cornelis was a dead man standing, his eyes rolled back inside his head, and like a felled tree, he simply fell overboard, and floated away on the tide.

The high-pitched scream of a woman closeted in fear fell on deaf ears while Anneken sat spellbound in total meltdown. She reached out and grabbed the boom halyard, then re-hitched it to its cleat before shifting and with both hands; she held on tight to the tiller arm. Anneken had no idea what just happened, in which direction she was now heading, or how she could possibly survive this night alone with a sick child. She held tight to the rudder and kept true to her new course. The wind was now blowing hard over her right shoulder, but at least the yawl was moving on an even keel and not threatening to capsize.

Hours passed with every bone in Anneken's body chattering with the chill of the wind lashing the tops of each rise and fall of the following sea. She dared not risk looking back. Her body's survival mechanism to generate any form of natural warmth was losing its unspoken battle. With one hand navigating and the other bailing out bucket after bucket of water, she seemed to be maintaining an even balance between survival and being swamped. Her daughter's welfare was all that kept her focused.

The swell was relentless as the bow was continually jostled high into the air, then a second later the pointed bow would slide down the face of the wave, nosediving into the waiting trough's thirsty swallow. Anneken wanted to feel the warmth of her only child; the steady heartbeat close to her bosom, but knew if she left the rudder for even a second, it would surely spell their demise. *At least she seemed to be asleep.* The shadowed silhouette of a rising moon behind the cover of shifting clouds told her she was heading east, and she knew this was the same direction Commander Pelsaert headed in his search for fresh drinking water. Anneken allowed her eyes to close and started to recite The Lord's Prayer, over and over. *Our Father, who aren't in heaven . . .*

Her freezing body started to resemble a human iceberg. Both her shoulders were hunched with two hands locked in a frozen clamp. She slowly opened one eye and was greeted by a haze of shimmering blue light with a border of burnt orange emerging over a horizon that could be mistaken for land—tall, upright and less than welcoming.

She cleared her eyes of the stinging salt water. With each swell negotiated, the landscape became more vivid, and now it seemed to materialise as something real. The sounds of breakers crashing into the solid surface of the coast were enough to make her cry inside. She had no knowledge of sailing or what was necessary to land a boat successfully on an unfriendly shoreline.

Had both my sick daughter and I survived this night just to meet our maker at the first hint of daylight? She prayed she was wrong.

Anneken changed course and followed the coast north when a divine light seemed to point towards a break in the reef, reflecting from a steep wall of limestone below a mountainous red bluff. To the left was a dry riverbed of white sand that was in stark contrast to the red soil that followed the lay of the land.

Anneken steered the yawl towards the only gap in the broken water that was enticing her into its unwelcome boil with each swell pushing her closer. She wanted to lean forward and feel for her daughter, still asleep under the scant dry shelter offered by the cut-down sail to act as feeble protection. She noticed a slight movement under the canvas, which was all the reassurance she needed to confirm her daughter was still holding on by a thread to her frail life while her vice-like-grip held steady on the tiller arm.

Anneken aimed the bow for the only spot void of any white caps and held tight to the railing with her free hand. The entire hull was slowly lifted into the sky, higher and higher. She craned her neck to see past the mast and ballooning sail. The yawl slewed sideways down the face of a wave and was in danger of tipping again. Anneken shifted her body as a counterweight. Seawater was now spilling over the port-side gunwale, and she leant as far back as her body would allow. Her bailing bucket and some coiled rope were swept into the maelstrom of the churning ocean and disappeared in an instant.

Please, God, save us from this hell.

A large flat-surfaced rock appeared from under the backwash, Anneken could see the seaweed and oysters attached to the pot-holed surface. It was solid ground, and that was good enough for her. She pulled hard on the tiller and braced herself for a heavy landing. The genoa sail ripped free and flew away on the wind like strewn tissue paper. The loose halyards swung wildly; she ducked her head as the last wave prepared to dump the yawl unceremoniously to its final end. The bow made the first contact, sending a shudder through the hull. The smaller aft mast snapped clean off and toppled over the stern. Anneken let go of the tiller for the first time in what seemed like days and allowed herself to throw her body weight forward onto the canvas to protect her child from being swept overboard.

Within an instant, she came to a sudden halt as the yawl teetered and layover to one side. She raised her eyes above the wooden rail to see the next swell pick the yawl up and gently drop it on the only patch of sand twenty feet farther inland.

The hand of God, her faith reminded her.

The last wave in the set failed to reach the beached craft, and now the yawl was high and dry. Anneken stood upright and removed the protective sail from her sick child. She screamed and reeled backwards, falling to the ground as the tail of an escaping ships' rat found refuge on dry land. Both her eyes widened as her teeth chattered while she absorbed her daughter's greyish skin colour, her lips were a mixture of purple and blue, and when she attempted to cradle the child in her mother's loving arms, she was as rigid as the broken masthead.

...*September 14*...

Commander Pelsaert felt a wave of vacillating emotions sweep over him as he recognised the summit of the highest island come into plain view. Making ready to drop anchor, he could only hope and pray the stranded survivors were in God's hands. On a nearby island, west of the shipwrecked *Batavia*, a plume of trailing smoke wafted from the distant skyline like a bent corkscrew. The sheer relief of seeing the first evidence of survivors was a sight for sore eyes.

The last scattered remnants of the VOC's flagship was in full view for all to see as the crew of the *Sardam* bustled for a position to gain a bird's-eye view of the remaining carnage. Like a macabre three dimensional painting, it was a stark reminder of that fateful night when the *Batavia* ran aground and struck Morning Reef on June 4, over four months ago now.

Pelsaert noted the *Batavia* had seemed to have broken up under the relentless avalanche that was the swell and incessant wind, which appeared to be an almost everyday occurrence in this part of the world. He issued his first orders to the *highboatswain*, ordering the *uppersteersman* to turn the *Sardam* into the wind. The sails were furled from the mizzen, main and the foremasts before being stowed as the anchor peg was knocked out. The loud roar of, "Anchors Away," resounded from the bow over the working quarterdeck, bringing the boat to a dead stop as preparations were made to lower the longboat into the water.

The tallest island was still two miles to their south. With barrels of water, wine and a generous amount of ditto bread at the ready, Pelsaert ordered the oarsmen to head for the nearest coral beachhead. His imagination was creating disconsolate portrayals about the general health of the stranded men, women and children. Soon he would be horrified at what awaited him on his arrival.

Wouter Loos and Jan Pelgrom de Bye van Bemmel watched on intently from the neighbouring high island as the longboat's oars stroked the rippled surface. They could clearly see a handful of armed soldiers, and the all too familiar face of the stricken *Batavia*'s maligned commander from their distant vantage point, as the bow slid onto the broken coral that made up the beachhead.

Both men paused while exchanging concerned glances. "Wouter, what did I tell you about Commander Pelsaert's resolve, he is a very determined man. I said he would return."

"Yes, you did. Surely a remarkable feat of sailing. Now, finally, there will be some law and order restored, and he can set about handing out some rough justice to Cornelisz and his deranged accomplices—which include both of us," Loos replied.

"Yes, Wouter, and let's not forget the gold and silver sitting on the ocean floor. I question both his, and the VOC's motives for their return journey to this remote wilderness."

Commander Pelsaert stepped onto the small island and surveyed the surrounding landscape, then beckoned the obvious question, "Where is everyone?" He was alerted to the familiar face of Wiebbe Hayes rowing a mastless yawl around the southern point.

Hayes sprang ashore and ran with a hastened step. Pelsaert remembered Wiebbe Hayes from the time they weighed anchor in Amsterdam. The Hayes of that time was of sallow complexion and a slight frame which had not experienced the heat of a southern sun. Now the man running towards him was sun-scorched brown in skin colour and looked to be as strong as a bull, dressed in a combination of rags and some kind of animal fur, while his feet seemed to be bound with strips of ragged cloth to offer some protection from the sharp coral.

"*Welkom-Welkom,* Commander!" he cried out. "Thank God you have arrived safely, but please—you must return immediately, for there is a party of treacherous scoundrels approaching from the south. They have in their possession a fully manned sloop. You are in danger, sir. These men are armed and evidently seek to overthrow you. They have it in their minds to seize your yacht." His apprehension was clearly visible through his sunburnt scowl.

Wiebbe Hayes was a veteran soldier, and a trusted man. Pelsaert needed to guarantee the safety of the *Sardam* at all costs and returned without haste to make preparations for an expected premeditated assault.

***

The stiff 18-knot breeze filled the mainsail and pushed the wooden-hulled sloop through the water at a steady 3-5 knots as it made sail towards the anchored *Sardam*. Jan Hendricxsz was at the helm. He was adamant about placing himself, and his own four, armed accomplices squarely between the shoreline and the rescuing yacht. There could be no chance of escape if they were to commandeer this vessel and set sail for the freedom of the open ocean. A life of pirating on board the captured *Sardam* awaited the entire group of mutineers, upon this very day's success.

After attempting for the third time, without success, to free their captured ringleader, Jeronimus Cornelisz, now being held prisoner by the competent and newly appointed leader of the stranded soldiers, Wiebbe Hayes, the remaining boatload of mutineers, now led by Jan Hendricxsz rallied and made a veiled half-hearted attempt to first welcome, and then board the *Sardam* under the guise of desperate and stranded survivors with only treacherous thoughts of mutiny fermenting silently in each man's mind. They planned to woo the crew to Batavia's Graveyard to celebrate the arrival of Commander Pelsaert, and then after plying their rescuers with wine, food, song and good fervour, and while in a drunken stupor, slay each and every man who refused to join the mutiny.

With ten loaded muskets and a cannon at the ready, pointing directly at the arriving mutineers, Pelsaert quickly quelled the hastily orchestrated attempt to overthrow the yacht and gathered each and all the ransacking and pillaging crooks, holding them captive to await trial and explain their deprecating behaviour. Jan Hendricxsz immediately confessed to personally murdering, with others, over twenty fellow survivors—women and children included. Jeronimus Cornelisz and Jan Evertsz were confirmed as the ringleaders, the instigators of the mutinous plot that resulted in the wholesale rape of women and the slaughter of innocent people.

While contemplating the fate of each guilty man, Pelsaert sent his captain, with the popular Fat Trumpeter, to search the other neighbouring islands, and to fetch a barrel of vinegar he spotted on the furthest island to the north. The crew and boat failed to return after yet another wild storm ripped through the Abrolhos, stirring the ocean into a whipping frenzy. The strength was of such ferocity; it caused the *Sardam* to slip its anchor.

The commander's patience had run its course. He was still recovering from a previous lingering illness, wasting no time dilly dallying, he pressed on with more crucial matters. Perplexities that needed to be dealt with personally, like applying some law and order plus some swift sentences to be handed out to the surviving rebels.

The trials, confessions and the final executions took place on nearby Seals' Island, where wooden galleys were erected to carry out the orders of the VOC. Jeronimus Cornelisz, Jan Evertsz and Jan Hendricxsz, along with six other misguided murderers, had either one or both their hands removed with a swift swing from a hammer and chisel, then strung up and hung from their necks, until dead. The remainder would be taken as prisoners back to plead their cases in front of Governor-General Coen after arriving back in Batavia.

On November 15, 1629, the *Sardam* weighed anchor and set sail for the unknown mainland pushed along by the prevailing south- by south-west wind under a cloud of fine weather. Pelsaert sailed until smoke trails from cooking fires could be seen rising from the shoreline about seven miles to the east. He considered the unlikely possibility it may be his lost captain sending a signal only to watch the smoke dwindle away. With the favourable conditions and the smallish swell on this day, Pelsaert saw fit to carry out the final sentence for two of the delinquents still on board.

Pelsaert considered the future of Jan Pelgrom de Bye. After pleading for his life to be spared, he contemplated the cabin boy's young age. Pelsaert asked his boatswain to prepare a flat-bottomed yawl. Wouter Loos and Jan Pelgrom, with their futures having already been decided, the incensed commander took his own pleasure in advising the two men of their gloomy fate.

Commander Pelsaert made his decision as a fitting punishment for their participation in the beastly behaviour while marooned on Batavia's Graveyard. The eighteen-year-old cabin boy Jan Pelgrom de Bye van Bemmel and the twenty-four-year-old soldier, Wouter Loos, were to be cast adrift and make their peace in the hands of God.

Pelsaert stood to attention on the quarterdeck and bid a farewell. "God grant that you may stretch your services to the company, and may God grant you a good outcome to know once and for certain what happens on these lands." Pelsaert then noted in his diary the latitude of 27 degrees 51 minutes.

Both the convicted men were given the basic necessities of life. Pelsaert handed Loos a compass, and a handwritten chart, showing a tall bluff where fresh water was plentiful. He also offered some trinkets, including some children's toys, mirrors and coloured beads.

"Sail your way east towards the brackish water, make your acquaintance with the local black men. A man's luck is to be found in strange places for you death-deserving wrongdoers," Pelsaert conveyed.

Commander Francisco Pelsaert had decided the time had come to leave behind these harrowing windswept and brutishly uncivilised lands to set sail for the return voyage to Batavia.

Loos and Jan Pelgrom gathered their thirty days of rations, and were cast adrift from the faster moving *Sardam*. With a favourable breeze and flat seas, they managed to row towards an elevated white sandhill that resembled a smaller version of the White Cliffs of Dover.

With only a light swell, the older and stronger Loos was able to negotiate the small natural entrance and ease the small yawl onto a sandy spit. They moved their meagre belongings inland about a half a mile and went about making their first land-based shelter, constructing a lean-to from long-dead trees with a thatched roof by stripping some branches from the local scrub near a permanent waterhole. These two marooned men from the *Batavia*, which now lay in tattered ruins on the bottom of Morning Reef, were now destined to be the first unwitting permanent European residents in the land to be known as Australia.

The Yamatji people were indigenous Aboriginals and nomadic wanderer's, travelling on foot-alone, the vast distances between waterholes, up and down the arid coast and the hinterlands of Western Australia in search of food. All were in abundance if you knew what to look for in this far-flung, unforgiving and unchartered country as the tribe followed the weather and nature's call to provide for their own mortal needs.

Jan and Loos were to attempt their first night of sleep in a foreign land as marooned convicted criminals. Loos was first to be stirred awake by the bizarre sounds of unfamiliar birds perched amongst the tall trees as they swayed with the strength of the ocean breeze. The following evening a first approach was made by a group of four blackfellas, including a youngish-looking woman. Guessing any of their ages was an impossible task.

At first sight, they looked like woeful people. The men were straight bodied, tall and lithe, which accentuated a large skull with heavy set brows. Their eyelids seemed forever to be half-closed to keep the flies from swarming on the moist parts of their sullen eyes, which resulted in them needing to lift their heads, as if spotting a bird, to view anything from a distance. Their hair seemed to be predominately the colour of burnt ashen coals, short and tightly wound.

Loos looked at his only companion. "Not one of this group could be considered as having handsome features," he shared with Jan.

A slightly more attractive teenage girl offered a smile from her full mouth, revealing a set of strong white teeth through her thick lips and a wide gape. A stalemate had formed between these men from contrasting cultures as they continued to hold ground from a curious distance. A carcase of a dead animal was laid to rest with a throwing action, landing with a dusty *thud* near Jan's feet. The Aboriginal elder intimated an eating action with his hands to mouth. Loos bent over and retrieved the furry animal with a long tail, muscular hind legs and a pair of smaller front arms with nailed paws.

Two tall-looking elders with long greying beards and leather-like skin the colour of cindered charcoal stood resolutely with one foot resting on the other knee, almost posing while leaning on their long spears with a small wooden shield held in front. They wore just the rind from a tree, like a girdle with some loose leaves and grasses to cover their nakedness. They didn't look menacing from afar, but fear ran amuck within the worrying minds of each white man.

The smiling face of the less than beautiful gin returned two days later, with what may have been her mother standing to one side. Both women were waving their arms and hands to indicate for the two marooned men to follow. Loos and Jan studied each other's facial expression with a nonsensical gaze for confirmation of what the other man may be thinking. With their dwindling supplies and no means or knowledge of how they could possibly survive this harsh land, they packed up their camp and followed from a safe distance.

The burning sun slowly set each evening over the western horizon for a further two days. Loos and Jan kept up the stiff pace in earnest, passing around a long lagoon set in from the beachhead which on high tide and with a decent swell, the waves would crash over the sandbar and mix with the freshwater pools behind. The red soil of mother earth was their bed, and the heavens were their canopy, camping next to the freshwater holes that this tribe knew well enough. There were no fences to negotiate or any livestock that needed caring. Their minds boggled when they cast first eyes on a giant egg laid from a bird bigger than any man, and could not be matched for pace.

The days were blistering hot with a stiff sea breeze, a welcome relief each and almost every mid-morning. The land changed drastically as they tracked farther north, with the sand giving way to a rock-strewn landscape with high cliffs, dropping vertically to the wild ocean below. There seemed to be no sign of any grazing land as they approached what looked to be their first river crossing. That afternoon they set up camp in a dry creek bed, and spent the sunset fishing, removing their fill of oysters that were in abundance. Jan followed the rocky peninsula towards a group of crystal clear blue holes and was dumbfounded to be confronted with a beached yawl sitting well above the high watermark over the next inlet. He yelled for Wouter to follow his lead and ran like the wind to see who might be about.

The craft was damaged beyond repair, and the smell of a rotting corpse filled the air with a foul stench. Jan followed a trail of discarded clothes and found an old sail he recognised as originating from the sunken *Batavia*. He stepped over a sand dune to be facing a half-clothed adult woman still cradling a young child in her arms. She was seated with her back, parked up against the white-knuckled trunk of a bent tree. The crabs and feral animals had done a good job removing the eyes and most of the stomach organs. The sun-dried and knotted hair was the only real indication they were both females.

Wouter Loos arrived at the damaged yawl and started emptying the contents onto the soft sand nearby. There was a half-full barrel of fresh water, a small bag with some children's clothing inside, and a trumpet. Loos placed it to his lips and failed to raise a note as he blew and spat into the damaged mouthpiece. Loos dragged clear another cut-out section of sail from a small space in the bow, and his eyes lit up when a small chest tipped over and spilt its silvery contents over the wooden-planked hull.

"The VOC's reason for its very existence," Loos shared with the younger Jan. "Coins and some jewels, Jan," he explained excitedly.

"And where do you think you will spend your first gilder, Loos? Not anywhere around here, I can assure you of that," the young cabin boy wanted to remind his older companion.

Loos refilled the half-empty chest and then noticed an odd-shaped ball made of what looked to be wood. He pried it from its trapped position and held it by an unusual handle. "So, what is this, then?" He raised it above shoulder height to offer a better perspective and to seek an answer to his own question.

"Open it Loos and cast a look inside," Jan suggested.

Loos placed the ball down on the chalky sand and rolled it many times. "There is no seam, no opening I can see, Jan."

Jan stepped around the stern of the yawl and offered his expert advice. His scrawny body and boyish, muscle-free-build struggled to lift the heavy wood above his head, but soon he was in agreement to the fact there seemed to be no way to see what may lie inside this polished, spherical-shaped lump of timber. An image of a man seated cross-legged with both his open palms holding what may have been planet Earth with another strange symbol was a backdrop that neither man had seen before. He picked up the discarded trumpet and recognised it as the one Cornelis the fat trumpeter was so fond of on their journey from Amsterdam. He decided to keep it as a memento of happier times while on board the *Batavia*.

The sounds of laughing birds early the next day was a sign they were to continue their way north, across a wide but slow-moving river until the landscape slowly changed, all the while following the tribal elders, gins and children; all barefoot and almost stark naked.

That very next morning Jan walked alone while following a worn path north for a few miles. The white sands and parched red clay that was their inland camp soon gave way to the rugged and rocky hard ground that formed the coastline as far as the eye could see. The swell had increased considerably and was pounding the rising cliff face in a relentless show of strength.

Jan was mindful of their two prized possessions, but the combined weight and the increasing interest from some black men was cause for concern. Jan scanned his surroundings with those very thought's occupying his mind. His curiosity was aroused by a small growth of trees with their white trunks bent over like an old man with a walking stick from the unrelenting wind.

Fascinating, he thought.

Jan looked out from his higher vantage point and noticed the water spouts from a pod of whales near to the shore. Mothers with their calves close by, heading in a northerly direction. He found some shade and answered his thirst with a fill of water when suddenly a corkscrew fountain of salted mist burst from the smoothed rock surface, showering his exposed skin with a cooling spray. It resembled the spouting whales as they meandered through the ocean, yonder.

The sun appeared from the shadows of white clouds, and suddenly in a dazzling display close by, a scattering of glittering quartz and green-tinted granite sparkled like diamonds. The sun's reflection unveiled a curious display of contrasting colours against the strewn boulders, sandstone pinnacles and deep crags bordered by needle-sharp pillars of limestone. A closer inspection revealed a blowhole from what was an underwater ledge. As each mountain of seawater rolled in from the untamed ocean, a soaring spray of salt water would rocket up a small canyon and spiral into the air in an awesome visual display of its raw power.

Jan sat and clocked the time between the arrival of each set of waves, then lay his body flat and peered down into the dark abyss that was the vertical hole. As the water dissipated, it revealed a man-sized natural cave below. The entrance looked large enough for Jan to drop his small body size inside. He ran back to their camp and summoned Loos to help heave the heavily weighted chest, and the wooden-handled sphere back to the blowhole on a hastily put together stretcher made from some fallen branches secured with some rope. Like carrying a wounded soldier in the field of battle, they lugged their only ticket back to civilisation and placed each item down at the base of the bent tree.

Jan kept his eyes peeled on the ocean below while counting under his breath. The largest swells were arriving in sets of four or five. He then lowered himself into the dark void. He felt with both his dangling feet for a ledge and a firm stance. "And now, Loos, light up that fire stick then pass me down the chest first, and be quick about it."

Loos lowered the brass-framed chest by rope, while Jan held it tight into his open arms. With the flame held out in front, he stepped his way over the uneven surface while moving farther inside the cave. It was bigger than he originally thought. He turned a corner and could see a rocky shelf sitting well above shoulder height. He swept his hand and felt the surface to be dry. Jan placed the chest carefully at his feet and returned to gather the wooden planet-shaped ball. Jan stopped and started his recount, waiting for the hole to blow again before returning to the base of the tight point of entry. He looked up to see Loos holding the rounded object by its own handle. "Also, Loos, pass me my shoulder bag, I have the skinned hide from that strange-looking hopping animal."

Jan hurried back to the cave's end with the mysterious wooden ball, then he pulled from his bag the salted hide. Previously, he had painstakingly carved with a knife both men's names, the year 1629 and a reference to the *Batavia*. Jan placed the hide over the top of the ledge, picked up the chest and slid it in as far as his arms would reach. He then secured the spherical-shaped object with a length of rope around an outlay of rock that jutted out like a man's extended arm. Jan was eyeing-off his handy work before a bellowing roar could be heard from behind and below. He braced himself and watched while leaning against the damp cave wall as the next set of waves arrived like a swollen river bursting its banks. The sound of the ocean swell spiralling up the hollow cliff face was deafening. Loos looked down from above as his face was soaked by the rising gush, causing his hat to shoot up into the air like a hovering eagle as he reeled backwards, struggling to hold a firm footing.

Jan counted again and then shouted back to Loos to help him out from the underground cavern. The two men spent the next hour rolling a large boulder using two sturdy limbs from the only trees visible in any direction. Foot by foot they rolled it closer and then positioned it over the hole, like a giant stopper on a port barrel.

The Yamatji tribe was about forty strong. They made camp near another waterhole twenty days' walk farther to the north, where they stayed for some time. A large portion of the coastal bluff had fallen away which allowed access to the ocean down a hundred-foot cliff face where a bounty of catchable and varying size fish awaited, weather and wind permitting.

Jan had formed an inquisitive relationship with the more than interested *wurrinya*. Soon they would be sharing bodily pleasures to the detriment of the older Loos. He was unhappy with this new arrangement, and he wasn't alone.

Loos sat around their small campfire and cut away a slice of meat from an ash-covered young rock wallaby. He looked over at Jan, sitting opposite with his newly chosen companion, both sharing a fallen stump. "Loos, what will become of us? What does the future hold for two shipwrecked and abandoned sailors in a land where we don't belong?" he asked his older and wiser companion. "The treasures we both stashed in that dry hollowed-out underground chamber, at considerable risk to ourselves. How will that be any of help to us now?" Jan wanted to understand.

Loos finished his chew before replying, "Jan, if we are ever to be successful in returning someday to retrieve and enjoy the proceeds of our good fortune, soon this information will dwindle from our memories and then be lost forever. If ever a passing ship offers our safe passage to the East Indies, this may well be our only assurance of survival?"

"Yes, a map of some sorts, Loos," Jan suggested.

Jan pulled from his small hessian shoulder bag a piece of dried bark with some charcoaled words etched on the surface. "You remember how I found the cave hidden from sight under that hissing blowhole with the three jaded wind-swept trees?"

"Yes, Jan. It was like a divining light was showing a path from the smoothed surface of that near-vertical small white limestone rock face. You spotted it first if you remember?"

"Yes, Loos, you have reminded me many a time now, I am truly a genius," he gestured, with a dismissing look ingrained over his sunburnt face.

"Well, I have recorded the location using symbols. From an early age, both my father and I often played a game, a bit like hide-n-seek," Jan confirmed.

"Yes, I know of this frolic. What is it you propose, Jan?" Loos answered with a renewed interest.

"Our futures are unsure, Loos, we both know that now. Our lives can be always remembered in mystique esteem if we can leave a trickle of information for others to follow in our footsteps. We may somehow live out the remainder of our desolate existence with the knowledge that someday our names will forever be recorded in the annals of history. Something for our families back home to cling onto as a reminder of our good intentions."

"You mean a treasure map where X marks the spot? I like your thinking, Jan," Loos replied excitedly.

"Yes, Wouter, but on something that will stand the test of time."

Life was becoming unbearable on this unforgiving land. The oppressive heat on any given day was never-ending. The wind was a constant burden as it swept in from the sea. Their lives had become a mere existence, and Loos was becoming filled with a disdained self-worth with his increasingly lonesome self as Jan spent more and more time with his black-skinned bride whose name was apparently Jibbiji. His discontent festered inside like a hungry tumour, growing as each miserable day ended in the same monotonous regularity.

An elder from the tribe had on more than one occasion shown his displeasure with this clash of white and black. Loos suggested to Jan that she may be this man's daughter and to tread carefully. "As white Dutch European people, we represent a lingering danger, which installs fear of the unknown to these deeply suspicious tribal leaders," he wanted to explain to his younger counterpart.

A show of strength the following day was a catalyst for what was soon to follow. Loos noticed as Jan and his new illiterate whore walked together towards the vertical cliff face that was a stepping stone to the never-ending swirl of the ocean, over one hundred feet below. The disgruntled shimmering black-skinned elder, with his long spear in full view, stood and followed the hand-holding couple to the edge of the precipice with a stone-faced glare. In his native tongue, he started to berate the unsuspecting pair. His body language was clearly portraying a feeling of pent-up frustration and anger.

Loos alluded to the possible outcome. *This was not going to end well*, he considered with a suspicious scowl.

His natural soldiering instincts coerced him to occupy a position nearer to the squabble, so he placed himself between the younger Jan and the threatening Aboriginal men.

In a quick action, the powerful arm of the black protagonist lifted into the air and let fly with his honed weapon of choice. The spear wobbled as it cut a path through the air, a slight humming noise could be heard humming above the sounds of a thousand buzzing flies. As a trained soldier, Loos was quick to react. Instinctively, he stepped in front of the young cabin boy to block the path of the incoming spear. The sharpened flint-end entered the flesh below his collarbone. He stood in both shock and surprise while trying to disengage the lance.

Jan was horrified as his screaming black partner ran to take shelter. Loos bent over and picked up a medium-sized boulder and made a run towards the poised spear chucker, who was now reaching down to his left side to withdraw a bulbous-shaped mallee root, held tight in his small loincloth. Loos launched himself as adrenaline surged through his veins, hell-bent on revenge. Time spent as an alien in a scorched and desolate land had taken its toll. He had reached a point of no return and wanted to inflict his deep-seated retribution to quell this unprovoked attack on a defenceless boy.

He thrust the rounded rock into the thick skull of his attacker. The black man was forced backwards, landing heavily on the bleached jagged rocks that littered the landscape like marbles. The dull sound of a human skull cracking open like an eggshell was soon followed by a gush of blood, pooling on the dried red clay. A constant swarm of curious flies rapidly descended to snack on the free meal.

Jan snapped out of his near frozen state of disbelief and ran over to lend some assistance as Loos staggered in bent circles. Another spear-chucker from afar lined up Loos' wandering torso and launched a second, shorter spear from the resin-covered handle of his woomera made from mulga wood. The sharpened quartz tip pierced a gaping hole in the breastplate of his chest. He staggered around for no more than a few seconds in an ungainly saunter, before crumbling to the ground, where his body quivered in its final death throes as his lungs filled with the flooding blood that ran through his veins.

Wouter Loos now lay dead.

Jan was mortified as Jibbiji rushed over to protect him from further harm. She stood between her man until the gathering tribe installed some calm over the tension-filled moment. Cool heads prevailed as the Aboriginal men gathered up the dead body of their elder and disappeared, not returning for some days.

Jan went about finding a suitable final resting place for his dead friend. This day the swell and wind allowed him access to the collapsed section of the steep cliff face. He located a small hollowed out chunk of rock and placed Loos' body inside, then covered him with a large hide from a slain kangaroo. He spent hours gathering rocks to place over the corpse to offer scant protection from the scavenging feral animals that were in abundance each night. The next three days, with just the root from a dead tree as a hammer and a sharpened piece of quartz, he laboured relentlessly, carving into a three-foot slab of limestone a headstone for Loos.

Jan cast a satisfied eye over the completed inscription, wishing the day would arrive when the hidden seamless wooden globe and his chest full of coins and jewels might one day be rediscovered. If it shaped to be of significant importance, he could take that to his grave in the dying hope his family back home could remember him in a proud recall of his life.

Five days later, the tribe packed up their limited belongings and made preparations to move on towards the south-east. Jibbiji, with her mother and two brothers, made their own plans to head north to meet up with the Spirit Bay Tribes. She didn't trust the elders with the safekeeping of her new white partner.

Jan made his last visit to the scantily prepared gravesite of his friend Wouter Loos and laid a flower. As a lasting memento, he placed three coins across the top of the headstone in lasting memory of the only other European to make permanent landfall in the Great Southern Land.

He looked out over the expanse of the wild Indian Ocean and bid a final good riddance to the islands that would be forever remembered by the ghosts of the former survivors of the VOC ship the *Batavia*.

Chapter-2

...1400 hours November 17, 1941
due west of the Zuytdorp Cliffs...

THE JAPANESE Imperial Navy submarine, *I-124* was a Type-B1, I-21-class commissioned on December 10, 1938. Her previously reported position was sailing alongside her sister sub, the *I-123* on a heading for Lubang Island, ninety-five miles south-west of Manila Bay in The Philippines. Their cover was supposedly laying down an impenetrable flotilla of underwater mines, to first act as a decoy and secondly, to destroy allied shipping; predominately bulk oil carriers running through the Sulu Sea. The reality of the situation was the *I-124*'s current chartered position would never be proven to be thousands of miles to the south-west, slowly cruising somewhere off the coast of Western Australia.

Lieutenant Commander Kishigamu Koichi was standing alert and at the ready inside the conning tower of *I-124*, accompanied by his executive officer and one other junior officer on lookout duties. All three men were scanning the horizon through their binoculars, searching for any sign of allied navy presence in the area. This day was of the utmost importance to Koichi for both himself, as a Japanese Imperial Navy submarine commander, but more importantly, for all the Japanese people. He waited for the radio officer to advise his captain when the all-important command, due at 1715 hours, had arrived, via their Kaigun Ango Sho, Type-D encryption code.

Soon his country would take the next step in securing total energy independence and will no longer need to rely on the greedy, oil-consuming United States, Koichi pondered privately, while he envisaged the photo of, Emperor Hirohito, occupying pride of place on the wall of his private quarters.

The *I-124*'s radio officer confirmed the encrypted message had now been received over the VHF teleprompter, alerting Koichi he needed to make his way back down the conning tower ladder and collect the typed command from Fleet Headquarters in Tokyo. He arrived at his cabin and closed the door and then entered the three-tiered combination to his private wall safe and retrieved Japan's decipher legend. Koichi's cheeks were still cold from the brisk ocean breezes sweeping off the ocean as afternoon prepared to give way to the evening sky, inside he felt a sense of warmth envelop him as this definitive point in history could soon become a reality. He thought of his wife and children, and a proud chill swept over him.

Lieutenant Commander Kishigamu Koichi copied down the typed numbers and numerals, and then slowly, with exacting precision, he relayed the completed alternative encryption to his leather-bound command journal. He stood to attention and saluted the emperor's photo, then ordered his XO to come to his cabin, immediately. As was the tradition in most navies, while serving on a submarine, formalities were often set aside between ranking officers on such occasions, due to the close confinement for enduring periods, spent either on—or under the sea.

A soft knock on his cabin door alerted Koichi to his XO's arrival. "Akhito, please enter. Come and take a seat next to your captain." A charismatic smile beamed through his enthralled expression. "Please decipher and confirm this encryption, then read back to me and ratify this order, please."

Akhito leant across the small table and went to work, following the same precise routine his commanding officer had only just previously performed.

"Sir, I confirm the command reads as follows: Lt. Cdr Kishigamu Koichi - JIN- Submarine *I-124* from Fleet Command, Admiral Yamamoto - *stop* - orders confirmed to proceed with extreme caution to latitude 26° 14`45" S and longitude 111° 12`

55" E, 112 nautical miles [207 km] west of Steep Point, Western Australia - *stop* - rendezvous with SMS *Kormoran*, German auxiliary cruiser, Commander Theodor Detmers - *stop* - continue with planned exchange of precious cargo -*stop* - be notified of enemy, Leander-class light cruiser reported leaving Sunda Strait Nov 19 [approx] heading due south entering the Indian Ocean, cruising speed estimated: 22-26 kt - *stop* - return earliest at full speed to Manila Bay- *stop* - godspeed - *stop* - end message."

"Thank you, Akhito. And now can you please place your officer's rank and signature next to my own into the command journal."

"With pleasure, Commander." Akhito finished his required duty and stood ram-rod straight while saluting his captain. "A day that will be forever remembered as a critically important time in naval history for the Japanese people, sir."

"Yes, Akhito. With the technology to break the American coded messages; we will now have the ability to track their main Pacific Fleet force. With all three carriers; *Enterprise*, *Lexington* and *Saratoga* hundreds of miles out to sea, our attack on Pearl Harbour will be guaranteed success. Japan's pathway in being recognised as a true world power, will be assured."

Both men raised a small glass of tepid sake.

"To Emperor Hirohito, Akhito," Koichi toasted.

"Emperor Hirohito," Akhito returned.

"Admiral Yamamoto has placed the burden of responsibility at our feet, and we shall not disappoint him. Please give the order to dive and enter in our new heading, Akhito."

"Yes, sir, right away."

...November 19, 1635 hours due west of Steep Point...

Lieutenant Commander Kishigamu Koichi ordered Sub *I-124* to the surface alongside the stationary, *Kormoran*. The sail hatch burst open while his crew prepared to unload their precious cargo of gold bullion from the for'ard hatches onto the waiting German cruiser. The two navy commanders exchanged respectful salutes in recognition of the significance of this clandestine meeting while adrift in the vast emptiness of the Indian Ocean. Koichi acknowledged the confirmation from Akhito that the encryption device was now stored safely below. The commander of the *Kormoran* quickly ordered all lines to be cast away and to engage the idling engines, after which the Japanese submarine slipped from sight beneath the ocean depths.

Chapter-3

...1635 hours November 19, 1941,
cruising south off the West Australian coast...

CAPTAIN JOSEPH BURNETT finished confirming the ship's log recording that he had, in fact, now successfully completed the required five anti-scuttling exercises as per orders from the Admiralty—noting the dates on June 16, August 3, 9 and November 17. These exercises were interspersed with many other non-gunnery drills, such as fire stations, abandon ship stations, steering breakdowns, and lowering boats for man overboard, collision stations, destroying confidential documents, underwater explosions and demolition parties.

He prepared to leave his private quarters to resume his preferred position on the upper bridge of the Australian Modified Leander-class light cruiser - HMAS *Sydney*. She was on her return trip to the Port of Fremantle after escorting the troop carrier, SS *Zealandia* for a hand-over mission, to HMS *Durban*, in the Sunda Strait.

Captain Burnett acknowledged and returned the salute from the three other officers currently on duty within the bridge: the navigator, the officer of the watch, and the assistant officer of the watch. Four ratings, a wireless telegraphy rating and runners, seven signalmen—the chief yeoman, the yeoman of the watch, the leading and two other signalmen also occupied the heart and soul of the Australian Navy cruiser. On each bridge wing – four seamen, in two pairs, were manning the twelve-foot-long rangefinders, two ratings stood by the depth charge release lever. On the lower bridge were the officers and ratings, maintaining the plotting office. The assistant navigator and chartroom personnel given the cramp workplace in the chartroom on the lower deck, it was necessary that four navigation personnel, including the assistant navigator, be stationed on the lower bridge. This included two wireless telegraphy ratings in the remote control office – one rating in the silent compartment – two men standing by the torpedo range indicator and two by the torpedo firing pistol on either side of the lower bridge – with the helmsmen and assistants in the wheelhouse.

HMAS *Sydney*'s full complement of 645 crew and officers were all looking forward to some well-earned R&R in Fremantle after spending eight months battling the Italian Navy in the Mediterranean Sea. The *Sydney*'s cruising speed of 24 knots placed her 120 nautical miles (nm) west of the town of Carnarvon. The radar officer on watch alerted the lieutenant commander of a sighting, bearing 190°, 26 miles to the south, "She looks to be slowing, sir."

Captain Burnett then ordered his executive officer to check the range and speed, questioning, "That seems strange. Why would a ship be reducing speed in the middle of the ocean?"

Five more minutes passed, "Speed and heading confirmed sir, she is now stationary and dead in the water."

Burnett watched intently through his binoculars over the distant horizon. "Position and distance again, Lieutenant?" the captain ordered.

The lieutenant leant over the shoulder of the radar control officer. "She is under steam now, Captain. Heading two-seven-zero degrees, speed increasing to ten knots and range, fifteen thousand yards. She is moving west into the setting sun, sir."

"Request the yeoman of the watch to activate the bridge wing signal lamps to prepare to identify her letters, let's see who this is—shall we?"

The radar officer let out a short, "Ha, that's weird?"

Captain Burnett looked over with a doleful expression, "This is the Royal Australian Navy son, and we don't do weird. What is it?"

"Sorry, sir, for a fleeting second, I thought . . . Well, I thought there was a faint print of a second ship?"

"Make the call, sailor. Can you confirm this second contact or not?" Burnett was agitated at the possibility there might be a second unidentified ship in the vicinity.

His full attention was now focused on the newly installed, Acronym Radar, "Arr... no sir, just the single blip, probably just a ghost shadow."

"Order the men to first-degree action stations, XO," Burnett further ordered. He was a cautious man, having only taken command of the *Sydney* in March of the same year, eight months earlier. Most impressions were that Captain Burnett was a capable ship handler. He was aware that he commanded a skilled and well-trained ship's company and was backed up by highly trained, experienced and battle-hardened senior officers. He was a man who would listen and accept the advice of others.

HMAS *Sydney* continued to reduce the distance between the still unidentified ship, over the horizon. Captain Burnett was playing back in his mind the final coded dispatch from Canberra received before departing Java. The Admiralty had requested all active naval vessels to pursue if at all possible, any chance of rendering an enemy ship to a point where an anti-scuttling party could board and possibly put a halt to any attempt to scuttle their ship in the hope of capturing information on current German and Japanese communication codes. This was a 'Priority One' request in the overall war effort. Captain Burnett wanted to give the *Sydney* and its men every possible opportunity to do, just that.

As the still-unidentified mystery vessel came into view, the captain repeated his orders. "Signal her a second-time Lieutenant and this time, raise the 'NNJ' flag."

"Yes, sir."

"Captain, she has responded with the 'VH' flag. She also requests we show our letters first."

"Does she now?" Burnett replied with a suspicious scowl. "Ask her which port she embarked and country of destination?"

The lieutenant read the incoming flagged response out loud to his apprehensive captain. "Dutch ship *Straak Malaaka*. Left Fremantle Port with peace goods destined for Batavia. Sir, it looks like she has raised the Dutch merchant flag, PKQI."

"What do you mean, looks like, Lieutenant? Either she has, or she hasn't... which one is it?" the captain replied curtly.

"Sir, the flag is slightly obscured behind the forward funnel."

"What's our distance now?"

"Sir, seven thousand yards off the port bow."

"Signal her again, Lieutenant. I need to confirm her identity NOW! Officer of the watch, take us to within five thousand yards."

"Sir, is that wise? Until she replies with the *Straak Malaaka*'s call sign of 'IIKP', we have to assume she is an enemy vessel."

"Need I remind you, Lieutenant, I am in command of this ship, five thousand yards please and alert the crew, full battle stations fourth-degree," Captain Burnett shouted the order, as the alien ship became a flurry of activity, above decks.

The sound of the bugle was broadcast over HMAS *Sydney*'s loudspeaker system, resulting in all crew immediately reporting to their designated action stations. All armaments, including torpedoes, were manned. Personnel also formed up in the shell rooms, cordite magazines and ammunition lobbies. As part of closing up at action stations, turret crews started the hydraulic pump motors for the training of the turrets and the elevation of the guns. The hydraulic systems were then tested by elevating and lowering the guns by training the turret around on different bearings. The firing circuits were tested with the firing of a 'dummy' firing tube. All twenty-four watertight doors and hatches were secured. The turbine power generators were brought online and the ring main separated into four separate circuits, each providing power to a separate part of the ship, including one turret each. A team of seamen under the command of an officer formed up at the steering gear compartment for emergency steering. It took just three and a half minutes to secure the ship to full battle readiness.

In each of the four turrets, there were twenty men – the officer of the turret – the petty officer of the turret – the phone number – seven men operating each gun plus three men manning the local control cabinet. The supporting spaces for the six-inch guns housed a further ten men in each of the four ammunition lobbies, giving a total of forty personnel – add to that the six men in each of the four shell rooms, increasing the final tally by another twenty-four personnel.

At action stations, the executive officer closed up at the lower steering position. The lower steering position housed a gyrocompass repeater and the other instruments required to navigate and control the ship, including engine room telegraph, rudder and steering motor indicators. If the bridge was rendered non-operational, and the captain was unable to command the ship, the executive officer moved aft from the lower steering position to the rear control position on the aft superstructure and commanded the ship from there. The route from the lower steering position to the aft superstructure was a relatively long one, requiring the English-born, Lieutenant Commander Jack Bacon to ascend three decks to get to the upper deck and then walk about one-third of the entire ship's length to ascend further ladders on the aft superstructure.

Commander Theodor Detmers knew at that moment, the gig was up. With the Australian cruiser bearing down on their position at flank speed, he ordered *Kormoran's* disguise to be lowered, and the Dutch flag be replaced by the Kriegsmarine ensign. All *Kormoran's* combined armoury of guns and torpedoes were to open fire as the Australian light cruiser approached, five points off their stern.

Both ships fired almost simultaneously. The first shots from HMAS *Sydney*, a full, eight-shell salvo from the main guns, were aimed at *Kormoran*'s bridge but whistled past while a single 152mm shell drove a hole straight through her funnel. Captain Burnett's attempt to disable and board the German cruiser, rather than destroy her, may prove to be decisive regarding the overall battle about to take place.

With *Kormoran*'s opening salvo, the gunnery officer sought to embody the light cruiser's bridge but failed on their first attempt, with the shells striking other parts of the ship or missing altogether. Two torpedoes from *Kormoran*'s starboard, above-water tubes were launched simultaneously. With the German cruiser's attack and the relatively close proximity of the target, this allowed the use of the five Flak anti-aircraft and six-15cm SKL/45 C guns to rake the *Sydney*'s flank, mowing down any, if not all sailors unlucky enough to be above decks.

There would be no respite as Detmers ordered a subsequent salvo with devastating accuracy. The second, three-shell attack destroyed the *Sydney*'s upper bridge, damaging her superstructure, and knocking out the gun direction control tower. HMAS *Sydney*'s communication capabilities beyond visual range were via the wireless Type-48 transmitter set in the main wireless telegraphy office, another Type-49 set was located in the second W/T office, and a Type-45 set in the auxiliary W/T office.

None of HMAS *Sydney*'s wireless sets had the capacity for voice transmission. The Type-48 transmitter was the ship's most powerful unit, capable of transmitting signals worldwide. It could, however, transmit only by Morse code entered utilising manual keying by a trained telegraphist. The ship remained on full radio silence, as was the normal wartime doctrine.

The telegraphist tried in vain to fire a 'plain language' message off to Darwin, advising they were under attack. The radio tower lay shattered on the forward deck. The foremast had taken a direct hit and toppled over, destroying one of the two 32-foot cutters secured by their own davits before dropping over the side. Captain Burnett, and all but one of the *Sydney*'s command structure on the upper bridge, were killed instantly.

Kormoran continued relentlessly, firing with four of her six-SKL's. Spraying the decks with a hail of iron; the third and fourth salvo's knocked the cruiser's 'A' and 'B' turrets out of action before the *Sydney* could fire a second time. The fifth hit the cruiser above the waterline in proximity to the forward engine room, causing mayhem with oil fires burning out of control. The walrus seaplane was split in two and now lay scattered about on fire—while still in her catapult.

Lieutenant Commander Jack Bacon attempted to make contact with both 'A' and 'B' turrets. They needed to switch to manual control. He was shouting into the mouthpiece in a frenzied shrill on the pretence of remaining calm. The open-mouthed gape and bloodied mess of his fellow officers made him feel nauseous. He was now the senior commanding officer and needed to take control. His attempts to contact both turrets fell on deaf ears as thick smoke billowed from their three-inch armour plating.

Kormoran's guns were now squarely aimed at HMAS *Sydney*'s two-inch plating below the waterline and upper deck. After the sixth German salvo, the *Sydney* was able to resume fire with her aft turrets. 'Y' turret only managed to fire less than four times with little effect, but multiple shots from 'X' turret struck *Kormoran*, damaging the cruiser's above-deck machinery, wounding the sailors manning one of the guns, as their own oil fires wreaked havoc on the foredeck. A direct hit on the remains of the *Sydney*'s command centre levelled the entire superstructure. Lieutenant Commander Jack Bacon's interim captain's role came to an abrupt end.

The next salvo's from *Kormoran*'s two PaK-36 anti-aircraft guns shredded 'A' turrets housing and tore the roof from 'B' turret. Commander Detmers ordered two more torpedoes to be fired. The first passed behind the *Sydney*'s stern, and the second blew her rudder to pieces. She now turned to port in an involuntary demarche, moving aft of *Kormoran*'s position.

HMAS *Sydney*, the flagship of the Australian Fleet and a crowd favourite, after her success in the Mediterranean, was now doomed. The *Sydney*'s main armament was completely disabled with both the forward turrets damaged or destroyed, while the aft turrets were jammed facing port, away from the *Kormoran*. As she continued limping away on a blind heading, her secondary weapons were now out of range.

The burning carnage below decks was unimaginable. Fire control was non-existent as the light cruiser's oil-based paint fed the spreading flames and burnt unhindered. Acting Sub Lieutenant Callum Bishop, through a sheer stroke of luck, was not currently at his battle station position, below decks. He was returning from sickbay, after a severe bout of diarrhoea and now found himself one level below the outer deck. He grabbed for the steel stair railing as another explosion threatened to consume the whole stepped structure, his left hand seared from the heated metal, while he steadied himself from another shuddering detonation below decks. Bishop arrived on the upper deck and looked on in abstract disbelief.

"Oh, my God," he gasped in total unbelievable shock at what he was witnessing with his own smoke-filled eyes.

The ship he'd served on for the last eighteen months resembled nothing more than burning scrap metal. Now the HMAS *Sydney* was almost unrecognisable as a serving RAN vessel. Her decks were strewn with bodies, which now resembled burnt briquettes of charcoal. The entire bridge had just—disappeared.

This can't be happening, he tried to convince himself.

He was momentarily blinded by the sun sinking over the western horizon when he noticed what he first guessed to be a pod of breaching whales breaking the surface of the water off their starboard bow. His gaze turned to stark horror as the conning tower of a Japanese submarine, shot up out of the oil-smeared ocean, beyond.

"What the hell?" he wheezed through the smoke, struggling to come to grips with what he could see with his own eyes.

He searched aimlessly for evidence of any lifeboats in the process of being launched. The remaining cutter had been reduced to a scattering of broken timbers, and both the two 35-foot motorboats, two 27-foot whalers, and a 36-foot pinnace were nowhere to be seen. All that was left was a 30-foot gig and a 16-foot jollyboat that needed to be launched using the deck-mounted crane which had long been pulverised and now lay on the ocean floor somewhere.

HMAS *Sydney*'s secondary life-saving equipment were several Carley floats. These consisted of a large-diameter copper tube formed into an oval ring divided by bulkheads into watertight compartments. The tube was covered with a layer of cork and then painted canvas. A platform of slatted wood was slung under the inner edge of the tube by rope netting, and a lifeline was fitted around the outside of the tube. Carley floats had been used in both the British Royal Navy and Royal Australian Navy warships since 1915. The two types of Carley floats used on HMAS *Sydney* were the pattern 18, which was fourteen feet long and had a lifesaving capacity of sixty-seven, and the pattern 20, which was ten feet long and had a lifesaving capacity of only twenty.

To Bishop's recollection, they were all now destroyed or rendered useless with a peppering of bullet holes riddled down the side of the only two floats that were in plain sight. Callum Bishop's bloodshot eyes almost popped from their sockets, as a pair of incoming oxygen-fuelled Type-95 torpedoes left a trailing phosphorous wake from the stationary Japanese sub's forward torpedo tubes. They were making a beeline for a direct hit on the bow, which was where he was currently occupying a space in a state of increasing panic. He searched desperately for anything that would allow him to get off this sinking time bomb.

A free Carley float had broken away from its strapping and was leaning against the ship's railing. Bishop ran for his life, and while grappling the raft, he hurled himself overboard and almost floated to the whipped-up ocean below, landing on the crest of a two-metre swell. The Carley float spanked the ocean hard, and his body was thrown clear. His arms and legs were flailing in the turbulent and oil-burning waters in an attempt to grab the float before it drifted away on the stiffening breeze.

The first explosion was ear-shattering. The entire front section of the *Sydney* lifted clear over the tops of the swell, silhouetted against the evening skyline in a macabre setting that would forever haunt the acting sub-lieutenant. A second torpedo split the hull forward of amidships, causing her bow to angle down. This proved to be *Sydney*'s Achilles' heel. The asdic compartment was the weakest section of the hull. With the added weight of the anchors and chains, the bow just peeled away like opening a can of sardines with the piercing shrill of tearing metal and began to sink into the black void below. HMAS *Sydney*'s front section now listed as water poured into her gaping holed superstructure, unabated.

Bishop watched helplessly as his fellow sailors started launching themselves from the stricken ship in a last ditched effort to just survive. It was a forlorn hope. The Japanese submarine carpeted the ocean with a spray of fire from her single-mounted 14cm naval machine gun. Bishop's Carley float and only means of survival drifted aimlessly behind a cloud of black smoke and the overwhelming smell of cordite.

The engagement was over, with HMAS *Sydney* heading south and now slowing, while *Kormoran* maintained her course and speed before both engines failed and bought the incapacitated cruiser to a mid-ocean drift. Detmers ordered all hands to abandon ship and prepared to scuttle the damned *Kormoran*.

The HMAS *Sydney* was wreathed in smoke from fires burning in the engine room and forward superstructure, and around the aircraft catapult. *Kormoran* discontinued her main attack, but the individually firing aft guns scored hits as the *Sydney* crossed the cruiser's stern one last time.

Shipwrights and other crew were assigned to carry out immediate battle damage repairs—known as 'damage control'. All RAN ships had a damage control organisation that included a cruising stations mode and an action stations mode. On HMAS

Sydney, the damage control headquarters was situated at the lower steering position, which consisted of three teams. The watertight integrity of the ship had now been compromised, damage control parties mustered at their assigned stations.

They aimed to slow down and preferably stop the ingress of seawater and thus preserve the buoyancy and stability of the ship. Damage control stations were located throughout the ship at or below the waterline and contained tools and timber for making repairs. The teams of highly skilled sailors worked tirelessly to assess the destruction, isolate damaged compartments from fire mains, and establish flooding boundaries and shore up the surrounding ship structure. They were trained to cut and fashion the timber into pieces that could cover breaches in the hull and to shore up damaged bulkheads, doors and hatches.

Pumps were bought online to empty a breached watertight bulkhead and counter-flood the magazine rooms before the heat caused a catastrophic event. The pumps all relied on electricity and were thus reliant on the ship producing steam to fire the boilers and turbogenerators. Six of the eight pumps on the *Sydney* were located on the port side of the ship below the main suction line. In addition to the turbogenerators, the *Sydney* also had two diesel generators behind the armour belt on the lower deck port and starboard, between frames 116 and 126. Even if all steam was lost, power could be provided for some time by these generators, assuming they were undamaged. The damage control teams were attempting to pump fuel oil between compartments to counter asymmetrical flooding.

Callum Bishop wiped the oil from his face and eyes. The taste of smoke and oil filled his mouth as he repeatedly spat out the foul-tasting fill. Both his arms were burnt, and his rib cage felt like it was poking his lungs from inside. For the first time since HMAS *Sydney* came under attack, he noticed blood leaking from a gash on the back of his head. A throbbing pain beat through his entire skull with timed regularity. He placed his hand on the floor of the Carley float to lift himself above the flat sides. Another shooting pain shot up his right hip. Small pools of blood were forming on the floor of the Carley float, with a gathering of interested flies and insects now buzzing around the coagulating dribble.

"Jesus bloody Christ," he exuded in a long drawn acknowledgement of his battered body. Callum Bishop was in shock and had lost a life-threatening amount of blood.

Bishop needed to knuckle down to deal with his newfound surroundings, drifting in a shitty little float on an unforgiving ocean, while injured will require all his training and skill, just to stay alive this night. In the parting distance, he could hear cries and morbid moans for help. He scanned the smoking and burning surface for any survivors. Suddenly the increasing noise of splashing water joined in the nightmare. Bishop paddled in the direction, calling out, "Hello, anyone out there? Keep calling out, mate. Hello... call out if you can hear me? I'm over here... shout so I can hear you."

He threw his only paddle behind him and leant over the side to drag the flagging body inside the raft. Large portions of flesh smouldered, and the smell caused him to vomit. With half his body in, Callum bent his back and grabbed the cord of what looked like a cook's apron and heaved the man into the float. He was staring at two eyes void of life, and yet the stranger still shook from both the cold and an inner terror.

"Come on, you lie down over here and rest." *You poor bastard.*

A bloodied bone was protruding at an unnatural angle from his shin. "Bloody hell, mate, you're in a real bad way, aren't you?"

A fading glow lit up the southern horizon for the next hour as Bishop was captivated in part hypnotic fixation as he watched the *Sydney* fade-away at less than two knots, on what little power that remained from her shot-to-pieces, three drum boilers and Parsons geared turbines.

The Carley float drifted in a south-easterly direction, following the trail of debris that scattered the ocean surface. At a little before midnight, the blackened, smoke-filled sky lit up like a fireworks night bonfire, illuminating the night sky in the distance, beyond the point of the disappearing horizon. The HMAS *Sydney* was gone as she sunk, bow down to her eternal resting place in 2,500 metres of water, west of Dirk Hartog Island.

Callum Bishop was in a distraught state. There were no other survivors to be seen as night slowly morphed into daybreak. He lay flat on the canvas floor, next to his traumatised stranger and slipped into a distorted, agonising abomination.

On the second morning of his drift, he awakened from his interrupted attempt to sleep by the slowly decreasing sounds of grief, misery and woe as the incoherent rabble drooled from the mouth of his passenger. Callum considered the obvious option to end this poor soul's agony. The gates of destiny awaited him, and death was enticing him to dance on through.

How could I do that, and what would I use?

The welcome distraction of crashing waves caused Callum to lift his head, only to be met by a better than decent swell battering against the fast-approaching unfriendly coastline of some obscure part of Western Australia. Callum was instantly reminded of the searing pain in his head with another eye-watering bolt of agony radiating from a piece of shrapnel lodged behind his left ear.

Lying belly down on the front of the oval-shaped raft and with just a single paddle, he stroked the rising ocean swell frantically. His strength was waning as he surveyed the endless towering hundred-foot sheer cliff face that ran in a north-south direction, as far as his swollen eyes could see.

"Bloody hell, I can't keep this up for long. Hopefully, there must be somewhere along this slice of desolate shoreline to land a simple cork dinghy?" he wanted to reassure himself.

For each metre he gained with the stroke of his paddle, to place some safe distance away from the jagged coast, the wind pushed him three metres closer.

I'm in dire straits now, Bishop had to painfully acknowledge, as he paddled in a direful paranoia.

The simple task of sliding overboard and succumbing to the call of the ocean was at the forefront of his mind. He could rejoin his lost mates and put an end to his pain and suffering right now. *The cook had been quiet for probably too long,* Bishop contemplated.

He estimated the swell to be about four metres in height. As a sailor stationed in Fremantle, he knew the locals would probably deem this weather to be a relatively calm day. With a renewed vigour, he took this to be a good sign. Both his arms were burning with the assiduity of paddling. He swapped hands and kept following the wind, north. Bishop noticed a broken section of a coastal bluff had slipped away as part of the precipice, with large boulders offering natural stepping stones as a means to reach the safety of higher ground. At its base was a flat piece of limestone.

"If I can just make my way to the front of that crag, I could try my luck and let the swell dump me on that pancake-shaped chunk of lime and sandstone? Bugger it. I've got nothing to lose." He searched deep within for some inner motivation.

Bishop watched on intently as the wind and tide pushed him closer to the shoreline with each mountain of water picking up the dwarfed Carley float and hurtling him towards the broken cliff face. The curling spray covered the two nautical travellers in sheets of salt water. Callum wiped his brow and soldiered on. Some odd formations were forming on the flat-looking rock, where a short section of the escarpment seemed to have a light covering of sand. A large length of timber with a wide girth lay across the edifice, like a felled tree trunk. He had no time for sightseeing as the third wave in the set picked him up and slew him sideways before he corrected his incoming line with backward strokes.

Anguish filled a scowled frown as an intense pain flowed up his bruised hip. But the plan was working. He leant over as far as his legs would allow and slapped the water hard. The last roller coaster spat him out onto the smoothed rock surface as the remnants of the broken white water flowed over his horizontal body. Bishop allowed himself to roll out of the float, plucking his officer's peaked cap from the raft while he scampered to the safety of higher ground.

The broken white water picked the Carley float up like a rubber toy as the backwash sucked it back out to sea. Callum tried in vain to gain a hold from the trailing rope. All he could do was watch on as a hopeless spectator while it continued its way up the coast with the only other survivor still on board. "Good luck, mate, whoever you were."

He sat up and witnessed firsthand the natural ladder that he will need to traverse in reaching the top.

"Shit, I don't even know where I am. Most of this bloody coastline, north and south of Dirk Hartog Island, is station country. The homesteads are bloody miles away from the coast. Either way, I have to get my way up there somehow. With the incoming high tide, I will be a sitting duck here," he knew this to be true while feeling the effects of his ordeal.

Callum then noticed a couple of strange items scattered to his right. "If I didn't know any better, that looks like an old ship's mast, with a couple of spars still attached."

Then, while the ocean remained calm for a minute or two, the sun could be seen highlighting what looked like the dark shadow of some wrecked remains of what must have been an old wooden ship, about five metres below the surface.

"Jesus Christ, strange happenings, not something you see every day."

As Callum surveyed his surroundings, some old earthenware, covered in crustaceans and bleached by the sun, lay to his right. It was time to make his first attempt at climbing to the peak of the almost vertical bluff.

Bishop grabbed an old timber yardarm not far from where he was sitting. Using this as a make-shift crutch, he attempted to stand on one leg. He hopped on over to the first boulder when something jammed between two rocks in a small pool of water caught his attention. He bent down and picked it up, then rubbed the surface with his thumb and forefinger. There was a symbol of a lion holding a lance, and turning it over revealed some foreign spelling and the date, 1711.

"Shit, this is an old coin. Like a Spanish doubloon." Then he remembered reading about the discovery in 1927 of the shipwrecked Zuytdorp which came to grief sometime in the winter of 1712.

"I've stumbled on the old remains. How's your bloody luck, Callum? Two days ago you got blasted out of the ocean and almost died, then the next day you find some lost treasure. Not much good to me right now," he half-joked, knowing this was the least of his burgeoning problems.

He placed his officer's hat on his head, remembering the picture he cherished so much still carefully tucked under the cotton lining of his only other living relative, a much younger brother, now living in the United States with his adopted parents.

Callum then started his first climb and dragged his broken body to about the half-way point, up the cliff face. There was a sizable gap in the rocks. Knowing the only way over would be to jump, he sat back down to regain his composure. He finally stood and steadied himself, then threw his makeshift crutch to the opposite side. Callum took three deep breaths and launched himself off his good leg to the next rung in his rocky climb, and hopefully to reach the other side, which had to be better than what lay below.

He missed by about a foot and fell clumsily. The front of his head cracked against the sharp edges of the uneven rock surface and old-growth coral as he landed in a crumpled heap back to the starting point of his initial climb. He knew the instant he hit hard ground and heard the sound of a bone snapping, he would now be fighting an uphill battle. Balancing on the horns of a dilemma that could result in his ultimate demise. Blood flowed unabated from his forehead, and his good leg was rendered useless in a clean break. He screamed in pain as his body convulsed in warm and cold flashes of torturous stabbing pain. He fought the body's urge to lapse into unconsciousness. Callum let out a dolorous howl and started to scream obscenities.

The fine spraying mist peeling off the backs of each wave was soaking his Navy officer's uniform. He needed to move. To stay in this same spot would be a sentence of death. He looked up from his horizontal position and spotted a small cave. Any protection from the elements was better than nothing. He wanted to rest and sleep. He was in a desperate state.

Callum spent the next two hours hauling his lame body over the notched natural wall until he was able to force himself inside the small recess. His elbows and knees bled and were filled with broken shell grit as he manoeuvred his body into a small crevice only to find a neatly piled stack of rocks. "Bloody hell," he snorted while panting loudly, "Some bastard has already beaten me here."

Inside the cavity were the remains of a rock-covered, above-ground grave complete with a headstone. Callum rolled his body to one side to allow a slither of sunlight to filter through so that he could read the engraved words.

The inscription was in Dutch, and the only decipherable word he understood was the name Wouter Loos and a scattering of random letters and strange looking symbols that meant nothing. Callum looked closely and thought there may have been an image of the sun and a date. The remainder was a mystery to him.

"This is some poor bastard's final resting place, 1629. Bloody hell, mate. Apparently, young Wouter Loos, you didn't find your way home either, did you? I think you and I, Wouter, might be heading for the same shitty and inevitable end. May we both rest in peace," he voiced while shrouded in a feeling of total abandonment.

Callum pushed himself into the far reaches of his small bastion and laid his head down to rest. He was exhausted and completely immobilised.

With the threat of a menacing sky, a fierce storm gathered in unrelenting strength. A tropical cyclone had formed off the coast of Carnarvon and was unleashing its full power with no mercy. Wind gusts of over 110 mph were pummelling the hundreds of miles of exposed coastline, and torrential rain poured from the skies unallayed, hour-after-hour, in a vertical blanketing.

For the first time in his life, Bishop was in a total state of dread, in fear of his life. The sound of an ear-piercing cracking noise from above filled the small recess. His body stiffened as the rock shifted. With a loud *thud*, the tonnes of Tamala limestone that formed a natural ceiling split then came crashing down on the acting sub lieutenant's shivering body.

After surviving the battle at sea between the HMAS *Sydney* and the German cruiser *Kormoran*, a freakish natural occurrence laid to rest a second body that now occupied a cave above an isolated stretch of famous coastline known as the Zuytdorp Cliffs.

Part-II

The Celestial Sphere

Chapter-4

...Present day...

THE PASSENGER located in seat 6-C packed away her laptop and settled into the business-class seat as the familiar *ping* of the seatbelt sign sounded from above. The first officer's voice announced over the intercom they were about to commence their final approach into Ngurah Rai International Airport on Bali, as the smiling, manicured British flight attendants busied themselves in preparing the Airbus A-300 for landing.

At 32 years young, Evina Bishop-Joiner was an alluring, attractive-looking woman. In the past, even in her early years while still studying full time at Columbia University, the academic community often struggled to come to grips with the simple fact that beauty and brains could operate on a single platform. Her current position as an associate professor at the Smithsonian in the division of Islamic Science was a testament to her dedication. Her relentless endeavour to be recognised as a serious research scientist—no matter what the cost, was proving to be very high with the current research project she had been relentlessly pursuing for almost ten years now.

She scanned the tropical oasis that awaited her below the rain-filled sea of dark clouds through her slightly scratched window seat and allowed her mind to drift back to that defining moment in the early days of her career, in a clandestine meeting, all those years ago.

The Smithsonian often received relics and odd artefacts at regular intervals for verification and dating. Little did Bishop-Joiner realise, the day she was mysteriously hand-delivered a wooden box by a courier service while approaching her parked convertible 64 *Mustang* in the staff-only car park, would morph into a ten-year-odyssey of discovery.

The moment she placed the unusually heavy package on her dining table in her rented flat in Maryland and cut away the thick packaging tape was to become an awakening to something of the utmost importance. A short note addressed to her by name awaited inside that simply read:

Mrs Bishop-Joiner, this is one of three celestial globes, and if you take the time to delve deeper, I think you will find the results an enlightening experience. Caution: the world is fuelled by greed and corruption. Trust no one.

It was unsigned.

With growing interest, she studied the metallic sphere with her analytical eye and immediately noticed an inscription written in Arabic. After further examining the globe back at the Smithsonian, she found it also to be un-dated and unsigned after which the director of the institute, Byron Clarkson, then suggested that she immediately instigate a search, and scour the museums of Europe and the Middle East to see if she could find any other similar pieces. The superlatively crafted and perfect example of seamless metalwork was a technical feat in itself. These globes weren't just beautiful; they were masterful in their uniqueness.

Many museums seemed to have in their possession, one or two of these globes but constructed of two identical sections, and she started to uncover signatures and dates. Gradually she built up a library of knowledge relating to their construction and history.

On her return to Washington, the Smithsonian Conservation and Analytical Laboratory agreed to conduct a full range of tests using X-rays and cameras to identify the faintest trace of a join anywhere on the inside and the outside surface of her strange celestial globe. Anything that might offer a clue as to how the sphere may have been cast. By tracking down and studying a large number of these globes, she was finally able to put together the pieces of her gathering jigsaw puzzle. At the very least, she could now identify the maker of the anonymous Smithsonian globe that prompted her quest to solve the mystery of why such a fine instrument was left unsigned and without a date stamp. More crucially, her detective work led her to identify the unique way the globe was constructed—something that had hitherto gone unnoticed.

A decade later, Bishop-Joiner was a now a key-figure within a small group of research scientists that were spearheading the discovery of Muslim heritage that originally was ear-marked with researching its impact on early civilisation and now had evolved into a full-blown search with regards to ancient Arabic medicinal remedies. She was on the cusp of unearthing a secret that started in the 1300s and continued onto the 1600s, with the 4th Moghul Emperor *Jahangir*, a key figure in her seeking answers to the questions that occupied every recess of her inquisitive scientific mind.

It is often said the legacy of the ancient Egyptians who left us their colossal pyramids, amazing temples and obelisks, that mankind does not credit them with the scientific know-how. Although the so-called 'experts' will speculate on how they erected such mathematically exact and stupendous structures, long before the Greeks—recognised as the first scientists, made their impact on the world stage. The great pyramid of Giza was already a relic of antiquity when Greek and Roman invaders encountered them, and both were as awe-struck by these astonishing stone skyscrapers, as people are to this day. A feat all the more remarkable, since until the 19th century, these sole surviving wonders of the ancient world reigned supreme as the tallest constructions to populate the planet's surface.

The undisputed fact was the globe in her possession was discarded due to a mistake in the encryption, rendering it useless as a map—but a map to what and to where? A second and third globe had been cast by the Moghul Emperor Jahangir that held within it, a possible location of something of such importance it could change the lives of millions of people. The impoverished and the poor. A feat welcomed by some but not shared by other, more rich and powerful men in positions to wield enormous influence. Money and greed ruled the modern world, Evina knew only too well.

She privately considered, *Maybe we are close to changing that for the better?*

After checking her e-mail account and filing the final draft of another editorial, Abigail Bishop-Price disconnected her free resort Wi-Fi connection and closed her laptop. Even though she was unofficially on holidays, as a journalist, her reporters' brain never switched off. She gathered her pool-side belongings and headed back to her two-room suite for a quick shower and a change of clothes to ready herself for the ensuing task of picking her twin sister up from the airport, located on the opposite side of Bali, in just under an hour.

The identical twins' father was an American serving naval pilot stationed on the Forrestal-class carrier USS *Kitty Hawk* during the Vietnam conflict in 1968. After his F/A 18-E/F Super Hornet was shot down by a surface-to-air missile, immediately after disposing of a Soviet-designed, North Vietnamese MiG, he was tagged as a hero amongst his men.

Wounded in action, he was flown to the closest positioned hospital ship. At that time, the Dutch-registered; MS *Oranje*, which currently was refitted to perform her role as an Australian hospital ship, was anchored off the coast of Da Nang, in South Vietnam. There he spent the next twelve hours in intensive care, waiting until the all-clear was given for him to be airlifted to Darwin hospital for emergency surgery to remove the life-threatening shrapnel from his stomach, shoulder and a small piece lodged behind his right temple, requiring more intrusive surgery not available on board the ship.

Melissa Price was a sought-after model in her teenage years and used this as a means to pay for her nurses' training. And because of her striking good looks and bubbly personality, her photo was selected from a pool of thousands as a recruitment poster for other women to join up and offer their services to the war effort. The previous campaign to lure nurses to join the ranks was based on pulling at the heart-strings of the average Australian, rekindling the sinking of the RAN hospital ship, *Centaur* off the coast of Queensland on May 14, 1942.

Join the campaign in ridding the world of the scourge of communism. Do your bit for the country and the brave men and women of the combined defence forces. This was a well-known slogan that was the most successful recruiting campaign during the entire war. Nurse Price was chosen to accompany the handsome, dark-haired American on the medical airlift, and it was during this time and the recovery period soon after that they became friends, and soon lovers.

The war was now over for Lieutenant Thomas Benjamin Bishop, and he received his orders to be flown back Stateside after his full recovery; which he managed to stretch out to nearly three months. Six weeks later the lieutenant arrived back to the shores of Australia with a diamond engagement ring in hand, and a proposal that would sweep his Florence Nightingale off her feet and the two were married within weeks.

After serving out her required eighteen months' service, Melissa Price-Bishop resigned her commission, and the couple moved back to the States to commence their lives as any other married couple. The twins were born within the second year of their wedding, and it was at this time that her husband was diagnosed with post-traumatic war syndrome, a relatively unknown after-effect caused by his time serving in Vietnam, suffered by thousands of returning veterans. The medically discharged lieutenant was subject to ridicule and countless unsubstantiated innuendo from the media and the public in general as to this then-unknown condition. He became isolated and withdrawn before finding solace in the bottom of a bourbon bottle.

Melissa then suffered the next six years in a near-state of hell as her husband couldn't sustain any form of paid work. The day she found him locked inside their bathroom with a tourniquet and a spent needle lying on the tiled floor was the day she packed up her seven-year-old twin daughters and caught the next flight back home to Sydney. Their divorce was ratified two years later in his drunken and drug-induced absence, while Melissa Price went about resurrecting her life as a single working mother.

On the day of the girls' joint 18th birthday celebrations, Thomas Bishop reappeared out of the fog of his previous life, unannounced and uninvited; at least as far as his ex-wife was concerned. Thomas Bishop had managed to sort through the problems of his life and reinvent himself. He was now re-married with an eight-year-old son named Nathan. He also now owned a successful employment recruiting agency and enjoyed a well-balanced life with a better-than-average income and lifestyle to match. He wanted to offer the chance for his twin daughters to revisit his new life, meet his son and their own half-brother, also offering to pay for a full university education—the only catch being it had to be in Washington State, where he now resided.

Melissa Price was outraged at this proposal, ordering him from her home and threatening to call the police if he refused. Twelve months later, Evina was boarding a flight to DC. The opportunity to travel, live and attend an Ivy League University was too much of an incentive, and through the tears of a distraught mother, she bid farewell to her younger twin and left Australia.

That was fourteen years ago now, during which time she had only visited her mother on a handful of occasions, and each time she was met with the same frosty reception. Abigail had not seen nor heard from Evina for the last five years, apart from the one or two yearly emotionless e-mails, until suddenly, like a bolt of lightning, she received an unexpected call. Evina was offering an all-expenses-paid holiday for the two sisters to 'catch up' and bury the hatchet of their troubled past.

Yeah, right? Abigail questioned alone. An olive branch she remembered Evina quoting, which didn't sit well with her. As a reporter, she could smell a rat a mile away, and in her mind, a very big one was about to land in Bali very shortly.

Evina needed to slightly duck her tall, athletic figure as she stepped through the exit door of her British Airways flight. She was dog tired and looking forward to reuniting with her twin sister, after being separated by work and half a world for the last five years. Evina lived, breathed and practically slept at the Smithsonian in Washington DC and her home State since she was a teenager while her sister was left to care for their heartbroken mother, back in Sydney.

Evina battled her way through Customs, and the obligatory scowl from the Immigration officers, then proceeded to the baggage carousel. Her mind was preoccupied with other matters as she contemplated the reason for her ensuing reunification with her identical twin, the only difference being that a recent photo showed Abigail was now a bottle blonde. *Like pepper and salt*, Evina surmised, as she tied her shoulder-length locks of natural brunette hair into a tight, cooling ponytail.

Abigail waited with a slight air of apprehension as the line of incoming passengers made their way through the final automatic glass sliding doors to be greeted by loved one's waiting in the public area with open arms and loving hearts. Abigail wasn't sure what the forthcoming reception might reveal with her highly strung and sometimes impertinent sister. As maternal twins, they shared a special bond, but as teenagers, the relationship was often pushed to the point where restraint was the better option. The 'I am the older sister' comment was often used by Evina, even if it was a mere three minutes; she loved to throw that snippet of fact as a means to break the deadlock of many a sibling rivalry.

The two sisters held open their arms and embraced as only twins can. A few male passengers' heads turned at the sight of two stunning-looking women, standing centre stage, feeling the warmth of the other's embrace. Abigail was unprepared for the open show of affection. A tear rolled down the cheeks of the younger twin.

"Come on, Abby, it hasn't been that long. Grab a bag and let's get out of here. I need a shower and a change of clothes, the humidity and heat are killing me in these cooler climate clothes."

"Always the soft at heart, Evina," Abigail scoffed. Her older sister offered a reassuring smile and proceeded to make a straight line for the exit. A resort-supplied Toyota *Celica* with a driver awaited their combined departure.

The driver placed the luggage into the boot and opened the rear door. "Welcome to Bali, Mrs Bishop-Joiner," as the heat enveloped her like an open oven door. The two sisters shuffled into the rear seat as the car headed off to their resort, located about 25 kilometres to the north-west, with the air-con struggling against the humidity and oppressive tropical warmth.

Evina was pumping her blouse to generate some cool air. She turned to face, Abigail. "Mrs Joiner, wow, what a joke that turned out to be? How's Mum, still angry about me giving Troy his marching orders? I'm sure she was counting the days until a first grandchild would occupy her dreary life." Evina posed the question to her sister, already knowing the answer.

"Well, from what your e-mail said, that isn't about to happen anytime soon, is it?" Abigail stated, still not sure of the details surrounding her sister's recent and unexpected marriage break-up.

"Troy is a thing of the past. Trust your older sister when I say to you that he *can't* be trusted, Abby, and please—spare me the 'I told you so' speech. And what about you? Has Mr Right turned up on his white stallion yet? The life clock is ticking away, little sis. I bet Mum never stops asking the same question?"

"I don't need a man in my life right now. To me, it's all about my career." Abigail proudly stated, knowing her sister was not far off the mark.

"Who are you trying to kid, Abby? You're talking to me now. You are a hopeless romantic who would ditch your career in a millisecond if you bumped into the right guy—and you know it. Anyway, we can't waste any time chasing after men. We're under a deadline, and we may not be alone."

"What does that insinuate, 'may not be alone', what are you into anyway, Evina?"

"All in good time, Abigail. I need a bloody shower then to change out of these clothes and a good feed first. Food and then maybe slip me a couple of margarita's sister and I promise I will tell all—well, almost all."

Evina disguised a nervous laugh as the taxi pulled to a stop at the main entrance to their resort.

"It'll need to be a late lunch, Evina," Abigail wanted to explain.

"Why is that?"

"I have an appointment with a rather interesting English man who has offered to teach me some basic ballroom dancing moves."

"He doesn't happen to ride a white stallion by any chance, does he?" Evina's gaze suggested her sister might be holding back on a possible romantic link.

"No. Each year *The Telegraph* hosts an annual charity ball, and my editor has insisted that I attend, but I cannot if I can't at least look like I know what I'm doing on the dance floor."

"So, all is not lost. Is this mystery man good looking?" Evina replied with a smile.

"I haven't actually met him as yet, but you'll be the first to know—okay, big sister."

If either woman had bothered to turn their heads and cast a glancing view behind them, they would have met with the ice-like-glare, from a set of eyes that mirrored a pond of stagnated water. The retired North Korean major general who was known as the 'Jindeugi' which translates to mean a 'Tick', was a person trained in surveillance and observation from close quarters, like the bloodsucking kind that latches onto its prey and without detection sucking the life juices from its unsuspecting victims.

For a North Korean national, Duckhwan Tao was taller than average. As he directed his own taxi to drop him off within the tree-lined parking lot that fronted the resort entrance, his slanted-shaped eyes were firmly locked on to the two women entering the main foyer while he kept a safe distance, finding some cover under the shadows of a cluster of native cotton palms. He followed the women through the main entrance and took a seat on a comfortable lounge chair near a small fountain as a centrepiece in the cavernous foyer.

The Jindeugi stretched his arms high into the air and yawned. The slight scar running down from his bottom lip to the tip of his squared jawline stretched and was always a stark reminder of the perils involved in the business that was his chosen profession. He slid his mobile phone from his inside jacket pocket and disabled the flight mode, then began to scroll down, ignoring the first two missed calls, silently cursing each name as it appeared. The only contact of any importance was the final text message, a non-de-script set of letters from the North Korean alphabet that each represented a number. He retrieved the prepaid mobile he'd previously purchased from the airport and entered in the corresponding nine digits that would connect him to his current employer on Christmas Island.

Chapter·5

JUST OVER 1,000 kilometres to the west of Bali, located in the middle of the Indian Ocean, is the flat summit of a dormant underwater volcano which rises from 4,200 metres below sea-level with just the last 300 metres remaining above the surface of the ocean. Kiritimati Island was first sighted by Captain William Mynars on board the *Royal Mary* on December 25, 1643, and later visited by Captain James Cook on Christmas Eve in 1777 while sailing on the ships *Discovery* and *Rezolyushn* before being renamed Christmas Island.

Six people of immense power had gathered for their 'once a year' clandestine meeting in a secured facility located ten kilometres south of the main settlement of Flying Fish Cove, which lies near the north-eastern tip of Christmas Island

The ancient ceremony of the Korean 'special tea rite' dates back to the *Goryeo Dynasty* from 918 to 1392 and is a prerequisite to an important business meeting, a time when substantial information would be received and passed on to others with enormous influence and immeasurable wealth. The two hosts of the ceremony were half-brothers from a different mother and a North Korean father. The eldest sibling, Dakho Um, known as the *Geulaendeu Maseuteo*, or Grandmaster, motioned for the remaining four men to take up their pre-defined positions, designated as Bugjjog, Namjjog, Dangjjog and Seojjog translating to epitomise the four points of the compass reaching out on a never-ending spiritual path to embody the entire world. No names were ever exchanged at these high-profile meetings.

The first man to be seated was Bugjjog: the Chairman of the Board of the American-based Novar Corporation with an annual turnover US $47,101 million. Namjjog was the President of Ruchedarkt. A German drug empire with the Ruche family still holding fifty-one per cent of stock: annual revenue US $45,708M. Dangjjog was a Japanese man of small stature, who wore a tuxedo with a top hat and cane. With his manicured waxed moustache and a quick-step shuffle of his small feet, he could have passed as the villain in a James Bond movie. He was the senior president of the Japanese-based, Taxeto Corporation: combined annual revenue last financial year was over US $36,437M, and the final member of this select group was Seojjog, the CEO of the Amgon group of companies, with their head offices located in Moscow with an annual income of US $36,042M.

Privately, some might refer to Amgon as the runt of the litter, with just the poultry 36 billion in turnover. Making money was a game to these men—a game they played for keeps with exacting precision. Dealing with one pesky research scientist was going to be no problem at all.

After a decade of mergers and aggressive company take-overs, this small group of men represented the four largest pharmaceutical companies on the planet. Between them, they now controlled over eighty per cent of the world's retail 'over-the-counter drug sales'. Their combined wealth was almost insurmountable, and the power they wielded was far beyond the reach of most governments.

Each person sat cross-legged, around the low-lying *Soban*, a large tray-like table made of ginkgo wood where a collection of earthenware cups and teapots were arranged in the table's centre in precise order. The Soban was generally classified by their shape and number of legs, the most popular of which is *hojokban* or 'tiger leg'. This table's surface was constructed in the shape of a hexagon to represent each of the four men present, plus the master and his apprentice.

As the host of these annual meetings, the younger brother, known only as the Doje, or *e'prentis* to the Grandmaster, was to commence the time-honoured ceremony by first heating the pot, cups and the decanting bowls with hot water. The Doje then sprinkled green tea leaves into the pot, thereby rinsing the leaves of any dust and slightly opening up the leaves. He then allowed this to cool to the correct temperature, which was of the utmost importance, depending on the type of bud and the season it was picked. Early April meant the tea would be steeped at exactly 60-65 degrees Celsius for two to three minutes.

After steeping was complete, both hosts began to pour the tea into the decanting bowl, which serves to rid the water off the leaves in the pot and also to give the tea an even mixture. Then it was poured into each member's cup. The guests would now wait until the Geulaendeu Maseuteo, and his Doje picked up their cups first, soon to be followed by each person in order of their position around the Soban. This ritual was repeated until they each finished, which would consume the next thirty minutes as polite conversations were exchanged, usually about world political events and unrelated trivial business matters, to relax each member of this secret organisation, before the business at hand would be discussed at length.

A large bronze handmade purplish-blue-coloured effigy of a Christmas Island robber crab, with the slash of a violet hue across the underside of its carapace, hung from the ceiling over the Soban. With its two front pincers raised menacingly as a reminder to all and present of their vice-like-grip on the 200-billion-dollar-a-year pharmaceutical industry. Indigenous to Christmas Island and as the largest terrestrial arthropod on Earth, they can grow to relatively gigantic proportions. The largest specimens can weigh up to four kilograms with a body length of up to 400mm and a leg span of around 800mm.

The likeness, with its giant front claws, represented the Grandmaster and his Doje as the head of this business empire and the other four legs symbolised the remaining men that occupied their positions around the Soban. The company name 'Anomura' was inscribed in raised lettering, in both English and North Korean on the underside. Its two marble-shaped eyes cast a wide view over proceedings within the confines of this specially designed multi-functional room.

The younger Doje was alerted by the slight vibration of his cell phone as it buzzed on the glazed table surface. He cast his eyes down to recognise the name of the incoming call, then raised his hand to motion the room to silence. "Duckhwan Toa, please present an update on your status, we wait in anticipation of your current whereabouts," the Doje answered.

The Jindeugi frowned and cursed silently. *Amateur hour.* "May I remind you, Doje, there is no such thing as a secured line. The eyes and ears of the world are forever listening."

"Yes, of course, I apologise—I will use only your code name, Sinto, as agreed. Please go on."

"I am yet to receive confirmation of the transfer of my sister from the Australian Immigration Detention Centre." The Jindeugi wanted a verbal acknowledgement.

"All is in order. I give you my word as a fellow North Korean. The Australians have completed their due diligence, and she has been placed at the top of the queue. She will be transferred by commercial airline to the mainland as soon as you complete your assignment as arranged. No harm will come to the only surviving member of your family as long as you follow orders. Do I make myself clear? Her life rests on your results. You are to proceed as planned. Pursue and eliminate Abigail Bishop-Price and this old man, then apprehend the associate professor and deliver Bishop-Joiner, with her research, in-person to the Grandmaster. It is imperative we gain forward knowledge of how far this research group has progressed in their search for answers to nature's vault."

"I have arrived in Bali. If and when the moment presents itself, and either sister makes a move, I can assure it will be done. I guarantee it will be spectacular as requested," Tao replied.

"Assurances are short-lived, Sinto, we deal only in results. I shall wait for your next, more detailed report, then."

He ended the call and nodded to his older half-brother, seated at the opposite end of the hexagonal-shaped table.

The Grandmaster placed his cup neatly on the Soban and ushered with a sweeping hand action to gather each person's attention. "Gentleman," he offered a polite nod of the head to each member of this elite group as a show of respect. "I wish to bring this annual meeting to order and start with a most pressing piece of business, that I think you will all soon agree, needs to be dealt with urgently as a matter of course. Doje, would you be so kind as to update our associates on what we have uncovered since we all last met."

"Thank you, Grandmaster, it will be my honour. As you will be aware after perusing the detailed reports in front of each of you, the Anomura organisation has spies and many well-placed sleepers hidden within countless governments and corporations around the world. Our combined wealth is circumspect on the population of the planet, remaining unhealthy. A healthy population is not good for business. If a million people catch influenza, we make thirty million dollars. The common cold, in its innocuous self, represents billions in revenue for pills that offer relief, not a cure—just a stop-gap measure until the sickness reappears. May I remind all that sit here today, we are in the business of prolonging the sick and the unwell. A long and protracted death from terminal diseases is the core of what we all do, and we have proven in the past that we do it very well.

"One year ago, it was brought to our attention, a team of research scientists from the Smithsonian, were tasked with deciphering a mysterious ancient Arabic text dating back to the fifteenth century. This, in itself, was no reason to raise this to anything more than a 'watch and monitor level of interest'. That has now changed. Nine months ago, we received confirmation, that an associate professor, a woman named, Evina Bishop-Joiner, who is the head of this small team of researchers, is perhaps on the cusp of unearthing something of major significance to our business empire. She has in her possession a celestial globe. We believe this to be an ancient mapping device, to what and where, we are still not fully aware—for now. Our own research leads us to believe, she is on the verge of unravelling a mystery that could impact on all our combined business in a way that will be unprecedented."

There were a series of unified gasps and nervous exchange of concerned glances as each member's undivided attention hung in the temperate air from the ramifications of the final statement.

"We have set in motion a plan to bring this woman to stand before Geulaendeu Maseuteo so she can be interrogated concerning what she believes to be on the cusp of unearthing and revealing its contents to the world, without consideration. I might also add, this woman is due to meet with someone whom Anomura have been monitoring for some time now plus we have an inside Australian political contact that may turn out to be more than useful in our endeavours to bring this situation to its inevitable final resolution.

"Now gentlemen, I draw your attention to the screen on your right. As you can see, it is a map of Australia. The areas you see shaded in red are our current landholdings, and the purple areas represent other stations and farms we have earmarked for future acquisition. After we secure the necessary water rights from the relevant authorities, we will be on schedule to reach our optimum acreage by the end of the year and move into the first stages of our production plans."

The four men seated all nodded in agreement.

"Moving on," the Doje continued, "if you could turn to page three of your documents folder, we will set about discussing a secondary proposed expansion into other markets."

All six men in attendance opened their red-textured leather-bound folder and were each presented with a portfolio of coloured photos. On display were children as young as 12, up to teenage years, of both sexes in varying stages of undress down to full nudity.

"Please make your personal sexual preferences, or both if you wish, we have it all. Highlight your individual selections by circling your preferred photo and as the final meeting tonight reaches its end, we can all enjoy some well-earned sexual gratification, courtesy of the detention centre the Anomura organisation funded and built right under the noses of the Australian Government," the Doje boasted with a satisfying glee.

Contrasting defiled, and perverse sexual images flashed through the minds of these four pillars of the business world that occupied their position of privilege around the Soban.

Chapter-6

IN 1991, the Australian Liberal-National Coalition Party, who held a comfortable ten-seat majority, called a snap election to gain a mandate from the voting public concerning the introduction of the controversial Goods and Services Tax—the GST. The media described it as the un-winnable election for the Federal Labor Opposition Party, quoting the never-ending daily news polls as an inference for their sensationalised headlines. Then a simple question to the incumbent Liberal prime minister set the wheels in motion for a disaster in the waiting, and the rest would enter the annals of political history.

The prime minister was a special guest on the hugely rated Mike Willesee hosted *Current Affairs* program. Each weeknight at the prime-time of 7:00 P.M., millions of Australians would be glued to their television sets in anticipation of the critical questions that needed to be answered. This election was all about the GST, and the general public was confused as to how it would be implemented throughout the retail sector. How it would affect their everyday lives and would they be better, or worse off—as most guessed to be closer to the truth? The question Willesee asked was, "Could the Prime Minister explain to the millions of viewers how the GST will impact on the ingredients for baking a simple cake?"

Within a few short minutes, the election campaign was now in turmoil for the Liberal Coalition Party. Unable to answer this simple question, the PM stuttered and bumbled his way through some garbled political rhetoric that made no sense to both Willesee and the live studio audience. For Willesee, this was an interviewer's dream come true. He saw blood and went for the jugular. This was a career-maker, and he seized his moment. The more questions raised, the more the prime minister buried any chance of convincing the public how the introduction of this new retail tax would be rolled out. His government was in a spiralling downhill fall with no way to stop the massive swing, resulting in the Labor Party forming government with a seven-seat majority, six weeks later.

In August 1976, a relatively unknown swimmer most people just called Jerry, was representing Australia in the XXl Olympic Games, hosted by Canada in Montreal. Jerry competed in the 200-metre individual butterfly where he set a personal best time of 1:59.96 to take out the bronze medal in front of a cheering Australian crowd. Later the following day he was to become a controversial selection as the third leg in the shorter; 4 x 100-metre medley relay team, after a positive drug sample was returned by the popular, Craig Gibbings. Two hours later he broke Mark Spitz' world record time of 54:27, set in Munich during the 1972 games with a time of 54:17. This then took the relay team from their expected fifth-place standing to a slender lead of 1.6 seconds against the unbackable American team, closely followed by the local favourites; the Canadians and the controversial East Germans, with the suggestion their entire campaign was underpinned by a 'state-sponsored steroids program'.

With just the final freestyle leg remaining, Andrew Simms stood on the starting blocks in absolute awe at what he had just witnessed. Less than a minute later he looked up at the giant screen, oblivious to his three teammates going into near-hysterical excitation as he first noticed the Australian flag appear in first place. The gold medal was theirs for the keeping, and the team would now enter the history books as the underdogs who took on the world's best—and won.

In 1994, Jeremy Collins was offered the pre-selection and entered the political arena as a front-runner in the marginal federal seat of Eden-Monaro in his hometown of Bega.

Nine years later, the Labor Party was on the verge of an unprecedented third election victory as the groundswell of support got behind the newly Party Room appointed Prime Minister Jeremy Albert Collins, due to illness forcing the previous P.M. into early retirement. Collins immediately called an early election, wanting a clear mandate from the people to ratify the Labor Party's decision and to reassure himself that he was the preferred man for the top job.

Each morning Collins rose at exactly five A.M., jogged to the nearby New Parliament House aquatic centre for a one-hour work out in the Olympic-size pool, accompanied by his two Jack Russell terriers named Rusty and Nail and just the single security officer. After a light breakfast and his third cup of black coffee, strong with three teaspoons of raw sugar, Collins leant back into his comfortable high-back leather chair.

His first task after arriving at his office each morning was to open the secured, yellow and green wooden-padded lockbox and read through the reams of paper that painted the daily picture of both world and local events. The old Bega railway clock, a gift from his constituents, sat proudly on the opposite wall. It read 8:00 A.M., which prompted the prime minister that the first Tuesday of each month, he had requested an informal 10:00 A.M. meeting with the head of the Australian Security & Intelligence Organisation, referred to as just ASIO.

Since the Bali bombings in 2002, which resulted in the deaths of 88 innocent Australians, and a combined body count of 202, plus a further 209 people injured from a total of over twenty other countries, Collins wanted to keep abreast of proceedings with relation to the, almost farcical Indonesian court proceedings, currently taking place in Jakarta.

The so-called 'brains' of the operation was a radical Muslim cleric named Abu Bakar Bashir. He might have been their spiritual leader, but that was it. The Indonesian police had already detained three of the actual bombers who'd all been given a 'death sentence' in a Hollywood-style trial. They were all being treated like rock stars and now tagged as 'heroes' in the local media to cheering crowds, each day as they were paraded by smiling police and army-supplied security, all posing for pictures, while being escorted from the prisoner holding cells adjacent to the Indonesian Supreme Court.

Collins had always professed to his Labor Party colleagues, that if you ever wanted to check on the heartbeat of the Australian public, walk into the front bar of any pub, buy a round of beers and talk with the locals, which is something he did, from time to time. "At least there you won't get any of the political bullshit for an answer," he would proudly state to his own fellow ministers.

His days were continually interspersed with endless meetings that occupied too much of his time with the countless lawyers, barristers and the emerging elite class that seemed to be steering the world of modern-day politics to a state of 'political correctness' that was illogical, and unworkable. It was beyond the realms of comprehension, bordering on insanity to the average man in the street. At ten A.M. today he was hoping that was all about to change.

Chapter-7

JACK KELLY was an Australian. Tall, lean and apparently, ruggedly handsome, or so said the two sisters who ran the only bar within walking distance of his small bungalow in the village he now lived in on Island Chang in southern Thailand.

Kelly was a man with two identities, two pasts, one forgotten, the other somewhat regretful which together mapped out an unknown future. In some circles of the Royal Australian Navy, some might even regard him as an unsung hero. The simple fact was, he was still listed as MIA [possible KIA]. Like having an each-way bet, this was unprecedented.

Right now he was seated on the rear teak decking, comfortable in the stern all-weather lounge on his 72-foot cruising yacht the *Thin Lizzy,* named after a goanna that was now getting fat in the jungle that bordered his home. His first mate, deckie, cook, cleaner and chief bottle washer was a Thai man named, Till, still yet to turn 21, a man he treated like another brother and trusted—no questions asked.

The *Thin Lizzy* was a one-off prototype, designed to travel the oceans of the world with the comforts of a five-star floating palace, and was in the final days of a six-week charter on behalf of a family joint venture. The Centre for Tsunami Research (NOAA) and the Pacific Marine Environmental Laboratory (PMEL) was tasked with the job of identifying the slow surface displacement of any active geologic faults along the ocean floor between Sumatra and Central Java. DART stands for Deep-Ocean Assessment and Reporting of Tsunamis. It's an enhanced recording device that sits at a depth of up to 5,000 metres, measuring changes in pressure due to altering water levels. The recorder transmits acoustic signals to a buoy which then relays the measured height of a wave to a satellite. This information is then used to forecast the progress of a tsunami sending information in real-time to tsunami warning centres in Alaska, another in Hawaii, and a third in Puerto Rico.

The cost of replacing a DART and its Bottom Pressure Recorder is estimated to be over US $150,000, so the relatively small cost of periodically maintaining the equipment is regarded as money well spent.

And at $1,200 a day, Jack Kelly agreed wholeheartedly. The charter was due to wind up the following evening. The two bigwigs of the entire operation were both Americans named Frank and Jesse James. When Kelly was first introduced, he wondered if it might have been a practical joke—it wasn't. Some parents just don't think the whole naming their children thing through. In keeping with the whole western theme, everyone referred to Frank as just Horse, like the larger-than-life character in the '60s TV series, Bonanza. The word 'draft' could have easily been slipped in—he was one big unit.

Frank was a keen big game angler and asked Kelly if he could invoice his company another week in return for two days fishing off the southern side of Bawean Island in the Java Sea. A fifty-metre underwater drop-off runs east to west, which causes the ocean currents to bring to the surface schooling bait balls of pilchards. The distance from the shore is enough that the use of dynamite by the local fisherman hasn't yet destroyed the local habitat and the reef edge is frequented by albacore tuna, wahoo and blue mackerel that will test the skills of any half-decent fisherman.

Kelly had a simple rule: 'no fishing charters'. They were messy and always included excessive intake of alcohol, which, when mixed with testosterone, usually ended in heartache. Not an ideal situation when you're a 100 kilometres away from the closest land. Frank James was a man that didn't take no for an answer, and money speaks its own language. So, the game chair was dusted off and retrieved from the below-deck storage, and younger brother Jesse was currently doing battle with what looked like a better-than-average tuna using a Shimano TLD-50 loaded with 20-kilo mono.

Nine hook-ups, three bust-offs and three edible fish in the icebox, was considered a good day's fishing in any man's books.

Kelly set the auto-pilot, then manoeuvred his six-foot-two-inch bulk down the internal stairs to the galley on the floor deck below. Till immediately started hosing down the external rear decking before washing all the gear down with fresh water. The skipper stepped onto the rear deck, then buried his arm up to his elbow into a large icebox. It was full with an even mix of salt water and slush ice to make up an ice slurry and inside were three nice-sized 15-plus-kilo albacore tuna the brothers managed to haul in on a trailing red and white Rapala lure. Kelly laid the first fish flat on the filleting table then expertly ran his surgical steel, bone-handled filleting knife across the diamond-edged butcher's steel and felt the blade with the tip of his finger before he went about dressing the long silver finely honed predators of the sea.

Kelly yelled out to Till, "My turn for the chef's duties tonight. I'll cut these fish into about sixty cutlets for the smoker. For dinner tonight, Till, let's set aside eight nice size fillets and wrap them in alfoil with some garlic, lemon butter and don't worry, there will be plenty of chillies sprinkled around for your Thai-trained taste buds, all right. You crank up the BBQ and get some coals glowing, mate."

Till looked up into the cobalt-blue eyes of his unkempt-looking, blond-haired skipper with the same amused expression he'd used so many times before as his boss always enjoyed poking a bit of fun at his love of hot, spicy food—with breakfast, lunch and dinner. A flock of seagulls swooped down and started squabbling over some discarded fish guts amongst the disturbed prop wash as Kelly loaded up the bread maker with a freshly knead dough mix.

Till then asked in his Thai version of English, "So, Boss, what time we make Bali tomorrow?"

Kelly looked at the ship's clock, "We'll drop Frank and Jesse off at Surabaya where they have a private jet booked to fly them straight home to the States. We can slap up a bit of breakfast, purchase all our stores and get them stowed before we head off to Nusa Lembongan on the high tide. I reckon we'll be anchored up before the sun sets tomorrow."

Kelly was careful not to slip on the freshly mopped deck as he headed inside to the galley. The only occasion this man found it necessary to wear shoes was either attending a wedding or a funeral, and since today was neither, he enjoyed the freedom of bare feet while at sea.

At 10:30 A.M. the following day, a fully loaded Mitsubishi *Triton*, packed with stores, and an abundance of fresh fruit and other groceries, reversed up Surabaya North Quay to the berthed yacht, sitting high in the water as the tide reached its highest ebb.

Kelly pointed towards the sky as a Learjet flew over, "Say goodbye to Frank and Jesse, Till," then he commenced the unloading, passing the boxes over to the waiting arms of his smiling deckhand. After the last box was stowed, Kelly sat in his comfortable air-cushioned captain's chair and punched in the GPS coordinates for their destination, a small island off the coast of Bali for his much-anticipated first time meeting with a woman named, Tamara Sherry. For whatever reason, the Indonesian authorities were adamant that he and Till were to meet with Immigration on Lembongan, about 18 kilometres west of Bali itself.

A crowd of interested onlookers, mostly local fisherman and their young families, had gathered along the entrance to Yellow Bridge that connects to Ceningan Island. They all gawked in fascination as the sleek lines of the freshly spray-painted green and blue fibreglass and kevlar hull cut a clean line through the shallow, unspoilt azure-coloured waters as the cruising yacht prepared to set anchor for the night.

From the flybridge, the skipper reversed the twin Man V12 1900-hp diesel engines, bringing the yacht to a dead-stop and allowed the bow to drift into an up-wind position. Till cast a toothy smile over the four-foot-long rubberised goanna that took pride of place clip-locked underneath the stainless steel bow rail. He knocked out the anchor release pin, allowing Kelly to drop the 55-kg Danforth anchor. The noise of the linked chain rattling through the anchor snubber startled a group of hovering gulls, as Kelly reversed the port-side engine to embed the dual flutes into the sandy bottom five metres below the keel before Till tied off the anchor safety rope on the bow cleat.

Till then asked, "You must really like your football, Boss?"

"Australians, Till. We are great travellers, mate, and it's both the AFL and NRL grand finals this weekend. Plus, I promised my two sisters I would meet with this Australian woman. Apparently, her position within the Federal Parliament gives her access to some very powerful people."

Kelly picked up the satellite phone and dialled the Two Sisters Bar on Koh Chang to pass on a message to Tiaan—a Thai lady that punched well above Jack Kelly's weight. But stranger things have happened in the land of love and luck.

Kelly's past was still dotted with gaping holes. The circumstances surrounding the first time he met with Tiaan didn't exactly exude an aura of confidence that he might make good husband material. After his return trip back to Thailand, he planned to pop the question that can scare the living shit out of many a fine man. *The best-laid plans*, he silently considered with an air of apprehension.

Chapter-8

PRIME MINISTER Jeremy Collins' private phone buzzed twice. Without picking up, he yelled through his half-open office door for his personal assistant to escort the taciturn, Director-General of ASIO Darcy Jones, into his office.

ASIO was established in 1949: post World War II at the insistence of Prime Minister Sir Robert Menzies. Its direct operation was answerable to the attorney-general's office under the *Australian Security & Intelligence Organisation Act 1979* and is tasked with the responsibility of investigating and identifying espionage, threats to Australian borders, sabotage and any politically motivated violence against Australians, both internally and abroad. It keeps a check on any interference from foreign enemies and allies alike, against the Australian Defence Forces. The position of director-general is a non-political appointment and is designed to be clearly separated from the influences of any incumbent government. With this comes great responsibility as a covert organisation that operates on the world stage. In a nutshell, ASIO is answerable to no one.

Darcy Jones cracked what he would regard as a wide smile through his pursed lips while he greeted Collins with a warm and firm handshake. Both men began the short walk to a pair of lift doors that would descend to a secure room, located three levels below ground. Only four other Australians possessed the security clearance to gain access to this electronically monitored secured conference room referred to as the 'Menzies Room' but today's meeting was between two people, and for a very good reason. Jones emptied the contents of his pockets, including his two mobile phones into a specially provided secured locker as was normal procedure, while Collins placed his right eye into the rubberised cup that would perform the laser ophthalmoscopy scan. The six blue confocal lasers scrutinise a microscopy diagnostic image of the cornea and match the results in less than three seconds.

The bombproof doors electronically opened, revealing three steps to a sunken room with a long boardroom table made from a single Tasmanian blackwood tree. Surrounded by eight high-back leather chairs facing a wall of computer monitors, a handful of large digital screens accompanied by an abundance of other electronic monitoring equipment, these were all controlled by a half-hexagonal-shaped control panel normally occupied by three—24-hour-a-day operatives behind a soundproof plexiglass divider. Darcy Jones looked on in surprise at the empty room. He had only cause to be invited into the Menzies Room on just the two previous occasions since the New Parliament House was completed, but never had he been in this room with just the prime minister. He asked himself why?

Collins placed his open palm on a second biometric scanner. It returned a luminous green imprint of all his five fingers and palm before a small window embedded into the console slid silently open. He then placed his hand inside and depressed a large grey plunger, and a red light blinked on a monitor in the shape of the Menzies Room until a small alarm sounded and the image also turned the same colour green in an instant to indicate the room was now secure.

The prime minister turned and faced the director-general, "Just you and me here today, Darcy. No other eyes or ears. Are you okay with that?" Collins wanted to point out.

"Well—that all depends. Why all the extra effort? Obviously, something important is on your mind. If I feel you're placing my position as director-general, or this conversation compromises ASIO in any way, I will ask you to cease, and I will leave. Is that understood, Prime Minister?"

"Loud and clear. Here, take a seat." Collins opened up a thick green-coloured manila file that was already conveniently sitting on the table. He extracted three pages and slid them over to where Darcy Jones was seated.

"Read through these, they arrived by secured courier three days ago, personally delivered by the British Consulate via diplomatic pouch, for my eyes only. Read it carefully, particularly the final paragraph, and then tell me what you probably already know and what you privately think—without any bullshit. Straight from the hip today, Darcy. Do you understand?"

Jones speed read the first two pages without alarm. He was well aware of all that was written. Then he turned the last page, and his eyes widened. He adjusted his reading glasses and read over the entire last paragraph slowly, a second time. He removed his glasses and looked up at Collins, still pacing the room on the opposite side of the table. "Bloody hell! When did this come to light? How good is this source? Have you had this verified by a third party as yet?" Jones fired his questions off in rapid succession.

"I just got off the phone with the Madam Director-General of MI6. Her and I go back a long way and were more than good friends. She owed me a favour from the time she was involved with the British Olympic team in 76. Equestrian if I remember right. Those bloody Indonesians are playing games with this country, and I don't like it one bit," an animated Collins let fly.

Jones stood and walked over to the triple-headed coffee machine, then pressed the button for a flat white. The sounds of grinding coffee beans filled the uncomfortable silence. Jones stirred in a cube of sugar, turned his head slowly to face the scowling Collins, and started to speak. "Prime Minister . . ."

Collins raised his hand in the air, "Hear me out first Darcy before you answer. I want you to clearly understand what I have to say. Then you can form a precise picture in your own mind, where I stand, okay."

"You have my full attention." Jones held a deep respect for Jeremy Collins. Since the Bali bombings, his monthly meetings with the PM had resulted in a special understanding in relation to current and past events. This prime minister, in his opinion, understood better than any of the two previous PM's he was tasked with delivering a two-hour debriefing every month, the difficulties and intricacies of dealing with a foreign country in affairs that would never make it to the front-page of any paper. Collins wore his heart on his sleeve and was a true patriot. Jones had, in the past, always preferred action to the long-drawn-out rhetoric of diplomatic solutions, and that suited his agency—just fine.

Collins leaned into the polished table, "Eighty-eight Australians lie dead, Darcy—and for what? Innocent people enjoying a holiday, then *BOOM!* In an instant, their charred and mutilated remains are spread all over the streets of Kuta. I visited the aftermath; saw with my own eyes, smelt with my own nose the stench of death. How many bloody Australian families have to bear the aftermath for their entire lives? Children growing up without a parent or grandparents. Christ— the Kingsley Football Club in Perth lost seven team members. Gone in an instant—and the Australian public both want—and deserve answers.

"All that unnecessary carnage just so these bastards can raise their status as a serious terrorist cell and impress their towel-head mates back in sand-land. This report is the final icing on the cake as far as I am concerned. There is no doubt in my mind now that the Indonesian Government played a role in this attack. They're protecting Bashir, and those three stooges they've conveniently showcased to the world media for execution are just the tip of the iceberg. Do they really think we are that stupid to believe they masterminded this—alone? No bloody way, and you and I both know that to be true.

"Australians have sat back for too long, Darcy, sitting on our hands and letting both the Americans and the Brits pull our strings. They both treat this country like a giant mushroom, keeping us in the dark while feeding us a line of bullshit. I want that to change, and that is why we are both locked away here— today."

Jones was not easily alarmed. As a former field agent, he had worked closely with the Americans, both during the Vietnam conflict and earlier behind the Iron Curtain in East Germany. At that time, even as an Australian operative, he reported directly to the British, who then passed on what they thought to be relevant information to the Australian parliament. He sympathised with Collins and knew what he said was closer to the truth than he even knew himself. As the prime minister, politicians come and go, but the rolling stone of espionage gathers no moss. This was a common acronym within the circles of ASIO. He had never witnessed the raw emotion and frustration that was evident with each word spoken by Collins. Jones considered privately, *Maybe the time is right to test the waters, so to speak?*

Jones stood up and circled the table, "Prime Minister, I want to discuss with you about your own private thoughts on what I know you are privy to. And what I mean is the covert actions taken by both the CIA after 9/11 and MI6, post the double-decker bus bombing on the Aldwych at London's West End in 1996. Like you said; all bullshit aside."

"Like I said before, Darcy, straight from the hip. This is no time for the political two-step. Yes—I am fully aware, and that is exactly why I have asked for this meeting today. Let's just cut to the chase, Darcy—shall we? What are our options in hitting back at these terrorists, off the grid? Does ASIO have the resources to carry out a Parliamentary Order, under Article-289, of the Act?"

"Article-289? Prime Minister, are you fully aware of the ramifications of such an order? This would be unprecedented, unheard of in the history of Australia," Jones stated, while excited at where this conversation may be leading.

"Darcy, this prime minister—probably more than any other previous sitting PM knows the sealed section of the Act intimately. I have read and studied Article-289 for the past four weeks—word-for-word. Ask yourself this? Why was this piece of legislation included by our Bicameral Federal Parliament and ultimately passed by both the House of Representatives and the

Senate in the first place? I'll tell you why—for this very reason. Someone had the foresight to write this in, with the presumption that this very real-case scenario could—and now has happened. If we don't act and act now, then it remains as just worthless words on a piece of sealed parchment. So, let me have it in clear language we can both understand."

"Is this conversation being recorded?" Jones was an experienced operative. He needed to cover all his bases before proceeding any further. PM or no PM, he wanted to protect his own position.

"Nothing is being taped. The legislation excludes ASIO from any form of prosecution—even under a parliamentary investigation. We have the legal means, now I want to know, do we have the capabilities to carry out a covert overseas operation?"

"Well then, Prime Minister, what I am about to divulge to you—here in this room, between just the two of us, will always remain exactly that. Do I understand this correctly?"

"What is discussed in the privacy of this secured facility, is, and will always remain between the prime minister and the director-general of ASIO. Section-289, under the Act, does require the prime minister to seek verification of the order by all the Joint Chiefs of the Australian Defence Force. That includes the Army, Air Force and the Navy, and a further confirmation with the deputy prime minister. This won't be a problem and is of no concern of yours. You still haven't answered my original question. Do we have the assets to carry out a sanctioned assassination on foreign soil?"

"Yes, we do, Prime Minister. We have a man trained and ready to go. You just give me the signed written order, and we will initiate contact with our man on the ground, and as you say, the rest is of no concern to you after you take affirmative action. The details will stay within this organisation. You will be notified, by me personally, when the operation is completed."

"A man, one man—is that what you're referring to, not a team?"

"That's exactly what I'm saying. This man only works alone. Trust me when I say that is the preferred option. One man, one set of eyes and no other witnesses. This man I refer to, Prime Minister, will get the job done. He has been under the ASIO umbrella for some time now and has never failed to complete a mission."

"Is he already on your payroll?"

"We have access to discretionary funds as part of our non-disclosed budget. The one the bean counters and the Senate don't have access to in Canberra. And yes, he is part of our team. How well-read are you regarding the history of the ASFU?"

"The Australian Special Forces Units? You're, of course, referring to the 'Black Scatter' program," Collins answered.

"Well, yes, and no. Let me enlighten you. After Singapore fell in February 1942, General Blamey, in one of his few master-strokes, had the foresight to see the need for a different approach to the Japanese incursion through Indonesia, the Java Sea and eventually Papua New Guinea as the Japanese Imperial Army marched towards mainland Australia.

"He formed small groups of eight-man teams, who underwent specialist training in counter-espionage tactics. Australian trained and Australian led in the field of battle, a first during the entire Second World War for our troops. The only forces in place in Papua at that time were reservists and conscripts. There were *no* full-time ADF troops; they were all still posted in North Africa, if you remember, courtesy of Churchill.

"Both he and Roosevelt, in a private meeting in London, had already agreed they'd both be prepared to let 'Australia fall' to the Japanese. Justifying this decision by saying they could reclaim the country after the war in the Pacific was won. Do you believe those guys? Shit, they're supposed to be our allies, for Christ's sake. These virtually untrained and inexperienced soldiers were tasked with hindering the Japanese advancement, alone.

"Blamey's new teams were to assist in destroying railway lines, bridges and ships at anchor, all to disrupt their supply lines. You know the Jap's eventually got within plain sight of Port Moresby. Next step after that was North Queensland. These small groups were solely responsible for that not happening, and probably the reason we're not all speaking Japanese right now."

The prime minister turned from his standing position, placed both his open palms firmly on his desk and eye-balled Jones. "That conversation between Churchill and Roosevelt was never proven," Collins challenged.

"Yeah, and either was the truth behind Kennedy's assassination. Both kept under wraps courtesy of the fifty-year Presidential Seal," Jones continued. "In 1962, John F. Kennedy laid the foundation for what was to become the first of the Navy SEALs. SEAL teams, one and two. Their primary objectives were to develop an unconventional warfare capability to conduct counter-guerrilla tactics and covert marine operations. As the conflict in Vietnam increased, and with more and more American soldiers dying, President Johnson took the SEAL initiative one step further. It became a known fact that there were stark differences between the American and the typical Viet Cong soldier. The CIA initiated a report at the direct request of Johnson. The report highlighted the simple fact that the typical VC soldier relied on the unbroken chain of command. As a fighting unit, they were highly skilled, but as an individual soldier, they lacked initiative and the ability to act alone if their command structure was decimated. It was often said that if a VC general instructed his troops to walk off the edge of a cliff, they would do so without question. It's a part of the Asian mindset, not to question his commanding officer, under any circumstances—ever. They followed orders like marching ants.

"Give the same order to a bunch of Australian soldiers, and they would just laugh, sit down and roll another smoke. The then-defence minister recommended that the ADF create a spur unit based on the success of these SEAL teams. Teams of up to eight soldiers with a trained sniper and lookout man. These units needed to think for themselves, acting without direct supervision and with a wider scope of deployment. They were to be a fast-acting, fully mobile unit, able to be called upon at a moment's notice. They could be transferred by submarine, or airlifted by helicopter, and dropped deep behind enemy lines, which were blurred anyway, for sometimes up to six months at a time. Their primary objective was to 'take out' the enemy's leadership. Assassinate with a single bullet their CO's. Cut the head from the snake, and the snake becomes useless. These teams became what is now known as the Tiger Force."

"Your man is a part of this elite force?"

"Was—Prime Minister, their true identities are sealed under Executive Order. You would no doubt remember the single refugee boat that arrived on Christmas Island back in 1993. The only survivors from what was initially a family of six were the husband, his wife, and a young son. The father who provided photographic evidence that resulted in the return of those Australian POW's and the one very lucky journalist, well that was the Tiger Force which officially has been disbanded, but unofficially the training regime continued under a cloud of secrecy."

"Jesus, Darcy? You guys in ASIO really do run your own show, don't you?" Collins came back with, questioning the chicanery that existed between ASIO and the highest office in the country.

"Plausible deniability Prime Minister. Can you imagine requesting permission from the then-prime minister's office or the Senate to agree to such a covert mission, we would still be locked in ridiculous diplomatic talks, and those men would all probably still be held captives somewhere in the jungles of South East Asia. Action first and bugger the consequences were words used by these men at the time, and rightly so."

"So—go on. What happened next?" Collins queried.

"After the POW's eventual debriefing back in Australia, we were advised they were originally a detachment of sixteen soldiers. The details of their actual rescue, to this day, are shrouded in a cloud of secrecy and the unknown. The sniper's scout wrote in his report that he was the only person to survive a bridge collapse forcing him and his sniper into a flooded river. Something happened over there, and we may never know what it was because of the bond between these brothers-in-arms is unbreakable and for life."

"I have been read-in, but now you're telling me—one man—single-handedly rescued these POW's *and* that female journalist from what we have to assume was a heavily guarded secret camp in the middle of the Cambodian jungle and somehow got them all to the safety of the extraction point? Bloody hell, who is this guy—Superman?" Collins asked.

"He is still officially listed as MIA, but his old scout is our man on the ground, and currently he is probably enjoying a cold beer somewhere warm, awaiting his next set of instructions."

"Fine, it's time we dipped our toes in the cesspool of water that is modern-day terrorism and hit back with a bloody sledgehammer. People and other countries need to know that the Australian public will no longer sit idly by while our citizens are used as cannon fodder for cowardly acts of mass murder for their own political gain. This country has stood side by side with both our allies in times of war, always on foreign soil and always to protect the interests of nations thousands of kilometres from our shores.

"Lest we forget Gallipoli. Our diggers would be turning in their graves if they knew the situation we find ourselves in today. It's time Australia stood alone and sent a clear message, that we too can play their game, and let 'em know, we're bloody-well very good at what we do. You will have the signed order by the end of business this Friday. Make it happen, Darcy." Collins walked out from behind his seated position.

"Yes, Prime Minister." Darcy Jones stood to attention and extended his hand to the man they simply called, Jerry.

"I'll send you confirmation of where and what time on Friday. Not here in Parliament House," Collins added. "I don't want people to start asking the question why the director-general of ASIO was meeting with the prime minister, twice in the same week."

"This is my twenty-four-seven mobile number," Jones offered. "It's an ASIO monitored line that will send a text message to my second secured phone. Until Friday, then."

"You have the green light to proceed. Good luck and godspeed."

"In my humble opinion, Prime Minister, under the guise of God and religion, more wars have been created than solved. I think we'll just keep this between our mortal selves."

Collins looked at Jones with an aporetic stare and then nodded, followed by an under-the-breath grunt. The slight hissing sound of the airtight sealed door slowly opening to his rear indicated that the meeting had come to its inevitable end. Both men left the Menzies Room, with their thoughts consumed by what had just transpired. One was excited at the prospects that lay ahead, while the other considered the political fallout if the reality of failure was to raise its ugly head.

Chapter·9

TOBIAS STONE checked his kitbag for the final time as he prepared to board the GAF-Nomad high-wing, STOL floatplane due to leave Darwin at 2200 hours. The director-general of ASIO hand-delivered his instructions, which Stone burnt after reciting them to memory. Most of what he needed to carry out his mission would be acquired after a rendezvous with a local asset after he is dropped off the coast of Southern Central Java to meet with a waiting fishing trawler. His back door entry to a foreign land was almost as simple as purchasing a ticket over the counter from a local travel agent. He had been down this path on many occasions before.

After a flight time of just under five hours, a lone trawler flashed its deck lights as the low flying Nomad circled back on its original flight path and prepared for a blind instrument-only landing. The pilots were accustomed to these fly-by-night approaches, but the nerves were always tested while landing any aircraft without a clear line of sight. It was like driving a car in heavy fog at speed with just your park lights. The dark-blue-coloured amphibious aircraft bounced across what was a relatively calm sea and eased to a slow crawl, with a spraying mist trailing the powerful spinning propeller blades, almost invisible against the natural ocean backdrop. A small rubber dinghy was launched over the starboard side of the fish-stained deck as the idling trawler swayed on the gentle swell while a dark-skinned man paddled the short distance to where the seaplane was drifting on its two floats.

The pilot removed his earphones and turned in his chair to face the now-empty seat with his hand mimicking a loud hailer. "Please check you have all your belongings safely secured in your possession before you prepare to disembark—and thank you for choosing stealth air. We hope you enjoy your holiday," Taffy Bromwich joked, as he watched his only passenger open the door-lock and step onto the port-side float.

"Always a pleasure, Taffy. Safe return journey, mate," Stone replied with a cool stare while his thick locks of black curly hair tucked under a woollen beanie hung loosely down the nape of his neck.

The co-pilot removed his harness and secured the door, checking the safety lever was firmly locked in place. Stone heaved his long canvas bag into the open dinghy and jumped in, taking the only other small bench seat towards the snub-nosed bow. Bromwich waited until the all-clear had been given, assuring the small craft had cleared their wingtips before powering down on the chrome, bone-handled centre stick and gathered speed. The sounds of the turbo-powered engines roared loud with a deep whirring growl in the distance as the floats cleared the small swell and lifted into the barren night sky above.

Today would be day one of the mission assigned with the code name, 'Blue Skies'. This was Stone's third assignment for the director-general of ASIO and without a doubt his most challenging. The Indonesian Government had previously arrested and tried three men: Imam Samudra, Amrozi Nurhasyim and Huda bin Abdul, who they professed were solely responsible for the three-pronged bomb attack on Bali in 2002.

It was all just a well-rehearsed show for the eyes and ears of the world press, with the courtroom packed to the rafters each day accompanied by the swarming media scrums all following the trial proceedings. This was merely a means for the Indonesian Government to 'save face' which was of the utmost importance and entrenched in the Asian way of life. Their apparent sentence of death by firing squad was to be carried out on the island prison of Nusakambangan sometime in the foreseeable future after all appeals had been exhausted, and this was to be the end of the matter as far as the Indonesians were concerned. Tried, found guilty and shot. All over - red rover.

Stone had in his possession three names. Two were Indonesian nationals, and the third was possibly either an Arab or a Turkish citizen, and all were members of the terrorist cell known as *Jemaah Islamiyah*. The bomb maker was identified by the intelligence report from MI6 as a man called Dulmatin, referred to as the 'Genius', and was ultimately the individual who made the call that set off the car bomb, packed with potassium chlorate, parked out the front of the Sari Club. The second name was that of Abu Dujana and was identified as the leader of this terrorist cell and responsible for delivering the thirty thousand US dollars funding and the precise instructions required to carry out the attack. The third and final name was Aris Munandar: a.k.a. - Sheik Aris. He was the link between Jemaah Islamiyah and al-Qaeda. British Intelligence suggested he may have fled back to Pakistan and could be holed-up in a mountain hide-away somewhere near the Afghanistan border.

As their spiritual leader, a radical cleric named Abu Bakar Bashir was currently being held in custody, also wanted by the Indonesian authorities for other related attacks in Malaysia and Singapore. Without his ultimate consent and blessing, the bombings would have never taken place. He was of no concern to Stone, which was a pity because he would have been more than happy to have clocked his card for the final time—free-of-charge.

And now all three men's names appeared as a memorised list and had been cleared by the five most powerful men and woman in Australia for a sanctioned targeted assassination, under Article-289 of *The Intelligence and Securities Act.* An imminent terrorist threat to the people and the lives of Australians travelling overseas. Simply put, it was revenge at the highest level of power, therefore—it was both justifiable and legal. Stone never allowed himself to get involved in the semantics of what was morally right and what was straight-out murder. *Live by the sword - an eye for an eye, and all that bullshit*, Stone surmised. He was a Darwinist and definitely was *not* a man that leaned towards any religious persuasion. In his opinion, faith was real, but the number one bestselling book on the planet was pure fiction.

The modern lines of the war on terror were never clearly defined, and the world was fighting a different type of battle. There were no front lines anymore. Just decisions made by men who hide behind positions of enormous power that needed to be acted upon by soldiers such as himself. The Australian Navy had spent hundreds of thousands of dollars training Tobias Stone, and the Australian people were about to see a return on their investment. They just would never be privy to any of the finer details.

Stone's biggest obstacle was not the bad guys. They would be oblivious to his arrival. His major problem was the Indonesian police and the inherent corruption that was part of everyday life in most Asian countries. A person's life was worth about as much as a small paddy field. A foreign operative working on their patch of dirt would secure you enough land and money to live a comfortable life. The carrot was dangling and within reach, which is one of the reasons Stone liked to work alone these days. The sanctioned assassinations needed to be carried out in privacy with no ties back to Australia if he was to have any chance of taking out his three designated targets. A sniper round from five hundred metres would be an easier option but would awaken the sleeping dragon that was the Indonesian police, headed by Da'i Bachtiar and he was nobody's fool. Tread carefully around the edges and trust no bastard.

An Englishman named John Jay, quoted in 1813, 'hope for the best and plan for the worst'. Stone often liked to remind himself that you needed to be able to flip a plan in a matter of seconds.

Stone's one and only contact while in Jakarta was with a British operative named, Bradley Monarsh, who with his own British-born Green Beret father, had worked together while in

South Korea during the debacle that was later to be known as the 'Korean blue house raid'.

On January 16, 1968, in an attempt to assassinate the South Korean, President Park Chung-hee, while in his residence commonly known as the blue house, for obvious reasons, a North Korean unit called the 124, left their garrison at Yonsan. Negotiating the demilitarised zone and then crossing over the Injin River, they eventually set up camp at the base of Simbing Mountain.

Four South Korean brothers named Woo stumbled across the secret camp while collecting firewood. A fierce debate took place about whether they should kill the brothers. Instead, it was decided to indoctrinate them on the supposed benefits of communism with a verbal guarantee they would not report their whereabouts to the local Changhyeon police. The Woo brothers did exactly that immediately after their release.

Three battalions from the South Korean 25th Infantry Group Division were dispatched and began searching the Simbing and Nogo Mountains. The 124 were split into four groups of six-man-cells and were given a new rendezvous point to meet and complete their mission. Failure was not an option under the North Korean regime.

At that time, Burma was still colonised under British rule. The Brits weren't directly involved in the Vietnam War but were well aware of the direct relationship between North Korea and the North Vietnamese. The link continued further down the slimy political trail to also include Russia and China. The Vietnam War was never about the country itself. The real war was putting a halt to the tentacles of communism creeping into South East Asia through the back door that was Vietnam and South Korea by these two military giants to the west. The British were made aware of the planned assassination attempt on President Park Chung-hee's life and sent a team of sixteen, sniper-trained Green Berets under cover of diplomatic immunity to meet with the Americans and finalise their plans. Firstly, they were to thwart the proposed execution, which would have resulted in chaos among the newly formed, American-backed government of South Korea, and secondly to attempt to capture alive the man known as the Jindeugi, and the leader of 124.

As the 25th closed the search perimeter, two groups of the 124 made it to the agreed location and changed into Republic of Korea Army (ROKA) uniforms of the local 26th Infantry, complete with correct Unit Insignia, which they had in their possession. They formed up and prepared to march the last mile to the blue house. Posing as ROKA soldiers, they approached the final Jahamun checkpoint and were challenged as to their identity by the Chief of Police Choi Gyushik.

The British plan was simple. With the element of surprise, confirmed intelligence on the enemy's strength and their planned point of entry into the ten-acre presidential compound that was protected by a twelve-foot-high perimeter fence, the final checkpoint gave them a five-hundred-metre clear line of sight. Each team of two, a sniper and his lookout man, would need to eliminate three 124 targets in under twenty seconds. It was a dream come true for the snipers, almost like a training drill. They lay in wait under their hutches with the scouts relaying the distance, wind speed and their designated targets. The Jindeugi was an expert warfare strategist and needed to be taken alive for interrogation.

Suspicious of the impersonating ROTA soldiers' answers, Choi Gyushik drew his pistol and was immediately shot by the Jindeugi. A fierce exchange of gunfire broke out with the 124 resorting to the use of hand grenades before the unit broke up and retreated back into the Inwang and Bibong Mountains.

Stone's father and the British team leader, a Major Bradley Monarsh snr, could only watch on through their infra-red night vision goggles, from their concealed positions in shock realisation as the fiasco played out only four hundred metres from their location, with strict orders not to engage and risk losing allied forces under friendly fire. An hour later, ninety-eight South Korean police and soldiers lay dead. Their plan to capture the 124's leader had been blown away by the hand of fate. Lady luck, or in this case, bad luck.

Just fourteen days later, the Jindeugi's brilliantly planned and execution of the TET Offensive was put into action, which ultimately was the turning point of the Vietnam War and a prelude to the Americans withdrawing from Saigon. Some days are diamonds and others just turn to shit.

Stone knew his information from Monarsh would be accurate but more importantly, it would be current. Unlike the CIA, MI6 could be relied upon, Stone knew from personal experience. The special relationship that had always existed between Australia and the UK was almost sacrosanct among the small community of special operatives that chose this as their way to serve their respective countries.

Stone paid for his estimated one-week rental accommodation in the slum district that bordered the Barito River in Jakarta after previously retrieving the prearranged dead-letter-drop from under a park bench opposite the British Consulate. Inside was a key to a locker located at the Manggarai Train Station.

He needed a safe house to conduct around-the-clock electronic surveillance of the shanty building opposite his second-story window that overlooked the busy Banjarmasin Floating Markets and eating houses. These days they mainly consisted of wooden-hulled boats now permanently moored, taking the place of the more traditional land-based stalls, all sharing the rat-infested canals with the seemingly endless kilometres of overgrown morning glory that clogged most of the waterways. After setting up his recording equipment programmed to sound a low-level alarm with a choice of ten different sounding birds when it detected movement at the doorway, Stone stripped down to his boxers, turned on the overhead fan and grabbed some much-needed sack time.

The slight chirping of a flycatcher, a common local bird species that helped rid the spiders from taking over the exterior of the building, alerted Stone to an instant awakening. He stepped over to his window and pulled the dust-covered, rotting curtain to one side and cast his eyes at the activity taking place across the road. Three men, all wearing a traditional Arab thawb, could be seen entering the near-dilapidated building. One was still talking on a mobile phone as he scanned a wide view of the neighbourhood before securing the door closed behind him.

"These pricks are never alone," Stone cursed under his breath. Sometimes collateral damage was part and parcel of the deal—but not on this occasion. Three names—three bodies only. *The sleeping dragon*, Stone recited silently.

A further two days passed with the only action being a young Javanese boy delivering parcels of food to the front door at midday. He would knock and then leave immediately. The door would soon after crack open, and the same person-of-interest each day bent down to collect the small cardboard box. On day three, a stray cat startled him, causing the contents to spill out onto the small wooden landing, revealing some of the menu items inside. As devout Muslims, their diet certainly *did not* include any form of Western food, but as Stone reviewed the video and zoomed in, he noticed a half-litre plastic bottle with the words in clear English describing a brand name, Danish Dairies. *That was possibly their first mistake?*

Two days later, he caught his second break. *Murphy's bloody Law*, he remembered his old Tiger Force sniper sharing with him on many occasions. The three men left the building for the first time in five days. Stone needed to get this job done-and-dusted and time was ticking away. As they prepared to enter their clapped-out vehicle, the target casually discarded an empty Coffee Chill into the gutter.

"Gotchya! That will teach you about littering, you lazy bastard," Stone grinned through his binoculars.

The next morning at 11:00 A.M., Stone pulled up a chair at a floating restaurant and ordered a tasting plate of BBQ pork ribs, some fried duck and grilled chicken with a small bowl of jasmine rice. After another forty-six excruciating minutes slid on by, the same young delivery boy stepped off the boat with a cardboard box in his arms. Stone watched on as he strapped the food onto his rear bicycle carrier and started to peddle the short distance to the litterbug's hold-up. Stone stood up and left some local cash on the table, then entered the grid-locked market street. He kept up a steady pace about a metre behind the bicycle, struggling to make its way through the hordes of locals, all hawking their fresh produce and other wares. The bicycle came to a halt as an emaciated, flea-ridden old dog meandered in a slow stride and blocked the path of the pushbike.

Stone swooped in like a descending wedge-tailed eagle about to gather up an unsuspecting rabbit; fast and silent. Discarding the safety cap, he removed a small syringe that was designed to fit into the palm of his hand then reached into the box of food and plunged the needle through the plastic lid of the Coffee Chill and kept walking, all in the one motion, back to his rented room. He still needed visual confirmation.

At precisely 3:00 P.M., the terrorist known to his loyal Islamic followers as the Genius removed the cap from his favourite beverage. He always felt a tinge of guilt as he placed the open container to his bearded lips and swallowed half the contents. He placed the remainder on the floor next to his small prayer rug. It was time to face east and offer his second *Dhuhr* call to praise Allah.

He knelt down and clasped his hands together. As he bowed forward for the first—and soon to be last time, white foam started to form around his open mouth. He reached for his neck as it began to swell. The nerve agent known as UX or S-2 is a toxin that was a dicotyledonous angiosperm. A plant species in the family Apocynaceae and commonly known as the suicide tree. It has a reaction time of under thirty seconds. Dulmatin's head bounced off the hardwood floor, and his body slumped to one side as a continuous flow of frothy white phlegm disgorged from the mouth of his palpitating body. He started to convulse uncontrollably. His bomb-making days were over.

Stone packed up his gear and left the building. He crossed the street and waited. Within minutes number two and three bad guys came running out, with mobile phones glued to their ears, screaming shit out in their local tongue. They were not happy campers.

Stone dropped his canvas bag into the muddied waters of the Barito River and flew up the rickety rear stairwell. He entered the building through an open window with his phone camera at the ready. "Strike one for the good guys," he murmured, as he viewed the shape curled up in a tight ball. He photographed the deceased and pulled from his own jacket pocket something he had been carrying since the time he left Darwin. It was not protocol, and certainly not part of his instructions from Darcy Jones. "But shit happens", he told himself. He placed near the corpse a small Aboriginal wood carving of a boxing kangaroo with the number 88 scribed across its puffed-out chest. *One down—two to go. Lest we forget the eighty-eight, you bastards,* Stone repeated before he left.

Chapter-10

A MOTORISED three-wheeled two-stroke taxi the locals called a bemo slowed as it approached what seemed to be an isolated location that matched the handwritten street name held in Kelly's hand while still seated in the back. The bike struggled to negotiate the final winding hill-climb to a private residence located in Balian Beach about 15 kilometres north of Kuta. The bemo pulled up under the dual lane front overhead awning, and the young Balinese driver indicated they had indeed arrived at the given destination. Kelly stepped out onto the cracked concrete surface and surveyed his strange surroundings. He quickly noticed a CCTV camera swivelling on its mount towards the idling trike.

"You want me to wait, mister? Take you back to the hotel later? I wait—no worries," the aspiring business-minded teenager offered in sporadic English.

"Sure do, maybe an hour or less," Kelly answered, while he unfolded some local rupiah and handed over half the negotiated amount, plus enough of a tip to keep the smiling driver more than interested. Then he asked, "You okay with that?"

The bemo parked down the street, leaving a trail of more oil than smoke. Kelly was about to walk over to the only entry door when it slid open, and he was greeted by a woman who introduced herself as, Isabelle. Her bright red lipstick only accentuated the collagen injections she'd obviously thought were a necessary addition to her surgically reinvented self. "Welcome to Bali, Mr Kelly. Come on inside. You can leave your footwear inside the door. Mrs Sherry is expecting you. Please, this way if you would."

Kelly stepped inside, and things changed dramatically. The lavishly decorated foyer caught him by surprise. It was a stark indifference to what any casual pedestrian might assume from the almost derelict-looking exterior. Stained suar wood with a vast array of indoor tropical plants featured throughout. A stone pool that looked to be over twenty feet long and about half as wide was designed as a showpiece. It was impossible *not* to notice as you needed to step around it while following a slender, wooden arched bridge that split the pond, leading to a second set of stained doors. The pool abounded with brightly coloured red and orange fish, with their long flowing tails and pectoral fins fanning out in a visual display that resembled an aquatic ballet, swimming in easy idleness, bobbing under the giant lily pads that covered half the pool's surface. Looking menacingly down from above was a six-foot-long deity of the *Leyak*, a mythological Balinese figure in the form of a flying head with entrails still attached.

Leyak is said to be able to fly in his pursuit to find a pregnant woman or a newborn to suck her baby's blood dry. This one drooled water from its gaping mouth, ears and over-sized nose reminding Kelly he will need to use the men's room sooner, than later, while still following red lips to a sunroom towards the rear of what was shaping up as quite a large home.

As a man that had endured more than most over the past years, Jack Kelly's nature was not to fear the unknown. The unexplained had been the salvation that had occupied his inner thoughts since his retrograde amnesia became a real-life reality some years previously. Today's meeting was the first of possibly many steps to confront the realities of his past actions and search out an answer to how he might mend the broken pathway between himself and his former employer—the Australian Defence Force.

Kelly knew he needed to be prepared for all the ensuing answers—good, bad or otherwise. In the deep apse of his displaced anamnesis, he knew that his past life may divulge a shocking truth. "The truth will release you," he remembered Mrs Sherry quoting in one of their few e-mail exchanges. He sucked in a deep breath and entered a room that may provide the answers he hoped would release him from his feelings of guilt and shed some positive light on what seemed to be his disconnected past.

Mrs Tamara Sherry was a Front Bench Minister in two previous incumbent federal governments. After her retirement from the political arena, she was then asked to take on a lead role in the recently formed Anti Corruption and Crime Commission—simply referred to as the ACCC. She was a woman known for her ability to find solutions and an expert at cutting through the bureaucratic red tape that all governments suffered. She was often referred to by the Australian media as the 'Mrs Fix It', with far-reaching powers and unrestrictive access to any Australian citizens' file. ADF and locked juvenile records included. Kelly entered to be greeted by the smiling face of a very attractive woman in her early forties who had obviously taken good care of herself. She was a real cougar. "Welcome, Jack. I'm, Tamara Sherry. It's so good to finally catch up with you in the flesh. Please, take a seat. You can call me, Tamara. Today is all about building a foundation of trust between the two of us."

Kelly was ushered towards two single lounge chairs with a small table separating the space. Two green-coloured files were neatly placed on the table's polished surface next to an open laptop. Both were marked *−For Minister's Eyes Only−*.

Tamara poured two glasses of ice water from a glass jug, "This place once belonged to my first husband. He loved to come to Bali for the surfing. I could never find it in my heart to sell it after he died."

Kelly sipped his water, "It's like stepping into the *Tardis*."

"My husband always said it was safer that way due to the long periods the house was left empty. He loved to say, 'if it looks like crap from the outside, no one will be interested in what's on the inside'."

Kelly straightened his back and leant forward in his comfortable chair, "So, where do we begin?"

Tamara then asked, "Do you mind if I record our conversation today?"

Kelly paused before answering, "Look, Tamara, don't take this the wrong way but..." He paused a second time. "For me personally, today is about filling in a few gaps about my being enlisted in the Australian Navy, and then how best to deal with my presumed MIA status."

Tamara leaned over and separated both the green files. She placed a finger on top of the folder to Kelly's left side, "This file is your complete locked juvenile record while you were a ward of the state. The other is your RAN file." Tamara then stood, "I just remembered that I need to attend to something urgent. I will be gone for about fifteen minutes. I trust in my absence, you won't use this time to read these files." She smiled and left the room.

Kelly didn't need her veiled suggestion to be spelt out any clearer than it was, so he picked up the first folder. He flipped through the pages and read about his twelve years spent in foster care up until the time he was found left for dead on the banks of a river when he was only 17. The rest he'd already pieced together alone. The second folder explained he joined the Navy at the age of 18. Then it went on to say he was a Special Wartime Officer, and later was accepted into the SASR training regime, then transferred to an elite counter-terrorist squad covertly called the Tiger Force. He rubbed the small SF tattoo on the nape of his neck. The last page filled in the first blank, explaining he was a sniper, and together with his scout, they both became separated from a six-member team in Cambodia during a monsoon. And now he was listed as MIA [possible KIA].

How can you be both MIA and KIA?

Kelly closed both files. Soon after, Tamara re-entered the room.

"Sorry about that," she half-heartedly apologised. "Family dramas back home—teenage kids... All right, where were we then?"

"Let's start with the MIA and possible KIA entry in my Navy file? I don't understand," Kelly asked.

Tamara sat back down, "Firstly, that Thailand passport you previously entered Australia with has now been red-flagged. You'll need to destroy it a.s.a.p. I have here a new Australian passport in the name of Phil John Kelly. I know you have no middle name, but *John* will give credibility to the reason you now call yourself, Jack."

Tamara handed the passport over. Kelly opened the first page. "Nice photo. How did you manage to get your hands on that—it looks recent?"

"That's because it is. Taken when you passed through the Customs checkpoint in Darwin."

"Right? But I recently used my Thai passport to enter Bali, and there were no problems."

"The Thailand Government are in the process of data chipping all reissued passports, and the one in your possession will not pass a security check—which means when you re-enter Thailand as, Phil John Kelly, this will officially be your first-time visit. Do you understand?"

"Yeah. Jack Uppmaya is a figment of someone's wild imagination."

"Jack Uppmaya has left Thailand, never to return, so that won't be a problem. Now, Jack, we have a friendly ally back in Australia that wants to help. I have spoken in depth about your unusual circumstances to a man I know quite well. Admiral Peterson wants to work on the best way to bring you back into the fold, but he needs some more time."

"Time—time for what?" Kelly replied.

"After the upcoming Federal Election. Until that happens, not much will need to change."

Kelly then asked, "Will I be charged—spend time in custody?"

"Not on my watch, you won't. That's the deal I struck. You are the only reason eight Australian POW's were returned to their families in Australia. If the media ever gets wind that the man responsible for that is now behind bars . . . Well, let's just say we also have a very influential reporter on our side—one who knows your story, intimately."

"That sounds ominous. Male or female?"

"Abigail Bishop-Price is definitely a female."

"How well do I know her . . . ?"

"Not *that* well."

"How and when do you propose I hand myself over to the ADF, then?"

"Soon . . . Admiral Peterson has the ear of the current PM. The election is due early next year. He wants to see that through, but the polls indicate Prime Minister Collins should be returned with a clear majority. The current Opposition is a shambles and is not expected to make any inroads to the Labor Party's seven-seat majority."

"So," Kelly quizzed, "that's only twelve weeks away, do I need to cast my vote?"

"Good question, I'll let you know. Do you have any other questions, Jack?"

"Just one—and it's real simple? Why... why are you, Mrs Sherry, going in to bat for a man you only met today?"

She returned Jack's questioning gaze, "I've met all but one member of your family now, Jack. Your brother Jaxon, your sisters, Leah and Serena, and then there is your mother . . . Your family has suffered enough. I know your last reunion in Sydney was short-lived, but I for one hope that is just the beginning."

Jack pondered her answer for a few seconds. There was something Mrs Sherry was holding back. "Since when does a woman who wields tremendous power and influence over the affairs of a country suddenly go all soft and gooey? What aren't you telling me?"

She paused and swallowed the last of her water. "Jaxon said you would pick it. He says you never miss a beat—the same as, Leah. She wasn't fooled for a minute."

Kelly smiled, "You and Jaxon are seeing each other, and not in the office—I'd say he's a lucky man."

"Yes, and that's why the secrecy. Now would not be the appropriate time for Jaxon and me to be seen strolling through Martin Place holding hands. Getting you back onside with the ADF is the first priority, Jack."

"I understand. That's fine by me." Kelly looked down at his watch. A full hour had passed by in the blink of an eye. "I must wind this meet up soon. I want to go and check out a bar where I'm going to watch the AFL grand final tomorrow."

Mrs Sherry stood, "Go, Port Adelaide."

Kelly returned, "The Lions by eighteen points."

They both shook hands when Tamara unexpectedly moved forward and gave Kelly a warm embrace.

"Like I said, Jack, thank you for what you did. Molly Pritchard made both myself and Jeremy Collins acutely aware of the importance of a returned soldier. The prime minister is also the Member for Eden-Monaro, and Molly Pritchard is a constituent with a big voice. I'll walk you out."

"That Molly, she sort of gets right into the pieces of your heart that are usually padlocked shut," Kelly replied before turning and leaving through the front door.

Chapter-11

TWELVE KILOMETRES AWAY, amongst the hustle and bustle of the streets of Kuta, Evina and Abigail had both showered, redressed in loose-fitting cotton clothes and were cruising the main street overflowing with the thousands of other tourists, deciding on an appropriate restaurant to order some local food and enjoy a few cooling beverages. As previously promised, Abigail wanted some direct answers to the exact reasons her twin sister had decided to arrange this hastily put-together so-called holiday in Bali. Abigail knew her older twin too well to believe the prepared answer it was time for the sisters to reunite and bury the hatchet.

Bullshit, she quietly reminded herself.

"This place looks all right, Abby. Come on, I'm starving." As individual women, both sisters were almost oblivious to the constant alluring intrigue they enticed. The disguised stares from strange men, craning their necks to gain a better perspective were only equally matched by other members of the fairer sex. Some would admire the sheer radiance of these two naturally eye-catching women, while others might seethe with hidden jealousy. Together, as a pair, they were hard to miss. A line of men drinking at the near-capacity bar all turned like a row of clowns in sideshow alley, while the twins were shown to a street-side table with a fan directly above.

"Four margaritas to start with, then we'll order something to eat", Evina almost demanded of the waiter, in her matter-of-fact tone. Abigail noticed a small crowd gathered to the right side of the three-stepped main entrance to the restaurant where a two-seater bench seat was strategically placed with a life-size statue of a seated, cement version of

Forrest Gump. A plaque hung above his head: 'life is like a box of chocolates'. Tourists were lining up to have their photo snapped, sitting beside the now-famous scene from the movie of the same name. Five minutes later, a procession of both kitchen and bar staff could be clearly seen, making a direct approach towards their table. Both women looked on with abstract astonishment, not aware of the local custom with each margarita ordered.

The staff formed a circle, while what looked like the manager broke into song, soon to be joined by the other budding tenors, all the while he was rattling the stainless steel cocktail shaker high above his head. Patrons that weren't already looking their way were all now firmly eye-balling the singing commotion, while both Evina and Abigail could only look on in bewilderment as innocent participants in the short pantomime that followed.

During the distraction, a tall man with a prominent scar forming a crease down his chin, wearing dark sunglasses and a Balinese straw hat that obscured the top portion of his face, politely edged past the twins table. He excused himself before placing the palm of his open hand under the wooden railing that ran the length of the row of tables facing Kartika Road. He casually crossed the same road and found a vacant table that offered an unobstructed view of the Bubba Gump Restaurant. He ordered a coffee before opening an app on his iPhone while inserting a single earpiece into his one good ear. His left ear was rendered near-useless by a gunshot that was meant for the space between his ink-black eyes while on an assignment in East Berlin. He survived the attempted attack to end his life, but the eardrum was perforated in the process.

The manager finished his Karaoke-style rendition of the *Ketchak* dance and filled both the frosted, salt-rimmed glasses to the brim, then exited, leaving the twins with embarrassed smiles imprinted across their identical faces.

"All in a normal day at the office in Bali, I can only assume?" a frowning Evina suggested. "Oh well, bottoms up,

Abigail. Cheers." Both girls drained the glasses in one easy flowing motion, drawing some small applause from the smiling line of male barflies. The same singing procedure was repeated a second time in quick succession as their second round arrived, causing a steady flow of new customers, all wanting to experience the Gump margarita.

"Business is business, I guess?" Evina remarked. "Maybe we should order a daiquiri next. The novelty is short-lived, I'm afraid."

The staff duly departed, and Abigail jumped straight into her no-holds-barred inquisition. She was in full reporter mode now. "All right, Evina, it's time to come clean. Firstly, I want to know what happened between you and Troy, and secondly—the real reason for your sudden yearning to catch up with your sister on the island of Bali after all these years? I'm all ears."

"Troy is a two-timing piece of shit, Abigail. When I was offered the chance and the financial resources from the Smithsonian to investigate further into these celestial globes, Troy was out of work—again. I managed to coax the curator, my boss, to allow him to accompany me as an assistant. He liked to dabble in amateur photography, so off we went to Europe, together as a team." Evina paused and sipped her drink, this time with the aid of the accompanying straw. "Then I left him alone in London for three days to search for some documentation in some obscure museum located in the small town of Pamplona, in Spain. I arrived back at our hotel a day early, only to find some red-headed skank lying naked in our bed. But that's not all—the slut had also been parading herself in public while dressed in *my* clothes, using some of my makeup, and was half-way through emptying the mini-bar. Pissed as a maggot, she was."

"Bloody hell, where was Troy?" Abigail feigned shock, but inside the news was not unexpected. On many occasions in the early days of her sister's marriage to the English-born wandering eyes of Troy, Abigail had interrupted his disturbing stare at his new wife's monozygotic twin. It made her feel ill inside.

"He was out buying some lunch to share with his new young *babe*," Evina spat out.

"I never did like that man, anyway. He had insidious eyes that belied his sly intentions," Abigail shared. "No love lost there as far as I'm concerned. And the second question? Why are you in Bali, and what's a celestial globe?"

"That's a bit more complicated. It would only bore you to tears, Abby, trust me."

"Try me anyway, sister, and none of your rehearsed answers, I want the truth. I can see something is worrying you, Evina. You're still my twin, and I could always sense when you were consumed by ambition, deep in your own thoughts."

"Well, it's just that on more than a few occasions, I could sense that someone was following me. One time when I returned to my hotel in Cairo, my room had been tampered with. I challenged the house staff, but they denied entering in my absence. It gave me the heebie-jeebies to be perfectly honest. The long and the short of it, Abigail, is I have arranged to meet with someone—here in Bali. This particular individual made contact with me over a year ago, while I was in Pakistan; Lahore, in fact. He revealed to me he has information that's relevant to what I and others in our small team have been researching for almost ten years now."

"Who is he? And when and where have you arranged to meet with this man? Do you know anything about this stranger?" Abigail asked as a sister would.

"I know enough that I need him to share what he knows. He's an Australian. We have only spoken on the phone one time. He was very adamant about that. All other contact has been through a secured e-mail server that can only be accessed via a password-protected encryption app he sent to me over the Internet. All very James Bondish, I know. He signs each e-mail with the name, Barnacle Bob."

Abigail almost choked on her margarita. "Barnacle bloody Bob? Are you kidding me or what? What is he, an old crustacean? What the hell name is, Barnacle Bob, anyway?" Abigail altercated with a bemused tone.

"Maybe he has an unusual sense of humour, it doesn't matter. But now, finally, he has agreed to meet with me personally. Abigail, without going into intricate details, our team is on the verge of something that is of great significance, and somehow, this man is aware of what that might be. Only a handful of people are familiar with our research, so how does he have involute knowledge of what that might be? My guess is he may be disguising the fact that he is an academic himself. I believe him to be the same individual who originally sent me that celestial sphere in the first place, back in the U.S. He is enticing me to unravel the mystery, and now he wants to talk. I sensed he may very well be elderly. When people prepare to welcome in the afterlife, sometimes they want to part with information and not allow it to be taken to the grave. I need to see this man, and that's exactly what I intend to do. Tonight, in fact, at a place called Paddy's Rebuilt, somewhere in Legian Street at eight o'clock. Have you heard of it?"

"A blind man could find the recently rebuilt Paddy's, Evina. Just follow the loud thumping doof-doof music that reverberates throughout the streets after nine o'clock every night until the early hours of the morning. It's dark and gloomy, the drinks are double the price, and the average age is about that of a juvenile delinquent. Why would an older man who goes by the name of, Barnacle Bob, want to meet there? It's not the setting for a private meeting, I can assure you. Do you even know what he looks like? You're not going alone, that's for sure," Abigail was adamant.

"Oh, yes I am, just watch me," Evina stated with an air of the older sister syndrome.

"You have no idea, do you, Evina? After spending so much time wrapped up in your own scientific ball of cotton wool, you have forgotten the world is full of idiots. An attractive white woman alone at night in Kuta? Somehow, I don't think so," Abigail fired back, wanting to stand her ground.

A compromise was reached with the sibling rivalry agreeing to disagree that Abigail would wait in a small cocktail lounge called the Expresso Bar on the opposite side of the street, with her mobile phone at the ready. If something *were* to go askew, Abigail would be ready to pounce.

"Maybe you can dress up as, Pirate Pete, and then the two of you can have a real serious one-on-one. I mean, *really*, Evina?" Abigail joked in an attempt to belittle her sister into realising the absurdity of this clandestine meeting with a perfect stranger. Evina did not possess the street-smarts of her twin sister.

"He told me to look for the sore thumb. I'll stand out like a sore thumb were his exact words," Evina continued. "You said *recently* rebuilt? Have they just refurbished Paddy's Bar?"

"Evina, pull your academic head out from that rabbit hole for just a moment. The old Paddy's Bar and the Sari Club opposite were destroyed in the Bali bombings over two years ago now. I know you're a dual national these days, but first and foremost, you will always be an Australian citizen. Remember, two hundred two people died in that explosion, including eighty-eight Australians. Let's not ever forget that. This is my first return trip to Bali since that chilling night."

"I'm sorry," Evina replied in an apologetic tone, "I didn't join the dots. Yes, I remember it well. October 12, 2002. That and 9/11. How can we ever forget? Let's lighten the mood and order lunch."

"Aye-aye me hearties", Abigail mimicked, with the accent of the pirate, Long John Silver.

Evina returned a glare that suggested enough was enough and summoned the waiter over with a wave of her hand.

The Jindeugi sat in silence while making shorthand notes in his native handwriting about the conversation coming through loud and clear on his earpiece. The secured e-mail server encryption the sister referred to had long ago been broken, a relatively simple task with the limitless resources available to the Anomura Group. The Jindeugi retrieved his prepaid phone and pressed redial. The Doje answered on the second ring. The Jindeugi updated his employer on what he'd just learnt and listened intently as new instructions were relayed, again in Korean. He finished the call and Googled the location of the Expresso Bar.

Chapter-12

STONE HAD NOW BEEN on the island of Bali for eight days. His only slender lead to locating the number two man on his target list was a partial vehicle registration number. The other relatively unknown slice of what may turn out to be useless information was that Abu Dujana had an infatuation with English-built cars. It was reported that he owned a collection of vintage Morris *Minors* and a couple of Rolls Royce *Silver Lady's* that were in desperate need of some tender loving care, but importing parts for a Roller may have raised more than a few eyebrows when you are the head of a local Jemaah Islamiyah terrorist cell.

MI6 received daily updates courtesy of a CIA satellite camera that could read a newspaper from thirty kilometres above a clear or cloud-covered sky. Two low orbiting geostationary satellites were reprogrammed to sweep over both the island of Bali and the capital of Jakarta each day during the trial of the three Indonesian nationals waiting to eat a bullet. The simple reason was terrorists were no different from murderers or arsonists. They enjoyed witnessing first hand, the results of their handy work. The U.S. had made giant leaps in the use of advanced facial and ear recognition technology. Once every twenty-four hours the satellites would download thousands of images from the crowds that converged on the court proceedings each and every day. They were configured to run a diagnostic matching the sixty-five points of any person's unique facial features on the off-chance they may identify any known or suspected terrorists, or any other people of interest from their giant database and share this with all three nations that held a vested interest in the trial's outcome. The Americans and British both lost people on that day in 2002.

MI6 had pinpointed on three separate occasions a late-model Range Rover with just the numbers, 17_9 on a set of plates that were registered in Bali, not mainland Java. Stone had been busy visiting the ten most frequented Mosques located on the island in the hope he might get lucky. This was day eight of operation Blue Skies, and Stone was now monitoring a black Range Rover with the plate number: B-1719 PJ. He'd followed the car back and forth from the same Mosque to a secured residence with enough security to allow Osama bin Laden to drop in for a visit. Each time the occupants left the vehicle, it was under cover of a secured car park at the back of the Mosque or in the privacy of an electronically operated, outer perimeter, heavily secured gate. Whoever it was enshrouded behind the ten-foot-high brick fence was a high-profile individual.

The Jindeugi, after receiving his updated instructions, needed to act quickly. He made the call to meet with his contact in Bali, a man named Abu Dujana. This was an arrangement that was only to be initiated if deemed as absolutely necessary. To take out two separate targets on the streets of Bali with a handgun would send the wrong message. This assassination needed to be spectacular and very visual. He was met by a car and driver outside the An-Nur Mosque, near the Sanglah General Hospital in Denpasar.

"Sugeng rawuh," the driver greeted the Jindeugi, while dressed in a full-length thawb with a traditional laced kufi as headwear. He welcomed the tall North Korean with both palms together as he bowed three times while opening the left-side rear door and ushered with the wave of his open hand for his special guest to make himself comfortable. The black Range Rover, with dark shaded tinted windows, headed off along one of the three routes that Stone had previously mapped.

"Your reputation precedes you, and my Rayiysay-syd has asked me to extend all common courtesies in offering any assistance to our friends in North Korea. We all fight the same war—do we not? The enemy of our enemy is always a friend," the smug-faced driver passed on while he cast a glancing eye in his rear-view mirror.

The Jindeugi nodded but remained silent. He didn't entertain at any time the hypocrisy that was modern Islam, with its warped ideals all in the name of their version of God. In his own version of the truth, there was only one Master, and that was parked snugly inside his shoulder holster with his silencer itching for some action in his jacket pocket.

An Indonesian-looking man with fake black tan hand-rubbed onto his lower legs, arms, neck and face stood next to his parked 125cc Honda *Eco,* sporting a tinted full-face helmet, grey cotton knee-length tattered trousers, and an old soiled button-less shirt. He rechecked the octopus strap currently securing a wooden cage strapped to his vacant pillion seat. Crammed tightly inside were three unhappy Ayam Cemani chickens. He looked like any one of the other thousands of locals going about the mundane task of everyday life in Indonesia.

Stone turned his ignition key and allowed the engine to idle, checking his right-side mirror before he gently pulled out into the flow of moving traffic with a clear view of the vehicle, three cars ahead. He immediately recognised the occupant in the back seat. "The Jindeugi—what was he doing in Bali, and why would he be chauffeur driven in a Range Rover of interest? Not for coffee and a freshly baked croissant, I'll bet?" Stone questioned alone. His internal senses were telling him no good would come from this visit.

The car pulled up at the secured entrance and was instructed to enter through the electronically controlled reinforced steel gate by the disinterested guard seated in his small pillar-box. Somehow, Stone needed to get eyes on the inside of this large residence that was built like a small fortress. An hour later he parked his bike under a tangled growth of old bamboo at the rear of the compound, which opened up to some free-range farming land. *No pesky neighbours to worry about.*

After parting with over 4.5 million rupiah at the Central Plaza shopping complex, he unpacked a Spark DJI Mavic-Pro drone with a miniature high-resolution real-time camera attached to the underside. He powered up the console, flipped open the six- by four-inch screen and turned on the power. Four six-inch propellers all fired up in their numbered sequence. He swallowed a mouthful of warm water from a plastic bottle with a picture of a pristine snow-capped mountain that was definitely not within a bull's roar of Indonesia and moved the left-hand toggle forward. The drone lifted into the air like a Harrier Jump Jet, only smaller and a lot quieter. He felt like a big kid on Christmas Day. Stone had to admit, this was fun.

He guided the drone about a hundred metres west of the perimeter fence at its peak altitude, then moved it in an easterly direction to take in a full-screen view of the house and surrounding grounds. He could see three females wearing a hijab, completing some washing duties from an inside laundry. A couple of kids were playing under the sagging, rope-strung clothesline. He moved around to the south and zoomed in with maximum focus without any signs of pixilation.

Bloody amazing, I gotta get one of these things when I get back home, Stone promised himself.

Another two guards were walking the inside perimeter, both with semi-automatic rifles hanging from short shoulder straps. Together they stopped and lit a cigarette each. Stone was now about to get a first gander at the location that seemed to be a Muslim version of an alfresco entertainment area. The shadowed silhouette of four people seated could be seen through three triangular-shaped sails tensioned over an area of paved limestone. He lowered the drone to hover directly above the fence line, then turned the camera in a 360-degree swivel to check for any other stragglers. Stone toggled both levers and caught a clear view of all four men seated cross-legged around a low-lying table. Three were sharing a hookah and sipping on small half-filled glasses of espresso. He could make out the faces of two, but the third and fourth member of this little gathering had their backs facing the camera. A neatly stacked pile of local currency was being thumbed by the second seated John Doe.

The unmistakable scarred face of the Jindeugi filled the screen on Stone's console as the North Korean was personally handed a wrapped package. Stone remembered being briefed about the night of the aborted blue house raid where he earned that scar from a gun-wielding South Korean police officer, moments after he shot the surprised police chief, point-blank. Stone tried to make-out what the contents might be, but the package was hidden mostly from his view by the table. Soon after, the North Korean got up and left.

The third member leaned over the large wooden low deck table to retrieve his mobile phone. Stone just needed to ID this final person. With little warning, the bearded foreigner stood and turned, looking straight into the camera with his phone held tightly to his ear.

"Smile, you bastard", Stone whispered in a satisfying tone. Abu Dujana started pointing and barking out orders in his local dialect. The other two cohorts jumped to their feet and soon joined in, all looking directly into Stone's small screen. "Shit, the drone's been made."

The first sounds of rifle fire rang loud, scattering a group of feeding birds in a tree behind where the drone was still hovering. Then a sweeping right-to-left trail of bullets zeroed in on its position. Before Stone could apply a retreating manoeuvre, his new favourite toy was pulverised by a hail of automatic fire, and the screen went blank.

"Time to go to Plan B." Stone needed to improvise. It was the name of the game. Always flexible and ready to change the blueprint at a moment's notice. He knew from his own timed run from the headquarters of the Bali polisia that he would have at least another twenty-three minutes before even the quickest police car would arrive at this address.

He threw the console, together with the hard plastic packaging, into a pre-dug hole and kicked in a covering of dirt with his foot. Then he rolled the Honda *eco* down an angled grassed verge and started the engine. He had his confirmation of the target, and now it was just a matter of following his alternative strategy to end Abu Dujana's time on planet Earth—and today. Before the police started becoming deadly serious about protecting the murdering bastard closeted behind the safety of the compound, like the cowardly chicken-livered terrorist he was.

Stone straddled his bike and rode around to the front of the compound. As he neared the pillar-box, he cut the ignition and rolled to a stop. With his back already facing the curious guard, he removed the spark plug lead and wound the starter motor, over and over. The guard approached from behind, intent on laying a boot into the unsuspecting local farmer to move him on, in quick fashion. He started ranting instructions in the local Malayo/Polynesian dialect. Stone stood and turned in a single motion. With the palm of his open hand, he let fly with a short blow to the tip of the unsuspecting guard's bottom jaw. His cheekbone dislocated and entered a small area below his left eye, piercing his brain. He went limp, while Stone grabbed him by the collar of his army-style shirt and dragged him back onto his seat, in front of a small black and white television. He removed his own 9mm Browning with the muzzle suppressor already attached and fired two rounds into the electronic gates' control board, disabling the two CCTV cameras, and fired another round each into both sets of rollers. Before he made his way back to the rear fence, he placed the second, in a set of three small wooden figurines, inside the shirt pocket of the dead man with his silent eyes glued to the TV.

Stone returned to where the chicken cage sat nestled amongst some long grass and rolled the bike into some waist-high trees. He grabbed the cage, opened the lock and turfed it over the wall. The sound of three pissed-off chickens was all the distraction he needed. He raced back to his bike, leaving behind the commotion of the chickens and the two fast-reacting guards he saw earlier. Stone unlocked the seat and grabbed his small pack that held all he would need to carry out Plan B. He swung in a tight circle a small grappling hook and felt for a secure hold before scaling the fence with little effort. He was in.

Stone could see the clothesline pegged with sheets and blankets. Good cover, so he bounded over the small pebble-shaped coffee rock and stopped at the laundry door to his proposed point of entry.

The element of surprise can never be underestimated. After the drone was shot down, nobody in their right mind would then expect an intrusion. They would all be preoccupied while searching their video surveillance to get eyes on who was controlling the airborne camera and trying to figure out where that person was right now. That individual was about to enter the building through a side door, unchallenged.

Stone stepped through the laundry that led to a big kitchen. The smell of food cooking suggested someone was inside. He turned the washing machine on and waited behind the door. A woman entered, cursing loudly in what sounded like Arabic. Stone leaned over and put her in a sleeper hold. Her body went limp. He moved her over to a pile of dirty laundry, then duck-taped her mouth, and clip-locked both wrists and ankles. Shuffling footsteps could be heard coming from the second entrance to the kitchen. Not combat boots. Another woman, he guessed correctly, while closing the gap of the door and waited for her to enter. She was only a teenager. Soon she was slumped next to the cook. *This wasn't their fight.*

He searched another two empty rooms and checked his watch. Stone stiffened as the sound of muffled voices echoed down a winding staircase. He could hear the heightened chatter of maybe three men. He couldn't tell if they were arguing or ordering lunch. To Stone, the Arabic language sounded like they were always angry when they spoke, anyway.

Stone crouched and moved over to a three-ring gas burner above a small oven. He opened the knob momentarily and smelt the releasing fumes.

Natural gas, not LPG. Probably all the way from the Northwest Shelf off the coast of Western Australia. That's bloody irony.

The half-inch copper piping ran behind a floor-to-ceiling cupboard, then it reappeared for a few feet before exiting the wall where he found the gas meter outside and shut down the main valve. Stone reentered the kitchen and went to work. He pulled out his KA-BAR knife and sliced the soft copper pipe four times. Then he taped a length of wire gauze filled with charcoal to mask the smell and covered it with a dustpan he found inside the walk-in pantry. In his own homemade version of nitro-glycerine, Stone found a half-filled pack of baking soda, an opened plastic container of drain cleaner and an unused bottle of bleach. He quickly read the warning labels - *thirty per cent mixture of both nitric and sulphuric acids.* Stone then thumbed two cartridges from his magazine and pried off the copper and brass projectile. He then made a neat mound of both gunpowder and baking soda in the centre of the glass turntable before he placed the bleach bottle half-filled with the drain cleaner inside the microwave and set the timer to begin its cooking cycle in ten minutes, and then he hit start.

Sweet mother of Satan will come out to play in exactly twelve minutes.

Stone stood motionless as the sound of a man's shoes walking on a tiled surface could be heard shuffling his way. He backed into the pantry a second time, pulled the door closed and pressed his eyes against the small wooden slats. A bearded Arab with a protruding hook-shaped nose, dressed in a three-piece Armani suit, answered his cell phone. He placed a laptop on a table and opened the fridge, pulling out a bottle of water and a small Tupperware container of food. He filled his mouth with one yellow Barhee date at a time and chewed before spitting the pips onto the floor while listening to his caller.

Bloody pig. Eat up, Abdul. Only ten minutes to go, Stone counted.

The conversation was in Turkish. There was a moment of silence before he switched to broken English. "Is that you,

Nasim?" Another small pause followed while the Turk listened on intently. "Yes, I have confirmed the second Sheik should be transported to Christmas Island and will be processed with the other refugees in due course." Another pause. "Yes, he has all the necessary papers." The Turk waited for a response. "I can confirm they were met by the Australian Navy patrol boat, as expected. Before reaching the point of no return, they were initially advised to turn back, but even *this* Sheik Aris is a wise man, Nasim. He forced some women and children overboard and ordered the captain to open the seacocks. The stupid Australian infidels fell for it. Their soft bleeding hearts will be their own demise," he scowled with a sinister satisfaction.

Stone was hanging off every word spoken with the mention of his native Australia and the Navy that he was still unofficially enlisted as a reservist.

Sheik Aris? That's Aris Munandar! His watch was counting back: 7:59 and ticking.

The Turk tapped the closed outer case of his laptop with his free hand. "I have all the details right here, Nasim. They are safe. We have wiped all the remaining hard-drives clean and destroyed every PC in residence as a precaution. You must agree now, Nasim, Bali has been compromised. We're packing up and leaving immediately."

You just signed your own death notice, Pinocchio, Stone promised.

Stone stepped out from the pantry and squeezed the trigger. A single round left the silencer from his Browning with a muffled *thud* into the apex of Pinocchio's spine. He fell to the floor, knocking over a chair in the process. Stone grabbed the laptop and bent down to relieve the dead man of his phone, still grasped in his ring-laden hand. A voice could be heard from the small speaker, "What happened, Kaeleb, are you still there...?"

Stone spoke as he dragged the body into the laundry, chancing a last look at the microwave timer counting down. "Sorry, mate, your terrorist buddy is indisposed." *Click.* He reopened the main gas valve and prepared to make the run across open ground to scale the fence while making his escape. He stopped by the side of the building. The two patrolling guards could be seen with the grappling hook in their possession. *Shit!*

Ten kilometres away, Indonesian Chief of Police Da'i Bachtiar was in the passenger's front seat of the lead vehicle as it cut through traffic with lights flashing. He listened intently to the hyperventilated diatribe of Abu Dujana, explaining the virtues of what police protection means to him and reminding him repeatedly the amount of ten million rupiah a month being deposited into his private account.

"Move it, go around the traffic," Da'i Bachtiar screamed at his probationary driver. "Use the medium strip. Run the bastards over if you have to. Just get this car to the address A.S.A.P."

Stone needed another escape route—and fast. He turned and ran back through the house. The voices from above could be heard coming down the stairs. *I need to find the bloody garage.* He opened a door that led to an expansive sitting room with a couple of well-appointed sofas, and the standard wall-mounted TV with a DVD player and a flash-looking stereo unit. He crouched down behind one of the sofas and waited. Heavy footsteps could be heard approaching the door. Stone stood and fired twice, *thud-thud*, two to the heart. He dragged the limp body and lay it down behind the sofa. Then a voice screamed from the laundry, "Abib-Abib, come quickly."

The only thing that did arrive in no-time-flat was a third and fourth bullet. The two Arab women in the laundry were both conscious, and when seeing Stone again, they both started to shuffle and slide their constrained bodies away and towards the door. Stone lifted each woman, then cut their leg ties and pushed them through the laundry door back outside. He fired a single round at their feet and watched them hightail it towards the clothesline.

Stone headed in the exact opposite direction. He reentered the lounge area and unbuckled his backpack then took out a stun grenade. He pulled the pin and taped it to the inside of the door handle with just a slice of electrical tape. As the handle is turned from the opposite side, the tape will unravel, and the surprise will fall to the floor releasing the safety clip with just a four-second timer before the cuboid fragmentation blast decides between life and death. He noticed a collection of DVD's sitting on a small coffee table. The covers told their own story. Porn. *Devout Muslims, my arse.*

The next door Stone raced through opened up to a long hallway with two opposite-facing doors built into the end of the corridor. He opened the right-hand side door first and caught a glimpse of the Range Rover, still parked in the garage. The second door had a steel plate pot-riveted over the front panel and was locked with a large padlock that looked like overkill.

What are they hiding in here? Stone wondered.

He fired two shots, and the clasp fell to the floor. The second he swung the heavy door open, his nose immediately recognised the wafting aroma. The room was dark, and he felt blindly for a light switch. There was none. He flashed his small Mag-Lite from left to right, and then stopped suddenly. "Holy shit! Will you look at that?" Stone allowed an animated smile to flash over his face, thinking about the twist of fate with what was neatly piled in two equal stacks. He booby-trapped the second grenade to the door handle of the garage. The vehicle was parked with its rear-end facing the front roller-door. He opened the driver's door, and his eyes lit up, after spotting the key still dangling from the ignition. "That's a bonus." He started the 4.2-litre supercharged Jaguar AJ V8 engine and reversed straight through the roller-door.

The sounds of two polisia vehicles with sirens blaring and flashing lights pulling to a stop at the front gate was a bit of a shock. Stone baulked. "They made bloody good time." He looked at his watch, counting back one more time: 2:39, then slammed the stick shift into first and floored the accelerator. *There must be another way out of this place, somewhere?* Wet mud and grass spewed from the spinning rear tyres. He turned then sped past the alfresco area and headed north, following the perimeter fence. Stone ducked his head as a guard emptied an entire 30-round clip at the moving vehicle. He turned the car to face the gun-toting Arab as he frantically tried to reload a fresh magazine. Stone poked his arm out the driver's window, then fired three times and hit him twice. Then he noticed a tractor parked under a dilapidated wood-framed shed filled with rusting tools and other farming equipment. His eyes lit up. *That's my way out,* while he remembered his old granddad.

Da'i Bachtiar exited the stationary police 4wd and tried to alert the seated guard, who looked like he was fast asleep. His constable shook him violently and then watched in shock as he slid in an ungainly slumber to the floor. The constable bent down and picked up a small figurine that fell from his top pocket and handed his police chief a wooden statue of a kookaburra with a small snake in its mouth, perched on the limb of a gum tree. Da'i Bachtiar placed it on the dashboard of the police vehicle and tried to push open the damaged gate. He screamed at the three men in the second vehicle to give him a hand. It didn't budge.

"Step back, all of you," he ordered, then let rip with a volley of small arms fire at the locking mechanism.

The probationary driver pointed to the damaged rollers. "Sir, they've already been shot to pieces."

"Get in the car and run this gate down. I need to gain entry. Hurry, I can see the Range Rover. He's trapped inside. Move it," he screamed at the young constable.

The second-year officer reversed the Toyota *Fortuner,* placed the T-bar into D and slammed his police-issued boot down hard on the pedal. The vehicle lurched forward, picked up some momentum and rammed the gate causing the airbag to explode, and the entire tonne and a half of Japanese fabricated metal and moulded plastic shuddered. Smoke and water started spewing from the radiator, and the gate barely had a scratch on it.

"Follow my lead," Da'i Bachtiar shouted, then jumped onto the crumpled bonnet and motioned for his men to lift him to the top railing. He dragged himself up and over the apex and fell to the ground, then dusted down his uniform as his men followed his lead.

"Over there," Da'i Bachtiar pointed. "The black SUV." Each man removed his handgun while the injured constable handed his chief of police a semi-automatic through the vertical bars of the jammed gate.

Da'i Bachtiar barked out an order, "Radio through for back-up and tell the desk sergeant to set up a three-kilometre roadblock. And see if the helicopter is available—on my authority?"

The Range Rover slid to a halt behind the shed. Four polisia were running across an expanse of sodden mud, slowing their progress.

The tractor was the old crank handle start model. Stone remembered his grandfather had something similar on his small banana passionfruit farm, not far from Lake Eildon, near Mansfield in country Victoria.

The crank was held by two clips on the side of the block. Stone removed it and inserted the T-shaped key-end into the harmonic balance. The accelerator and gear shift were both manually operated by hand. He moved the power lever to about a quarter, then hand-pumped some diesel to fill the injectors and heaved hard on the crank handle. It moved a half turn. Stone took a deep breath and placed all his body weight and shoulder strength behind the crank and wound again. Slowly it gained some centrifugal motion and began to speed up. He could hear the three pistons rising and falling in their sleeves. A first cough spat from the vertical exhaust on the front of the open cabin, soon followed by a puff of oil-rich black smoke. The first injector fired. Stone kept turning like a mad-man.

"Come on, old girl, taste that diesel and fire up, darling." Numbers two and three cylinders ignited, black smoke was puffing from the rusted exhaust. *Pop – pop-pop – pop-pop-pop,* then the whole block rattled and kicked over. The toxic smell of diesel fumes was cause to hold your breath. The loud knock from the big-end bearings was like music to Stone's ears. He jumped up into what remained of the cabin and parked his backside on the single steel saddle seat. He leant on the gear lever and moved it sideways before going forward into the unsynchronised single-geared crash box, then increased the power to maximum and turned the crumbling steering wheel directly towards the brick perimeter wall. The 28-inch ribbed tyres dug into the soft surface with their rubber teeth and moved forward. The old Komatsu tractor was getting up a decent head of speed. Stone tied off the wheel with a piece of cord and jumped out.

The polisia were closing in. Two officers stopped and took a couple of long-distance pop shots. Da'i Bachtiar knew better and kept stumbling through the mud. He was almost clear and soon would have an unobstructed view of the black SUV and its driver.

The tractor was hurtling along, bouncing down a lazy hill with only about twenty metres until it would collide with the single brick wall. Stone looked at his watch, hopefully for the last time. He closed the driver's door and took off after the tractor. He started to countdown. "Ten, nine, eight..."

Da'i Bachtiar was on firmer ground now. He dropped down to one knee, then flipped the safety and started firing short bursts of three and four rounds at the escaping intruder. The third volley caught the Range Rover's rear quarter panel. He adjusted and moved his arm to the left in time with the increasing speed of the moving vehicle. He fired another three short bursts. The rear door was peppered with a single file of neat holes. There was nowhere for Stone to take cover. He lowered his head as the passenger's rear window exploded. *Seven, six, five, four...*

The tractor hit the wall with its raised concave-shaped shovel. The two-tonne weight knocked down a complete section, taking with it both the support pillars. The tractor bounced into the air and came down hard in the water-filled rice field beyond the wall, and just kept going like a runaway freight train. Stone braced himself. The four 20-inch magnesium wheels hit the rubble and became airborne. With a giant splash like a good old-fashioned belly flop, the Range Rover followed the cleared path into the paddy field. He reached over to the centre console and engaged the diff-lock. Now all four wheels were working together as one unit. He quickly waved goodbye as he accelerated past the old bumbling Komatsu and cut a straight line across the open field.

"Three-two-one..." The Sony microwave sounded a small audible ringtone as the timer ticked over to 02:00. The gunpowder ignited and blew the microwave door clean off its two hinges. A giant gas explosion erupted from the inside of the compound. Stone looked in his rear-view mirror in time to see the roof of the large residence almost separate from its load-bearing walls. The windows all blew out in a single motion, spraying glass in a hundred-metre-wide radius. Within a millisecond, the two grenades exploded.

A group of local farmers were bent over in the ankle-deep water, all wearing their wide-brimmed straw hats. They stood to attention as one, relieved for the chance to straighten their aching backs from hand-harvesting this year's rice crop with just a well-honed sickle. They watched in a captivating intrigue as the white man behind the wheel of the mud-splattered car sped past in a bow wave of parting water and chopped up rice stalks.

As Stone reached the road, a second explosion, much larger and so much more powerful, shook the Range Rover on its coil suspension. The percussion wave flattened the rice field, and the dozen or so locals were thrown backwards in a flying display of flailing arms and legs. The blast radius continued its destructive path. Stone smiled as the images of the two neatly stacked boxes of C4 plastic explosives flashed through his mind. *Arr, the sweet smell of Semtex.* "Remember the eighty-eight. That's karma, you bastards." *Some days really are diamond.*

Stone was far from reaching safe ground. He knew there would be a perimeter set to keep him caged up in a tight cordon. He still had the one ace up his sleeve, and that was the cops would not be looking for a dark-skinned Indonesian man with ripped farm clothes. Stone found a quiet street one block back from the main road, dumped the car and stole an old women's bicycle, which even had the added luxury of air in both tyres. He paid for a new orange-coloured straw hat from a street vendor and was casually waved through the roadblock another kilometre farther down the road.

"Now it was time to catch up with that North Korean mercenary and see what he was up to." Stone needed little convincing that it would end in heartache. *Surely, Bali has suffered enough?* he silently considered.

Chapter-13

THE FOLLOWING MORNING, the Jindeugi was dressed in a set of full white coveralls with a clipboard in one hand, wearing a peaked cap with the title: Bali Gas & Power embossed across the front in raised embroidered lettering. He parked his bike in the alleyway that ran down the side of what was named the Expresso Bar, directly opposite Paddy's Rebuilt. His watch read a little after 7:00 A.M. The first of the kitchen staff weren't due to arrive until nine.

The North Korean picked the rusted padlock which secured the small-gauge steel cage that housed three, 60 kg liquid petroleum gas cylinders and lifted the lid, hinging the small chain to a clasp on the adjacent wall. The Jindeugi tapped each cylinder with a Philips-head screwdriver. The first bottle was empty, but two and three were both full with their full 32 kg tare weight of highly volatile LPG. It only took a couple of minutes to secure the pocket-sized device in his possession to the inside-back of the centre bottle, concealing it from any casual onlooker. Another prepaid mobile rode piggy-back, held on by two black plastic zip-ties.

The small explosive device was designed to ignite a phosphorus fuse. Reaching a temperature that would melt solid steel, capable of searing a hole the size of a golf ball through the strengthened pressurised gas bottle. The igniting contents would then set in motion a mind-blowing, flesh-burning, highly fulminating chain reaction—followed by a heated fireball that was designed to kill and maim any person unlucky enough to be within a fifty-metre radius. The Jindeugi also knew it would be a simple task to trace the source back to Abu Dujana, with the inevitable full forensic analysis which would surely follow.

Less than twelve inches away, the eastern wall was made from single, 40 x 20mm builders' block. In most Western countries, with rigid building standards, this is only ever used as an inner-brick, with a second, more solid clay brick making up the exterior walls. The builders' block was of inferior quality and was porous. They were prevalent throughout the poorer Asian countries and the Expresso Bar was no exception.

Chapter-14

KELLY INSTRUCTED the bemo to drop him off at the front of Kuta's main surfing beach. A decent swell was being enjoyed by the swarming contingent of surfers that flock to this island paradise in pursuit of that perfect wave break, which was in abundance throughout the winding and mountainous coastline. He walked the short distance and entered his room at the Four Points Sheraton. He stripped off and stepped into the black-tiled shower recess, washed away all the day's sweat then towel-dried before he phoned Tiaan, back home on Koh Chang. Kelly updated her with a blow-by-blow description of the morning spent with Mrs Sherry, then collapsed into the queen-size bed with the air-conditioner oscillating a wave of cooling air and a welcome relief from the relentless humidity. He was in a deep sleep within minutes.

The sound of the 42-inch digital TV stirred Kelly awake. He lifted his head and fumbled for the remote to end the loud screaming from a Japanese game show host revving up the studio audience. He showered a second time and phoned Till.

Kelly left the resort and followed Benesari Road until Poppies 2, then walked down to the next intersection on Legian Road and saw for the first time the Bali Memorial to the 2002 victims of the terrorist bombing. He stepped past the array of potted plants and flowers and climbed the five stairs. The plaque was bordered by palm trees, and it looked to be carved from both marble and stone. It resembled an open book with the centrepiece in the shape of a leaf. Twenty flag poles formed a guard of honour as a back-drop to represent how many countries were affected.

His skin went clammy, and the hairs on the back of his neck stood up as he sat down to read the individual names of each of the 202 victims, written in gold lettering set into the base of the leaf with their corresponding country of birth and their country's national flag displayed alongside.

Bloody hell, eighty-eight fellow Australians and two hundred two people in total. Fuck me, he contemplated alone and in silence. Kelly took some time-out to consider the senseless slaughter of so many innocent people. It was a poignant moment. He remembered hearing about the bombings while on Koh Chang, but to stand here today, on ground zero where the attack took place was a personal reminder that his life problems were of little significance. He was alive and enjoyed a calm and peaceful existence with his extended family, free from the threat of terrorism.

Kelly knew from his hotel informational paraphernalia, the Stadium Bar advertised live Australian Rules football and also sold Bulmers cider. As a lead up to the big game tomorrow, the TV network replays eight hours of previous finals' games to set the tone. The bar was only another kilometre down the same stretch of road.

He grabbed a vacant corner table and ordered a cider accompanied by a handled glass of ice. A large group of fellow football-loving drinkers lined the long island-shaped bar, all the while screaming at a replay between Essendon and Collingwood being telecast under lights at the MCG. The Magpies were leading the Bombers by a single point with the third quarter siren about to sound. The full-forward was lining up for a goal, unaware there were only seconds remaining. The crowd was urging him on to get his kick away before the siren sounded. He missed anyway.

Kelly tried to immerse himself in the game, but his mind was consumed by the awakening of past events during his 'off the record' chat with Mrs Sherry.

The man, once known as Lucky Phil, leaned back into the comfort of his cane chair and started to search the bar.

Jack Kelly was and always had been a people watcher. He liked to play a game with his own-self in trying to ascertain what makes people tick; why some act so indifferently to others? He had a habit of always sitting with his back to the wall and scanning the room to view all that he currently shared the same space with at any given time. His natural instincts were to look for oddities; things that looked to be out of place. He shifted his head to the left to gain a wider perspective past a row of three large centred wooden columns that had to be over four-foot in girth. A young family was preparing to depart. Mum was packing the baby away in a pram while Dad seemed more intent on keeping his eyes glued to the game.

As they moved away, Kelly's heart skipped a beat. He swallowed hard and stood up from his cane chair. A lone man was draining the last mouthful from a tall glass of a crimson-coloured frothy liquid. As he placed the empty glass on the table, their eyes met.

I've seen that face before somewhere.

And judging by this man's startled reaction, the familiar-looking face was thinking the same. Kelly shifted his chair back, using the backs of his knees. For a second, his view was obscured by the thick column. He pushed his way past the table and prepared to casually walk on over. From the time it took to get clear passage, the man was gone—in an instant.

Kelly turned his head both ways. There was a rear open door near the entry to the kitchen with hanging strands of a plastic fly screen still swaying. He pushed through to be greeted by the kitchen staff. An old female cook looked to her left and pointed. Kelly upped his pace and shouldered his way through the swinging door that led to a rear alleyway. A single, helmetless rider on a motorbike could be seen turning the corner at speed. Kelly noticed a thick of jet-black curls flowing from the rear of his head and a T-shirt that read, 'I survived Woodstock' with the images of Jimi Hendrix and Janis Joplin sharing a joint. He bolted to the corner, reaching the junction in just a few strides. The tight road led back to the chaotic traffic snarl that was an everyday occurrence in Kuta. The familiar stranger was gone.

Was that Tobias, Kelly wondered while struggling to place the face, *and if so, why did he run?*

He swaggered back up to the emptying bar as the final game score flashed on the TV screen. The game had finished with the Bombers winning by a goal on the death knock. Two barmen were fussing about behind the bar. Kelly interrupted their conversation, "Excuse me, the man sitting at that table a few minutes ago," Kelly turned and pointed to the vacant table with trails of ruby-red ladies legs oozing down the inside of the tall glass, still sitting on a damp coaster, "is the man who ordered that drink a regular? Have you seen him before?"

"Sorry, no. Maybe this man comes here one time."

Then the second man joined in, "Snakebite. We sometimes refer to customers by their unusual drink orders. I have never been asked to make this drink before—ever."

"Snakebite?" Kelly almost shouted. "You mean cider and red cordial?"

"Cider and Ribena," the barman corrected.

Somehow, somewhere, Kelly had seen this unusual mix before. He remembered ordering the very same drink, but not for himself. He resumed his spot back at his table, visualising the strange man's facial features and trying to place the eyes. Now with more questions than answers clattering around inside his head was something he'd come accustomed to these days. He checked his Bali version of a genuine gold Rolex. The local time was 8:30 P.M.

Chapter-15

EVINA'S STRAPLESS DRESS exuded a casual elegance and only accentuated her classical natural curves in an exquisite example of unspoilt beauty. She was now ready to meet with her driver in the resort foyer for her long-anticipated meeting with the now-almost famous, Barnacle Bob, thanks to the continual ribbing from her sister. The twins had just finished another heated discussion, with Abigail insisting she should accompany her sister to the planned meeting at Paddy's Rebuilt. Evina was adamant that she would go alone. She didn't want to spook the man that could hold vital information in her pursuit of the answers to so many unanswered questions.

The two sister's parted company, and Abigail watched on intently as Evina crossed the road and prepared to enter Paddy's Rebuilt, alone.

Evina needed to adjust her eyes to the darkened interior. A young Balinese waiter greeted her inside the spacious foyer with an impressive array of fish tanks occupying the wall opposite a small front reception area. Inside the largest glass tank were 500ml plastic water bottles bursting with a single live giant manta prawn.

The well-groomed waiter motioned for her to follow him to a vacant table. She pointed to the bar and eased herself into a swivelling, cushioned bamboo barstool. Evina rearranged her above-the-knee dress with her free hand to cover her shapely sun-deprived legs and placed her small bag on the bar top. "Margarita, please," she ordered, almost regretting her request the moment the barkeep turned with a wide grin, remembering the last song and dance. She gently turned on her stool and scanned the dimly lit expanses that made up this Western version of a nightclub in Bali. Chrome and glass were in abundance. A huge Perspex dance floor could be seen with an array of changing coloured lights beaming up from the floor in a kaleidoscope of shifting shades. Framed cartooned murals of famous Hollywood actors lined the walls above a numbered order of private booths that ran the length of the wall opposite.

Abigail was right about this place, Evina regretfully now agreed.

Paddy's Bar seemed to be only about a quarter full, with a steady flow of new arrivals spilling through the entry at regular intervals. With her night vision now adjusted to the darkened club, Evina searched for the sore thumb.

In a double-bench-seated-booth, closest to what was obviously the entry to the kitchen, a light beamed through as a waiter bumped his way through a set of swinging doors with a tray of food. Evina noticed a single man sitting low in the corner. He was still wearing a woollen beanie that covered most of his head, but the flash of light revealed a long silver beard. He was an elderly man, and he certainly did stick out like a sore thumb against the hustle and bustle of brightly coloured flowing dresses, high heels and men neatly dressed in the hope they might get lucky.

Evina paid for her drink, slipped out from her stool and casually made her way over to the booth. The elderly man slid out from the confinement of his privacy, stood and extended one hand. "Mrs Bishop-Joiner, I believe? Your photo on the Smithsonian website does not do you justice. Please, take a seat and allow an old man to enjoy the delights of being in the company of a cultured and finely polished woman. It's been a while, I can assure you."

Evina felt his firm and calloused hand then slid into the smooth leather seat, opposite. A small candle flickered from the centre of the table, sending a distorted hue of purple from the surrounding vase as she placed her margarita glass down on a coaster.

"Well, it seems you know who I am? Who should I refer to you as, certainly not, Barnacle Bob?"

The old man let out a half-hearted chortle as he rolled an old coin along the tops of his left-hand knuckles. "Just call me Bob for now. Names are not important. Robert is my middle name. Barnacle Bob is who my two grandchildren liked to refer to me as when spending time on the *Bhagwan*."

"The *Bhagwan*?" Evina questioned.

"My old cray fishing boat. It was, at one time, the largest boat in the whole fleet. A fine vessel that served my family well. I see you have already ordered a drink."

Evina placed the two shortened straws between her lips and emptied the contents of what was a half-sized cobalt-blue confetti speckled copy of an authentic margarita glass. Double the price and half the size. "I'll have a refill if you're offering?"

"Of course," as he gestured with his open hand to the hovering staff. "I've always admired a woman who enjoys a drink. My experience is that they can be trusted. Can you be trusted, Mrs Bishop-Joiner?"

"I've always liked a man that gets straight to the point. Are we at that pivotal moment now, Bob?" Evina fired back with her quick-witted reply.

The waiter delivered the round of drinks and left. Evina eyed off her table companion's tall glass with an unsettling stare, full of a thick-pulped orange liquid and a piece of celery poking over the rim.

Barnacle Bob looked up and met Evina's glare. "Just carrot juice, my vodka drinking days are well and truly behind me. I assume you're wondering why I wanted to meet with you tonight, after all this time exchanging e-mails? Your investigative brain must be in almost total meltdown with unanswered questions?"

"The celestial sphere I received by courier that started this whole episode of my life—that was you, wasn't it?" Evina wanted to set the rules of engagement.

"Yes, it was. It was actually left to me by my deceased brother. I'm afraid he was the brains of the family. I have sort of just carried on with his legacy."

"How did your brother come into possession of such a rare and historical artefact, just out of curiosity?"

"It was payment for some legal work he did on behalf of some rich Indian prince who, at one stage, owned Murchison Station. Richard originally thought it was just an unfinished world globe until the Internet arrived."

"A prince—how did he get his hands on it?"

"You would have needed to ask him that. Richard's dealings with him were shrouded in secrecy, so I never gave it another thought, to be honest. How well do you know your early Australian history, Mrs Bishop-Joiner, and I don't mean, Captain James Cook? Earlier—much earlier."

"Give me a hint," Evina prodded.

"June 4, 1629, to be precise. Does that date ring any bells?"

"The wreck of the *Batavia* off the coast of Western Australia. The Houtman Abrolhos Islands, to be exact," Evina answered.

"Very good. Morning Reef, to be precise, a place I got to know very well. Notwithstanding the sinking of the HMAS *Sydney*, the loss of the *Batavia* is the most well-known shipwreck in Australian history, but its relevance to India is not appreciated and often overlooked. The first recorded marine expedition to India took place around 500 BCE when Vijaya arrived in Sri Lanka. Kaundanya sailed to Champa in 100 CE, and the Roman trading ships appeared in India around 200 CE. After the foundation of the Islamic Kingdoms, Europe lost free trading rights with the East. Looking for alternative trading routes, Vasco da Gama arrived at Calicut in 1497. The race to be the first country to establish a firm footing in the spice-rich islands of Indonesia was almost a prerequisite to war, as far as the VOC was concerned."

"So, your brother, Richard, I'll assume he had some interest in all these historical facts?" Evina wanted to stay on point and learn as much as possible about this man and now his brother.

"A man named, Max Cramer, who I took on many a scuba diving expedition around the Abrolhos, eventually became a good friend of mine. He was attributed to the discovery of the *Batavia* in June of 1963."

Evina's heart skipped a beat. She swallowed some more of her cocktail. Her team had already uncovered a direct link between her mysterious globe and Francisco Pelsaert, the much-maligned commander of the VOC-owned *Batavia* and her following fleet after it ran aground. And now, this strange, obscure old man was about to share something that may not be known to others. It was always the way of research. Books and historical references can only disclose so much. Local knowledge is always the key to peeling back the layers of what may be true and what actually can be proven as historical fact.

Barnacle Bob continued, "I originally worked in the asbestos mines in a town called Wittenoom, up until I managed to save enough cash to buy my first rock lobster boat. I was a cray fisherman for forty-one years. Geraldton and Kalbarri were my home ports. The Abrolhos Islands were my backyard—and I knew every square inch of my home paddock, Mrs Bishop-Joiner. Those early days in the Fifties and Sixties, there *were* no carrier boats as is the case today, to ferry stores and bait across the dangerous expanse of the Indian Ocean that separates the hundred-kilometre-stretch of the north to south running, low-lying coral atolls from the mainland. If you needed bait, you were forced to catch it yourself in the off-season from July to November. It wasn't easy either, in the small-sized wooden open-hulled boats that were used back then. With my brother, Richard, we often spent days on end being belted by the huge swells and the daily deluge that are the Roaring Forties, whipping up from the Antarctic with relentless ferocity. It was no picnic with the twenty-five- to forty-knot winds, sometimes blowing with no respite for weeks on end. It was no bloody wonder the *Batavia* came to grief in the dead of night. It wasn't an easy life, but it was full of excitement. Man against the best the ocean can dish out. They were testing times."

"I can see the glint in your eyes, Bob. A man of the sea— through and through. I think you are blessed to have lived that lifestyle."

"Blessed and bloody lucky," Bob replied. He straightened himself into his high-back leather seat and looked Evina in the eye. "Pelsaert was a shrewd businessman. At the young age of twenty, he was appointed as a Junior Merchant, which required skills in diplomacy, a lot of patience and a nose for business. At twenty-two, he was promoted to Opperkoopman or Senior Merchant. He possessed excellent linguistic skills, also versed in both Persian and Hindustani. With the VOC requiring its employees to be available twenty-four hours a day, it was no wonder a man like him had other business interests on the side to line his own pockets. He got greedy and paid dearly for his haste. His captain should never have been that far east, and he mistimed his turn to the north, all in his attempt to arrive in Jakarta in record time and sail onto India to present his gift to the new Moghul emperor.

"Anyway, one particular afternoon, Richard and I were pulling the last of a line of ten beehive cane pots when a violent storm came in from the south-west. We were forced to take shelter on the leeward side of what is now known as Beacon Island. We guided our thirty-two-foot-long boat between the winding deep water channels that will eventually bring you out on the eastern side, under the protection offered by the island mass itself. This day we had already lost one anchor in trying to hold the bottom and were not about to risk our second and last anchor. That would have undoubtedly spelt our demise. So we eventually ran the bow onto a sandy beachhead and knuckled down to wait out the shellacking.

"The storm passed, and with the light of day, we could see a large shape sticking vertically out from the water in the distance. At first, we thought it may have been an old tree trunk, or a discarded timber choc that often fall from the swaying decks of the many container ships as they pass through while heading for the Port of Fremantle. As we moved in closer, it soon became clear we were looking at a huge anchor at low tide. I mean, it was colossal, and it was blatantly obvious that it was old—very old.

"In the clear light of day under a cloudless sky and calm waters, which are a rarity in those treacherous waters, we were astounded at what lay on the shallow ocean floor."

"You mean the *Batavia*? Are you telling me you and your brother found the wrecksite first?" Evina's eyes opened wide. Her exuberance was fathomable.

Bob leaned back into his backrest and gazed at the dim ceiling, "I remember it well, September 1958, five years before I eventually showed Max the location. But more importantly, Mrs Bishop Joiner . . ."

"Please—call me, Evina. Names *are* important to me, Mr Barnacle Bob," she interrupted, unable to resist the quick dig.

"All right, Evina. What I was about to explain is that we were not the first men to dive on the wreck—not by a long shot."

"How did you come to that conclusion?" It was in her scientific nature to challenge everyone and everything.

"The anchor had clear signs that a rope had been tied off previously with rub marks through the eye and down the shaft."

"My God. Take me through what you saw. This is amazing. This is history, and both you and your brother's name, posthumously, should be recorded."

"Trust me, that's never gonna happen, and I hope after this conversation, you'll understand why." Bob turned his head, placed a handkerchief to his mouth and coughed. A low, raspy gurgle resonated from behind his hand before he neatly folded, and pushed the hanky inside his studded shirt pocket.

Evina noticed some red droplets of blood. *He is sick!*

"It was amazing, Evina. What little remained of the *Batavia* was like a giant FAD. There were schools of fish scattered throughout the shallows numbered in the thousands. Enough bait to fill our cray pots for years to come, right on our front doorstep."

Evina wanted to shout but couldn't. "FAD! What is a FAD?"

"Fish attracting device," Bob replied like it was common knowledge.

"I mean the wreck itself, Bob? What lay on the bottom?" Evina almost begged.

"Oh—you mean the treasure? The carpet of scattered gold and silver coins lying on the sandy bottom like glittering oysters. Chests full of ancient booty plundered from all points of the compass by Spanish, Dutch and English, state-sponsored pirates."

Evina's eyes lit up like a sparkler. "Yes! . . . Yes!"

"Well, I'm sorry to disappoint you, but there was none of that. Just the skeleton of the wreck lodged firmly into the seabed. Don't get me wrong, we did manage to recover some loose coins, but whatever else lay there for over three hundred ninety years was gone. No doubt plundered by scavengers and looters. I mean, the Aboriginal people have been visiting the Abrolhos Islands for over forty thousand years, so they had a decent head start. Mostly what was salvageable is on display at the W.A Maritime Museum in Fremantle now."

"I hope to go there when I next visit my sister in Australia," Evina added. "You mentioned Pelsaert was in a hurry to arrive in Jakarta. Why?"

"To understand, Francisco Pelsaert, you need to go back before the time he took command of the *Batavia*. Pelsaert was a businessman before he was a commander with the VOC. The English East India Company was established in 1600, and the Dutch East India Company; the VOC, followed soon after, in 1602. Pelsaert's original charter with the VOC was to re-establish relationships with India to expand their trade links with the Moghul Court. Pelsaert had painstakingly gained the favour of the fourth Moghul Emperor Jahangir. Now, with his untimely death two years earlier, the process would commence one more time with his firstborn son, Prince Khurram. With the presentation of his precious offering, he was on the cusp of shoring up relationships between the two trading nations, once again.

"Pelsaert was engulfed with a burning desire and single mindlessness in applying some of his own business nous; resulting in his establishing the indigo factory at Agra, which was his first introduction with the Court of the Great Moghul. There he learnt about the prospects, of bringing cheap trinkets and selling them at a very high profit. On his previous return trip to the Netherlands, Pelsaert explored the possibility of selling collectable items to the Moghul Court. His sole purpose for his journey on the now stricken *Batavia* was to present a priceless artefact of immense importance that once belonged to Prince Khurram's father, as an offering of good faith. Timing was of the utmost importance as the Islamic Kingdom gained a firm foothold in the Court. His own personal dream of fame and fortune now lay dashed on the bottom of the ocean floor."

"How is it that a rock lobster fisherman from Western Australia has procured all this wealth of knowledge about Pelsaert and the Moghul Court?"

"Like I said earlier, Evina, Richard was the brains of the family, but be patient. We will come to that later. Do you know of a man called, Tom Pepper?"

"Yes. Pepper was responsible for finding the *Zuytdorp* wreck."

"Right again. My father liked to spend time with Tom on Tamala Station. He would anchor his boat almost right at his doorstep, at a place called Prickly Point within the sheltered waters of Shark Bay. Tom Pepper was a European stockman. He was almost considered a celebrity in his local community, after he and his Aboriginal wife, Lurleen, accompanied by her sister, Ada, stumbled on the wreck of the *Zuytdorp*, laying at the bottom of the cliff's that are a prominent part of the West Australian coastline. With her rich cargo laid bare on the seafloor in a bed of gold and silver, this created immense interest within the maritime archaeological community.

"The Zuytdorp Cliffs, wild in their beauty and dangerous in their intentions, are a small section of what is sometimes up to two-hundred-foot-high rock escarpments spanning hundreds of kilometres, allowing limited access to the ocean. This particular place was always a favourite fishing spot for Tom and his extended family, as it offered relative ease of access to the flat-bottomed rocks below. Stretching more than two hundred twenty kilometres from Pepper Point in the north to the southern town of Kalbarri, they are the longest fault scarp in Australia. Pounded by the Indian Ocean with wave-cut benches, blowholes, spouts and slips, these dangerous cliffs are a stark reminder of the dangers that lurk for the unprepared mariner.

"The Zuytdorp Cliffs consist of Tamala limestone, which stretches down much of the West Australian coastline. The cliffs formed about five to ten thousand years ago when the Earth's crust shifted along a fault line during an earthquake. In November of 1941, Tropical Cyclone Evelyn had just ripped over the coastline. Tom was keen to drive the western boundary to check on livestock and, if time permitted, chase a few Westralian dhufish that often ducked the worst of the storms, spending time closer to the shallow rocky ledges.

"Tom, with both me and my dear old dad, jumped in the station's old single-cab Land Rover Ute and headed off in a westerly direction. The damage from the three-day-old storm was nothing out of the ordinary, with a few fallen trees and a couple of sheep somehow managing to wander off the precipice, now destined for the dinner plate of the wild dingoes. Apart from that, it all looked relatively okay.

"Tom finished his rounds, and we drove the last thirty kilometres of the dusty track to the Zuytdorp Cliffs. With just a couple of handlines, we all scaled the broken rock-face and baited some hooks with small black crabs before Tom and Dad cast out their rigs."

"It would be fair to say that Tom and your father were close friends, then?" Evina asked.

"I can count on one hand, my close friends and the people I trust, Evina. Dad was the same. Something you should always remember. Both Tom and the old-man loved fishing and the great Australian wilderness. Tom always enjoyed his time on Dad's old boat with the smell of the sea and the spectacle of the setting sun on the distant horizon each evening. On this particular day, Tom laid down his gear and stepped his way to a scattering of rock pools in the distance, to trap another couple of small crabs for bait.

"From the corner of his eye, Tom caught the quick flash of a reflection, about halfway up the vertical bluff. With his curiosity sparked, he started his scramble to higher ground. The pungent odour of rotting flesh was almost overpowering. There was nothing unusual about that. That whole area was inhabited by wild goats that have adapted to survive the long dry spells by drinking salt water. It makes them go a little crazy, but Mother Nature provides in her own mysterious ways. It looked like a section of the top cliff had caved in, probably due to the cyclone.

"Tom crouched down and started to excavate some of the rubble. The smell was almost unbearable, as he called my father over to give him a helping hand. A small cavity started to appear from behind. Tom was a powerfully built man. He started throwing the fallen rocks over his shoulder. Some required him to stand and use the full force of his hardened stockman's arms. Eventually, he'd made enough room to gain a shadowed look inside. Tom placed his body flat and extended his arm to feel around. His hand brushed against something soft. He clasped his fingers and pulled the object clear.

"They were both amazed to find a navy officer's cap complete with its woven black mohair hatband. The inside of the cap was still lined with blue corded silk, and the leather inner hatband was stamped 'MADE IN AUSTRALIA - RAN'. I remember how Tom spat on his fingers and wiped away the dirt and grime that covered the embroidered officers' badge, positioned above the peak, and you won't believe what it revealed?"

Bob fumbled for his handkerchief a second time.

"Are you okay?" Evina asked with genuine concern.

"Sorry. Who would ever know that asbestos can kill a man forty-five years later?"

"I'm so sorry, can I get you something?"

"Thanks, but I'm fine."

"So, you were there, with Tom and your father?" Evina continued.

"I was only knee-high to a grasshopper. Our two families spent many a Christmas together."

"Tell me, what was the inscription on the cap?"

"Ultimately, it was this inscription that led me to contact you. It simply read, RAN - HMAS *Sydney*."

"The *Sydney*?" Evina almost cried out. "The only known survivor was the remains of a ships' cook who washed up sometime later on Christmas Island still lying on the floor of a Carley float that was identified later as originating from HMAS *Sydney*. You have to be kidding me? How can this be? Surely that can't be right?" Evina was struggling to believe what Bob was telling her.

"That's pretty much what Tom and my father both said. How can this be? I was only nine years old at the time, but I can still recall the exhilaration and the sense of adventure at what we uncovered next. It was amazing. Tom asked me to crawl inside with my smaller body size using his Zippo lighter. The small cavern lit up like a bushman's campfire. I remember bumping my head on the rock ceiling as I pulled back hard and fast, trying to make some sense of the macabre scene, only a few feet away. The rotting threads of an Australian Navy uniform were lying flat on the cave floor. Inside were the decaying remains of some poor soul. Bits of flesh hung from what was once this man's face. A few tufts of black hair resembled wilted wild spinifex. Tom raced back up to the Land Rover and grabbed his torch.

"Behind the body was another rock pile. The way each boulder had been laid out suggested it was man made. This was starting to get weird. We found bits of an old kangaroo hide as I searched deeper. A two-foot-high slab of white limestone looked out of place. I started to carefully remove some of the rocks when every nerve-end in my body started to dance from head to toe. A perfectly preserved skull, with a full set of angled teeth, appeared from under the pile.

"Tom and my father were both speechless. 'What is this place?' I remember we asked ourselves. Two bodies tucked away in the middle of nowhere. My father told Tom they needed to get back to Tamala Station and alert the authorities."

"I don't recall any mention of these two bodies in any of my research. Surely this would have been big news at the time? What was to become of the corpses and more importantly—who did they belong to?" Evina was trained to be sceptical. It wasn't that she had any reason to doubt Bob's story. But she worked on logic and undeniable proof as a scientist.

"You need to understand, Evina, Tom Pepper was married to an Aboriginal woman. He lived his life as a nomad, immersed in their culture and historical beliefs of the Yamatji tribal way of life. For a gravesite to be desecrated would anger the Spirits and affect their Dreamtime after death. The Yamatji people call it a Sorry place. Tom was probably more Aboriginal than a white man, and there was no way he wanted to risk the wrath of his family. This was their land, and this was his life, and his choice. My father had to respect that."

"Are you telling me the gravesite is still there and undisturbed? What about the unusual slab of limestone? What was that all about?"

"It was a headstone with a carved inscription written in Dutch including the latitude of twenty-seven degrees—and it was signed. I read it out while Tom copied it down on the inside of a pack of smokes. "

"Bob—please, let's just slow down here a moment while I grasp what you're telling me. No bugger it, I need to know. Did you have it translated?" Evina's heart rate was increasing by the minute.

"The bloke who owned the Denham Hotel back then was a huge man. He was known as the Flying Dutchman, because of his reputation of turfing you out the door in a flying action if you caused any trouble."

"Bloody hell, Bob, tell me what it said, for God's sake."

The old man with the long white beard leaned to his left and pulled open a previously concealed small cloth shoulder bag. He placed his hand inside and retrieved a sealed Perspex container. Inside was an old ripped open and flattened out soft-pack of cigarettes with the logo still clearly displayed of a single-humped camel. He slid it over the table in an action that suggested he didn't want anyone else to see what it was.

"These are the original letters and numbers, as I called them out to, Tom. Next to that is the translated version."

Dear God, does it ever end? Evina thought to herself. She picked up the container and turned it over in her hand and read out the English translation in nothing more than a loud whisper. "Here lies Wouter Loos in his 24th year. Dec 1629 - Jan Pelgrom de Bye van Bemmel, VOC *Batavia*. Lat 27." That was followed by seven symbols and eight random letters.

$$\approx\approx\approx \text{ ß-m } \zeta \diamond \gamma \text{ bel uil } \downarrow$$

Evina nearly spilt her drink a second time. She finished the contents and quickly waved for another. Goosebumps were prickling over every inch of her body. She started to perspire and pulled a wet-one from the inside of her Gucci bag. This could be one of those career-defining moments, that same moment in time that all scientific researchers hoped and lived for, but usually never have the chance to experience. Evina wanted to ask the sixty-four-thousand-dollar question. Was she about to find the location of an artefact so important that it could change the world—forever? A better world. She was almost struggling to breathe while she fought back the urge to give this strange, unassuming man a giant hug.

"Tom and I replaced the rocks and left the site as we found it. It's still there today, so you can check the authenticity of this story yourself if you wish. I have the exact location scratched down on this mud map I scrawled out that day," Bob offered as an afterthought.

Evina's mind was spiralling. She wanted to scream out. *If you wish... yes... I wish very much. Oh, my God! Was this guy for real? Was this actually happening?* Her academical brain was red-lining..

Bob continued, "Reading Pelsaert's journals from the time he left Jakarta on the *Sardam* to return to the site of the wrecked *Batavia,* he wrote that he struggled to find Batavia's Graveyard reading Captain Jan Evertsz, own carefully mapped latitude. It was a proven fact that his captain was sometimes out by as much as a degree or two, and in navigational terms, that equates to missing an island by miles—or in this case, about forty miles to the south. He was certainly not an experienced cartographer like the brilliant, Cook. His maps still stand the test of time today, a miraculous feat in itself."

"Yes—yes, but where did the spot on the headstone lead you to? Please put me out of my misery, Bob. The suspense is killing me."

"Pelsaert left the Abrolhos and headed east- by nor-east which would bring him to about where the white cliffs of Menai Hills are and twelve kilometres south of Hutt River, which is twenty-eight degrees in latitude. The next day his journals say they proceeded under small sail, but with a top-gallant gale and a stiff breeze until noon. That's when they encountered the small inlet Pelsaert previously attempted to make land on the continent in his desperate search for fresh water on his return trip to Batavia. This is the same location he marooned Wouter Loos and Jan Pelgrom de Bye.

"Now if you consider he sailed for a maximum of seven hours, while still looking for his lost captain and four other sailors, he would still be under small sail while they searched for smoke on the shoreline. We know the distance from White

Cliffs to Hutt River is twelve kilometres; Wittecarra Gully is seventy-three kilometres farther to the north. At an estimated sailing speed of 1.7 kmph, this would place them at the mouth of Hutt River. To reach the alternative, the *Sardam* would have needed to reach speeds of somewhere in the vicinity of nine to ten kmph. The best speed the yacht achieved on their entire journey back to Batavia was only 11.4 kmph."

"So you don't believe Wittecarra Creek is the actual location where Pelsaert marooned both Wouter Loos and Jan Pelgrom de Bye?" Evina had to agree, the summation was sound.

"It's only based on my own experiences running a cray boat for forty-odd years in those waters and a bit of basic common sense."

Evina took some time-out and considered Bob's theory for a moment.

"There is one other thing, Evina. I want you to listen carefully and heed my advice. There are hidden dangers that lurk behind every corner. I want to share . . ."

Barnacle Bob stopped mid-sentence and looked over Evina's shoulder. A tall man with blond hair had suddenly appeared from nowhere and looked like he was about to ask Evina for a dance. She shifted her attention from her guest opposite to the stranger now standing to her immediate left. At this moment in time, Evina didn't care how good looking this guy was, everything that Barnacle Bob continues to disclose could be of the utmost importance. It's always the littlest things that amount to something bigger. *I need to blow this weirdo off—and now.*

Chapter·16

KELLY WAS BECOMING BORED and needed a distraction. He paid his bill and left the Stadium Bar. He followed the street back towards the Bali Memorial and was soon playing a game of sidewalk shuffle while following a group of teenage school leavers looking for their next watering hole. Kelly started to follow the group of partygoers as they spearheaded a clear path ahead, then decided to cross over to the less congested side of the road.

Suddenly, over the buzz of the crowd and traffic, he heard, "Skippy . . . Kelly, over here."

A woman's voice could be heard as Kelly dodged between the never-ending flow of motorbikes, cars and tourist buses. He stepped onto the high wet season kerbing, careful not to fall down a hole in the concrete big enough to swallow a pram, and searched for the source of the commotion.

"Mr Kelly, I'm here, in the bar." The blonde-haired woman was still seated and waving a welcoming hand.

Kelly recognised the face, "That reporter?" No man alive can forget the defined features of a good-looking woman. Kelly stepped into the Expresso Bar and stopped next to her table. Abigail stumbled from her chair, stood and embraced him with more than a friendly hug which caught him by surprise. This was a little unexpected. As she pulled away, the slight glazing of her eyes revealed the reason why.

"Pull up a chair, Kelly. It's really good to see you again. You obviously found your way out of Cambodia. What are you up to tonight, all alone, and in Bali? Let me order you a drink. The cocktails are two for one until ten o'clock. Yippeee."

Oh boy, this should be fun. "What are you doing here, and why are you drinking alone?" Kelly asked. He noticed a couple of men seated opposite silently cursing him for his untimely arrival. They looked like they were ready to pounce like a pair of horny lions. *Sorry, boys.*

"Waiter, two more of those pretty blue drinks for me and my friend, Kelly," Abigail slurred in a cheerful tone. "I'm here with my twin sister. She's not actually here, now, but here— what I mean is here in Bali with, Barnacle Bob."

"Barnacle Bob?"

A loud *hiccup* followed by a small *burp* confirmed that he needed to get Abigail out of here and to a safe place. She was smashed. "Your twin sister?" Kelly quizzed.

"Ye-siree. Evina is her name. We're maternal twins... but she is older." *Hiccup.*

"Where is she right now?" he asked again.

Abigail placed her elbow on the table and bent her head with one eye closed and pointed with her index finger to the bar across the road, now with a growing line of patrons waiting to enter. Kelly had never met her sister, but if they were identical twins, it shouldn't be hard to spot her.

The Jindeugi was seated in a corner position along the short side of the L-shaped Expresso Bar. His eyes were half-glued to the TV screen as Korea played a World Cup qualifier against Japan. He glanced at his watch. *Ten minutes to go.*

He was waiting until nine P.M. This was the time the nightly entertainment would kick into full-stride, and the loud rock 'n roll music the Western world loved so much would fill the bar and drown out most, if not all, the muffled blast. As the Korean goalkeeper pulled off a spectacular save, then from the reflection of the mirrored backdrop to the bar, the Jindeugi was alerted to someone about to join Bishop-Price.

The Jindeugi swivelled in his retro-looking barstool that was numbing his backside. With his brightly coloured, yellow, red and streaks of green Hawaiian shirt and a pair of cream cargo pants with comfortable loafers, he blended into the swelling crowd like a chameleon lizard. He wanted to take in a full view of the person who had just arrived. His line of sight was slightly blocked by the swaying leaf of a large indoor elephants ear plant from the over-head fan, spinning directly above.

Who the hell is this guy, then?

His plan was showing its first splinter, as it looked like they were asking for the bill, and now he needed to think on the fly. He flicked on his prepaid phone and scrolled to the only two numbers in the list of contacts, stopping at the entry with just three digits. Six, four and three were three numbers he will never forget thanks to the constant reminder of his tinnitus ear-ringing. The Jindeugi finished his pineapple juice and left some rupiah on the bar. He pushed his way through the swag of happy patrons with his finger at the ready while scowling at all the obnoxious drunk faces in the crowded bar, drinking alcohol, scantily dressed and covered in layers of makeup. He was disillusioned with Western civilisation, with all their combined wealth. To someone like him who'd tasted the poverty of a peasant childhood, these people wasted their lives on materialistic objectives and superficial life ambitions, but he had his orders: Bishop-Price and the old man.

"Welcome to the Expresso Lounge Bar, let's get this party started," the lead singer from a three-piece band rocked through his microphone.

The Jindeugi shouldered his way past a stocky bouncer who looked Russian and stepped onto the pavement outside, then crossed the road. As he walked north along Legian Road, he pressed redial, sending a signal to the second prepaid mobile attached to the side of the explosive device on the centre LPG bottle. He stood, silently waiting for the ten-second delay to count back to zero. "Five, four, three, two, one..."

Kelly stood back up, "Come on then, Abigail. Grab your bag and let's go find your twin sister." He summoned the waiter and paid the bill. "Two Heineken's and four cocktails? You really are a journo." He helped Abigail to her feet and with their arms locked they began the assisted stagger across the road to Paddy's Rebuilt. Kelly went straight to the head of the line and slipped the doorman some cash, offering an understanding wink with the attractive blonde hanging off his arm. The burly built bouncer returned a knowing smirk and guided him to a tip-hungry waiter.

"Table for two," Kelly instructed. "Somewhere quiet and near the ladies' room, please." He seated Abigail and ordered a glass of ice water and a stubby of cider. Abigail was about to enter stage two of her night on the turps. Her face turned a lighter shade of green. She sipped on the water and then stood up and ran to the nearby restroom.

Kelly took this time-out to locate the missing sister, inquisitive to who this Barnacle Bob character might be if he was at all real or a figment of a drunken woman's intoxicated imagination? He scanned the dimly lit room. The dance floor was still empty as the DJ was preparing to change that with his sound checks almost shaking the collection of framed Hollywood stars lining every vacant spot along the wall. A row of private booths ran along the entire east wall. Kelly followed his adjusted night vision to the last booth. The swinging doors of the nearby kitchen flew open, and he focused his attention on the two people seated. *An older man, and that definitely has to be, Evina?*

Kelly stood and walked the short distance to the booth. Evina turned and offered an unwelcome glare. "Can I help you?"

"You sure can, Evina."

"I'm sorry, I don't seem to recognise *you?* How do you know my name?"

Kelly stepped in closer, giving the old man who was more than likely the larger than life, Barnacle Bob, the once over. "My name is, Jack Kelly. And, Evina, in about one minute, your twin sister is going to come stumbling back out through that door," as Kelly turned and pointed to the ladies' room. "And just quietly, she's in no condition to be left alone. I found Abigail across the street, and the two-for-one cocktails have had the desired effect—trust me."

Jack Kelly... that rings a bell? Where have I heard that name before?

"Abigail? You mean, she's here, right now? —I told her to wait," Evina snapped, angrily.

The door to the ladies' room flew open, and Abigail almost fell out looking slightly worse for wear. She was wiping her mouth, and her sleeveless dress looked dishevelled, now struggling to cover her increasingly exposed bra.

"Abigail," Evina shouted as she cleared a path from behind the bench seat and grabbed her sister by the arm. "I leave you alone for one hour and now look at you, you're an absolute mess."

"Hellooo, Evina, letzzz dance." *Hiccup – Burp.*

While all this bedlam was unfolding, Barnacle Bob slipped the small coin he'd been rolling along the tops of his fingers into Evina's open bag. This conversation was over, and he needed to leave, not wanting to draw attention to himself.

Abigail stumbled awkwardly in her high-heels. Kelly grabbed hold of her other arm again and motioned for Evina to help him seat her back at his table on the other side of the dance floor. With her sister almost unable to stand, Evina glanced over her shoulder to see Bob opening his wallet and preparing to pay the drinks tab. She wanted to stop him. There was still so much she needed to hear from this quite old man of the sea, but her sister was in no state to be left alone. With Abigail supported by both Kelly and Evina, they prepared to make their way through the swelling crowd. As they reached Kelly's table, the waiter assigned to her booth came running to her side. "Excuse me, miss, excuse me. You left these two bags on the seat."

Evina grabbed her clutch bag, then immediately recognised the shoulder bag Bob had kept by his side. "Yes, please. I will return it to my friend. He's waiting for us outside. Thank you."

Kelly cast a worrying eye towards Evina, "What do you wanna do?"

"Come on; let's get her out of here. I'll see if I can catch Bob out the front and return his bag. Then it's back to the resort for the two of us. I'm so bloody angry right now. Sorry, Jack. I don't mean to sound ungrateful for your help, but tonight was very important to a lot of dedicated people."

Tobias Stone was casually enjoying a feed of what he hoped were beef satay sticks he'd just purchased from a street vendor while standing to one side of a flickering streetlamp. He slid his three-inch-long, single lens, night vision scope back into the rear pocket of his Billabong boardshorts and snapped some digital photos of the man standing less than fifty metres away from a palm-sized digital camera. The Jindeugi was repeatedly pressing redial on his phone, and still, there was no response—nothing. Stone wanted to laugh. He jumped on his second Honda *Eco* in as many weeks and negotiated a sharp U-turn. He pulled over to the side of the road, only a metre from the frustrated North Korean.

"Here, mate, catch this. I think it belongs to you." Stone tossed something into the air with a high loop. The Jindeugi was caught off guard but did manage to catch the incoming phone with his other free hand.

"The next time you and I cross paths will be the last. You got that, arsehole? *Arrivederci.*" Stone grabbed a hand-full of throttle and sped away. The Jindeugi was incensed. *What just happened and who was that man? This situation is getting out of control. People keep popping in and out of this night. Always expect the unexpected,* he thought, *but this was too much. I'm being followed.*

Something snapped inside as he just noticed the two people from inside the Expresso Bar, now accompanied by Bishop-Joiner and the old man, all walking along the opposite pavement in two different directions—alive and well.

What happened to the bomb? My sister—someone needs to die.

He pulled out his Daewoo Precision K5 9mm, complete with a four-inch Dead Air Wolf muzzle suppressor, and raised it to arm level, then fired off two quick shots. Barnacle Bob felt a pain in his left shoulder, soon to be followed by a second burning hot feeling in the square of his back. He lifted his hand and felt the warm sensation of something wet, and a deep red colour filled the creases of his calloused hand. He fell to one knee and started coughing. This time no handkerchief was going to disguise the steady flow of his own blood filling the inside of his agape mouth, now pooling in a neat circle on the stained footpath. He gurgled as he started to choke. He wanted to spit and empty his mouth of the foul taste that was the fluid from his punctured cancerous lung. His final thought was now he won't have to suffer the long and drawn-out suffering from a slow death in front of his family before he collapsed face-first onto the street.

People began to take notice of the body lying in the gutter, assuming that he maybe had one too many from the bar only a few metres away. A concerned bystander bent down to see if she could lend a hand, then she started screaming.

Jack Kelly was accustomed to being shot at and had the scars to prove it. He looked back over his shoulder and saw the old man lying with his head hanging over the high kerbing. Immediately he looked for the source of the muted thuds he thought he'd heard seconds earlier. His eyes locked onto the Jindeugi, now moving his aim to the right and straight in his direction.

He reacted in a split second, pushing the twins into a small alcove. Two wood splinters flew off the frame of a door, then a hanging ceramic flower pot shattered only inches from their scant protection. Just then a large curtained VIP bus packed with Chinese tourists *hissed* with the sound of its air brakes and stopped. The passengers facing the footpath started clicking off photos of the crowd building around the bleeding corpse. Kelly gathered up both the girls and threw them into the back of a three-wheeled bemo parked close by while they had some cover. The driver was happy to have his next fare until Kelly tossed him from the front seat and crashed the gearbox into gear with his foot, almost lifting the front wheel into the air as he floored the small 90cc motor. The twins were thrown back, but Evina managed to grab her drunken sister before she fell out the small window in the rear.

"Hang on girls, this might be a rough trip," Kelly hollered over his left shoulder.

"Yippee, this is so much fun, Evina. We should go out more often. Faster—faster, Kelly. Have you met my mysterious Navy Special Forces friend, Jack Kelly? He is so cute, but . . . I know, I have my career to think of," Abigail cheered with the excitement of a young school leaver. Evina needed to gather herself. She was staggered that someone might be firing a gun at this man she had only just met. She leaned forward, "What's happening, is someone shooting at us?"

"Just hang on to your sister, we're about to turn," Kelly answered back.

Evina did exactly that, and just as well. Abigail was proving to be a real handful as she slid around the back seat, hooting and well-wishing pedestrians as they flew by at speed on two wheels.

The Jindeugi re-holstered his weapon and grabbed the closest bike with a key in it. He sped along the footpath, scattering people like tenpins until he came to an intersection and jumped back onto the road over the gutter, landing with one leg hanging out sideways and changed directions. He noticed the long flowing blonde hair in the distance and accelerated.

Stone watched on with his mind stuck between a rock and a hard place. The professional inside him was saying, let it go, mate, it's not your concern. *Murphy's Law*, he remembered, and that was the trigger he needed, as he recalled who taught him that exact saying. He put on his helmet and joined in the pursuit.

Kelly had no idea where he was heading. He pulled out his phone and passed it to Evina. "Find the number for Till will you and ring it, please? Now would be really good."

She fumbled for the phone. "What's your password?"

"Can you be trusted with such vitally important information, I mean it looks like you have a few enemies? It's 0061, but keep it to yourself or I may have to shoot you myself," Kelly fired back in friendly banter.

A voice answered, "*Sàwàt dii khràp*, Boss. Where you pack the fish sauce? I make Tom yum fish tonight, very good."

"Fish sauce, can this night get any weirder?" Evina had to ask herself. She was about to hand back the phone when the rear taillight exploded behind her.

"Ooohh, fireworks, great. I love fireworks, especially sparklers, they're my favourite," Abigail wanted to share with her sister. "I looove you so much, Evina. I just wanted to say." Evina looked on and couldn't hold back a smile at her sister, oblivious to the fact their lives were in danger.

"Jack, he's shooting at us again. Step on it," Evina shouted.

"Step on what, this is all she's got, I'm afraid? Not to worry. Hold on tight."

Kelly swerved into the oncoming traffic with his horn blaring. He dodged another bus and turned a sharp left, hoping it wasn't a dead-end. A sign read Suli Road which looked narrower, so he veered off at an angle and was soon free from the traffic but kept the two-stroke at full revs until he started to lose power. The bemo was slowing. He glanced down at the speedo. It was teetering at just over 25 kph.

"Bloody great, what a heap of shit?"

Blue smoke mixed with black oil was spitting from the exhaust. Kelly was looking left and right, for anything that might provide a safe haven before the trike coughed its last breath.

Stone could see the Jindeugi in front, and he was gaining with each second. The bus pulled away, and they both entered the same side-street. He was only a matter of metres behind now. The Jindeugi looked in his mirror and noticed for the first time, another bike was hot on his tail, and then he recognised the helmet. He turned and fired another two shots on the fly.

Stone weaved as a piece of his front fearing broke away with a ricocheting spark, forcing him to let go of the grip. The bike wobbled, and he slowed to avoid hitting a bin overflowing with rubbish. A broken umbrella stood upright from the top of the piled rubbish. Stone grabbed it as he passed and accelerated.

Kelly glimpsed a set of reversing lights backing out from a private garage. He also slowed and allowed the car to drive off, then suddenly turned again and stopped inside the empty bay before the remote-controlled door came to a squeaky close. An upright freezer pushed hard up against the wall offered a small reflection from its power-on green light. He killed the ignition and placed a finger to his lips. "Shoosh. Everyone quiet now."

"Is this where the party is? Where are all the pretty lights? Yee-hah . . . Let's party hard." Abigail thought it was a pertinent question.

"Abigail, shut up." Evina placed her hand across her sister's mouth just in time to catch a full projectile vomit.

"Oh, no, please—this can't be happening," as she forced Abigail's head over the side of the back seat. The sound of regurgitated cocktails being emptied over the smooth concrete surface filled the dark space, followed by that awful smell.

Kelly placed a hand to his nose and sucked his next breath. "What are sister's for if you can't share these special moments together, I always say?" he mumbled through the cracks of his fingers.

Stone lined up the rear taillights and pulled in close. The slight slip-stream gave him enough momentum to pull alongside; the two bikes were now hurtling down the small street together like waring chariots. Stone turned his head slightly to the left. He raised the umbrella and speared it into the front spokes of the Jindeugi's motorbike.

The effect was both instantaneous and spectacular. The front-wheel locked and skidded, causing the rear end to skip high into the air, like a bucking bronco. The rider was smart enough to try to lay the bike down and make a desperate attempt at landing with anything but his head on the bitumen surface. He collided with the road, absorbing the full brunt on his left shoulder. The wind was knocked from his lungs, but he could deal with that. He slid to a stop and had the presence of mind to jump straight to his feet as the bike careered into a stormwater drain in a shower of sparks and disintegrating plastic cowling.

Who is this guy, a Hollywood stunt-man? Shit, he's good, Stone had to acknowledge.

The North Korean reached for his gun, only to realise it had fallen from the inside of his loose-fitting cargo pants. He searched the road, looking left and right. Stone turned the bike with his headlight facing the Jindeugi, which highlighted the handgun ten feet away, resting inside a pothole in the dead-centre of the road. The Jindeugi covered the short distance in one giant leap, barrel-rolled, and was back on his haunches within seconds. He propped and took in a consoling breath while steadying himself on one knee, setting up for the kill shot. *Five bullets left in the mag, I'll only need the one.*

Stone was a sitting duck. His bike was idling only metres away from the bleeding North Korean with no choice but to be an unwilling participant in what will be no more than simple target practice. The Jindeugi raised his gun arm and steadied his aim. Stone flicked on his high beam, startling the Korean like a fox fixated under the spell of a spotlight. Stone accelerated and popped the front wheel. With his front rim free-wheeling in mid-air, he aimed straight at the Jindeugi. Stone felt the first bullet ricochet off the underside of the bike's sump. The second shot was higher and blew a hole in the front tyre. The North Korean tried to jump clear of the incoming bike, but he was too late. Stone rolled off and allowed the riderless Honda to collide head on, sending the Jindeugi spiralling into the night with both his arms and legs thrashing at the vacant air, uncontrollably. Stone heard the sound of flesh and bone coming into hard contact with the road.

Ouch, that's gotta hurt. The sound of sirens in the distance prompted Stone to pick up his damaged bike and wobble off down the next road. He only got about a hundred metres up that street when the front tyre rolled off the rim. He left it where it stopped and started to hoof it out of there. Stone jogged past a row of houses when his finely tuned ear picked up the unmistakable sound of an engine cooling. *Tick-tick-tick.* That was followed by the sound of someone throwing up.

The drunken sister, how's your luck, Tobias?

He stopped near the entrance to a private dwelling. The sound of someone's voice talking on a phone from the inside of a closed garage could be heard. He waited and listened.

Kelly and the twins remained tight-lipped, surrounded by an almost eerie silence. All sounded as it should on the home-front, outside. Suddenly the voice of Till broke the tension of the moment from the back seat of the bemo. "Skipper, are you still there? The fish sauce, I can't find it anywhere? I make Tom yum and cook sticky rice. Hello... hello, is anyone there?"

Kelly picked up his phone and spoke in a hushed whisper mixed with the desperation of their current dilemma. "Till, listen carefully. Fire up the *Thin Lizzy* and meet me at the water taxi depot on the northern end of Double Six Beach. And Till, that would be *now*, mate. *Rĕw-rĕw*. Quick-quick. You understand?"

"I want to eat first, but I need the fish sauce. Tom yum fish no good without fish sauce, Boss."

Evina shook her head in disbelief. "Bloody hell, give me that phone, Jack, and I'll explain what he can do with his fish sauce."

"Who's that skipper, she wants to eat tom yum, too?"

"Till, *now*, mate. Taxi depot and ring me when you get close. Get your arse into gear Till and move it."

"Got it, Boss, I come now... soon-soon."

"Oh, and Till. There are two new bottles of fish sauce on the top shelf of the pantry. Grab a chair, and you should be able to reach them, okay."

"Got it, Boss, but you want me to come and get you first, yes?"

"Yes, Till. You come and get me now. The water taxi depot. You got that?"

Kelly looked over at the dark silhouette of Evina. He was sure he could see the fire burning from both her eyes. "Till is only a small Thai man. He can't see the top shelf in the pantry, but he makes the best tom yum you'll ever taste," Kelly offered as his only defence.

Stone smiled as he strolled away. He Googled the words, thin lizzy. The first hit was a website about a band. He scrolled down and stopped at a photo of a flash-looking blue and green cruising yacht and read the caption. "The *Thin Lizzy*, named after an Australian goanna, is a superbly designed one-off-prototype cruising yacht for your next Thailand getaway with a unique flavour. Travel in style and pure luxury with a difference. Sounds good to me." Stone had just booked his passage out of Bali, and he loved tom yum fish. "This guy Till sounds like he knows how to cook. I'll see you soon, old buddy.""

Chapter-17

THE ROLLER-DOOR creaked open while a set of headlights lighted up the short drive-way.

"Grab your sister, we're out of here," Kelly wanted to advise Evina. Abigail had well and truly arrived in that place between happy and hangover.

A very surprised Indonesian woman remained glued to the driver's seat when she laid first eyes on the two girls. Kelly moved in. Without the luxury of time, he ushered the startled lady from the driver's seat, and into the garage before rolling it shut. "Sorry."

Evina was already in the back seat with her sister's head buried in her lap. Kelly was about to reverse out when he noticed the owner of the car standing outside the driver's window waving her hands.

Didn't see a side door.

He wound down the window. In reasonably clear English, she held up the cloth bag Bob left behind back at Paddy's Rebuilt. "I think you must have left this inside your taxi," she said.

Evina thanked her from the back seat while Kelly placed it on the passenger's front. "Lady, I'm sorry, but we need to borrow your car just for about an hour. You can pick it up at this hotel. I'll park it in the underground car park, so it's safe, okay." She seemed to understand, but just in case, the card Kelly handed to her was of the hotel next door to his own. He turned in his seat and addressed Evina, "What hotel are you two booked into?"

"The Meridian in Seminyak, I think I can remember the way if you can get me to the big roundabout. What should we do now, Jack? What the hell is going on? Who was that man shooting and following us? God—this is a nightmare."

"Well, Evina. I was sort of hoping you might have some answers. Right now yours and my biggest problems are the Bali police. I sure as hell don't want to be asked those same questions with the answer—sorry, we don't know, all the while on the inside of a jail cell. My recommendation is to grab your passports and let's all get the hell out of Bali."

Evina remained silent as Kelly headed for their resort. As he neared the entrance, he pulled over a block short. "What do you want to do then, Evina? It's decision time—right here—and right now."

"Yeah, I'm with you. There's nothing here for me in Bali now. Keep an eye on, Abigail. I'll be back in fifteen minutes."

Kelly turned in his front seat, "Evina, whatever money you owe, just leave the cash in the room. No official check-out, okay. In and out, real quick, through the back door, not the foyer."

Kelly hailed down a taxi and asked him to park behind the now-stolen vehicle. Evina arrived back with a look of anguish on her face, "I need a hand with our suitcases, Jack. I think my sister has packed her entire wardrobe. I can't believe it."

Kelly helped the driver with the luggage. With Abigail hanging off her shoulder, the two sisters followed him in the taxi. Kelly heeded his own advice and was in and out of his hotel room within ten minutes. They all squeezed into the small yellow cab, and Kelly gave instructions to take them to the north-based water taxi drop-off point. The taxi finally pulled away just as two police cars with their lights flashing turned sharply left into the hotel next door. *She sure didn't waste any time. That complicates things.* Kelly's phone rang. "Till, where are you now?"

"I wait now at the water taxi. I think you want me to go very fast. I here now, Boss."

"*Dū khun ni sib*," Kelly answered.

"What was that all about?" Evina asked.

"That's Thai, it means, I'll see you in ten," he replied.

"I searched the name of your boat while you were grabbing your bag. It looks to be quite stunning inside?"

"And thirsty, but we'll get to that later," Kelly replied.

The last of the six bags that belonged to the twins were stowed in the two for'ard staterooms. It would have almost been easier to winch Abigail on board using the boats Hiab. Kelly instructed Till to cast off both the bow and stern lines. He engaged the port-side bow thrusters and pushed away from the dock. Kelly scrolled through some screens on his GPS, looking for a safe place to anchor until first light. He moved his mouse pointer and clicked 'go-to' and watched the screen initiate a destination point behind Sumbawa Island. *Three hours and we should be fine.*

Kelly throttled *Thin Lizzy* to a comfortable cruising speed of 22 knots and settled back into his cushioned skipper's chair. It felt good to be finally back on board, albeit under slightly different circumstances than he previously expected. He was about to pour a coffee when Till came into the main lower bridge area from the internal stairs. "Boss, you want to eat now? Tom yum very good. Your friend says it's the best he ever taste."

"That would be she, Till. The best *she* ever tasted. If you haven't noticed, our guests are both ladies."

"No, no, Boss. Your other friend. He says very good."

Kelly needed to clarify, "Till, what *are* you rattling on about? Have you been sneaking in some shots of Whisky khao?"

Kelly could hear another set of footsteps climbing up the spiral stairs. He turned his head. Abigail was passed-out, and Evina was enjoying a hot shower. "Who the hell is it, Till?"

Tobias Stone stepped onto the last stair with a bowl of Till's tom yum and a small cane basket of sticky rice.

"This really is very good, Till. Good to see you again, Lucky Phil . . . Whoops, sorry. It's Jack now, isn't it?"

"Till, give us a minute. Go down and prepare Evina something to eat and see if her sister needs a hand. I need a bit of time with my dear old friend, Stony."

"Bit of excitement tonight, Jack. Good to see you still haven't lost that golden touch. Some nice drifting in that clapped-out bemo."

"So, that *was* you in the Stadium Bar? The eyes never lie. I didn't get it until just now. Why did you run, and what are you hiding from, or should I say—from who?"

Stone wandered over and looked at the GPS. "You need to change course, Jack, and set a heading west."

"Is that right? And there I was, thinking this was my yacht, *and* I was still the captain."

Stone placed his bowl on a coffee table with an image of a goanna engraved on the smoked-glass top. He turned and pointed his Browning at Kelly, "West, old buddy—and now. Please."

"You going to shoot me in the back—again, Tobias?" Kelly rubbed the scar on his shoulder as a gentle reminder.

"I only nicked you on the left shoulder, Jack. And I did it for your own bloody good."

"My own good! Sorry if I don't share your idea of what's good and bad. Maybe you're just a bad shot."

"West and now, Jack. We want a heading of three-one-eight degrees. I'm not kidding, and I *will* use this if I have to."

"Why three-one-eight, the only speck of land out there is Christmas Island?"

"That's right and international waters."

Kelly reentered the new coordinates and engaged the auto-pilot. *Thin Lizzy* responded, turning in a long wide arc.

"Can I put this down now, Captain?" Stone was holding the handgun by the barrel. "The chamber is empty, anyway. We need to talk."

Kelly walked over to the L-shaped bar at the rear of the saloon. "Cider and red cordial, I see you're still drinking those snakebites?"

"Old habits die hard. Wild Turkey Rare Breed if you got it? Straight-up, no ice."

Kelly grabbed two 30ml shot glasses and motioned towards Stone to take a seat on the single lounge chair opposite.

"Let's start with you shooting me in the back, shall we? Sorry—shoulder," Kelly corrected.

"So all that shit about you suffering from some sort of memory loss wasn't a smokescreen? Are you telling me it was legit?" Stone was genuinely interested in his answer.

"The last time I saw you we were both in Cambodia—weren't we?" Jack's mind was flickering. "But I don't recall why. You're a living, breathing link to my past, so enlighten me, Tobias."

"Maybe you're better off not knowing, Jack."

"Better off—for you or me?"

"Do you still remember how to shoot straight? You were the best sniper I ever worked with."

"And best you don't forget that—old mate," Kelly smiled back.

"If memory serves me correctly, twenty-two confirmed kills, and you were still only twenty-four years young. Not bad. We were a good team—you and me. And now look at the two of us—together once more," Stone grinned.

"We're not together again, Tobias. You just happen to be on my yacht. Which begs the question . . . Why?"

"Jack, nothing much has changed, except now I get to pick my own jobs and the money is a hell of a lot better than the piss-ant salary we both used to get paid. Nice boat, by the way. You'll need to update me on how you wangled that deal. Anyway, I need to use your satellite link and Internet connection."

"You got a hot tip and want to put a bet on or something?" Kelly lightened the mood.

"Funny guy. I still have a flutter at the track, but no." Stone pulled out a Toshiba notebook and a Motorola cell phone from his backpack. "It's important that I upload the contents of this hard drive and the history logs of this phone."

"Another pissed-off boyfriend or husband? You never could keep your dick inside your pants."

"You're on a roll tonight, aren't you, Jack?"

"Give it here." Kelly opened up a drawer and pulled out two USB cables. He inserted one into the number one port on the side of his laptop, then double-clicked on the blue Internet Explorer icon. "It's all yours, Don Juan."

Stone typed in an ISP address. Both men looked on at the spinning icon. Within a minute, a logo filled the screen.

MI6, London office secured web server - security clearance required.

Stone leant over the keyboard and glanced back over his shoulder at Kelly. "Do you mind, this password is secured." Kelly turned and poured two more Wild Turkeys.

"What's your sat phone number, Jack?"

Kelly answered while smiling, "It's secured by a password," before he rattled off thirteen numbers. Stone entered each one into the secured website. Not more than a minute later, the deep throaty groan like that of a horny frog reverberated through the small speaker.

Kelly picked up the sat phone, "I'm assuming this will be for you. I hope for your sake, it's not a Thai woman named, Tiaan."

"Nice ringtone, Jack."

"It's a pisser, isn't it," he smiled back. "You're unbelievable, Tobias. Who the hell are you actually working for these days, anyway? Actually, don't answer that, I don't think I want to know."

"I wasn't anyhow, Jack. Need to know." Stone tapped a finger to the side of his nose.

"I'll be downstairs in the galley with, Till," he responded with his eyes rolling.

Stone waited for Kelly to leave. "All right, Brad, you should be able to upload it now." He could hear Monarsh busily typing away at a keyboard through the phone's speaker. "Let me know when you're done, and I'll do the same with the mobile."

"Roger that, about half-way through now. And Tobias, I have to ask, really, just to satisfy my own curiosity. Why are you not talking right now with your own ASIO people? Why MI6 first? Darcy Jones won't take kindly to you changing the pecking order."

"Just a hunch, Brad. Covering all my bases, it may lead to nothing, but I need to make sure."

Stone waited patiently when the slight bell of a small chime sounded. "Okay, plug in the phone now," Monarsh instructed. "That won't take nearly as long." Stone completed the change over and waited a second time.

"We're done. Give me a couple of hours, and I'll let you know what we find. Happy hunting, Tobias. Nice work in Jakarta. I see the last one went off with a bit of a bang."

"Sometimes, Brad, you just get lucky." Stone folded the laptop and put the phone in his trouser pocket. He grabbed his empty bowl and negotiated the internal spiral stairs. He was greeted by two other female passengers sitting with Till and Kelly, occupying both sides of a breakfast bench with their heads buried in bowls of tom yum fish. "Nice to see you're both still alive, and you Abigail, it looks like some colour has returned to your cheeks," Stone remarked with a, 'you should know better' tone.

Till filled Stone's bowl a second time and he joined in the delights of his Thai cooking skills.

Evina finished her soup first. "Well, Till, I'm so glad you found the fish sauce, your tom yum was delightful." Evina wiped her face with a Scott Towel and then fired her first question at Stone. "So—who might you be, then?" Then she turned and faced Kelly. "And, excuse me, Captain. Where are we headed? I mean, it's not often I arrive in a country by plane and leave in the middle of the night on a yacht after being shot at by a man I don't know. Somehow I don't think the Indonesian Immigration is going to be too pleased."

"His name is, Tobias Stone," Kelly answered.

Stone stood up. "Let *me* answer the other burning question, Mrs Bishop-Joiner." He reached a hand into another kitbag and placed a small device in the centre of the breakfast bar. Four sets of eyes were staring at the strange-looking apparatus that looked like some sort of high-tech iPod. "The man who shot at you tonight is known as, the Jindeugi. His real name is, Duckhwan Toa. A retired major general in the North Korean People's Army who now acts as a freelance operative—a gun for hire, if you prefer. What you're looking at is a . . ."

"A detonator, or a hot fuse," Kelly decided to finish the sentence.

"That's right, and this one was attached to a 60-kg, LPG cylinder about ten feet away from where you were seated at the Expresso Bar, Abigail. Nasty business. Luckily for you and my old friend here, the call to set the ten-second timer into action was never answered."

Abigail instantly stopped eating, offering her full attention to this man seated opposite. "A bomb, is that what you're saying? This was set to explode and kill me?"

Stone looked at Abigail. "Possibly, but that old man was definitely a target, and the Jindeugi didn't miss him."

"Barnacle Bob is dead, Jesus, Evina, what happened?" Abigail was dumbfounded. The previous few hours were all a bit of a blur.

"I don't know what happened. A man started shooting from across the road, and Bob got hit. I didn't actually know he died. Are you sure that's correct, Mr Stone? You think his injuries were fatal?"

"Mr Stone was my father. Just Stone or Tobias will do. Barnacle Bob? Well, yes, he's dead, there's no doubt about that."

Stone turned to face Evina. "Who was this man, and what was your connection to him, anyway?"

"I only met him for the first time last night. All our previous contacts have been by e-mail," she answered truthfully.

"E-mail, what was the nature of your business?"

"It's private, and I'm not at liberty to discuss it with you."

"That's your answer, Evina," Abigail spat out. "We were both almost killed—twice in one night, and you come out with that!"

Kelly finished his bowl of soup, "I think it's about time you all laid your cards on the table because when Tiaan rings in the morning, she is going to ask why Till and I are heading towards Christmas Island and not back home to Koh Chang. She can get a little feisty. Who wants to take that call?" Kelly was standing over the sink doing the dishes.

Stone posed the question, "Who is, Tiaan?"

Kelly answered, "Hopefully, the future mother of my children."

"Christmas Island? I mean, I know technically it's a part of Australia, but I want to go to Western Australia," Evina explained.

"They have an airport, Mrs Bishop-Joiner. You can book a commercial flight to Perth," Stone offered.

"I don't want to go to Perth. The Zuytdorp Cliffs are where I'm headed, and for that, I need a boat. This is a charter vessel, is it not, Jack? How about I charter the *Thin Lizzy*, what's the going rate these days?"

"Twelve hundred a day plus fuel, but the seventh day is free," Kelly happily answered.

"Sounds good to me, Jack," Evina confirmed.

Stone butted in, "I have both US and Australian dollars."

"Hang on a minute," Evina replied, "I asked first. Do you take American Express, Jack?"

"Technically, I was the first to board, so I think that gives me first option, plus I expect mates' rates, Jack," Stone continued.

"I'll bet you do, except it's not your money you'll be forking out," Kelly answered back.

"Who the hell are you anyway, and why Christmas Island?" Evina almost demanded.

"As you say, I'm not at liberty to discuss that—" There was a slight pause. "Look, Mrs Bishop-Joiner, all I need is to be dropped off, then you can have the entire yacht to yourself—free to go wherever you like. Do we have a deal?"

Both Evina and Stone looked at Kelly for some verbal confirmation.

"Fine by me," he said with both arms raised. "You've just booked yourself a charter, Tobias. Welcome aboard," he replied with a sheepish smile.

Evina placed her bowl in the sink and picked up a tea-towel. Till was fascinated and looked on with curious regard.

Evina turned and asked, "What's the matter, Till, haven't you ever seen a woman wiping the dishes before?"

"Not a fàràng woman—never." He laughed while dipping the ladle for a third helping.

"Ah, shit. That reminds me," Kelly interrupted. "That bag you left in the bemo, Evina. Till, where did you hide it, mate?"

"I go get it now, Boss." Till opened a broom cupboard and slipped the strap from a self-adhesive plastic hook. He handed it to Evina. She hung the damp towel over the drying rack and sat back down next to her hung-over sister. She removed the contents one item at a time and placed them on the table. All eyes were now fixed on a naval officers' hat and some documentation inside a plastic sleeve as she read a detailed DNA report from the University of W.A. Tears started to roll down her cheeks. Evina reached over and grabbed a handful of tissues.

"What is it, Evina? Are you okay?" Abigail asked, concerned for her sister. *Evina never gets emotional.*

Evina's thoughts were taken back to Bob, and the comment he made about the officer's peaked hat leading him to track down her whereabouts.

Stone picked the hat up and turned it in his hand. "RAN - HMAS *Sydney*. Who did this once belong to?" he asked.

Evina finished reading a handwritten letter signed, Barnacle Bob, while Abigail perused a photo of the HMAS *Sydney*'s entire ship's complement of 645 officers and sailors taken before she headed off to the Mediterranean Sea. A red line had been circled around the head of an officer in the back row, third from the left. Evina gently eased the black and white, slightly yellowed photo from her sister's grasp and instantly recognised the face of Callum Bishop.

"That officer's hat you have in your hand, Tobias, was owned by our Uncle Callum."

"Uncle Callum?" Abigail asked, surprised by the statement.

"Yes, Abigail, Callum Bishop. I never told you this before."

"You never tell me much of anything, Evina."

"Our American father always kept a photo of himself and another man taken while dressed in different naval uniforms. It took pride of place on his office desk in the study. It wasn't until I was about nineteen that I realised the other man wore the uniform of a Royal Australian Navy officer, in his full dress-whites. When I asked Dad who he was, he went all funny and walked away. At the time I left to attend my first day at Columbia University, he pulled me into his office and closed the door. This was our father's older brother. The age difference was I think about sixteen years. Our dad was given up for adoption at birth in Michigan, and Callum was resettled in Australia with his American-born, adopted mother, while his adopted father was an Australian Naval officer."

"Whoa, slow down a bit, Evina. You're telling me—this is our father's brother, and this was his officer's hat? The HMAS

Sydney was lost at sea. They say there were no survivors. How could this be?" Abigail was stunned.

"Read this, Abby. It's a conclusive report that the DNA from a hair follicle recovered from inside the hat is a 78.48 per cent match with you."

"Me?"

"Yes, you. Bob somehow must have somehow got his hands on something personal that could be tested. Not a difficult thing to do," Evina confirmed.

"My DNA is on file with the federal government. It's a requirement when you're assigned to report in a war zone. I spent three months in both Kuwait and parts of Afghanistan while the CIA was trying to assassinate, Saddam Hussein," Abigail explained.

"Those pack of government clowns couldn't safeguard a personal lunch box," Stone added.

"Abigail, Callum's gravesite is still intact somewhere along the Zuytdorp Cliffs. The location is right here. Bob has drawn a small map. That's why I want to head to Western Australia."

The maritime barometer with a small nautical clock inserted inside a wooden frame mounted above the sliding door to the open rear deck ticked over to 0200 hours.

Kelly said, "Well, we've got five hundred seventy-six nautical miles of sea to negotiate before we arrive at Christmas Island in hopefully under thirty hours, so I suggest we all get some shut-eye. Tobias, I know officially you are now a paying customer, but you can take first watch. Four hours, then I'll relieve you. We all pull our weight on this boat, old mate," Kelly enjoyed explaining.

Before Kelly hit the sack in his skippers quarters located right behind the bridge, he sat Stone down in the big chair. "Right, Tobias. This digital display to your left is a series of three randomly selected numbers that I have set to flash in bright green every five minutes. You have exactly thirty seconds to enter the exact sequence using this numbered pad. If you miss the call, an alarm will sound that will let everyone on the boat know that you have fallen asleep at the wheel. You got that?"

"Like a dead man's stick on a train?" Stone wanted to mention.

"Same-same, but different. Goodnight."

The twins headed down the three stairs to the twin staterooms. Abigail turned to her older sister. "Evina, I don't want to be alone tonight, can I sleep with you?"

"You're not going to be sick again, are you? Never again, Abigail."

"I may never drink again," she moaned.

"Yes, Abby, famous last words."

Part-III

The Golden Handcuffs

Chapter-18

PRIME MINISTER COLLINS was about to complete the third of the four disciplines he liked to practise in the New Parliament House indoor heated pool. His daily routine consisted of four laps each of back- and breast-stroke, then his favoured butterfly before finishing the session with a final ten laps of freestyle.

Today his schedule was full. His monthly meeting with Darcy Jones had been postponed twice already. Parliament was about to sit for the final time this year, and this meant he would also be required to chair the Joint National Security Committee (JNSC) meeting at 10:00 A.M. this morning. He never felt at ease in the presence of both the semi-retired General Miles Connelly and the unsinkable Admiral *Boomer* Peterson. Connelly was all class, a real gentleman but with a brain that was always two steps ahead of the play. He was a quiet and almost unassuming man. Collins always remembered his father saying, 'watch out for the quiet ones that sit in the background, son. That's where the real fight will be, not the bully with the big mouth.' Connelly had eyes on the prime minister's chair, and that was a good thing for Australia.

The bully was the admiral. A giant of a man with a handshake that would rattle a loose tooth. He would look a man in the eye and loved to quote; "To me, it's plain and simple, black and white." There was no grey in Boomer Peterson's professional or personal life, and he wore his heart on his sleeve. There was nothing he wouldn't do in protecting the oceans that surrounded the largest island continent on the planet. "Any country who wants to have a crack at Australia will have to come through my Navy first and good luck with that," the admiral would love to repeat. Unlike General Connelly, the admiral never played by the rules. To him, they were only there to be bent. "The terrorists don't own a rulebook, so why should we?" he often used as his end justifies the means speech.

Collins coasted the final two metres and touched the pool wall with his open palm. He stood and slid his goggles over the top of his mop of dripping black hair and was greeted by a pair of polished shoes standing at the pool edge. He bent his neck to see the Attorney-General Franklin Sandhurst, standing with his steely gaze suggesting this was not a social visit.

"We need to talk . . . Somewhere in private." Sandhurst's tone hinted that all was not well in his analytical legal brain.

Collins towelled himself dry. Sandhurst followed the PM into the change rooms, careful not to wet his handcrafted, Brando semi-brogue oxford cacao, Italian leather shoes on the puddles of water over the tiled floor. The attorney-general closed the door behind him, leaving the single federal security officer standing guard.

"What's on your mind, Franklin? This is a little unexpected for you," Collins got the ball rolling.

"I've just spent thirty minutes listening to my opposite number in Jakarta explain to me some rather interesting recent news events that have raised a few alarm bells amongst the Indonesian Government."

"I'll bet that was fun. How is that condescending prick?"

"This is no time for your crass remarks," Sandhurst snapped back. "They're still our closest neighbour and an important trading partner."

"We all read the papers and watch CNN, Franklin."

Sandhurst opened his briefcase and pulled out three coloured photos. "You won't see these on the front page of *The Sydney Morning Herald*. They were sent to my office e-mail account an hour ago." He handed Collins a single photo.

Collins viewed the first of three matt printed images.

"In case you are not aware of what this is, Prime Minister, it's a listening device found on the Indonesian President's private line in his palace."

"A bug?"

"Correct."

"Is there any direct evidence pointing back to Australia?" Collins inquired.

"Well, no, not to my knowledge, but..."

"Well, then, why don't we just send them a free can of Mortein, great for killing bugs? Just ask, Louie the fly," Collins joked.

"This is no laughing matter, I can assure you. Diplomatic relations are already set to breaking point with the protracted trial proceedings currently underway."

"You know I'm no diplomat. This government doesn't dance to the beat of their drum. And the other two photos?" Collins questioned.

Sandhurst handed them over. "These were both found within the crime scene regarding the suspicious deaths of a high-ranking cleric, and the second one of the kookaburra was discovered in the pocket of a murdered guard after the residence he was protecting was blown to pieces. Correct me if I'm wrong, but didn't our SFU's in Vietnam like to leave a calling card, similar to these wooden figurines?" Sandhurst's quick-thinking legal mind only ever asked a question after already knowing the answer.

"The CIA satellite images report traces of a large stockpile of Semtex exploding. If you play with fire, Franklin, you can expect to get burnt. Can I hang onto these photos?" Collins had already made that decision.

"Prime Minister, it is common knowledge that you have requested a monthly meeting with the director-general of ASIO since Bali 2002. ASIO answers directly to my office, and I have requested that Jones be present at today's JNSC meeting. I fully intend to ask him to explain all of this. Darcy Jones needs to be reigned in and kept on a tight leash. He's a maverick and seemingly becoming what might be referred to as 'a loose cannon'," Sandhurst wanted to spell out.

"Is there anything else, Franklin? I have a tight schedule today."

"Ten o'clock, Prime Minister. It should turn out to be an interesting meeting today."

Collins finished dressing and started to make his way to the ministers-only dining area for a quick breakfast and coffee. He looked closely at the two wooden figures. *A bloody kangaroo and a kookaburra? What the hell were Jones and his man on the ground up to?*

Since Bali 2002, the PM had requested a six-weekly, JNSC meeting with the nation's top six heavy hitters. It was a given that each and every person with the highest possible security clearance would offer an hour or two of their time to discuss and protect Australia's interests.

The prime minister, the director-general of ASIO with General Connelly and Admiral Peterson, were already seated across the boardroom table in the Menzies Room when the last two people with the credentials to enter were escorted through the secured entry. The attorney-general took up his same chair, and the Deputy Prime Minister Miss Helena Wilks was the last to be seated.

Helena Wilks was a product of the current political climate. Across Australia women had continued to be significantly under-represented in Parliament and executive government, comprising less than one-quarter of all parliamentarians and one-fifth of all ministerial portfolios. Internationally, Australia's ranking for women in national government continued to decline when compared with other Commonwealth countries. The representation of women in Australia's Federal and State Parliaments hovered below the 'critical mass' of thirty per cent regarded by the United Nations as the minimum level necessary for women to influence decision-making within the Parliament.

The Australian Federal Labor Party's Executive Caucus had decided to use this disparity between the heavily lop-sided sexes to its electoral advantage. The national papers had been running left-wing articles sprouting the bias towards men; the inequality in salaries, hours worked and perceived dedication to the job. The 'Men Only Club' one female reporter quoted. It was all paper selling propaganda, but perception was the reality of politics, so the Labor Party promoted the first-ever female to the position of deputy prime minister. Helena Wilks was handed the challenging Immigration Ministerial Portfolio tasked with dealing with the ever-increasing refugee crisis, arriving in alarming numbers to the shores of Western Australia on almost a weekly basis. The game of kick the political football never ceased. It was no coincidence that Miss Wilks was very easy on the eye, and the cameras loved her. In her new role as minister, the hope was the media may oblige her with some breathing space as she dealt with a rising problem that was on every thinking Australians lips.

She possessed a dress sense that portrayed a sophistication expected with the job, but she could also sling it with the average Joe Blow in the street. Wilks was highly intelligent, with a quick wit and a dogged determination to see that women's rights were high on the government's agenda. She also possessed the genetic qualities of her great auntie, Edith Cowan, who was a pioneer for women's and children's rights at the turn of the century becoming the first woman to enter any Australian Parliament when she was elected to the Western Australian Legislative Assembly in 1921. The fact Wilks had expensive tastes and an appetite for a lifestyle that was far beyond her means was seen as a minor obstacle in the Labor Party's pursuit to play the women's card to their political advantage—and it worked like a charm.

Helena Wilks' star burnt brightly as the steps to her political castle were paved with gold until the moment she opened her phone to answer a text message to see an image of her older sister behind bars in an Indonesian prison cell in the city of Makassar. The only accompanying words were, 'we'll be in touch.' That was over a month ago, and a lot can happen in a relatively short time in the grubby world of modern-day politics.

Boomer Peterson wasn't a male chauvinist pig as such, but he always cringed at the sight of the deputy PM. Her appointment by the Labor Party to simply appease the female vote irked him no end, but in the face of democracy, his hands were tied.

How can a person with no ADF training; an individual who has never had to face the enemy in the field of battle earn a spot at this table?

She struggled to grasp the 'real world' seeing life through her own political ambitions. The only saving grace was that she knew her place and usually refrained from entering into matters that she knew little about.

Collins stood at the head of the boardroom table and acknowledged each person with a sweeping glance. "First of all, Helena, you need to be made aware of this," as he walked the table and stood over her left shoulder. Wilks shuffled in her chair as Collins placed the original, signed Article-289 on her rectangular PU leather desk mat. She glanced at the details and recognised the four signatories. The fifth line was titled Deputy Prime Minister of the Commonwealth of Australia: The Right Honourable Member for Bowman, QLD, Miss Helena D. Wilks.

She was irate at the empty space. "This is an Article-289, and my signature is required to invoke this. Why was I not informed? This is blatant fraud," Wilks replied sharply.

"Deputy, if I may?" Boomer was already prepared for this expected response. He faced the deputy PM and let loose. "The threat of terrorism does not take a leave of absence just because you decide to take some vacation time on some secluded Indonesian island in the Banda Sea. We now have to assume the Indonesians are monitoring all calls from this country through their exchange, and we *all* agreed, this sensitive matter needed to be acted on as a matter of priority."

"Not *all*, Admiral," Jones wanted to clarify. "I wasn't party to this."

"Breaking ranks a bit early, aren't you, Darcy?" Boomer replied. He was not a big fan of the director-general of ASIO.

"I have the authority to act with or without your knowledge," Collins interjected. "Read the fine print, Helena. This is not a pissing contest, so let's just move on." The prime minister made sure everyone understood.

Wilks gestured towards the attorney-general, and asked the country's highest legal officer, "Is that right, Franklin? Is this even legal under the constitution?"

"Does it matter now, what's done is done? This is *all* privileged and cannot be discussed beyond this secured room," Sandhurst wanted to clarify.

Collins placed the photograph of the listening device in front of Darcy Jones. "Is this one of ours?"

"Prime Minister, ASIO does not answer directly to your office."

"No, but you do to mine," Sandhurst cut in. "So, is it one of ours, and if so, why and for how long has it been there?"

"Are you asking me a direct question about an ongoing operation, that's not your normal style?" Jones responded defiantly.

"Well, I'm doing it now," the attorney-general fired back.

"I can't confirm nor deny this particular bug is ours, it may be, or it could be the Americans or the Brits. You almost need to book a space since 2002," Jones returned.

"And what about this dead cleric and the explosion at the private residence of a certain, Abu Dujana? Is that also something you cannot confirm? I think you need to understand, Jones..."

Darcy Jones was in no mood to be questioned about operational protocols. Results were the only thing that mattered in his world. He leaned forward in his chair with both hands planted on the boardroom table and cut the attorney-general off mid-sentence. "In this business—this country's business, a secret is no longer a secret when you share it with others. People's lives are at stake here. When the operation is completed, you will have my complete report, as usual."

"I don't believe this," Wilks stood up with her arms raised in disgust. "Are you telling me this Article-289 was to eliminate these people in Indonesia? Do you know the ramifications of such reckless actions, Prime Minister? This government and the Defence Expenditure Committee, which I chair, are into the final stages of a protracted two-year negotiation, to build eight Armidale-class patrol boats under the designation of the SEA-1444, for the Indonesian Navy. The people who work for Austal in Western Australia are counting on those contracts."

Franklin Sandhurst shifted in his high-back leather chair at that last comment. He wasn't aware that the contract had been ratified.

"And while we're at it, Miss Wilks," Boomer interrupted, "why don't we just throw in a couple of Oberon-class subs. What the hell, we can refit the HMAS *Melbourne* and give 'em the old carrier as well. It's always the same with you politicians: money and votes. In case you haven't noticed, there are over two hundred million Muslims sitting right on our front doorstep, so unless you want to start wearing a burka and resorting back to the dark ages, I suggest you start listening and stop worrying about your own political future," the admiral remonstrated from the opposite side of the table.

"Big boys with big toys, is that how this works? You all need to step into the twenty-first century. The Cold War is over," Wilks responded with an air of cynicism.

General Connelly had remained silent up to this point. It was time to fire a broadside across Wilks' bow. "Deputy Prime Minister, your position at this table is simply a legislative requirement in the event the prime minister suddenly drops dead." Connelly met Collins' stare. "No malice intended, Jerry." He turned and directed his full attention back towards the deputy PM. "You're not required to offer your opinions, but you *are* expected to leave the party politics for discussion within the sitting Parliament. It has no place in this room. The world is full of bad people wishing to bring harm to this nation and its citizens, and if you don't believe me, then perhaps you should accompany me to the Sturt Football Club on the upcoming third anniversary of the bombings and speak with the families of Bob Marshall and Josh Deegan."

The room fell silent for a brief moment while each person contemplated the 88 dead Australians.

The deputy PM decided to change her tact. "Perhaps a women's perspective is exactly what's needed, General? Instead, we find this country heading for a diplomatic nightmare that will reverberate throughout the free world. Indonesia is our closest trading partner. We don't go to war with countries that help to bring Australia's current account deficit back to a surplus. You do remember what that is—don't you?" Wilks circled the room with a menacing eye.

"Helena, nobody is questioning your passion or the lengths you have gone to, to procure these difficult negotiations under an extreme pressure cooker situation. The Indonesian question is a tinderbox waiting for a spark, but we need to look at the bigger picture and question where all of us as a nation want this country to sit on the world stage. Australia is no longer prepared to play second fiddle to the British and Americans. This is our backyard, and we need to take the necessary steps to protect that—at all costs," the prime minister declared.

"Where does operation Blue Skies stand at this very moment?" General Connelly directed the question at Darcy Jones, who looked less than comfortable.

"I am in contact with our handler and expect an updated report at the appropriate time," he lied. "Stay the course gentleman—and ladies, of course," Jones turned to offer Wilks a courteous bow of the head—it was anything but. "The operation is ongoing therefore I won't discuss any details until it comes to its safe conclusion," Jones added.

"Handler? Is that what you call your spooks these days—a handler? They're no more than hired assassins, funded by our own government to eliminate people protected under the provision of 'innocent until proven guilty' in a court of law from a jury of their peers," Wilks blasted across the table.

"Some people give up that right the minute they become radicalised and pick up their first semi-automatic rifle—usually before they finish kindergarten, Miss Wilks. Sit down and let people who understand our enemies deal with Australia's security. No further outbursts—please." General Connelly's strength of voice made it known to all that the subject was now closed.

"The next question without notice is electronic phone security," Collins broke the awkward silence and continued on with the day's agenda.

Helena Wilks considered privately the precarious situation her outspoken gay/lesbian sister had placed her in. And now she was being blackmailed, more than likely from one of the people sitting in this very room. She needed to protect her own position, and her sister was going to help her achieve that—whether she liked it or not.

An hour later, each person left the Menzies Room, collected their personal belongings from their allocated secured locker before being escorted by a Federal Police officer to their parked government-supplied vehicles. Collins sidled up to Darcy Jones and whispered into his left ear, "A quick word in my office before you go."

Collins closed his office door. "So, Darcy, operation Blue Skies? Anyone might think you've been trying to avoid me. Where are we and what's the current status of your operative? Things are heating up. This was supposed to be a covert operation." Collins slid over a two-day-old copy of *The Sydney Morning Herald* with the photo of the burning and demolished house in Jakarta on page five.

"I'm not due to make contact until the mission is complete. Our intelligence suggests the third person of interest is no longer on Indonesian soil. Our man's operational parameters do not extend beyond their borders. I would suggest he would try to confirm that information and return to Australia."

"Not *our* man, Darcy. This guy is your responsibility and lets both not forget that," Collins reminded Jones.

"Are we done here, Prime Minister? I have a country to protect."

"So do I, Darcy. The difference being, I was voted in by the people with a seven-seat majority. I don't like being kept in the dark. The Indonesian Ambassador has asked for an unscheduled meeting with the deputy PM tomorrow morning. The shooting that took place in front of all those witnesses in Kuta, can you add anything to that? The dead man has been confirmed as an Australian citizen, but now the rumour mill is saying there may be some other Australian nationals involved."

"Rumours are for the gossips. I deal with realities and facts that can be verified, Prime Minister." His smile was less than sincere.

"Well, here's a fact for you. If the third name on that list is confirmed as *not* currently residing within Indonesia, you bring your man home. You don't want to make an enemy of me, Darcy." The PM locked eyes with the head of ASIO; man-to-man with a glare that only succeeded in pissing-off Jones even further. He was no politician and nor did he entertain the games they played.

Jones left the PM's office and walked down the ministerial wing that also allows access to the Senate and the House of Representatives. Below the tapestry of the Great Hall is a removable division that opens on to the Member's Hall with a water feature at its centre. He passed the access to the Public Galleries that lead to the impressive marble staircase that ends in the main foyer below.

His chauffeur opened the rear door of the white Holden *Statesman*, and Jones slid into the rear seat. He retrieved his second mobile from his locked briefcase and typed in a three-digit number, then pressed *send* and settled into the leather seat to wait out the expected three minute reply time. *He's not coming home until I say so. Aris Munandar is the final link and must be eliminated.*

Stone was already two days overdue with his second field report, which in itself was nothing out of the ordinary, but Darcy Jones did not reach the heady heights as the director-general of ASIO by being a fool. He had more at stake than just the success of Blue Skies. *Was Stone going to prove to be a major pain in the neck?*

Chapter-19

AFTER BEING RUN DOWN by Stone's free-wheeling motorbike, the Jindeugi picked himself up from the edge of the same culvert where his stolen bike lay in pieces. He dusted himself down as best he could, but the shooting pain down his right side and soaking blood seeping through his ripped shirt where the bike's side-stand had punched a neat hole below his navel, together with his gravel rash would need to be cleansed and sterilised. His clothes were in shreds. He checked his immediate surroundings for any stray prying eyes, then hobbled towards a sign he remembered spotting earlier.

An A-framed advertising board was boasting a free shampoo with every dog or cat spayed in November. The only visible light was a low, resolute reflection from the front reception computer monitor. The Jindeugi picked up a rock and threw it through the smaller of the two front aluminium-framed windows. He didn't have the luxury of time. He found the vet's surgery at the rear of the building, turned on the overhead fluorescent lights and located a bottle of rubbing alcohol with an unopened pack of fresh gauzes. Inside a flimsily locked cabinet were two single bottles of Bupivacaine and Lidocaine anaesthesia, plus a complete set of needles and sutures. He found a pill bottle with a picture of an elephant nursing a sore leg. The Jindeugi swallowed two of those, hoping they were painkillers and not some kind of weird Indonesian aphrodisiac. He stripped his ripped shirt off and dabbed at the bloodied hole with the alcohol, then went to work with the arced needle. With bandages wrapped around his upper leg and arms, the only piece of clothing he could lay his hands on was a white knee-length doctors' coat. He felt inside his cargo pants pockets as the painkiller started to take effect. His prepaid mobile was smashed. His first task was to report to the Doje, a requirement he was not looking forward to, but his young sister's welfare was a powerful motivation.

The Jindeugi checked the contents of his travel wallet, left the veterinary clinic and found a bicycle leaning against a fence, which he gingerly peddled until the first bemo came into view.

The Jindeugi entered his first-storey one-bedroom apartment that backed onto a small shopping centre. After showering, he redressed his wounds and opened the small safe to collect his passport and his second operational cell phone. He had an unread 6-4-3 text message. The Jindeugi needed to find an Internet café. He parted with some rupiah and was shown to a PC in a privately screened booth. The only other occupants at this early hour were a group of four teenagers playing some game called Grand Theft Auto.

He opened up the web browser and typed in the single word, 'Tick'. Three minutes passed when the command was answered by the 32-bit encrypted web address. He tapped in the coded answer to his translation app on his phone and read the message in Korean. Even the Jindeugi was surprised at who was attempting to make contact with him. The only other man that was aware of the significance of the three numbers; 6-4-3 was asking for a private conversation. He entered a second encrypted cypher followed by a time and the number for a public telephone booth within walking distance of the café. He looked at his watch. He had three hours before he would need to report to the Doje.

The Jindeugi opened the swinging glass door and waited for the phone to ring. Bang on time at 0330 hours, it sounded a bell tone. He placed the receiver to his ear and leant his back into the small bench to gain a full view of the road outside. A digitally distorted electronic language translator resonated through the earpiece like a Dalek from the *Dr Who* series in fragmented English.

"Don't speak, just listen. I have information that will be mutually beneficial to both our causes. To prove my authority, go to this web address at 0500 local Bali time. Don't be late. Your sister, Mi-sun, is looking forward to talking with her older brother."

The call finished abruptly while the Jindeugi was still memorising the web address. He knew this person's position gave them access to unlimited resources.

But my sister? I need to get back to the Internet café.

With fifteen minutes to go, he moved in and sat down on the wooden bench seat that was bolted to the floor. After entering his password, the desktop came to life, and he typed in *https://ci-detention.gov.au/staff/private/term-106/* and waited. The connection was made, and he was presented with a stark white room with just a single chair under a vacant table. A microphone and a jug of water sat on a tray with an empty glass.

Could this really be Mi-sun as promised, and if so—what does this person wish for in exchange? the Jindeugi silently questioned.

The Jindeugi was becoming agitated. The time was now two minutes past the bewitching hour, and then suddenly there was movement. Two people entered, one was dressed in blue overalls while being escorted into the room with both their heads out of camera shot. The woman sat down and adjusted the mouth-piece to match her head height. The Jindeugi needed to swallow repeatedly to clear the lump forming in his throat as the sight of his younger sibling came into full view.

The distant, unseen female voice of a translator instructed her they had five minutes and advised the call would be recorded.

"Duckhwan, is that really you? I can't believe I'm talking with my older brother." Tears flowed freely from her olive-skin cheeks.

"Are you okay, Mi-sun? Are they taking good care of you?" He was her older brother and ultimately his responsibility. The family unit was everything to him.

"Yes, I am fine. The Australian authorities are very kind and even helpful. Nothing like what has been brainwashed into us as children while attending school. We have been lied to and deceived by our Great Leader."

"There is nothing great about General Secretary Kim Jong-il. What have the Australians told you?"

"I was advised of my legal rights as a refugee and explained in detail the procedure involved in processing each person based on their individual circumstances. The guards never beat us. Instead, they give me books to read about Australia. It looks absolutely picture-perfect, Duckhwan. The animals are so different. They played a video, and I saw my first kangaroo; it was really quite amazing watching it hop around. My case officer is a very understanding woman. She thinks my application for refugee status is strong, and I may be moved to the mainland soon. Then earlier this morning I received advice I was to be transferred to another facility. I'm so excited. When will I see you again? I miss you so much."

The Jindeugi needed to turn his head and look away from the webcam, momentarily.

"Are you all right, Duckhwan? You seem distracted."

"Just a bit of dust in my eyes, Mi-sun. Who advised you of this move and did they say where and when? You need to stay focused and don't trust anyone. Your brother will take care of everything."

"I was told maybe as soon as tonight or early tomorrow. Do you think this is good news? Do you think one day my brother may be able to visit me in Australia? They say I could live in either Sydney or Melbourne. Did you know there are already other North Koreans living in this country as citizens? They say they have well-paid jobs, own businesses and they can cast a vote to democratically elect their own government. Do you think this is true?"

"Yes, Mi-sun. That is all very true. I have seen these things with my own eyes."

"One minute to go, folks," the interpreter announced.

"Duckhwan, where are you now? I worry about you and what you will do to escape North Korea."

"Yes, I am working very hard right now to make sure you're safe. Everything I do, I do for you, Mi-sun, remember that always little sister."

"For the first time in my life, I feel happy inside. I can see a future, for both of us here in this country."

"If you're happy, then so am I. You are always in my heart. I love you."

"Times up," the gruff voice announced.

"Take care, Duckw . . ." The screen went blank in an instant. The Jindeugi wiped his eyes with the sleeve of his shirt and made his way out of the café.

He didn't need to access his contacts list. The Jindeugi dialled the number from memory, then cancelled the call. He took a moment and then inhaled a deep breath while checking his watch before pressing redial. The Doje answered on the second ring.

"Sinto, I am here with the, Geulaendeu Maseuteo, and we are not pleased with your progress. We gave you an order that Bishop-Price needed to be terminated. Only then can we prepare the sister and the rest of her team for interrogation, and yet you have failed. We need to know how advanced their research has progressed, and the only way we can achieve that is by instilling the fear of God into the remaining members of these scientists. Bishop-Price needed to be splattered all over the inside of that cocktail lounge. Are you still in Indonesia? Where are these women now?"

"I ran into some unexpected company, Doje, which complicated things. It was unavoidable. I am in pursuit of Bishop-Joiner and her sister now."

"The old man is dead, is that right?"

"Correct."

"And who was this other person, Sinto? Is that going to be a problem?"

"Nothing I can't deal with."

"I hear Mi-sun's application for refugee status is coming along quite nicely. It will be a shame to see that hit a snag, Sinto. She has been through a long and arduous ordeal to reach this point. I will now change that with one phone call. She might enjoy a change of scenery. This is your last chance. The Grandmaster wants this finished—without any further delays or mishaps," the Doje sneered. The line went dead, and the Jindeugi sat in silence while he considered the ramifications of his conversation.

The Geulaendeu Maseuteo moved his cumbersome overweight body in a bad attempt at swimming to the edge of the indoor sunken pool bar and sipped on a guava juice. He turned and floated his Buddha-like body shape onto an underwater bar-side stool. "We need to send a clear message to this pesky team of scientists. If we eliminate Bishop-Joiner, her sister and the other three people that are now involved, that will deter the Smithsonian from carrying on with their search. The remaining members of her team will run and hide, and then we can pick them off, one by one. Request a copy of any satellite imagery to find out how these other people left Bali. It won't be by air, so that only leaves a boat. Then confirm the order to move the sister and send out the code to activate Chungho Goe. We can't take any more chances on Duckhwan Toa failing us. He has been away from the homeland for too long and is becoming careless and soft."

"A wise move, brother, I will make the call immediately," the Doje replied.

The Jindeugi's thirty years as a military strategist was alerting his inner-senses that he needed to think this whole mission through, carefully. He had failed to accomplish his objective, and the trail had gone cold on both the sisters. The evil-kin-evil hidden behind the helmet who disabled the detonator outside that club had to be a professional.

What was his interest in this operation? And the second man that helped the sisters' escape—who was he and how does he fit into all of this?

Too many unanswered questions and too many loose ends. All this was for the safe passage of the Jindeugi's sister to pass the rigorous Australian refugee test status, and now the Doje was threatening to derail that entire process. He needed to sort this mess out himself. Take control and protect his sister. She was all that mattered. *My own life is of little importance.*

He flagged down a passing taxi and instructed the driver to take him to Ngurah Rai International Airport.

The electronic departures display showed no flight details to Christmas Island. He approached the first of a line of ticket counters and was told to find the QANTAS counter at the far end. He purchased a one-way ticket to the city of Darwin on the Australian mainland, leaving in three hours. There he could connect to a direct flight, late the following evening that would put him on the same island as his sister. The Jindeugi offered his fake passport and Visa Card supplied by the Doje. He ordered some terminal food and coffee, one of only two Western pleasures he allowed himself to indulge in, the other cost a lot more than a cup of instant coffee. He allowed himself to power nap with one eye locked on the departures screen.

The first boarding call was announced at 8:00 A.M. Bored passengers frantically raced to the final gate in the hope to be first to board with the thought that maybe they'll arrive earlier than the others at the back of the queue. The Jindeugi placed the only picture he possessed of his younger sister back into his leather wallet and was the final passenger to pass.

Chapter-20

CRUISING AT A COMFORTABLE 18 knots, *Thin Lizzy* was gliding over the backs of a gently rolling two-metre-swell with a slight 6-8-knot breeze, south- by south-west blowing across their port bow. It was almost perfect conditions for the otherwise sleeping giant that was the powerful and unpredictable Indian Ocean.

Stone glanced over at the unusual nautical clock mounted inside a metre-wide set of bleached shark jaws that once belonged to a 3.5-metre great white. The caption underneath read: 'TIMING IS EVERYTHING – STAY ALERT'. His watch was due to finish in just over an hour and a half. He'd already tipped capful after capful of water into both eyelids and even resorted to sticking his head out through the sliding double-glazed side window to awaken his senses. The cold stinging spray from the sleek bow soon put a stop to that. The dead man's digital display turned green, and he entered the three numbers for what seemed like the thousandth time. It'd been twenty-nine hours since he'd last slept. Stone leaned back into the gas-rise, leather pedestal chair covered with a pure Australian lambswool seat cover and slid into the waiting comfort of the two retractable armrests. The monotonous rising and falling of the ocean swell was enticing Stone to take the gamble.

I just need five minutes, that's all.

Stone allowed himself the small luxury of allowing both his heavy eyelids to close just for a second—or two or three . . . Suddenly, the slapping of the sea against the fibreglass and kevlar hull was drowned out by the sweet sounds of Diana Ross singing her number one hit in 1973, *Touch Me In The Morning.*

Stone bound from the skipper's chair and cracked his head against the shelf above which housed the UHF/VHF radios. He was startled and confused. *What just happened? Diana Ross. What the . . . ?*

Kelly slid out of bed and looked at his bedside clock. The bright red LCD was showing 0435. *Not bad Tobias, longer than I expected.* He threw on some jeans with a clean T-shirt and found Stone still trying to work out what button to press to stop the music.

Till arrived seconds later, "Good one, Boss, you change CD at last—Deep Purple too loud."

Kelly was standing behind Stone as he sat upright in the skipper's chair. "Get some sleep, Tobias. You can use my bed, and I'll wake you for breakfast." It wasn't a suggestion.

He lowered the volume as Stone turned and sleep-walked his way into Kelly's quarters while stripping down to his boxers. "You always did love your Motown, Jack. I owe you one for that. Goodnight."

Till nestled into his preferred horizontal position on the three-seater lounge and was back asleep within seconds, something the seventy million Thais are experts at. Kelly turned on the Breville Oracle espresso coffee maker and bought up the latest satellite images to check the weather forecast for the next twelve hours. He checked their current position and then opened up his world data mapping software and typed in Christmas Island. A 24-inch-screen mounted to the left of the main console zoomed in on the dormant volcano.

Kelly Googled the island's history to form an understanding of why Stone's sudden interest. The total land area covered 135 square miles, with a population of 2,000, mainly Malaysian/Chinese Buddhists. Phosphate was found and mined in 1899 with over 100 million red crabs on the island.

"Wow, that should make Till happy. Chilli crab for sure," Kelly quietly chuckled.

The island was made up of sixty-three per cent national parks and monsoonal forest. *What is so important that Stone wants to travel five hundred seventy-six nautical miles to visit this speck of rock, personally?* Kelly privately questioned both Stone's private and hidden motives.

Two hours later, the gurgle of the sat phone woke Till. Kelly picked-up. "Top of the morning to ya, Tiaan." The call lasted over twenty minutes while Till prepared for a Western-style cooked breakfast in the well-appointed galley that any chef would be proud to call his own.

The clock ticked over to 0900, and now the time had arrived to bring *Thin Lizzy* back to life. Kelly scrolled through his iPod and stopped on Supertramp, then hit play. The twelve Bose speakers throughout the yacht and the internal intercom came to life. Within minutes the twins could be heard showering. Stone stumbled out, still scratching his balls. The smell of fresh bacon, eggs and sausages with fried tomatoes wafted up through the spiral stairs from below.

"Well, good morning, handsome man. Sleep well, did we?" Kelly loved to stir Stone up a bit, still standing while wiping the sleep from his eyes. "Breakfast—five minutes." Kelly engaged the auto-pilot and flew down the stairs.

"Oh, boy," Abigail dribbled through a half-full mouth. "Has food ever tasted so good? Till, let me be the first to say your blood is worth bottling. Thank you."

Nothing makes a Thai person happier than when you compliment them on their cooking prowess. Abigail had a friend for life now.

Evina asked Kelly, "I want to access my iPhone and the Internet. There's some information I need to research. Is that possible while we're at sea?"

"Well, the *Thin Lizzy* is equipped with two radios, a satellite communication dish, plus we have plenty of empty wine bottles with their own corks if you want to send a message the old-fashioned way. Or you could just log on to the free Wi-Fi. Remember, you are a guest. The password is written on the inside of the pantry door."

Till was busy picking up the skipper's dirty laundry after making the queen-size bed. Tiaan had trained him well. The sat phone rang again. Till stepped out and answered the incoming call. *"Sàwàt dii khràp."*

Bradley Monarsh was back in London and was looking out his office window that over-looked The Thames. One of the bonuses of the MI6 building. He looked at his phone with a puzzled stare. "Stone, please?"

"You want stone, what type of stone you want? I see boss have Rolling Stones," Till offered.

"Ha? Stone—Tobias Stone, he should be on board the boat. Who is this?" Monarsh quizzed.

"My name is, Till. Who are you?"

Stone climbed the last stair. "It's all right. I'll take it from here." Till handed him the phone. "Is that you, Brad?"

"Who's, Till?"

"A bloody good cook. What's up, you got anything?"

"I hope you're sitting down, Tobias, because we've struck a rich vein. Your instincts were right again to take down this cell in Jakarta. This is a real scoop. It maps out the whole South East Asian network and the money trail from Pakistan, and that's just the tip of the iceberg. Our tech guys are doing back flips. We owe you one, Tobias—big time."

"And . . . ? There's always an and or a but . . . I can hear the excitement in your voice."

"You're going to love this, Tobias. Firstly, this guy, Aris Munandar, he is the connection between Jemaah Islamiyah and al-Qaeda. He controlled the flow of money from Pakistan to Indonesia, Malaysia and Australia."

"Australia?" Stone questioned.

"Yes, that's right. There is forming evidence to suggest these people are in the final stages of setting up a nest of sleepers en masse. Sheik Aris is the end game. He is the head of the snake. We estimate they have successfully landed over seventy people under the guise as refugees. There is something big being planned."

"I'm still operational. Is this Sheik on Christmas Island or not, can you confirm that?"

"Tobias, this is how it works. They send three people with the same paperwork and identities. Lookalikes to protect the main asset, which in this case is the Sheik, himself. One has already been located on Manus Island and has been quarantined, but…"

"But that still leaves the other two, right?" Stone filled in the rest.

"Either way, Tobias, someone needs to identify the real Sheik, and that means eliminating the possibility he is currently playing the 'I'm a poor refugee' card with the Australian authorities."

"How do we tell the real Sheik from the fake one?" Stone asked.

"Arr, the real Sheik Aris has a birthmark on his left buttock in the shape of a crescent moon, rather unique, and this one won't rub off with alcohol."

"You want me to check these guy's arses to see if one of them is the genuine article?" Stone was picturing in his mind a disturbing image.

"For king and country, Tobias. You know how it is. Just make sure you don't shoot him in the backside."

"What happens if he's not our man?"

"Two down and one to go. There is one other lead which we are working on with ASIO. I'll keep you informed. It's a bit flimsy at this time."

"Earlier you said, *firstly*. What's the second instalment?"

"You need to be careful, old mate. There is something rotten in the Land Down Under."

"Won't be the first time, Parliament House is full of 'em."

"This is a bit more serious. Listen up. Are you aware of something code-named HABIT?"

"I've got a few bad ones, but no, never heard of it."

"Well, it's good to see there are still some secrets because not many people are supposed to be aware of its existence. HABIT stands for Hacked Access Bug Identified & Tracking. In the past, the UK shared all our information with the Americans until we found out they didn't like to reciprocate. A bit like buying a fridge from the CIA, they send you the unit, minus the freezer, but the cheques in the mail. When they feel the time is right, they send the rest of the fridge, and finally, they might offer you the cord so it can be plugged in. So, up until that point, what you have in your possession is absolutely useless and probably obsolete."

"What else would you expect from the Company boys? Shit, Brad, both you, me, and our fathers all worked with them in Europe and Asia in different wars. Always another underlying motive. They like results, not happy neighbours."

"Yes, quite so. Anyway, the Thatcher government decided Britain should keep its cards close to our chest and deal with the French and the Germans. We buy their planes and then sell them back the software to fire their missiles. Then the French sell that onto the Germans who trade in encryption technology. They are the masters. Remember the Enigma device, simply brilliant and unbreakable at that time without an actual machine."

"Yeah, I drive a BMW," Stone added.

"Well, they decided about two years ago that what has been created by one man can be cracked by another man—or woman. What they're referring to is that all encryption code is ultimately written by a human for the sole purpose of denying access to a computer with code and algorithms written by another human. Man designs a code to crack another code that is written for a computer that has code written by a man, who wrote the original code which now the same computer has the capabilities of deciphering due to another code that was written by another man."

Stone scratched his head, "You're giving me a headache. That sounds like the All-Bran puzzle."

"It's a circle with no end. Together all three countries agreed you will never stop the hackers, so why bother wasting all your resources on something that ultimately will fail and become worthless? The best plans are always simple. You and I know all about that, Tobias. We attacked the problem from a completely different angle. Instead of stopping the hackers, all you need is to identify that a hack has been launched, redirect it to an exact duplicated phone, then piggyback the connection back to the source. Hack the hacker, and sometimes you get lucky and catch the bastards red-handed. The problem was solved. This way, we can reroute the hack back to its original source and hopefully to our advantage. It was all the brainchild of a fifteen-year-old kid in Germany with an IQ off the charts."

"I'm still listening, Brad, but you're drifting from my areas of expertise."

"Yes, right? The cell phone you retrieved from the Arab. Someone had already wiped its past calls history, but the RAM keeps the last four connections in its short-term memory. We traced a call to a cell tower in Canberra. In the UK, only the PM, sitting ministers and the nation's security services have access to HABIT. The same rules are *supposed* to apply to your government in Australia."

"Can you pinpoint which tower so we can narrow down the search grid?" Stone asked.

"The tower in question, Tobias, is located on Parliament Drive."

"Okay, has someone bothered to knock on the front door, with a big gun in their hand?"

"Well, probably not, because there are too many doors to knock on," Monarsh advised.

"What do you mean?"

"There is only one address on Parliament Drive, and that is the New Parliament House on Capital Hill."

"No shit! That's interesting. A rat amongst other rats. Maybe we should save the Australian taxpayer a small fortune and bomb the whole bloody building," Stone suggested.

"Just because the call was answered by that tower does not eliminate the fact it may have been from someone other than a serving politician. There is a swag of other options, a day visitor with access, perhaps a relative or a spouse using someone's phone?"

"Maybe the morning tea lady? It's always the tea lady, they know everything. Could it be a casual civilian walking his dog out and about enjoying the view over Lake Burley Griffin?" Stone asked.

"No, we can ignore that. The reason is the public has no access to this tower. It is government-owned and to access it, you need to register your phone and enter a password."

"So somewhere there will be a record of a name that could be of interest?"

"Along with a bundle of others, yes," Monarsh answered.

"Anything else?"

"You'll be the first to know, Tobias, happy hunting."

"See ya, Brad." Stone replaced the sat phone back into its soft rubber cups. The twins were hot on the tail of Kelly as they entered the saloon from the external stairs to access the Wi-Fi and get online. Social media was a real problem, and Stone needed to set a few ground rules first.

"Good timing, everyone. Now that we're all together, it's time we all talked." Stone motioned with his hand for each person to take a seat.

"I'll listen to what you have to say from here, Tobias," Kelly said as he took up his position in the skipper's chair while casting a watchful eye at the GPS and satellite images of the clockwise moving low-pressure system shifting in a southerly direction from the north-west.

"Well, to start with, I can't allow you to access the Internet, and secondly before you leave this boat, you will both need to sign a 64-OSA." Both ladies sat forward in their seats, looking like they were about to explode.

Abigail fired the first volley. "A 64-OSA, why?"

"Excuse me, but what's a 64-OSA, anyway?" Evina asked.

"Official Secrets Act. A zipper on our mouth," Abigail explained.

"You're a reporter, Miss Bishop-Price, and I was never here," Stone's voice suggested the decision had already been made. Both women looked at him with daggers in their eyes.

"Evina, Abigail—let's just hear what Tobias has to say before you give it to him with both barrels," Kelly offered as a truce.

They slowly eased back into their seats with their women's hackles set to stun.

Stone turned to face the skipper's chair. "Jack, we may have a problem?"

"*Really*, Tobias?" Kelly had heard those same words before, and he knew Stone was usually right. "What is it?"

"Our impending arrival may have been compromised, and we could have some company when we arrive on Christmas Island."

Kelly looked at his GPS, "We've only sixty-three nautical miles to go. When can we expect this problem to arrive?"

"I can't be sure, but we need to be prepared. Have you any fire-power on board *Thin Lizzy*?"

Both Evina and Abigail's ears pricked. "Fire-power, you mean guns?" Abigail's reporters' mind asked. She had been in the line of fire once before.

"Can't hit 'em with sinkers, Abigail. So, Jack—what about it? You hiding anything I don't know about? If I know you as well as I think I do, the answer will be yes. It's time to come clean," Stone prodded.

"What are you expecting, Tobias? A couple of rocket launchers and maybe a deck-mounted torpedo tube? This is a charter vessel, not a bloody navy frigate." Kelly pressed the intercom. "Till, I need you up here to take the helm."

The twins looked at each other with contrasting thoughts. One was becoming concerned what Kelly and Stone may come back with; the other could see the framework of a great story unfolding and made a mental reminder to start taking notes.

Kelly pointed at the twins, "You two stay put, and we'll be back in a minute. Tobias, follow me."

He led Stone down to the engine room. They both stood on the bottom stair and cast a view at the source of *Thin Lizzy*'s heart and soul. Kelly headed to the port side steel-grated gangway.

"This is cleaner and bigger than some houses I've stayed in, Jack. Lead on," Stone said as he followed close behind.

They reached a bulkhead, and Kelly leant over then turned, in an anti-clockwise direction, a T-piece that sat on top of a false valve. Stone heard a distinctive *click* noise. Kelly swung one of the two Onan generators to one side. A door fell open, supported by a pair of pneumatic pistons.

"There ya go. I knew I could count on you—still the same old, Lucky Phil. Very nice." Inside was a Colt M-1911 service pistol, a Remington 870 pump-action shotgun and a semi-automatic Heckler & Koch, over and under assault rifle all with spare magazines, full and ready to go. "I'll grab all this, plus I have my 9mm upstairs," Stone smiled.

Till yelled out through the intercom. "Boss, the radar is going, *beep-beep-beep.*"

Kelly looked at Stone, who was already checking both rifles. "It looks like your friends may be on their way."

"When was the last time you fired these, Jack, the bloody Civil War?"

"I think about the first time I will make love to, Tiaan. I don't travel the world, meeting interesting people and then shoot them."

"It wasn't that long ago you did exactly that. You know the old saying, Jack? If you want to speculate on a man's future, you need to look no further than his past. For better or for worse. You can't run away from previous actions forever."

"Stone the prophet. You sound like you're auditioning for the role as one of The Three Wise Men. That was the *old,* Lucky Phil. This is the new Jack Kelly version."

"Arr, Jack. You can take the boy out of the country, but never the country out of the boy. A leopard never changes its spots."

Kelly knew Stone was right. He could feel the adrenalin levels in his body peaking. His brain was running different scenarios. He was alert, and it did feel good.

Chapter-21

IN THE MID WEST region of W.A., Colin Gibson was regarded as a bit of a legend amongst the local Geraldton community for two reasons. The seaside town was a city located 423 kilometres north of Perth and not ashamed to be rated as the third windiest city in the world but could also boast more days of sunshine than any other town in Western Australia, if you believed the tourist brochures. Colin was built like the proverbial brick shit-house, well over six-foot-tall, with broad shoulders and hands the size of a watermelon, and a heart to match. He turned his hand to shearing after spending the summer holidays as a 16-year-old working as a roustabout, following the shearing teams throughout the region and parts of the Coral Coast farther to the north.

It was a tough life, but the comradery between these hardened bushmen were the building blocks of a lifelong string of friendships. The largest property on the shearing roster was Boolathana Station, located 167 kilometres north of the small town of Coral Bay. A spread of over 350,000 acres with over 20,000 Merino and Dorper sheep, the shearing contract was split between two teams and the rivalry between the men was fierce to the point it would often end in fisty-cuffs after a few too many frothy ales were consumed.

The owner was a man named Clancy Thornton, and was a likeable character with a well-tuned sense of humour, and he also loved a bet. To keep the interests of the men focused on the job at hand, he would add $500 each season to the amount offered for any man who could topple the Mid West record of 466 ewes sheared in a single eight-hour-day, currently held by a man named, Big John Malory, from Mingenew. For eleven years the record had stood the test of time, and the pool was now over $5,000.

Colin was easily the top shearer on his team, and that amount of money represented a car for his new bride back home and a couple of new fishing rods for himself.

The rules were simple. Electric shears, the Tally-Hi method was acceptable, and the record needed to be surpassed by two. The shearer would have his own personal holding corral, each sheep was only allowed the one bleed to the body, all dags were to be removed, and he would need to pull his own jumbucks from the yard. The time allowed was split into two, four-hour sessions.

At 8:00 A.M., the bell sounded, and Colin dragged his first woolly from the dusty yard and went to work. With a firm grip under the sheep's bottom jaw, he sat the animal on its arse and dragged its head between the tops of both his upper legs, keeping all four hooves off the slated wooden floor. His shears hung from the rafter above and to his right as he allowed his body to rest against his height-adjusted sling. His first blow started from the brisket, near the breastbone all the way down in one long blow to the open flank, and then the process was repeated on the opposite flank. After which he just kept running the shears until the last blow around the neck, then let the fleece drop to the floor and push the skinny, bald-looking sheep through his legs to the outside yard.

With 254 clean-skins in the corral, the bell sounded for lunch. Colin was trailing Big John by five, but still on-track. The real challenge didn't begin until the final hour. Colin sat down to his fried liver and bacon, and the side bets started to mount up. Men were wagering the equivalent of an entire week's worth of wages on the outcome. Colin sculled a litre of water and went back to work. He needed to average 53 an hour to reach the afternoon mark of 212.

With one hour remaining on the clock, the interest amongst the men started to gather boisterous momentum. Most reckoned the record was a mountain too high to climb and this young teenager, even though he was well-liked amongst his peers, who was he kidding, they mostly agreed?

The remaining working men started to lay down their combs and were forming a crowd, some egging Colin on; others wishing he would break a leg. The fifteen-minute bell sounded, and he still had 14 sheep left in the yard. Soon number 466 was pushed down the chute. The record was equalled. Colin's arms felt like led weights, and his back ached like never before. He wiped the sweat from his eyes as the entire two teams, including Clancy, had now formed a natural arena.

An old-time cook known as Tucka was the official timekeeper. Colin glanced over and could see him looking at his watch. The wooden spoon was in his right hand, and he looked like he was slowly raising it to sound the cowbell. Colin fought back the urge to straighten his back, he sucked in a long breath then ran his comb down the first hind leg, then the spine of the final sheep's back, after thirty-five blows, Colin clipped the last dag and the fleece fell away. He allowed his comb to swing away and heaved the final sheep through his legs to join the other 467. Tucka banged the bell three times with a smile from ear-to-ear. Colin was a winner, and the record was his for the keeping.

The crowd swarmed like a beehive, offering their praise and congratulations. Colin's back burnt with pangs of pain as he was repeatedly slapped on the shoulders while being applauded. Someone stuck a big brown bottle of Swan Lager into his open hand, and he downed the contents in a single action. The men settled their bets and Clancy Thornton handed over the $5,500. "Well done, young man. The name Colin Gibson will now sit proudly above the new record as the man who knocked Big John Malory from his perch. The beers are on me," Clancy yelled out over the giant roar erupting inside the woolshed.

The second reason Colin was held in such high esteem is a tragedy that changed so many people's lives forever. The Northampton Fishing Club only consisted of fourteen members, but they were a tight-knit group who all shared the same enthused passion for the love of fishing—the bigger, the better. Twice a year they would organise a trip away for a week at a time, and the Steep Point trip was always the one destination the men marked in their calendars as a 'must go'.

After a five-hour-long-haul over corrugated dirt roads, sand drifts, dodging the holes and rocks hidden below the tumbling spinifex in four 4wd's, the club arrived at the most westerly point of mainland Australia. The two-hundred-foot-high vertical cliffs meet the deep waters of the Indian Ocean and are regarded as one of the three best land-based fishing spots in the world. The southern tip of Dirk Hartog Island is a stone's throw away to the north, which provides the natural entrance to the silky waters of Shark Bay, and the small seaside town of Denham was a normally gentle two-hour steam to the east. On a good day, the swell that is pushed up from the Antarctic by the Roaring Forties across thousands of miles of open ocean will average two to three metres, on the other three hundred sixty days of the year, it can reach as high as ten metres. It was no place for the faint-hearted.

Rod fishing for the plus-20-kilo Spanish mackerel, blue and yellowfin tuna and an abundance of other great table fish that frequent these waters offered its own challenges. A reel needed to hold at least a thousand yards of line. You will require a flying gaff to haul your catch up from the depths below all before you lose it to the packs of marauding tiger sharks that are hungry for a cheap feed. All your consumables must be carried in, including fuel, fresh water, bait and food. It was an isolated area, which was its biggest attraction.

Colin's favoured spot was a small inlet called False Entrance located farther to the south. It was one of the few places that allowed you to scale the broken rock face and get within casting distance of the sea with a lure. Safety-first was the number one rule of the club. Never fish alone and never put your life at risk for the sake of a bloody fish was foremost in the men's minds. Colin, with his two fishing partners, sat on top of the red sandstone igneous rock surface and spent the next twenty minutes counting the sets and the distance each wave would reach while at its highest peak. Add another two metres to that spot, and this would become their casting platform, well back from the dangers of even the biggest swell.

The three men walked past the now-famous blowhole that was cause for demolishing the front-end of a Fisheries officer's Toyota *Hilux* the previous year. Plough discs often doubled up as a hotplate for cooking the nightly meals. On one spectacular day, the senior fisheries officer from Denham wanted to show to a junior subordinate the power of the venting sea and escaping mushrooming geysers as each swell rolls in and shoots up the vertical, hundred-foot rounded shaft gouged out of the vertical cliff face with a great sounding *whoosh*. He picked up a discarded and rusted disc, then stood back from the blowhole. He timed his run and dropped the ten-pound circular steel dish into the shaft. Seconds later it came flying out and shot high into the air like a small spinning UFO and landed squarely in the middle of the bonnet, destroying the engine of his parked government-supplied vehicle. The Toyota was a write-off, and the senior officer was reposted to a desk job back in Perth with his pride shattered and career grinding to a screaming halt.

Colin had successfully landed one good-sized mackerel and experienced two bust-offs. He wound his Penn Fathom star drag 30-series over-head reel at frantic speed, skimming the Halco lure across the ocean surface. As he lifted his rod high into the air to clear the jagged rocks below, the trailing treble managed to snag some giant kelp lurking on the water's edge. He jiggled and pulled, not wanting to lose a third lure. At over ten bucks a pop, today was already going to be an expensive one. He laid his rod down and with his closed hand following the taut line, and was able to get down close enough to the floating tangle of seaweed to cast his eyes on the silver and blue lure.

All he heard was a voice screaming from behind, "COLIN—LOOK OUT." He turned to see his long-time mate

Narley, and then the roar of an incoming thirty-foot-high freak wall of water came crashing down on his turned back.

Colin's first instincts were to reach out and grab hold of something. The so-called experts tell you to relax and let the surge take you until it turns and begins its retreat, then brace yourself and hang on tight. Colin's body was picked up like a piece of a broken surfboard and flung forward in a spiralling, rolling motion. His world went black as he held his breath and tried to remain calm. Easier said than done. The flat rock surfaces are littered with pot-holes, some the size of your fist, others big enough to swallow a man, whole. As he continued tumbling uncontrollably, his head was pushed into a pot-hole, and he felt his body lifting vertically, feet-first and backwards. The strength of the rushing water was beyond belief, and now he was at the full mercy of the wave's powerful surge. His body continued to be pushed in the opposite direction to where his head was facing when he heard a snapping noise from within. All his immersed pain and any feeling ceased in that instant.

The local Denham police accompanied by a Silver Chain Nurse were the first to arrive on the scene, four hours later. The thirteen other club members had erected a small shade as Colin lay motionless in the exact same spot. It was painfully obvious to his mates, looking at the hideous angle his body was concerning which way his legs and upper torso were facing, that he was in a diabolical situation and some even considered Colin may actually die where he lay. At five P.M. that day, the closest Search & Rescue helicopter arrived, needing to refuel twice on the 1,000-plus-kilometre journey from Perth.

The town of Geraldton was in shock as word spread of the tragic accident. Colin's vertebrate had snapped, and he was now a paraplegic from the waist down. He would never walk again. He spent the next two years in a rehabilitation centre at Shenton Park Rehab, in Perth, where both he and his wife, Tanya, were learning how to adjust to the constraints of his new, wheelchair-restricted life.

Clancy Thornton was no stranger to tragedy, having lost his own son in a helicopter accident while mustering cattle, and he'd also witnessed the slow death of his wife, Victoria, as she withered away from the ravages of cancer. He rallied the townspeople and the shearing community to help fund the necessities of life in readiness for Colin and Tanya's new life upon their eventual return to his hometown. Clancy donated a block of land he owned in the seaside suburb of Sunset Beach, near the Bluff Point shopping centre and not far from the Wintersun Hotel. Teams of tradesmen beat a path to the building site each day to erect a new special needs house. Rob Brown, or Brownie as he was better known, owned the local Retra-Vision franchise and donated an entire household of furniture, including white goods.

Ken Pepper owned the local Toyota dealership on Cathedral Avenue. With his own money, he ordered a specifically designed and custom fitted long-wheelbase Toyota *Land Cruiser* that allowed wheelchair access via an electronically operated rear lift.

The day Colin and Tanya arrived back home, the streets of Geraldton flooded with the tears of the entire town as they were presented with their new home, completely unaware of what had been happening in their prolonged absence. The local tackle shop was owned by a man everyone called Skuppy, and this is where Colin had spent thousands of his hard-earned dollars building up his sizable collection of boat and beach rods. He owned over fifteen different reels with countless lures and general tackle. Skuppy arranged for Colin's wheelchair to be fitted with rod holders and donated two Abu Garcia casting reels with an electronic retrieval system that could plug directly into the chair's battery-supplied power source.

This was all the excuse Colin needed to go wet a line, and that's exactly what he was doing at a relatively easily accessible fishing spot, just south of Carnarvon called Bush Bay, when after casting out Colin's whiting rig into the only channel of water deep enough to hold fish, Tanya spotted a shape on the distant ocean horizon.

The nine-metre tides experienced in this part of the world was at its lowest ebb. For over half a kilometre the receding water leaves a thick black mud bottom as the mangrove swamp becomes fully exposed. This is home for the famous northwest mud crab with a claw the size of a man's arm. The other two men were busy poking the bubbling holes with lengths of steel rod with a hook bent into the end, trying to snare the crab's claw and skull-drag it to the surface.

Tanya called out to Colin, after which he turned his wheelchair and followed her extended arm towards the outer bay. It looked like the bottom section of a wooden-hulled boat. It was as if the entire superstructure had been sawn clean off. The boat wasn't under power and was floundering on some exposed reef farther out to sea. There was nobody to be seen above decks. As the tide turned and the sun began to set over the western horizon, the group headed back to their camp with four nice-sized muddies ready for the pot.

The boat eventually refloated with the incoming tide and started a slow drift towards the shoreline. Colin's closest mate, Cooley, finished his beer, placed his plate in the washing tub and pushed his way through the thick nestle of white mangrove bush.

"Where you off to, it's your shout?" Narley wanted to remind Cooley. He was still busting open the claw of his chilli crab with a set of nutcrackers. "I'll have a JD and dry, the stomach is too full for another beer," he replied while rubbing his tummy like a fat good luck Buddha.

"Mother Nature calls, Narley. I'll be back before you know I've gone."

Cooley stepped away from the light of the campfire and relieved his swollen bladder. From a distance, he thought he could hear the sound of muffled voices drifting on the freshening sea breeze. He zipped his fly and made a pathway farther through the waist-high scrub. The dark shadow of the boat was in clear view against the moonlit night sky. The voices continued, but the language wasn't English. Cooley did a quick mental check on how many stubbies he'd drunk. *Only the three*, he reassured himself.

Suddenly the turban-covered head of a bearded man stood tall above the gunwale and lifted his long robe. He was facing out to sea when he plonked his backside over the side and began to take care of business. "Bloody hell, mate, that's a sight for sore eyes," Cooley whispered to himself as he swatted a couple of hungry mosquitoes.

The man shook his rear-end when a second person appeared from below decks with a lantern and some tissue paper. Cooley executed an about-turn and retraced his steps back to camp.

"Hey guys, you're not gonna believe what I just laid eyes on?"

"Try me, Cooley," Colin answered first.

"That boat we saw earlier, well, it's drifted up to the beach now."

"Really, how close is it?"

"Close enough that I could see the bloke's tattoo on his white tush."

"What are you talking about? What bloke and a *tattoo*? How many beers have you had tonight?" Colin's wide grin could be seen through his thick beard.

"No, seriously, I could see it as clear as day; a tattoo on his arse in the shape of a crescent moon."

Chapter-22

KELLY CHECKED his radar, and its circular sweeping pattern identified two separate contacts. He expanded the scan to a 30-kilometre-radius. A small fixed-wing plane was heading their way directly from Christmas Island. The second was on the outer reaches of the radars search capabilities, and it was of another boat—much bigger, and well over 300 feet long. It was on a heading of 280 degrees from the east. Both heading his way from opposite directions, Kelly confirmed. He turned and looked over his left shoulder towards the twins.

"Look here, ladies, I'm not sure what to expect, but if Stone says there is trouble brewing, well its best we take precautions. Gather your belongings and head back to your quarters until we can sort out what's goin' on."

"Like two scorned teenage girls, heh Jack. Well, bugger that, we're not entirely useless. We can help, can't we Evina?"

Abigail turned to check on the level of moral commitment she could expect from her twin sister. "Abigail, let's not rush things. Jack seems to know what he's doing."

"Don't be a pussy, Evina. Let's not forget *you* are part of the reason we find ourselves in this predicament in the first place."

"Well, either way, you're not staying here on the bridge," Kelly spoke with an air of authority. "Till, take the chair. Increase our speed to twenty-eight knots and run *Thin Lizzy* in a zigzag pattern on this heading, straight to the port at Flying Fish Cove."

"Okay, Boss. But what does zig and zag mean?" Till stood with a vacant look on his face.

"The same as a snake in one of the ponds back home, like this." Kelly moved his arm in a wriggling action, then followed the twins back down to the galley with Stone's Browning under his shirt.

Stone had already laid out on the galley table the entire armoury, which wasn't that much, but beggars can't be choosers. Kelly grabbed a pair of Porro Prism high-powered binoculars hanging from their strap and walked to the bow. He steadied himself against the 14-foot tender, still strapped to its davit, then scanned the horizon in the general direction the plane was heading. A reflection from the setting sun in the west flashed momentarily. Whoever it was had just changed course and was now making a beeline straight for *Thin Lizzy*. Kelly hurried back to the rear outer deck. "We still don't know if they mean us any harm, Tobias? It might just be a tourist on a sightseeing trip?" Kelly ventured.

"Do you believe in coincidences, Jack?" Stone returned the question.

"Never," he replied in a sombre tone.

With the binoculars glued to his face, he followed the descending flight path as it banked left and prepared to circle the fast-moving yacht.

Abigail was standing by his side. "Where is it now, Jack?"

He pointed with his extended arm while keeping both eyes peeled. It was a seaplane, and as it made a sweeping low turn, he could see a man with one leg braced on the starboard float cradling a rifle between his legs. "Inside *now*," Kelly ordered. He turned to face Abigail. "Where's your sister?"

"Tobias is showing her how to reload the spare magazines."

"That's quaint."

In the next instant, a spray of semi-automatic fire splashed small rivulets of water in a line across the wash from the twin propellers. "That bastard is shooting at my boat," Kelly yelled.

"Here, take this." Stone was holding the shotgun in one hand and the Heckler & Koch in the other. "You're the bloody sharpshooter. You still do remember how to shoot—don't you?" Stone quizzed.

"We'll both find out soon enough, won't we? Never needed to fire at a moving plane before—or have I?" Kelly responded.

The plane banked hard right and prepared to make the second approach over amidships, using the 72-foot length of *Thin Lizzy* to increase their target area. Kelly moved to the side railing. He raised the Heckler & Koch and braced the rubber butt-end into his right shoulder. He estimated their distance was now about three hundred metres. Kelly raised the barrel ten degrees and emptied the entire round of 32 NATO 7.62 calibre cartridges in four short bursts. Pieces of fibreglass splinters flew from the yacht's port-side walkway. A front reinforced window shattered as Stone let loose with the shotgun, pumping four cartridges of buckshot as it flew past.

Kelly replaced his empty magazine. "Now I'm really pissed-off," he spat out. "That clown is filling my boat full of holes."

"That won't happen if you could remember how to shoot straight," Stone answered, half-joking—half-serious.

The wings tipped the opposite way, and the plane made a slow, deliberate second returning run. "They're going to hit us from the stern, with the sun at their backs and in our line of sight. Smart move, that's what I would do," Kelly explained to Stone.

Both men leaned the tops of their legs into the rear gunnel and took aim. "This time, die, you bastard," Kelly murmured.

Chungho Goe grinned at the pilot as he laid his rifle down and dragged a canvas bag closer, then pulled out an object shaped like a port barrel with a handle. He turned a dial clockwise, labelled EDS for EXPLOSION DEPTH STATUS. He stopped at the word, *IMPACT.* Goe held it by the handle in one hand while holding on tight to the seat belt with his free arm and leaned as far as he could from the cockpit co-pilot's door.

Kelly squeezed the trigger. Sparks flew from the single prop, and the plane's passenger's front window shattered, causing the pilot to veer suddenly to his left. Goe was forced to let go of his barrel a couple of seconds early or risk falling. Both Stone and Kelly watched the white-coloured barrel shape drop from the sky and impact with the dispersing wave from the boat's wake. A huge explosion erupted in a fountain of bubbling salt water and spray, covering both men as they were thrown back, causing them to land heavily on the teak decking.

"What the hell was that?" Kelly cried out while wiping his dripping face. The yacht rocked violently from side to side.

"A bloody hand-held depth charge. Do you believe these guys?" Stone answered.

"Seeing is believing, Tobias. What have you been up to lately to piss these people off so badly?"

"I'm not so sure it's you and me they're after, Jack."

Kelly turned and offered Stone a confused stare. The piercing screech of an alarm sounded throughout the entire boat, forcing him to change his focus. "That's the fire alarm, and that can't be good. Here, take this," Kelly handed Stone his rifle. "I need to go check on the engine room."

The automatic fire control system initiated instantly. All the air vents closed automatically and the single air-tight engine room door slowly sealed electronically. Kelly arrived at the door and viewed the wall-mounted monitor on the adjacent bulkhead slide through its four screenshots. The four internal video cameras showed no signs of fire—not yet, anyway. He changed screens manually and could see a fine jet spray of diesel shooting from a split on the starboard engine injection pump hose. He opened a side cabinet and placed a re-breather over his face, then entered the engine room with a fire extinguisher in his left hand. The main power board was located down the end of the port-side gangway. Kelly isolated the fuel pump, and *Thin Lizzy* slowed as both engines went through their shut down procedures. There was nothing else to do here, so he made his way back up to the rear deck to help Stone.

Till suddenly yelled down from the flybridge above. "Boss, you have a call."

"A call? Tell them to ring back, Till. We're busy at the moment."

"No, not the phone, the radio. This man says he from the navy and wants to talk with the captain."

"The navy? That must have been the other radar sighting. Probably a patrol boat, searching for fleeing asylum seekers."

"The Australian Navy?" Stone almost cheered.

"Who else were you expecting? We *will* soon be entering Australian territorial waters, so yes... I would assume they're Australian." Kelly gave Stone a dumber than dumb look.

"The *Thin Lizzy* is slowing. We'll be dead in the water and sitting ducks," Stone stated the obvious. "I'll take the call," as Stone handed back the rifle and raced upstairs.

"Not a good time, Tobias, to be chatting with some old Navy buddies."

"Trust me, Jack. The man I want to speak with owes me a favour. Hang in there mate, I'll be back," Stone explained in his best impersonation of *The Terminator*. Till was still seated in the skipper's chair with the radio mouthpiece in his hand. Stone replaced it back on its clip and picked up the sat phone.

The HMAS *Ballarat* was an ANZAC-class FHH frigate returning to her home port of HMAS *Stirling* at Fleet Command West in Fremantle after a six-week deployment escorting oil tankers, cargo ships and some private yachts through the perilous Straits of Malacca. After passing through the Sunda Strait that morning, her surveillance radars had picked up two unknown contacts on a heading of 285°. Fleeing refugee boats were problematic and needed to be dealt with from time-to-time. Lieutenant Commander Scott Larson ordered his radio officer a second time, "Have you raised the captain of this unidentified vessel yet?"

"Yes, sir. A man identified himself as, Till, and advised he would go and find his boss. Still waiting. I think I could hear small arms fire in the background before the line was terminated from their end."

"Keep trying. XO, this second contact, I want confirmation of what that is."

"Yes, sir."

The officer of the watch interrupted, "Commander, I have another incoming call on the secured line. This one is from Fleet HQ, direct from Russell Offices in Canberra."

"XO, you have the bridge."

"Yes, sir. XO has the bridge."

Commander Larson left the bridge and closed the door to his small adjoining office before answering the secured satellite call. He already knew who was on the other end of the line, a first for him while at sea. "Lieutenant Commander Scott Larson speaking, Admiral."

"Commander, right down this authorisation code and repeat it back to me."

"Admiral, I confirm 7-6-3-1–BT–8-0, sir."

"Correct. That, Lieutenant Commander, is your ticket to carry out an order on my direct authority. Do I make myself clear?"

"Arr, I'm not sure, Admiral."

"Well, let me spell it out for you. It's time you proved to the Australian public if all that training you've received at the Navy's expense has been worthwhile. I'm giving you a direct order, and if you don't want to end up captaining a Sydney Harbour ferry, I suggest you don't miss," Admiral Boomer Peterson growled down the line like an angry grizzly.

The printer on the commander's workstation spat out a single-page document, confirming his orders in writing. Larson leaned over and lifted the A4 sheet from its tray.

"Yes, Admiral, as clear as day. I have your orders now." The sound of the phone being slammed down rang loud inside the lieutenant commander's ear.

"I have the bridge, XO."

"Yes sir, the captain has the bridge," the XO repeated.

"Officer of the watch, sound the alarm for full battle readiness. This is not a drill, I repeat—this is not a drill. This is live action." A pulsating horn sounded throughout the *Ballarat* as its complement of 22 officers and 141 sailors each took up their designated positions.

"Weapons control, enter this code into your computer and prepare for a firing solution. You have your orders."

"Yes, sir."

The officer of the watch looked on in excitement as the orders were displayed on his screen.

"XO, full countermeasures at the ready, please, just in case. What's the infrared tracking telling us? Report, please."

"Sir. Confirmed two contacts at two-eight-zero degrees. A small fixed-wing plane and a vessel travelling due west towards Christmas Island. Speed . . . It was twenty-eight knots, but they seem to be slowing now. It looks like she may be under attack?"

"Range?"

"Sir, range now twenty-three kilometres."

"XO, increase our speed to flank, on a heading of two-eight-two." The two 8840hp MTU 12V-1163 TB83 diesel engines immediately responded and quickly pushed HMAS *Ballarat* to her maximum speed of 27 knots.

"Initiate the vertical launch system and prepare to fire on my command."

"Yes, sir."

"Officer of the watch. I want that firing solution *today*, please," Larson barked out.

"Yes, sir, I have a firing solution, and the target has been identified. Moving at one hundred forty knots and turning . . . The new heading is two-seven-zero."

"Fine, then. On my command."

Stone glided back down the stairs and was standing again at Kelly's side. "Glad to see you could make it back in time for round three. Same MO as before, off the stern. Just the one mag left and the shotgun," Kelly updated Stone.

"The shotgun is all but useless." Stone was now holding his 9mm. "It's all we got unless Boomer can come through."

"Who's, Boomer?" Kelly asked.

"A man who loves to rattle a few cages," Stone answered matter-of-factly.

The fixed-wing plane completed its turn and made a new heading towards the now stationary yacht, gently rolling on the benign swell. Kelly and Stone shared a knowing glance. Words weren't necessary, they both knew the drill. The twins held each other in what they were thinking, maybe a final sisterly embrace. Till opened the fridge and pulled out a bowl of papaya salad. Evina looked on in dismay. "How can you eat at a time like this, look outside—can't you see what's heading our way?"

"I'm hungry and need to eat. Papaya salad very good and gives you power. You want to try?"

Chungho Goe held his final depth charge and set the dial to IMPACT a second time. He tapped the pilot on the shoulder and indicated with his hand while pointing a finger. He wanted to go lower. This time he would not be distracted. Goe lined up the stationary yacht. The two men could be seen on the outside deck with their guns raised and at the ready. "This is going straight onto your open deck," he muttered to himself over the drone of the single-engine, in his local dialect.

Kelly exhaled the carbon monoxide from both lungs and remained dead still. He closed one eye and blanked out all else except the sight of the incoming aircraft. Kelly could clearly see the Korean, extending himself from the side door with the barrel-shaped depth charge held clear. He opened fire with a burst of eight rounds. "Missed the bastard," he hissed through clenched teeth.

Lieutenant Commander Scott Larson looked relaxed, but the reality was quite different—he *was* slightly apprehensive. This would be the first time he had fired a live AMRAAM missile at an actual target. At $165,000 a pop, he surely did not want to miss.

"Range, please?" the commander wanted confirmation.

"Arr, range now eighteen kilometres, sir."

"On my order, XO. Fire one."

"Fire one, sir. One away."

The eight-cell, Lockheed Martin Mark 41–Mod 5 spat out the Rim-7 Sea Sparrow as the first fuel cell ignited with a small gas explosion and pushed the missile clear of the cell sleeve. As it shot up into the air, it hung awkwardly in mid-air until the second fuel load ignited. A blue flame burst from the rear, followed by a shower of sparks with a thick grey cloud of smoke trailing in its wake. In seconds it gathered momentum and reached its pre-programmed cruising speed of 4,256 kph. The sensor on the Sea Sparrow's nosecone was reacquiring its target every .5 of a second and communicating this information to the onboard computer and guidance system. As the aircraft closed the distance, the Sea Sparrow recalculated and made the necessary adjustments.

"We have clearance, and the missile is green. Acquiring target now. Target illumination is acquired, Commander. We have a lock."

"Arm the bird, XO."

"Arming the missile, sir. Sea Sparrow armed and we still have a green light. We are live and good to go."

Kelly leaned into *Thin Lizzy*'s stern rail with the tops of his legs and steadied himself. "Come on, you piece of shit, just a little closer." He fired his second burst, resulting in two single rounds deflecting from the bottom of the wing's outer skin. Goe flinched but held firm. The whites of his teeth were there for all to see as he parted his lips into a curdled grin. Kelly emptied the last of his clip. The plane kept coming. Goe was counting down, wanting to time his drop to perfection. "Five, four, three . . . Shit, what's that . . . ?" he gasped in near disbelief. They were the final words Goe would ever usher from his lips, and the pilot looked like he'd just laid eyes on the *Millennium Falcon*.

Kelly caught a first glimpse of the vapour trail out of the corner of one eye. A millisecond later the Sea Sparrow's annular blast fragmentation, 41-kg warhead exploded with a kill radius of 3.7 metres. The light plane disintegrated into a thousand pieces in a shattering spread of burning metal and showering red-hot shrapnel into the Indian Ocean. The only thing left with any mass was the remains of the engine block, which plummeted into the sea with a spectacular thirty-foot-high forward splash like a dam buster's bomb that didn't bounce.

"Hey, I told you Boomer would come through," Stone rejoiced.

Abigail and Evina both ran to the deck rails to witness the grand fall from grace. Kelly ejected his empty magazine and flipped the safety on. "I need a drink, who's with me?" Kelly wasn't asking.

"Great idea, cocktails all round," Abigail cheered. She hugged her sister again, this time out of sheer love, not from the fear of being blown to pieces by some crazed North Korean with a depth charge. Till kept spooning food into his mouth.

Lieutenant Commander Scott Larson waited for the confirmation with a touch of anxiety mixed with the excitement of a young boy firing his first slug gun at a live rat in the barn.

"Commander, I can confirm the target has been destroyed. The vessel is now dead in the water. She seems to have lost power."

"Continue our current heading, XO. Stand down the crew. Let's see what all the fuss was about, shall we?"

As *Thin Lizzy* came into view, the officer of the watch zoomed in with his binoculars towards the stern of what looked like a pretty smart-looking cruising yacht. "Sir, I see four, no sorry, five people on the rear deck."

"Do they look like they are in distress? Do we need a medical alert—are there any signs of injuries?"

"Well—no, sir. Just two men and two women drinking what looks like margaritas. A small man is holding a sign that reads, 'we need a tow'."

"Did you say margaritas? Reduce speed to three knots, ahead all slow, XO. Pull alongside and prepare to hail the captain."

"Yes, sir."

Chapter-23

COLIN FOLLOWED Cooley and Narley while trying to side-step the annoying saltwater snails to the water's edge, leaving Tanya to deal with the dishes alone.

"You see, I told you, right where I said it would be," Cooley proudly announced while pointing at the awkwardly angled boat.

"No doubt about it," Colin confirmed. "I thought it was an old derelict that must have broken its moorings somewhere in Carnarvon. It barely looks seaworthy. Wade out and look inside, I'll wait here."

"Really, don't you have a flipper attachment on your wheelchair yet?" Narley laughed and then climbed over the tilted deck rail before he disappeared below decks. Within a minute, his head popped back up while shouting, "Nothing worth much down here. You can clearly see people have been living inside, and it smells like a camel's arsehole. The entire boat looks a bloody shambles. What a heap of shit."

Colin turned his chair and switched on his single headlight. There were three sets of footprints still as clear as the mud they stood in, all leading away from the rippling shore-break. Suddenly a loud scream caused each person to stop in their tracks. They all turned as one towards the campsite. In an unprovoked harmony, each man shouted in synchronised terror, "TANYA!"

"Go, go—quick, I'll catch up," Colin yelled at his mates. Cooley and Narley both ran like wildfire back to the campsite. Colin powered his chair to top speed, which wasn't much better than a brisk walk. He needed to manoeuvre the tyres around some shifting sand twice, careful not to get bogged. He could see the flickering flames of the fire on the other side of the windbreak formed by a row of small trees. What confronted him next sent shock waves through the working parts of his body. He was both rattled and confounded.

Cooley lay on the ground with blood oozing from the back of his skull. Colin thought he may have been dead. He wasn't moving, and it was difficult to see if he was still breathing in the dim light. Narley was being held by one man while the other bound his arms and legs. Tanya was still seated by the fire with a third stranger holding a knife to her throat. She was visibly frightened, shaking and sobbing. Colin moved his chair in a threatening action. "Let her go now."

The bearded man lifted Tanya to a standing position and yelled something out in another language. The second man threw Narley to the ground, picked up a burning stick from the fire and waved it in Colin's face while screaming, "*Tawaquf, tawaquf.*" He then bent down and disconnected the main lead to Colin's battery. Colin's headlight extinguished, and the frightening scene in front of him darkened with the withering fire.

"Who are you, people? What do you want with us? You're all off what's left of that heap-of-shit boat, aren't you? Where did...?"

Before Colin could finish, the third man slapped him hard across the face with his open hand. "*La kalam, akhrus.* Shut up," he shouted in broken English.

Kenny Barndon arrived at the southern end of Bush Bay at exactly 8:15 A.M., each Tuesday and Friday. As part of his scheduled rangers' duties, he was tasked with replacing the heavy-duty liners in the council-provided bins, checking on the single ablution block with just the one unisex bore-water external shower and carrying out checks to make sure no one was bogged or had missed their ETA if they were boat owners.

He pulled his Toyota tray-back into campsite-7 and was shocked at what he'd stumbled onto.

"What the f...?" He turned off the ignition and leapt from the cabin before it came to a rolling stop. He first removed the gag and untied a young lady. She was distressed and inconsolable. Narley was awake with eyes wide open. Kenny released him from his ties, while Tanya slowly turned Cooley over and felt for a pulse. "This man needs to get to a hospital—and now," she shrieked at the uniformed ranger. He retrieved a small first aid kit and handed it to Tanya, then immediately fumbled for his two-way radio and called up base headquarters.

An ambulance met them halfway along the North West Coastal Highway. Cooley's unconscious body was transferred, and with lights flashing it soon disappeared on its way back to Carnarvon. A short time later, a police vehicle flashed his high-beam, and Kenny pulled over to the side of the bitumen. Narley and Tanya were helped into the rear seat and given a blanket each with some cool drinking water before arriving at Carnarvon General Hospital for precautionary medical checks.

A single police officer began his initial line of questioning and just kept scratching his head. He phoned the desk sergeant and ran a quick brief by him. The sergeant rang the only two detectives in town and his boss, who were all together, six kilometres out to sea with a beer in one hand and a fishing rod in the other. This was the easy-going lifestyle that was Carnarvon, which was about to be turned on its head.

"So, let me get this right?" Detective Neil Hoosan continued his interview later that afternoon. "You think they looked and spoke like Arabs and one of them had a tattoo on his backside?" He chanced a sideways glance towards his partner of two years and rolled his eyes. "And I gave up a day of fishing to listen to this story," he was already lamenting himself.

"If you don't believe me, see for yourself. The bloody boat is—well was, sitting high and dry in the mud," Narley answered his expression.

Detective Hoosan turned and looked at Ranger Kenny. "Did you happen to witness this mystery boat?"

"No, but I didn't look for it either. Camp-seven is at least a good fifty metres back from the shoreline. We loaded everybody into the pickup and high-tailed it outta there."

"Well, we'll know soon enough. Two uniforms should be arriving at Bush Bay about now," as Hoosan looked at his watch.

"How's your friend doing, has the doctor told you anything yet?" the second detective queried Tanya. She thought he sounded genuine.

"He's in an induced coma. What about my husband? Those bastards have taken off in our 4wd with Colin in the back. Why would they do that? What could they possibly want with a man in a bloody wheelchair?"

The internal phone in the small interview room buzzed three times in a low digital tone. Detective Hoosan snatched it from the wall mount. "Yes, what do you have?" There was a pause while he was updated. "Okay . . . Yeah." He listened on. "Are you serious? All right, we'll need to alert Perth. They'll want to run a full forensic analysis. Set up roadblocks at both the Billabong Roadhouse and another at the turnoff to Karratha. Alert the Geraldton police. I would hazard a guess they will probably head south. Tape off the entire area and get a couple of caravans and some external lighting down to Bush Bay. This could be a long night." He hung up the phone and turned to address Tanya. "Well, it seems your story checks out. We will set you both up with a room each tonight at the Carnarvon Hotel. Tomorrow you'll be interviewed again in detail by the Perth detectives and probably the Department of Immigration. It looks like we may have a group of loose-cannon asylum seekers who somehow made it this far south without drowning. It shouldn't be long before we pick them up. They'll stand out like a camel lost in a snowstorm."

The two detectives left the room, Detective Hoosan yelled out to the front desk, "Shirley, be a dear and tell the wife I won't be home for dinner tonight, will you." He turned and faced his partner. "This is turning into a dog's bloody breakfast."

Chapter-24

A SMALL CROWD had already formed as *Thin Lizzy* was towed into Flying Fish Cove behind the HMAS *Ballarat*.

Kelly ordered Till to lower the tender and used the 50-hp four-stroke Yamaha outboard to ease the 72-foot yacht into a berth at the end of a small marina. He'd already ordered a replacement fuel pump and new hoses with fittings to be flown in from Darwin and hoped they would arrive within two working days.

Kelly stood on the bow and looked on in a state of shock. Abigail sauntered over and asked what the problem was. "Look what those bastards did." He was pointing to the four-foot-long rubber replica of the goanna the yacht derived its very name from, strapped to the stainless steel handrail above the bow. Half its tail had been shot off, and now Thin Lizzy looked stunted.

"Do ya reckon there's a pub on this island?" Kelly asked.

Abigail took a second to answer, "You need a drink that bad?"

"I want some information and the local pub always has the answers. Go round up the troops."

From the marina they all followed Gaze Road north, passing by the Tourist Information Centre. The Golden Bosun was more a restaurant/bar than a pub but overlooked the ocean to the west and looked clean and inviting.

Kelly and Stone lined the bar with their bums firmly planted on a barstool each. The twins decided to spend some time checking out the local shopping.

"Let's talk, Tobias. I know you're working for the Australian Government, so that means ASIO, but you're sending sensitive computer information to your mate at MI6. So there is someone you don't trust. Who else knew you were in the first instance, coming to this island, and secondly: the *Thin Lizzy*? That was my own last-minute call to leave Bali, so how did someone find that out and who else on this speck of phosphate knew of our arrival? You expected trouble, and that's exactly what we got—big time. I've got the bullet holes to prove it."

"Jack, you're only half-right. Like I said, that reception wasn't for us. We need to talk with, Evina. She is the dark cloud in this shitstorm."

"What about this detention centre on the opposite side of the island? Is there someone you need to pay a special visit to inside those walls?"

"I need to check out someone's backside," Stone replied with tongue in cheek.

Kelly put down his glass and gave Stone a disconcert glance. "You can't be serious...?"

"I kid you not, Jack."

Kelly finished his cider. The barman returned with a big smile, only to be matched by his bigger beer belly. "You want another round of drinks, fellas? You must have come in on that floating gin palace behind the Navy frigate. Engine trouble?"

"Same again, please." Kelly stood and extended his hand. "I'm, Jack, and this here is, Trevor." Stone stood and reciprocated.

"Everyone just calls me, Barrel," the big man replied, as he accentuated his robust beer gut.

"I need some minor repairs done on my cruising yacht, Barrel. Who's the best person in town for that?" Kelly asked.

"Arr, that would be, Ed. He runs Ed's Marine Engineering business down the slip-way. Got the Navy contract, so he knows what he's on about."

"Is that the same Ed I saw on the way into town who owns Ed's Liquor and Ed's Hardware?"

"The one and the same. Ed's really smart," Barrel answered, proud as punch.

"Trevor and I were hoping to do some sightseeing while we're on the island. Does anyone own a floatplane we could charter for half a day? Trevor's happy to pay top dollar, aren't you, mate?" Kelly rubbed Stone's shoulder and grinned.

"Top dollar, for sure," Stone replied.

"The only seaplane I've ever seen is the one owned by the Anomura Group. Sometimes it lands in the bay and drops off weird food parcels from overseas somewhere."

"Could that somewhere maybe be Korea?" Stone asked.

"Ed could tell you. He owns the seafood import/export license. Bloody good fisherman too is, old Ed."

Jack asked Barrel, "This Anomura mob, where are they located?"

"Do you like playing roulette?" Barrel asked.

"I bet Ed does," Kelly couldn't resist.

"They bought the old casino, pretty quite bunch though. Keep to themselves, mostly." Barrel stopped and looked over Kelly's shoulder. "Speaking of the devil, here's Ed, now."

A sprightly silver-haired old man with a receding hairline, dressed in grease-stained overalls made his way towards the bar.

Kelly turned on his stool and stood. Ed approached the two strangers. "Are you the skipper of that bloody great big yacht tied up at the end of the marina, then? I've just been talking to the deckhand, Toll. He wanted to know where the best crabs are hiding. Pretty sure he didn't quite grasp the concept of what a protected species meant, though. Where's he from, anyway? Bloody good cook. He gave me some of his fish soup to try."

"Till is from a country where nothing is protected. Hi, I'm Jack, and yes, I am the skipper. I need some repairs carried out if you have time? I've heard you're a busy man, Ed."

"Did you run into a hail storm or something? Bloody dirty great big holes everywhere," Ed smirked knowingly.

"Need to replace a front quarter-panel window and a hose on the injectors. Hopefully, they both should arrive the day after tomorrow," he advised Ed.

"No worries. I'll see you on board when the hoses and clips arrive. I've got the cartage contract with the airline and the window we can cut a new one to fit."

Ed left as the twins arrived. Every man's head in the bar all turned at once to check out the new arrivals.

"Not much action on Christmas Island, I'll wager, Jack?"

"Not that kind, anyway," he replied.

"Margarita, please," Evina ordered from the still-startled barman.

"It's Margaret's day off today. I can call her if you want to catch up. Are you a friend?" Barrel asked with a look of genuine sincerity.

Kelly had been perusing the blackboard menu above the bar, which included a list of locally concocted cocktails. He stood from his stool, "Barrel, bring us four steak sandwiches, two baskets of those deep-fried scalloped potatoes with sweet chilli sauce plus extra sour cream. And we'll also order four of those Red Crab Crush cocktails. Cheers, mate." Kelly turned to face the twins, "Come on, ladies, let's grab a table."

The drinks arrived first. Abigail's eyes lit up like a lighthouse at the four short-stemmed Hurricane cocktail glasses filled with a red-coloured mixture with bits of watermelon plus a slice of pineapple with a small umbrella sticking out the top. "Wow, what have we got here?"

"A shot of vodka, malibu and peach schnapps, mixed with cranberry and pineapple juice with a dash of grenadine. Bottoms-up, and here's to our eventful but safe arrival on Christmas Island. Cheers everyone," Jack toasted.

"Good bloody idea, I say," Abigail smiled back. "And maybe after a couple of these, Evina, you might finally want to come clean about your mysterious celestial spheres."

"Yes... you seem to have pissed-off some very powerful people," Stone wanted to add.

All eyes were now squarely aimed at Evina. She sensed the attention and asked, "What? Why are you all staring at me like I just grew a beard?"

"Time to spill the beans, Evina. We need some answers." Stone was insistent. "The flying welcoming reception party, that was for you. Why is someone trying to have you eliminated?"

Evina kept herself busy dipping some chips into the two sauce dishes. The table remained silent. "All right, I suppose I owe you that much," she reluctantly answered.

"Oh—do you think, Evina? I mean, they only saved your life—what, three times now in the last two days. Cough it up, sister, we're all ears," Abigail remonstrated.

"Not here, okay. Tonight, back on board the boat, I promise. What are we all eating for dinner, anyway?" She wanted to change the subject.

"I'm pretty sure Till would have liked to be taking care of that as we speak, except he's confined to the boat and dock area only. There is no visa on arrival for the Thais in this country."

Stone stood and left some Australian dollars on the table. "I need to make a couple of phone calls and check a few things out. I'll see you all back on the boat tonight."

The dinner dishes were washed and dried, and Till retired for the night, happy he would not be woken by the musical sounds of Diana Ross, a second time. The remaining four people settled into the saloon with a decent bottle of Wynns Coonawarra Shiraz from Kelly's small wine cellar.

"Fire away, Evina. You have the floor, as they say," Abigail prompted.

Evina placed her half-filled glass of Shiraz on the table and gathered herself. "All right . . . Ten years ago, I was hand-delivered a celestial sphere that was rather unusual in its characteristics and construction. I believe now that this globe, still at the Smithsonian, is one of a set of three with each sphere telling a story that dates back to the 1600s and the nine-year-old Prince Mirza Nur-ud-din Beig Mohammad Khan Salim."

"Jesus, that's a mouthful for one person's name," Kelly butted in.

"As a young boy, Prince Salim spent the entirety of his youth, up until he reached the age of fifteen, raised under the protection provided by the Moghul harem. This was not just a place where women lived, babies were born, and children grew up inside these walls. Within the precincts of the harem were schools with playgrounds, markets, bazaars, laundries, kitchens and bathhouses. The harem held a strict hierarchy; its chief authorities being the wives and female relatives of the emperor. Below them were the concubines, mothers, stepmothers, aunts, grandmothers, sisters, daughters and other female relatives that lived in the harem. There were also ladies-in-waiting, servants, maids, cooks, female officials and guards.

"In his youth, Prince Salim suffered from severe bouts of asthma. His mother, Mariam-uz-Zamani, would tend to his suffering by removing Prince Salim from exposure to the prevailing winds that would carry pollen from the west. The tiny spores would gather in her son's lungs, causing his breathing to become laboured. It was a time of great distress as she sought advice from the palace physicians who offered little respite or solutions to her problem.

"Safiya Yeboah was a captured slave from a country that had been bled of its human resources via the often favoured trans-Saharan caravan routes through the Red Sea, and across the Atlantic to the Indian ports of Janjira, Surat or Bombay. She arrived in India as a slave and was purchased with a thousand others, just like her, to become a lady-in-waiting in the Moghul harem. As a young girl growing up in the turmoil that was her native Africa, she was the second daughter to the village healing woman, a Witchdoctor who possessed hand-me-down knowledge of the miracle of natural healing for curing the sick and debilitated.

"Safiya introduced the prince's mother to the herb called 'visnaga', which she grew within the gardens of the harem. She showed the emperor's first and most favoured wife how to mix the herb and to prepare the correct dosage for her young, sick child, to relieve the infliction of his asthma. The results were a miraculous turnaround. Prince Salim's symptoms ceased almost immediately, and before the year-end, he was completely rid of this heart-wrenching affliction, much to the amazement of the other five thousand residents of this inner-sanctum of women and children.

"The forever-grateful Prince Salim and Safiya soon became close companions. A bond had been struck that would see her wealth of knowledge shared and recorded into an original fifty-page manuscript. It was complete with hand-drawn pictures, dried pressings with a chronological reference to an exhaustive list of herbs, flowers and tree roots, that in the right hands and the acquired knowledge, could be procured into nature's own endless list of remedies for a myriad of everyday ailments and sickness. The body and nature working together to heal itself."

Evina paused and sipped her wine. "I'm sorry, the scientist inside of me tends to run rampant when I start thinking about the ramifications of such knowledge," Evina wanted to explain.

All eyes were still centred on Evina. No person moved or spoke. Abigail broke the stalemate first. "Evina, do you see anyone interrupting or leaving the room? Please go on, it's all very fascinating, and the importance to you is blatantly obvious."

"Well, okay then, you asked for it. Prince Salim's father was the third Moghul emperor and was known as 'Akbar the Great'. After his death, Prince Salim bestowed upon himself the name, Emperor Jahangir, meaning 'Conqueror of the World'. His knowledge base grew and in many ways was a follow-on from 'Ayurveda', a combination of the two Sanskrit words ayur:

meaning life and veda: science or knowledge which is one of the oldest systems of medicine in the world. Many Ayurvedic practices predated written records and were handed down by word of mouth. Three ancient books known as *The Great Trilogy* were all written in Sanskrit more than two thousand years ago and are considered the main texts on Ayurvedic medicine— which is still widely practised in India.

"Jahangir was a keen student of the arts, literature and science, and he sought out information about other cultures from his scholars. First and second century A.D., the *Shen'nong Bencaojing*, or *Divine Husbandman's*, written in China during the first century included three hundred fifty-four entries; of these, two hundred fifty-two are herbal medicines. This early herbal laid the foundation for traditional Chinese medicine. In the sixteenth century A.D. on the other side of the world, in 1552, thirty-one years after the Spanish conquest of Tenochtitlán, an Aztec physician, named Martinus de la Cruz wrote a herbal in the local Aztec language. Called the *Badianus Manuscript*, it's the first herbal of the Americas and details therapeutic uses of two hundred fifty-one Mexican plant species. Written under the order of the son of the first viceroy of New Spain, who was interested in herbs and spices of the New World and the medical knowledge of the Aztecs, the herbal conveys Aztec knowledge of medicinal plants and their pharmacological actions.

"The herb visnaga provided the Egyptians with a remedy for inflamed kidneys and was mentioned in the Ebers papyrus. A herb that is used to ease the pain of kidney stones and is the source of a drug used to treat asthma. Visnaga derivatives have a powerful antispasmodic action on the bronchial muscles. Jahangir knew only too well of this, from his own first-hand experience. Ginkgo is effective in improving circulation to the brain and in improving the condition of some Alzheimer's patients and those suffering from senile dementia. The tree is native to China, where its seeds are used in herbal medicine to relieve wheezing and to treat incontinence, and its leaves are also used to treat asthma.

"The Canon of Medicine, compiled by Persian polymath, Avicenna, and completed in 1025 AD is the more contemporary medical practice, which had been largely influenced by Galen and Hippocrates has ultimately always been widely accepted, certainly by Western civilisations, as *the* encyclopaedia of medicine. It was divided into five books and firstly translated from Arabic to Latin, by Gerard of Cremona in the late twelfth century.

"What you need to understand is that the life of a research scientist is mostly reading books, trawling dusty old museums, referencing documents and parchments. History does not give up its secrets willingly. We stumble around in the dark, and suddenly an all-revealing light is switched on. Barnacle Bob was that light."

"Barnacle Bob, who the hell was he, anyway?" Stone asked.

"The old man who was shot," Abigail explained.

"Yeah, I get that part, but how does he slot into all this history?"

Evina continued on with her rendering, "The celestial globe in my possession is one of a set of three. It is unsigned and has no reference to a date. My initial observations revealed it to have a mapping error until a freakish event occurred in Nepal. The story is both tragic and blind luck, really. A Spanish professor, also a good friend of mine, was preparing for a climb up Mount Everest when he came across some Nepalese kids kicking, what he assumed to be a soccer ball, around in the streets. The ball headed his way and being an avid fan of the game, he returned it with his best strike, which resulted in him fracturing his foot and ending his chances of completing the climb. The ball was the second globe protected by the hide of an old goat, and that particular ascent to the summit resulted in the deaths of six people after an earthquake measuring 7.8 caused an avalanche that swept through Pumori."

"Fate intervened. Just wasn't his time," Kelly added.

Evina agreed with a nod of the head, "And as it turned out, this second globe was also unsigned and not dated with the exact mapping error. The Moghul Empire's most knowledgeable astronomer and metallurgical, Master Muhammad Salih Thattvi, might have made one mistake—but two, I don't think so." Evina took another sip from her wine glass.

"I'm sorry, but I have to ask. What is a celestial globe, anyway?" Kelly wanted to know.

"Do you want the technical version, Jack, or just a wrap-up?" Evina asked.

"Let's go with the former to start with, Professor," Kelly replied.

"Celestial globes show the apparent positions of the stars in the sky. They omit the sun, moon and planets because the positions of these bodies vary relative to those of the stars, but the ecliptic, along which the sun moves, is indicated. Great circles transform into straight lines via gnomonic projection. The gnomonic projection is said to be the oldest map projection ever devised and was developed by Thales, in the sixth century B.C. The path of the shadow-tip or light-spot in a nodus-based sundial traces out the same hyperbola formed by parallels on a gnomonic map. The gnomonic projection is used in astronomy, where the tangent point is centred on the object of interest. The sphere being projected in this case is the celestial sphere and not the surface of the Earth. It was considered a major feat in metallurgy."

"Whoa, slow down, Professor. I knew I should have asked for the latter, and I need to grab another bottle of red," Kelly intervened.

Evina returned from her en-suite toilet and waited for Kelly to reenter before continuing on. "Simply put, Jack, imagine a world globe, and you place a rubberband around its circumference and then stretch it out. The rubberband is space with the planets, the sun and the constellations all looking back down at planet Earth as its centre. The axis of the rotation terminates in the north and south celestial poles, the sphere is encircled by the celestial equator. The two points where the ecliptic, the path of the sun, and the equator cross, therefore, mark the position of the sun at the spring, called the vernal and autumn equinox. The position of any point on the surface of the sphere can be given concerning the equator or the ecliptic.

"In the equatorial coordinate system, the position is determined by right ascension and declination. Right ascension is the angular distance along the equator from the vernal equinox; declination is the distance north or south along the equator along a great circle passing through the point in question and the two celestial poles. In the ecliptic coordinate system, the position is specified by celestial longitude and latitude. Celestial longitude is the angular distance along the ecliptic, again from the vernal equinox; the celestial latitude is the distance north or south of the ecliptic along a great circle, passing the two celestial poles."

"Well, why didn't you just say so in the first place? Simple really," Kelly replied, taking the opportunity to poke a bit of fun at the associate professor of the Smithsonian.

"As a person who spends so much time at sea, Jack, I would think the ability to know where you are on the planet without the use of instruments might be of interest."

"Point taken," Kelly conceded. "Please continue."

"Trade between Europe and the East was fast becoming threatened by waring factions within the Moghul Empire. Jahangir sought advice from England, resulting in Queen Elizabeth 1 sending an emissary named, Sir Thomas Roe. Sir Thomas was an English diplomat of the Elizabethan and Jacobean periods. In 1614, he was elected as a member of Parliament for Tamworth, and then from 1611 to 1618, he was appointed as the first ambassador to the Moghul Court at Agra in India. The principal object of his mission was to assure protection for the East India Company's invested interests and their factory located in Surat.

"Sir Thomas soon gained Jahangir's confidence. Together they indulged in alcohol and opiate binge sessions, all the while enjoying the local sexual delights on offer that normally would be frowned upon within the circles of the British aristocracy. Jahangir also wanted to seek advice from Sir Thomas about his recordings and knowledge of 'natural healing' based on the ever-increasing encyclopaedia he was scribing. He explained in detail the medicinal remedies that could be found in the forests and gardens of the poor and disadvantaged at virtually no cost to themselves.

"Sir Thomas was astounded at what he was reading. He questioned the legitimacy of such wild claims and asked for proof of Jahangir's written theories. Over the ensuing weeks, Sir Thomas, recorded how he was witness to the power of this wealth of knowledge. He claimed he saw with his own eyes, a young boy with an ugly raised pussed stye on his right eyelid. He wrote about a mixture of equal amounts of onions, cropleek and garlic being pounded together with a portion of wine and bull's gall. These were then poured into a brass bowl and allowed to stand for nine days and nights, then strained through a perforated cloth and applied to the inflicted eye with the touch of a bird's feather. Within a matter of hours, the abscess showed signs of healing. Within two days Sir Thomas was presented with the boy, now completely free of his ailment. He was more than impressed.

"Since childhood Sir Thomas himself had suffered from the effects of painful and debilitating migraines. After a three-day opium binge, with little sleep, he awoke to what he knew to be another painful episode. Jahangir prepared half a dish of barley, one handful each of betony, vervain and other herbs that are good for the head, and after they were well boiled together, he gathered them as one, wrapped them in a cloth and laid them to his friend's sick head. What happened next was a life-changing moment for, Sir Thomas.

"Within the hour the throbbing subsided, his feeling of unwell lifted and his fever disappeared completely. By early evening he was able to lift his head and bathe. That night he shared the emperor's table and devoured his meal with gusto. 'It was truly a miracle' Sir Thomas explained to, Jahangir. He witnessed in disbelief as peasants, and the gentry alike would be miraculously cured of diseases of the liver and kidneys. Measles and other poxes were rendered defeated, that would, under normal circumstances, see a person to an early grave.

"He insisted on Jahangir sharing the source and how a person could grow and administer these natural wonderments, insisting these miracle cures be shared with the world. These are the theoretical basis of the five elements of life. The earth, air, ether, plus fire and water that make up the physical being. When they are dynamically combined to manage all processes within the human physiology, they become the basic building blocks of human life, and through them, we can determine the fundamental healthcare that works towards prescribing a way to a healthier being. Identify the patient's unique constitution, their 'Tridosha System' then one can correctly diagnose the cause of the imbalance and able to decide on the correct herbal protocol. The three doshas, which are Vata, Pitta and Kapha, they represent our genetic blueprint and fashion how we respond, both psychologically and physically, to our environment. The constitutional type, Vata, is a combination of air and ether. Pitta is the combination of fire and water; Kapha, water and earth. These elements are the foundation of all life."

"He who possesses the power to heal?" Stone added. "I can see dollar signs and lots of them."

"Yes, very much so," Evina confirmed. "The power to heal, the 'Magnum Opus' of the Islamic world in the field of medicine, all provided by God himself. My research shows the third globe was entrusted to Sir Thomas Roe but was taken from him while returning home by a man named, Captain Walter Nelson. At the time Nelson sailed under the protection offered by Queen Elizabeth I and the insignia of the British flag. He, like many other privateers, were basically pirates with orders to plunder the riches offered by the returning Spanish galleons, splitting their booty with the Crown. As tensions between the English and the Spanish fleets increased, Queen Elizabeth I ordered Nelson to be stripped of all his wealth resulting in his yacht the *James Royal* being scuttled.

"The celestial globe Nelson stole from Sir Thomas was presented to the Crown with all his other riches. Queen Elizabeth I intended to hand the sphere back to the VOC, even after Sir Thomas Roe argued it belonged to him. She answered it was only ever entrusted to him and therefore still belonged to the Moghul Empire. The real reason was, both the VOC and the East India Company's interests were under threat by the Islamic Kingdoms, and a gift of this magnitude might sway the new emperor. Now, let us jump to where the link continues with Commander François Pelsaert."

"The *Batavia?*" Kelly questioned.

"Yes, the *Batavia*," Evina answered. "Pelsaert knew he had in his possession something of immense importance to the Moghul Court and his own journals show on his return journey from Djarkata, he was to present his gift to the new emperor. He needed to shore up relations between the East and the West, not just for the VOC, but for his own well laid out business plans. Christians versus Muslims. A time-honoured battle of the minds for the religious fanatics and the creation of wealth for the capitalists. But the mystery ended when the *Batavia* ploughed into that reef. That was until my meeting with, Barnacle Bob."

"Can we just call him, Bob, from here on?" Abigail suggested.

"We still need to verify the gravesite along the Zuytdorp Cliffs and the inscriptions carved by Jan Pelgrom de Bye on Walter Loos' headstone. That *could* point us to where this third celestial globe may well be resting. I have them right here. Bob wrote it down on a soft pack of Camel. See, take a look," as Evina handed over the empty sealed packet of cigarettes.

"Well, the first part is simple enough. Latitude twenty-seven degrees," Kelly shared with Evina.

"How so?" Evina asked.

"It's like holding half a map," Kelly replied.

Evina's eyes lit up. "Yes, but I may have a theory that might change that."

"You still haven't addressed the question of *why* is someone trying to have you killed?" Stone wanted to hammer home. Operation Blue Skies was still live and ongoing. The strike would only be completed when he eliminated the final pin. No more distractions.

"And what *is* the pot of gold at the end of *your* rainbow, Evina? The big question is; what's in it for you." Kelly also wanted to clear the air. He and Stone thought alike.

Evina returned a soft scowl. "All I can say is some powerful men would prefer to see me and my team fail. The pot of gold is not what you might think it is. Its dollar value is not in what it's worth in monetary terms, but more about what it may cost a near billion-dollar-a-day pharmaceutical industry. I'm an associate professor and scientist. I have a hypocritical obligation to share this with the world, and I don't mind saying that I am offended that you might think otherwise."

"I'm sorry, but it needed to be asked," Kelly backed down.

"Share *what* with the world?" Abigail wanted to know.

"It may be a book. We're not one hundred per cent sure as yet."

"A book! You spend ten years tracking down the next bestseller," Abigail blurted out.

"Maybe it's the ultimate 'how-to manual' from IKEA. Now that *would* be worth all the effort," Kelly couldn't resist the jibe. Stone laughed while nodding his head in agreement. Kelly remembered the one and only time he and Tiaan ended up arguing after she returned home one time from Bangkok with an IKEA flat-pack. Three hours later it lay in pieces on the floor and eventually ended up as nesting shelves in the chicken coop.

"This is not just any book." Evina finished her glass of 92 Happs Shiraz. "Nice wine, Jack. This could be the *'Book of Remedies'*, but let's not get ahead of ourselves, just yet."

"West Australian Margaret River," Kelly smiled while raising his glass.

"Presuming, you actually find this third globe, how will that help to locate this *Book of Remedies?*" Abigail's reporter's mind was kicking into another gear.

"If this third celestial globe is both signed and dated, this will provide a reference to the positions of the Zodiac at a specific moment in time. I think the sphere will point to a location or locations that could provide the next link to the book's final resting place."

"So this sphere is just another stepping stone to a supposed destination that may, or may not reveal a book that might not even exist. This could take you a lifetime, Evina, and you still may be none the wiser," Abigail wanted to point out in a sisterly way.

"Welcome to my world, Abby. We do know Emperor Jahangir became fascinated with the world map after he was presented with evidence of other countries healing herbals. China, Spain and the Aztecs, even the Egyptians. Each time a ship returned to port in Calcutta, Jahangir would request a private counsel from his captains' regarding these distant and faraway lands. His favourite captain was a man named, Willem Janszoon. He commanded a smaller yacht named the *Duyfken.* After a four-year absence, both the captain and crew were assumed to have fallen victim to the call of the ocean. Then one day the *Duyfken* limped into the harbour to the excitement of a welcoming crowd of onlookers with what resembled a dead tree sprouting from the deck of the damaged yacht. He had been swept off course by a severe tropical cyclone and was forced to beach his ship in the protection of a river after his mainmast was snapped. He ordered his men to search for a suitable timber and fell a tree for a replacement. Janszoon pointed out to his emperor. Never had he seen such a hardened wood, explaining how his carpenter's tools were all but useless in trimming the trunk. The ship needed major repairs, and Jahangir ordered the makeshift mast to be delivered to his palace using a team of bullocks.

"In the 1600s, the great battle of Sekigahara was waged between two waring Japanese clans, with forces loyal to Toyotomi Hideyori in the east and the west clans, commanded by Togugawa Leyasu. The conflict ended in a decisive victory and was the beginning of the last Feudal Military Japanese Government. Togugawa Leyasu was the founding father of the Tokugawa shogunate. The first appointed Shogun was, Tokugawa Lemitsu, and on issuing his third decree; the Sakoku Edict, this resulted in Japan entering a period of isolation. A closed country intended to eliminate foreign influence, enforced by strict government rules and regulations. It was a prime example of the Japanese desire to seek total exclusion.

"The Shogun sent his highest-ranked naval commander, Kuroda Nagamasa, to seek council with the Moghul Court and present to, Emperor Jahangir, a sealed order signed by, Emperor Go Yōzei, outlining the new trade agreements between Japan and India for essential items only. While in the presence of, Emperor Jahangir, Kuroda Nagamasa began moving in a numbered sequence a series of interlocking wooden slides to open the marquetry wooden-crafted Himitsu-Bako; his surreptitious personal lockbox and presented his own emperor's orders to the Full Court. Jahangir was more fascinated by the unusual puzzle box than the business at hand, preferring to leave that to his subordinates and sought a private council with the Japanese naval commander. He wanted to seek further information on its origins, how it was constructed and could it be replicated? Nagamase explained to Jahangir, it was part of a Japanese tradition known as, 'Hakone-Yosegi-Zaiku' and originated in a small town called Hakone-Odawara in the Ashigarashimo district. As a sign of goodwill, Nagamase presented the Himitsu-Bako to Jahangir as a parting gift.

"Jahangir then instructed his most experienced and expert palace craftsmen to dismantle the puzzle box and to build for their emperor, three of the finest lockboxes ever created, using the wood from the tree trunk that was salvaged from the damaged *Duyfken*. As Captain Janszoon had previously pointed out, the timber was harder than any man had ever seen before and required the leading metallurgist's forging specific strengthened and sharpened tools to hone the wood. It took over three months to finish the ornate and beautifully crafted Himitsu-Bako puzzle boxes with the image of past emperors emblazoned on the lid, seated cross-legged with a rising sun in the background.

"The chief metallurgist was instructed to construct a wax cast and to pour a gold-leafed casket where he sealed the bound parchments and placed this inside the finished Himitsu-Bako. Two of these caskets were to act as a decoy while his own son, Prince Khurram, secretly plotted his own grab for power and influence and was now slowly gathering impetus. The third I believe is where he placed the *Book of Remedies.*

"He then ordered Captain Janszoon, together with two of his most capable seafarers, to carry these wooden caskets to three furthest points of the compass, east, west and the southern tips of the world. Only one other has ever turned up in a three-hundred-year-old shipwreck discovered off the Madagascar coast in 1974. The wood was still in reasonably good shape, with a carved image burnt into the lid of a seated Emperor Akbar. The other amazing revelation was when they dated the timber, it was found to be over four hundred years old, and where do you think it originated from? Anyone care to hazard a guess?"

All eyes were on Evina as she circled the room with her inquisitive hazel eyes, waiting for an answer she knew would not be forthcoming.

"Australia—the Northern Territory, in fact. The Australian ironwood tree is one of the hardest woods known to mankind."

"Evina, that's absolutely amazing. Now I can understand your infatuation in tracking down this book," Abigail gasped. "Australia? Now I'm really intrigued."

"Well, good luck in your search to find your book, Evina. I'm hitting the sack. Got an early start in the morning.

Goodnight, all." As Stone headed for the stairs, he wanted to catch Kelly's eye. He nodded his head to indicate—downstairs. The two men walked to the end of the small cement pier.

"I spoke with the Darcy Jones earlier today," Stone spoke slowly as the two men walked shoulder to shoulder. "So, I asked him what he knows about this Anomura Corporation. He seemed to hesitate for a moment too long, and I also think he was a bit thrown back when I reported my current location."

"What are your guts telling you, Tobias?" Kelly asked.

"I should be asking you that. See what you can find out from this Ed character tomorrow? He seems to have his fingers in every pie."

"I can do that. See you in the morning."

"Probably not, but I will catch up before I leave. The *Ballarat* is due to weigh anchor at 2200 tomorrow night, and I've booked my berth."

Chapter-25

SHEILA WHITE read her letter of acceptance for what must have been the third time in almost as many minutes. This was her ticket to a bright future and finally, the time had arrived to turn a new page in her so far, uneventful, dreary life. She could now remove the shackles of constraint from an overbearing but loving mother and a farming father that cared more for his prized pigs than his 21-year-old daughter.

Her letter of employment was confirmation she had survived the gruelling and sometimes intrusive security checks she'd been subject to over the last ten weeks by the Australian Federal Police. Unlike the other 132 failed applicants, Sheila had survived the cut and was now part of the secretarial pool within the ADF. After moving from the tiny town of Captains Flat located 70 kilometres from the nation's capital in the Australian Capital Territory (ACT), her government subsided flat in the suburb of Majura Park was like being given the keys to the city for the young and extremely shy, country bumpkin.

Her first assigned posting was rather an unusual one. The Ben Chifley building was due for completion in just over four months. It was purpose-built for the expanding staff recruitments to accommodate the 1,800 expected full- and part-time employees of the intelligence watchdog ASIO, representing an increase of over 1,000 personnel, due to the demands of the new world order and the ever-increasing threat of terrorism, both abroad and on home soil. As the building neared completion, in a defined and precise order, each department would shift its entire operation from their existing premises, the short distance of one kilometre to the opposite end of Constitution Avenue.

Her boss, for reasons that were of no concern to Sheila, had decided to maintain his old digs. Even though his new corner office with sweeping views of the Old Parliament House located on Capital Hill and the Molonglo River as it gently meandered its way into Lake Burley Griffin was the first to be completed. The director-general of ASIO was old school, and he liked to keep his finger on the pulse, which meant being within earshot of both the Admiralty and Army HQ; both within walking distance of his old office.

A typical workday for Sheila comprised receiving her daily office assignments from the director's personal assistant each morning. From that point on, she was left alone except for the welcome interaction from a few contractors tasked with dismantling the labyrinth of office partitions to make way for the new occupants if, in fact, there were any. In her short term of employment, Sheila had only been confronted with the head of ASIO on two occasions and both times she was met with a curt, "Good morning," while he whisked past surrounded by a swarm of fussing minders.

A white government-plated vehicle that looked like the hundred others that make up the underground parliamentary carpool slowed before stopping at the front entry checkpoint to the Russell Offices. The female driver glanced down to check her skirt was still hitched high above her knees. The on-duty sentry guard stood from his stool and leaned through the open pillar-box window as the attractive deputy prime minister held her ID at arm's length. She offered a welcoming smile as the young second-year able seaman's eyes widened to be greeted with a bird's-eye view of her full breasts from a loosely buttoned white chiffon see-through blouse. He half-heartedly ran his eyes over the remainder of the car and was satisfied that this welcoming distraction of the female kind was alone. He waved her through and then went about rearranging his aroused man parts.

The vehicle moved slowly forward, following the designated yellow dashed line, then suddenly turned to the left, and with the engine idling, the boot flipped open. Within seconds, a lambswool blanket was removed from the body of a second person. A slightly nervous woman climbed from the confines of the rear trunk, brushed herself down and walked briskly to the front entrance of the building, titled: Department of Finance and Deregulation, which was a front for the now-defunct offices of ASIO. She pushed the lift for the second floor and entered the ladies' room, checked her lipstick in the half-length mirror before rearranging her styled, shoulder-length auburn hair with a ruffle of her manicured fingers. It needed to look slightly tousled without looking unkempt.

The sound of high-heels stepping over the hardwood hallway floor that led from the stairwell caused Sheila to raise her eyes above the level of her front office desk partitioning. At first, she thought she was hallucinating, it almost seemed too perfect to be true, but within seconds her smile stretched as she recognised the bright red lipstick glowing from a perfect set of lips and the familiar smiling face of her newfound lover.

Those deep blue-coloured eyes that had caused Sheila's heart rate to double with just a subtle wink and that swanky hip-swivelling walk which initially attracted her to this brash sex goddess while at the Transit Bar located inside the Petrie Plaza pedestrian mall in the heart of Canberra's gay entertainment district. The previous Friday night was an awakening for the normally reserved, young girl from the pig farm and was ultimately her first step towards fulfilling a sexual yearning and secret desire to allow her mind and body to finally succumb to the internal calling that had confused her since she was just 13 years old.

As the middle-aged bombshell swaggered down the last ten metres of the corridor, the tender-looking face from her one-night-stand could feel her nipples hardening and that familiar moist feeling tingling between her inner-thighs as her first-time lover approached; unannounced. This was a rarity, Sheila thought, as she rolled back her mind to the only other time she worked up the courage to strike the first-time conversation with someone of the same sex. That ended up in disaster with the resulting venomous tongue lashing, her first introduction to the lesbian mindset.

Gay women could be such bitches, but Penny seemed to be very different, Sheila needed little convincing.

Sheila stood up from her desk and met her intriguing lady of the night at the glass door entrance to the director-general's office, not sure of the protocols involved in an unscheduled meeting such as this. They shared a soft touch of the hands in a secretive but sensual way that was sending Sheila's hormones into a frenzied spiral. Her face was blushing, and her sexual yearning for more was conjuring up erotic images of her and the sex bomb that was now standing only inches away. The woman known to her as just Penny leaned into Sheila's private space and kissed her gently on the lips. Sheila thought she was going to faint, right there and then. Penny then offered to wipe her stained lips clean with the touch of a wet index finger and then suggested she make a quick dash to the ladies' room to touch up her makeup.

"How did you know I worked here? Oh, it doesn't matter now. I'm so glad to see you, and you look great by the way," Sheila greeted Penny with an open show of uncurbed enthusiasm. "We can have lunch together in the canteen. I'll be right back."

Sheila grabbed her bag from inside her bottom desk drawer. She needed a moment to gather her senses, not wanting to seem too eager, but eager as a beaver she was. The moment the door swung closed, Penny moved like a cat burglar. She entered a four-digit code and pushed the director's office door half open. Inside her Versailles jacket was a Federal Order.

Penny placed the A4-sized paper on the fax in-tray behind the expansive L-shaped desk that looked too clean and organised. It was marked urgent. She dialled the memorised number and pressed *send*. The connection was made, and the Australian Coat of Arms that proudly sat at the top of the page, fast disappeared as it swept through the facsimile and dropped out the other side into the waiting hands of the lesbian lover.

After returning from the little girl's room to an empty office, Sheila's total confusion was only matched by both her disappointment and the feelings of ultimate betrayal. It was totally unexpected as she felt the loneliness of her cell-like office close in around her. She wiped her eyes dry and resumed her boring day duties, alone once more. Politics was a dirty game played by experts—and Sheila White had just learnt a cruel lesson in life.

The deep growl of the larger-than-life Admiral Peterson, yelling through his open office door could be heard reverberating up the corridor. "Barbara, get me the PM on the phone, and I don't care where or who he's with." At the same time, an unexpected visitor was being escorted through his half-open door.

"You're a long way from home, aren't you, Miss Wilks?" Boomer was more than curious as to why the deputy PM was standing opposite his desk. Helena Wilks needed to cover the real reason she was visiting the Russell Offices.

"Cut the crap, Admiral. That JNSC meeting yesterday was almost farcical. You know as well as I do the importance of not rocking the boat of a friendly trading partner. I've spent a mountain of time and personal energy to place this administration into a favourable position with the Indonesian Government."

Admiral Peterson cast an inquisitorial eye over the pretentious Miss Helena Wilks, as she continued on with her rant. His own Navy career had already cost him two failed marriages, and both his ex-wives enjoyed the luxury of expensive tastes. He knew something about women's clothing, with firsthand knowledge of the exorbitant costs associated with maintaining *that* certain look.

He started to add up in his head the sum of the deputy PM's current attire. Jimmy Choo patent leather shoes, a Gloria Coelho straps design dress, an Erika Cavallini checked ruffled rim jacket and her Dolce and Gabbana clutch bag. He stopped when he broke the two thousand dollar barrier, and that didn't take into account her weekly visits to the women's salon and the gold jewellery that dripped from each hand. He reminded himself to ask Barbara to find out what the current salary was for a level-7 minister.

"I need to know the details of this operation, Blue Skies," Wilks continued. "I sit at the same table with the rest of the JNSC members and yet I have no dossier or personal knowledge of this ongoing operation on foreign soil."

Boomer Peterson stood up and closed his office door. "You need to talk to the prime minister about that, not me. You've already broken more than a few legal statutes in discussing that subject outside the security of the Menzies Room."

"Well, I'm here and talking to you now, so, cough it up. There is a lot more at stake here than even you are aware of, Admiral, and I certainly do not intend to just quietly sit by while you four cronies start another bloody war with an important ally."

The admiral's intercom buzzed, "Yes, Barbara."

"Sir, the PM will be on the line in one minute."

"Did you re-route HMAS *Ballarat* to Christmas Island?" Wilks half-heartedly demanded.

"It's a scheduled refuelling stop and to carry out some minor repairs. It was an operational matter and does not concern the deputy prime minister's office. Is there anything else I can't help you with today? I need to talk with the leader of this country." The admiral's tone hinted this unscheduled meeting was about to come to an end.

Helena Wilks stormed out and headed back downstairs. She remembered to smile at the CCTV cameras capturing her images as she strode from the Admiralty building. She turned the ignition key of her government-supplied car and headed towards the main gate, stopping just the one time to pick up her waiting passenger.

"Did you get it done—any problems?" Wilks asked. Her voice showed the first signs of the pressure she was under.

"Just a broken heart. Nothing that some time won't heal. You owe me big time for helping you out today," the less than interested sister replied.

"You don't consider for a moment, that ensuring that you didn't rot inside a foreign jail as payment enough. You're a spoilt bitch, Anna, and will never learn. Where do you want me to drop you off at now?"

"Somewhere where you're not," Wilks' ungrateful sister answered with spite that was borne from childhood.

Chapter-26

STONE STIRRED AWAKE at six A.M. He showered and dressed in a pair of creased, tailored trousers, a striped business shirt, and slipped on a pair of ankle-high black boots. All he needed for the first part of this day was his phone and wallet. He grabbed his small backpack and walked the short distance to where the car rental company had parked the yellow Ford *Focus* hatchback at the entrance to the marina. The scenic drive towards the western side of the island snaked its way through thick, lush rainforest on a road that was in good condition, only because of what greeted you at the other end. The detention centre was built into the highest point of a small incline. It consisted of both an outer and inner interlocking wired ten-foot-high perimeter fence with recoiling razor-wire strung along the entire top section. With its guarded main entry, the whole place screamed overkill. Stone considered the simple fact they were on a small island surrounded by the Indian Ocean. *Where do they think an escapee would go?*

Stone pulled up at the first check-point and flashed his identification, complete with badge and photo. He opened up his iPhone and showed the e-mail from Australian Federal Police headquarters in Canberra to the current Chief of Security; signed by a Mr Mitchell Lacey. The detention centre was managed by the successful tender, which in this case was a company called Havanack Security & Mine Site Services. There was big money to be made when it came to providing personnel for a job the Australian Government did not have the expertise to perform themselves. It was easier this way for the minister to lay blame on a private firm rather than accept responsibility if something went foo-bar.

Stone was directed to drive a farther five hundred metres past three distinct rows of pressed-steel buildings with sloped roofs. He slowed to be greeted by a tennis court smack-bang in the middle of a large area of freshly cut lawn.

A tennis court—really?

He parked his vehicle next to the administration block. The largest building was the communal centre where the asylum seekers ate, showered and passed the days playing table tennis, dealing cards or devising ways to kill more Australians. People were walking around aimlessly, others were crouching in small huddles, and some kids could be seen kicking a soccer ball into an old fishing net strung between two trees.

He locked the car with his pack in the boot and was met by a uniformed female officer who looked like she needed a shave. "Your Officer Merryweather, then? ID please," she snapped, in a deep, well-rehearsed voice. Stone flashed his wallet a second time while the five o'clock shadow copied down some details to an arrival's sheet secured to a clipboard. She handed him a day visitors' badge with a small jaw-clip attached, then indicated she wanted him to follow.

Stone explained, "I'm due to meet with a doctor before we interview the detainees."

"The doctor is based here twenty-four-seven," she answered like Stone was expected to know that. He continued following the officer down a hallway that was devoid of life. No pictures, plants or people bitching over the weekend footy results. Just blank white walls and sectioned lino floor that smelt of bleach with black heel marks everywhere. Stone considered for a moment if Ed had the cleaning contract. She stopped at the far end and gestured for her visitor to enter. "Mr Lacey will be with you in a minute. Take a seat."

"I prefer to stand and tell, Lacey, I don't like to be kept waiting, you got that?" *Now, who's the boss?* Stone turned and grinned as she hastened her step.

A tall man in his thirties entered from another door. His black denim cargo pants with leg pockets were tucked into a pair of lace-up boots with a matching shirt displaying the company's logo splashed over the front pocket and both lapels. A thick leather belt held his two-way radio and an old-fashioned cruncher, the same batons the riot police like to use. *Another weekend warrior*, Stone figured.

"Officer Merryweather, I'm Mitchell Lacey, and I'm the man in charge of this facility," he stated with an air of authority. "Sorry to keep you waiting. We just need to finalise the last of the paperwork. The Department of Corrections is very particular. We don't often have visitors to our part of the island."

You don't say, Einstein. Stone scribbled a name on the bottom of a release form. "Can we get going, Lacey? Where is this, doctor?"

"Doctor Ross will be meeting us in the interview room we have provided. Follow me. Will you require any special needs items today?"

"Special needs?" *Just a .44 magnum if I find who I'm looking for.*

"Yes, like towels, tissues, any special food requirements or soft drinks." Then Lacey asked, "What about tea or coffee?"

"I'm just here for the interview, Lacey. Not lunch."

"Right then, please come this way." Lacey stopped and pointed with his extended arm to enter another room. It was bigger than Stone expected, with a table and four chairs. A cushioned two-seater couch occupied one wall. There was a water cooler with a tap in the corner and a plastic box full of baby and children's toys pushed into the opposite corner. A writing pad and pen sat on the table. Stone counted how many ways a man could get killed in this room; he stopped at ten when the doctor entered. She looked like this may have been her first gig since finishing university and needed to pay off her HECS debt. "I'm Doctor Ross. You're from the Federal Police, then?"

"I think we've established that already. Where is the individual that goes by the name of, Riduan Ananas?" Stone wanted to get this show on the road.

Footsteps could be heard shuffling down the scuffed hallway. The door opened, and the detainee was escorted to the chair opposite wearing sandals, a traditional thawb with a bisht and a kufi. He was running through the fingers of his right hand, a strand of prayer beads called a *Misbaha*, and he held a copy of the *Koran* in his free hand. His head was lowered, and no eye contact was made. The guard prepared to leave, "I'll be right outside. If you need me just holler, Doc," as he closed the door behind him.

Ananas was mumbling and reciting some scriptures under his breath while fingering each of the thirty-three beads.

The Sheik is left-handed, Stone remembered in his brief while he sat down and remained silent. He was studying the facial features of the photo he held in his trained memory. Picturing Riduan Ananas against the face imprinted into his mind. A face he will never forget. "Does this man speak or understand any English, Doctor Ross?"

She tapped away on her iPad while still standing. "It says here he only speaks Indonesian and some Malaysian. No English. Do you need an interpreter? That can be arranged, but it will take time."

"Not necessary." Stone locked onto the bearded man's face. "I want you to look into my eyes, Ananas."

Ananas didn't move. Stone slapped the table hard with his open hands. The doctor flinched. "There you go, he understands." The underlying hatred was there for all to see if you knew what to look for. Stone had seen it many times. "You know the Sheik—Sheik Aris?" Stone sarcastically posed the question. Ananas' eyes shifted down and left, then he turned his head sideways. "Oh, yeah, you sure do, you scumbag piece of lying shit."

"You can't speak to the interviewee like that. It is forbidden. That could be deemed as being racist," the doctor argued. She wasn't sure of her boundaries, but she wanted to stay her ground. Ananas let slip with a small quiver on his top lip.

"Well, we wouldn't want to look like racists, would we, Aris Munandar?" A small glimmer in his eye was all the confirmation Stone needed. This guy knew who that was, but he wasn't the actual Sheik. "Doctor Ross, please check this man's backside for a tattoo."

"Excuse me?" Her expression was that of shock.

"A tattoo in the shape of a crescent moon on his left side buttock disguised as a birthmark. That's the reason you're here today." Ananas suddenly shifted in his chair. His body language was giving up his secrets, like reading the morning paper.

"Ask him to strip and show me his backside. Trust me, Doctor Ross. He understands everything we say. *Now* please." Stone was insistent.

"I can't do that. We need an interpreter to explain his legal rights. He has the right to a hearing and an appeal."

"Doctor Ross, give me the room."

"I don't understand."

"The room, I want you to leave me alone for a minute or less—with our English-speaking friend."

"Officer Merryweather, this is highly unethical, and I won't take part in . . ."

Stone stood, opened the door and ushered the young Doctor Ross into the corridor. She felt annoyed. He closed the door, and a brief moment later she heard the shuffling of a chair. She thought she could hear the sound of a distressed voice verbal something in Arabic. That was soon followed by a loud *crack,* followed by a muffled *thud.* The door reopened, and Stone gently grabbed the doctor by the arm as she stood shell-shocked in a frozen stance. Riduan Ananas was now lying face down on the couch with his buttocks exposed. "Now, Doctor, tell me if that is a real birthmark or a tattoo."

"What happened to this man? How on earth did he end up like that?"

"I explained to him how much a lawyer costs in Australia, you know, to represent him at his hearing and explain the appeals process thoroughly. I think he passed out. Now do your job, please."

Doctor Ross regained some lost composure. She opened the door and went to the room opposite and came back with a pair of 8 x 420mm, Luope medical binoculars on her head and a pair of angled forceps. She tightened her surgical gloves and bent down before she stretched the brown shaped crescent moon with the tip ends. "Huh? This is definitely a tattoo," she stated, a little puzzled.

Stone was looking over her left shoulder. "Are you positive, one hundred per cent sure?"

"Yes, there is no doubt. Look at the pigment. You see when it stretches how it loses some of its elasticity. It's definitely not a birthmark." She stood and turned to face an empty room.

Stone strode back down the hallway and entered Lacey's office, unannounced. He was on the phone when Stone leant over the table and ended the call. Lacey looked up and met Stone's glare and decided not to argue the point. "Riduan Ananas, put him in isolation and on a twenty-four-hour suicide watch."

The man who loved to boast that he was in charge of this breeding ground for Islamic fundamentalists looked on in dismay. "Now, Lacey. Make it happen." Stone was in no mood for semantics. It was all business now. "The second refugee I requested to interview, a Miss Mi-sun. Where is she right now?"

"I thought you would already be aware of her transfer. The order came directly from Canberra yesterday. I have a copy here in my files." Lacey opened up a three-draw locked filing cabinet and retrieved a folder. He placed the open folder on his desk and slid out a printed copy. The Australian Coat of Arms indicated it was indeed a bona fide Federal Order. Stone read the two paragraphs.

"Can you give me a copy of this, for my records, you know what the bureaucrats are like with paperwork?"

"Absolutely, I like to dot all my i's and cross my t's. I'll be right back."

Stone stepped in behind Lacey's desk and made a mental note of the computer's terminal number. He tried his luck and started a half-hearted search, hoping for a password before he heard returning footsteps.

"How and where was she transferred?" Stone demanded.

"I am not advised of where, but it was unusual that she was taken away by a private vehicle. They had the necessary documentation, and that's all we need to release her from our custody. Why do you ask? Please don't tell me there may be a problem—is there?"

"I'll assume you have security footage of the transfer and the vehicle?" Stone added.

"Oh, yes, Havanack Security & Mine Site Services only installs the best. We have the latest SP thirty . . ."

Stone didn't allow him to finish, "Mitchell, just bring up the vision, if that's not too much trouble?"

"Right, it won't take a moment." Lacey swivelled his flat-screen monitor. Stone watched closely until a dark SUV turned and headed back out through the main gate.

"Remember what I told you about, Riduan Ananas. Someone will be here to transfer him, and very soon." Stone handed back his visitor's pass and drove out of the detention centre.

Why is it that all the bad guys drive black SUVs with tinted windows? The FBI has a lot to answer for.

Stone drove the Ford *Focus* back along Blowholes Road and turned north into Baseline until he found Golf Course Road. He passed a tourist sign that read: Soon Tien Kong Temple - 5 kilometres. An almost dilapidated larger sign indicated Christmas Island Resort & Casino - next right. Stone parked the car at the coastal entry to Waterfall Bay.

He jogged the last two hundred metres, crossed over some damp recently reticulated grass before coming to a stop. The old casino was surrounded by a high brick perimeter fence that was obviously a recent addition. There were no guards posted at the wrought-iron gate, and just the single CCTV camera was mounted on the drivers-side pillar.

They don't look like they're expecting any company? Stone thought.

He scaled the two-metre-drop and found some cover. The whole place felt like it had fallen victim to some strange, weird time-warp resulting in all the guests just vanishing into thin air, leaving the remaining buildings intact. It was eerie.

With his single-lens scope, Stone scanned the cream-coloured cement rendered front entrance supported by a series of round pillars and an abundance of glass. The remnants of what was once two tiled kidney-shaped pools sat empty between the coast and the main resort building. The entire complex consisted of coastal shrubs made up of tree palms, ferns, herbs, sedges and grasslands with the primary rainforest acting as a natural backdrop to the west. Two vehicles were parked on a side access road. One was a stretch limousine, while the other was a black SUV. Stone needed to get eyes on the number plate. He raised his scope vertically. A tall steel-framed cell tower stood out like a lighthouse on the pressed-sheet-aluminium roof. To the left, a heat plume could be seen rising in two distinct areas. The first looked like a generator room that was separate to the main building, and the other must be a huge air-conditioning unit supplying cool air to the entire complex, Stone decided.

There was some taller grass to his left. He used this and crawled on his stomach to gain a different angle at the plate. He wanted confirmation. Suddenly the double doors creaked open, and a pair of Korean-looking Sumo wrestlers wandered out and jumped in the SUV, both packing a holstered handgun. Stone remained flat on his stomach and buried his head in the dirt. A couple of ants crawled up and over his nose, he blew a breath from his bottom lip, and they dropped away. The noise of the whining turbo drifted past and turned a corner before he lifted his head.

AGH-629, it's the same SUV. How does an armed foreigner have in their possession a Federal Order to remove a refugee from a facility under the direct responsibility of the Australian Government?

A small sparrow flew from the branch of a tree and swooped down to gather an unsuspecting dragonfly. Stone followed its flight path and noticed a reflection from the sun low to the ground. He crawled over for a closer inspection. *A bloody tripwire—.*

The SUV stopped outside a second secluded building in the eastern corner. The two guards both stepped from the car and were greeted by four more of their buddies from inside, in what looked like staff quarters.

This is a shift change. Who are these people and why all the muscle?

Stone was about to make his way back to the stashed rental when the sound of a clattering garbage truck speeding down the final stretch of road scattered a group of scavenging guinea fowls, sending them scurrying for cover. He watched as it slowed and then stopped at the main gate. The driver's side window lowered, and a tattooed arm could be seen entering a pin code. The CCTV camera swivelled on its mount towards the cabin before the heavy gates slid open, and the garbage truck drove on through. Stone followed its course towards the plant room. In big letters on the rear of the crusher were the words: ED's HYGIENE SERVICES.

It was time to make his exit and place a couple of important calls.

Chapter-27

TOGETHER, KELLY AND TILL had already removed the old split diesel injector hoses by the time Ed arrived alongside the berthed *Thin Lizzy* in his own 50-foot ex-long-line fishing boat that was converted into a floating workshop. Till strung out two balloon buoys and secured both the bow and stern lines.

"Nice rig you got there, Ed," Kelly complimented him.

"I do all the Navy boat repairs, and it's easier to take Muhammad to the mountain."

"Makes sense."

Ed then asked with a hungry smile, "What smells so good, Toll?"

"I cook fàràng food. No Thai for breakfast, Boss tells me. You want to eat?"

"Later, mate. Just a coffee for now. So, Jack, let's get to work, shall we? The QANTAS flight that arrived from Darwin was thirty minutes late today. Bit of bad weather, nothing unusual. I have your part and the hoses."

"Follow me, Ed." Kelly led the way.

Two hours later the repairs were completed, less the bullet holes and the goanna's blown rubberised tail. Ed washed and joined the twins on the rear deck for a Till-prepared special brunch.

"Don't often get to share a meal with two pretty ladies. Let's all chow down," Ed shared.

It was time for Kelly to find out some answers. "So, Ed, how long have you lived on the island for? Not much would happen around these parts that would pass by someone like you, I'd expect?"

Ed was shovelling down Till's cooked breakfast. "I've been here since the end of the Second World War. Back then I flew reconnaissance for the RAN from South Java across the Sunda Strait looking for Jap subs trying to sneak into the South Java Sea. Both my co-pilot and I ran smack bang into the tail-end of a north-moving cyclone, then we got pushed wide and were forced to ditch about eight miles short of the coast. After ten hours floating, we were both rescued at sea by a passing cargo ship heading for Christmas Island. Lost a good man that day. When the war finished, I got my papers and came straight back to build a memorial for, young Dave. He was only twenty-two. Been here ever since. This is great, by the way, Toll. What is it?" Ed asked while chowing down.

"Sometimes it's better if you don't know, trust me on that one, Ed," Kelly offered. "This Anomura Corporation, what do you know about them?"

"Foreigners. They don't mix with the locals, I know that, and once a year they fly in on a swag of private jets for a five-day get together at the old resort. They're all here now, plus they don't spend a cent with any of the locals."

"Do you mean the casino?"

"Yeah, after the Ansett Airline strike in 1989, the place went broke. They bought it for a song. I would have paid double, but the chance never presented itself. All very hush-hush. You know they were also the successful tender to build the detention centre. I mean, our own government handing over taxpayers' money to foreigners. Hell, there was another one on the QANTAS flight today, which is unusual."

Kelly was curious, so he asked, "Why is that, Ed?"

"Well, you see, the Anomura Corporation also owns Haversack Security & Mine Site Services. They have the contract to run the detention centre on the other side of the island. A six-week, fly in - fly out roster, but they don't use a commercial airline. They bring 'em in on private charter planes, bypass Customs and Immigration and put the staff straight to work. A damn strange arrangement if you ask me."

"This man on the flight today, did he happen to have a scar on his chin?" Evina asked in a tone suggesting she wasn't happy.

"Bugger me, how did you know that? He was a tall bugger, that one. They never smile, and you can't tell if they're happy or about to rip your head off. Is he an associate of yours?"

"Not bloody likely," Evina fired back.

"Do you know where he went—where he's staying on the island?" Kelly asked.

"No, but it shouldn't be too hard to find out. Leave it with me. So, what are two Navy boys in civilian clothing doing on Christmas Island, anyway?"

"Navy boys?" Kelly was genuinely surprised.

"I can spot a squib a mile away. The way you walk and talk. The twinkle in your eye when you're around the ocean, a man can't hide that from, old Ed."

"Retired now," Kelly answered with the first thing that popped into his head.

"Yeah, right?" Ed offered with a wink and a wry smile. "Thanks for breakfast, Toll."

Till released the two rope lines and placed his foot on the deck rail to push Ed clear.

Ed leaned over the side rail. "The local copper Harry tells me Toll you're confined to quarters. I suppose you could do a lot worse than being stuck on this floating marine version of paradise." Ed placed a round-shaped canvas bag at his feet. "Inside are ten drop nets, complete with ropes and floats, Toll. Any bit of meat or fish heads will do the trick. Just drop 'em over the side, roll a cigarette and then pull 'em up real quick and Bob's your uncle, blue swimmer crabs for dinner."

"*Poo?*" Till asked.

"Sorry—what was that?" Ed returned a disconsolate glare towards the unassuming Thai deckhand.

273

"Poo," Jack needed to explain. "The Thai word for crab is boo, but they pronounce the b as a p."

"*Khàwp khun khràp,*" Till replied.

"Cop, what crap?" Ed answered, totally confused now.

"He says, thank you."

"Ah, no worries. I'll catch you all later. Hey, Jack, where do I send the bill?"

"I'll fix you up now if you prefer, Ed."

"Na, I'll swing by later. Not many pretty women on Christmas Island, if you know what I mean. Is either of you ladies interested in chasing a few bonefish on a fly? I'd be happy to act as your personal guide. Christmas Island boasts one of the few spots in the world where they still survive."

"Thanks for the offer, Ed. I think we'll take a raincheck," Evina replied with a smile.

"Okay, but you don't know what you're missing."

Ed swung the wheel hard to port and eased his floating workshop away, still grinning at the twins.

Chapter-28

KELLY WASN'T DUE BACK for another hour after buying some stores and organising the fuel boat to come alongside.

Evina was starting to go stir-crazy, and Abigail wasn't far behind. Stone had disconnected the Wi-Fi, and it was now the third day since either had accessed their Facebook or e-mail accounts, and there was no mobile data coverage. This was unprecedented.

"This having no Internet is ridiculous. I need to study the Western Australia Bureau of Meteorology's website to look up the historical data on cyclones and their effects on the river catchments in the lower reaches of the Murchison. I'm going to my room, Abby, to write some notes on what I need to research before we arrive in Western Australia."

"Have you got any lip gloss in your bag? I'm fresh-out, and I can feel my lips starting to crack," Abigail asked.

"Yeah, I think so. Here, have a rummage around while I fetch a bottle of water from the fridge."

Abigail probed inside Evina's bag and blindly fumbled around with her fingers. Eventually, she tipped the entire contents out on the table. A small coin fell to the cork floor and rolled behind a space between the pantry and a wall-mounted fire extinguisher. She crouched down on all fours and searched the dark recess.

"You won't find the lip gloss down there, sis."

"Thank you for sharing your wisdom, Evina. A coin rolled out. Hang on." She squeezed her hand in tight and managed to slide two fingers over the rounded edge. "Got it, finally. Here, take this will you while I wash my hands."

Evina viewed the coin closely, "I've never seen this before. Are you sure it came from inside my bag? It doesn't look familiar."

"Positive," Abigail confirmed.

Evina turned the cupro-nickel coin in her hand. The obverse side showed a side profile of a man's bust. She read out the circled inscription. "Hutt River Province. HRH Prince Leonard - 1977." She flipped it over to the reverse side. Struck into its centre was a pair of scales with an ink quill on either side surrounded by a scratched and faded esoteric effigy of a man enveloped by a rising sun with his hands outstretched and holding a small object that was difficult to analyse without magnification. Evina had a fleeting thought that it may have looked vaguely familiar.

"Is it real or a fake? . . . And Hutt River Province—never heard of it," Abigail stated with a look of disregard.

"This is the coin Bob was rolling over his knuckles. Why would he want me to have it? I'm going to see if I can reconnect that bloody Wi-Fi. Surely it can't be that hard?" Evina moaned.

"I might stay down here and help Till net some more of those crabs," Abigail voiced as Evina stormed off in the distance.

Stone drove back along Golf Course Road with his phone on speaker. Under his arrangement with the director, Darcy Jones was to be Stone's *only* operational contact. Like a dirty family secret, this resulted in having limited access to the wealth of accumulated information held in ASIO's respective databanks. He was a lone wolf and worked off the grid—or so Jones wrongly assumed.

His first call was to a tech geek that worked at one of the off-site subsidiary companies that could never be connected to ASIO. Their sole purpose was gathering and analysing data. Inside this building, the entire staff were employed to listen for chatter, surfing cyber-space for Internet-based chat rooms and search for patterns, random events that may connect to another random event that could lead to a link that might decipher a conversation that could lead to a terrorist cell and so it went on to infinity. The games nations have to play just to stay in the game.

When Stone spent time in Sydney, he liked to stay at what was once a grand circa 1920s home converted into a ten-bedroom boarding house in the harbourside suburb of Milsons Point that was once owned by his late grandmother. After doing a deal with a developer, Stone was now the proud owner of the exclusive top-storey penthouse apartment which doubled the value of his inheritance the day he was handed the keys. The prime minister's secondary residence was built on Bennelong Point in the adjoining suburb of Kirribilli. Kirribilli House overlooked the Sydney Opera House on the opposite side of the harbour and was just down the road, which meant it was usually nice and quiet.

From Stone's balcony, he could reach out and almost touch the north-side pillars of the bridge, and the smiling, larger-than-life clown face located at the entrance to Luna Park was ever-present, tucked away behind the Milsons Point jetty. Most nights he would jog from his room and head for the north pillar stairs which led to the pedestrian access that spanned the most picturesque harbour in the world, with Circular Quay on your left and Darling Harbour to the right. The Sydney Harbour Bridge was a hot spot for jumpers, and this is where he first met the only living person Stone could now regard as the closest thing to family, with her bare feet dangling from a giant steel girder about thirty feet above his jogging line.

After Stone spotted her, he didn't break stride until he reached the city-end and the only point of entry if you wanted to scale-up. The safety fences are a joke. And soon he was sitting twenty feet away on the same steel-grey painted beam. With eight lanes of constant traffic plus the two train lines, a constant vibration shimmied through the entire structure.

Stone glanced casually to his left, then focused both eyes forward towards the Opera House. "What time do you think you'll end up jumping?" he casually asked.

"Huh, where did you come from? Who are you? Leave me alone." The young woman was startled, preoccupied while immersed in her own life problems.

"I was thinking about waiting for the next Manly ferry to pass Fort Denison, then make my move. Do you want to go first or wait for me?" Stone further added.

"Don't talk to me, you sound like a nutter. You, me—it's all the same. I don't care; I don't care about anything anymore."

At least she was talking.

"Are you going to dive or land feet-first? They reckon the impact strips a person naked. Your clothes get ripped straight off. I'm not excited about strangers looking at my willy. What about you, are you shy?"

"I'm more than shy, I'm a bloody introvert. I *have* no friends," she replied hastily.

"You have one now. My name is Tobias—what's yours?"

"Tobias, from the Greek name of Tobiah. That was the name of the hero of the apocryphal *Book of Tobit*, which appears in many English versions of the Old Testament."

"Well, there you have it—that—I did not know. Where did you learn stuff like that?" Stone was impressed.

"I went to school, you know. I have a functioning brain."

"I remember reading somewhere that if you land feet-first, the impact with the water, from this height cracks every bone in your body. You end up resembling a squashed jellyfish. I've been told from a reliable source the sea rescue people almost have to suck you out of the water with a giant straw. But if you go head first, into what will feel like cement—well, I don't want to mess *my* face up either. My parents would both be really angry after paying all that money for my teeth and braces," Stone continued.

"Where did you learn all *your* stuff, they don't teach you *that* at school?"

Stone stood up and yawned. "Well, nice to meet you, whoever you are. Here comes the ferry now." He took a deep breath and stepped to the edge.

"No, don't. WAIT," the stranger yelled. "Tell me—why do *you* want to jump?"

"I tell you what—I'll make you a deal. I've got enough money on me for two drinks at the Fortune of War down at The Rocks." He shuffled in his pocket and pulled out some loose change. "You know it's the first pub built in Sydney. Mind you, the publican at The Australian reckons they made an error and still professes his pub's headstone, dated 1823, is three years earlier than his competitors. Not much use wasting good money. I'll shout you a last drink, and *then* I will tell you why, okay. Catch you later." Stone stepped his way back along the steel girder and did not turn around.

Fifteen minutes later, as he sat on a ripped upholstered barstool inside arguably Australia's first pub, a voice from behind brought a thankful smile to his face. "My name is, Felicity, and I don't drink alcohol."

That was five years ago now.

Stone passed by the T-intersection that leads to the detention centre. He dialled in Felicity's terminal number, texted three numbers, and then waited. Three minutes later, his iPhone buzzed.

"I won't ask where you are, but is everything all right, 007?" Felicity laughed.

"Are we secure?" Stone needed to confirm.

"Is the Pope Catholic?" Felicity was almost insulted.

"I want you to run a search for me, but it means hacking into a private secured server and maybe more."

"We don't use the word 'hacking' anymore, Tobias. We visit, look, and leave. Political correctness."

"Don't start me on that. Can you do it?"

"Give me the details. Am I part of a live operation now? I want a code name—you know, like Emma Peel, in *The Avengers*."

"I worry about you sometimes with your vivid imagination. ASAP, Miss Peel. Cheers." Stone quoted Lacey's terminal ID and hung up.

The second call was to Admiral Boomer Peterson. Stone was transferred to the Admiralty at Russell Offices in Canberra. Boomer picked up with his usual gust and raucous welcome. "Stone, this is becoming a bit of a habit."

"I need some toys, Boomer. A swamp needs to be drained. The HMAS *Ballarat* is still at anchor in Flying Fish Cove. What are her current armament capabilities?" Stone asked.

"The *Ballarat* was returning from the Sumatra Straits to Fremantle when she bumped into you. Those damn Malaysian pirates are becoming a real pain in everybody's side. She's at full battle readiness. SASR standard onboard armoury. What do you need?" the admiral enquired.

"You got a pen, handy?"

"Fire away, if you'll excuse the pun," the admiral joked.

"Oh—and Admiral. A Jemaah Islamiyah cell member is masquerading as a refugee on Christmas Island. He is being processed as Riduan Ananas, but I can assure you that is not his real name."

"Thanks for the heads up, Stone. Commander Larson can deal with that problem as well. Special delivery."

"One more thing, Admiral. I'll need the blueprints to the old casino on Christmas Island."

"Fancy a bit of roulette, Stone?"

"The Russian kind," he answered before ending the call .

Admiral Peterson leaned back with both hands folded behind his thick neck into the captain's chair salvaged from the HMAS *Melbourne*, a Majestic-class light aircraft carrier which he first commanded in 1955, and then remodelled at considerable expense to himself. He considered for a moment why Stone, a man he trusted without question, was by-passing his normal chain of command?

The Admiral swivelled his chair towards the window. *Stone is Darcy Jones' fix-it man, and now he was sharing information with the Navy, not ASIO. Why? Stone was no fool and could smell a rat a mile away. There's someone he doesn't trust, and that can only be one person. Darcy Jones?*

Chapter-29

A BIGAIL WAS WRESTLING with an angry crab, trying to master a rather unusual phenomenon. Till had just finished showing her how to render the feisty arthropods into a state of suspended animation. For the second time, Till placed two fingers around each claw and eased the crab from Abigail's flimsy grasp with its carapace facing towards him. "Look, you watch. I do it again." He moved the crab three times in a circular clockwise motion, and then repeated the same, anti-clockwise, two more times. Gently, he placed the crab on its back and there it lay, perfectly still with both claws pointing at the sky.

"Seriously, that's unbelievable, Till."

"You no kick bucket, okay. Crab wake up and very angry. They run, run," Till knew from experience.

A tall man with jet-black hair was striding up the short pier and stopped just short of *Thin Lizzy*'s stern. For the last fifteen minutes, he'd been observing their movements and knew the twins were alone with just the small Asian man. In near perfect Queen's English, he addressed Abigail. "Lovely day. Seems to me the crab are in plentiful supply."

Till turned, "We cook spicy *poo*, you want to eat?"

Abigail now noticed the scar down one side of his chin, and she remembered her sister mentioning the Korean man with the scar.

Before she could answer, he slipped out a handgun with a long barrel. The Jindeugi jumped down to the outer deck. "Upstairs, now, the both of you." The Jindeugi prodded Abigail in the back while they negotiated the internal stairs. He pulled a pack of plastic ties from his rear pocket and zipped one around both Till and Abigail's wrists and ankles, then forced them back down on the lounge. "Now, let's go find your sister, shall we? And please, Miss Bishop-Price, don't make me need to gag you."

Evina was soon being forced at gunpoint towards the spiral staircase to join her sister and Till on the three-seater couch. The Jindeugi made himself right at home, grabbing a bowl of fruit and bottled water as he passed through the galley.

"You're the bastard who shot Bob, aren't you? At least tell me your name," Evina snarled.

"I have many names, just like your friends. You should really be more selective regarding the company you keep, Mrs Bishop-Joiner."

Kelly was next to arrive. He propped at the edge of the pier with two over-flowing brown paper shopping bags held in his arms. The tide was out, and *Thin Lizzy* was sitting low in the water. He yelled out, "Till, give us a hand, will you, these bags are bloody heavy?" Then he crouched down on his haunches and balanced both bags on the pier, before jumping down to the deck. "There's never anyone around when you need them." Kelly shifted the first bag over the gap between the boat and pier, careful not to rip it open.

"Till's preoccupied," a voice from behind spoke. "Grab your shopping and move it upstairs," the Jindeugi ordered.

Kelly turned suddenly. "You... the man opposite Paddy's... the shooter." He didn't anticipate this.

Kelly was told to sit on the floor. The Jindeugi threw the first plastic tie and ordered Kelly to secure his ankles, and then he inserted the end of a second tie into its zip-lock and handed it over. "Around your wrists, then pull it tight with your teeth." Kelly did what he was told. The Jindeugi leant down and pulled hard on the loose ties. The plastic squeezed Kelly's wrists to the point it formed a white band.

"You and the small Thai man, I have no knowledge of who you are or what your connection is with the other three members of this merry little band, but it will be irrelevant. Tell me, Mrs Bishop-Joiner, I want to know? What is it that's so important you would spend ten years of your life pursuing?

Was it worth your marriage? Not that he was a good man, anyway. That whore your husband was shacked up with was not the first. Whatever it is that you wish to reveal to the world has a lot of very powerful people extremely nervous. The same people I worked for have access to unimaginable resources and the resolve to follow this through to its inevitable end. And you! You are just one associate professor, alone and with a moral compass that will lead you blindly to an early grave. Did you ever take the time to think this through to its grand finale?"

"You don't know anything about me or what I do. Not everyone is hell-bent on the destruction of human life. You're nothing but a cold-hearted killer. I want to prolong life and ease suffering to the people that can least afford it," Evina shot back.

"Very profound, indeed. You kill one person, they call it murder and you go to jail. Kill a million, and they bestow upon you the Nobel Peace Prize. If you want to find the real criminals, don't bother looking inside a jail cell. The Kremlin, the White House and the boardrooms of the corporate world, that's the cloak they hide behind. You don't vote in a president, Mrs Bishop-Joiner, he is auctioned off to the highest political donor. The pharmaceutical industry alone donated over five hundred million dollars to political campaigns throughout the democratic world last financial year.

"The American gun lobbyists—this firearm I hold in my hand and the thirteen bullets inside. Ask yourself this—who provides the finance for the factories that make these weapons? Who decides it's time for a good old-fashioned war so they can off-load their stockpile of ammunition and resupply? Not presidents or prime ministers. Your own country has been to war many times, and for what? An ideal based on untruths, distortions with an unquenchable thirst for more power. The almighty dollar is a powerful motivation. Wars have been started over less."

"Democracy might not be perfect, but until a better system is found, it's all we got, I'm afraid," Kelly spoke up.

"It only takes one person to make a stance—to make a difference," Evina added.

"And you have decided that will be you. How do you feel about that, Abigail? Do you share your twin sister's resolve?" the Jindeugi questioned.

"You said, *'worked for'*. Past tense," Abigail pointed out to the Jindeugi.

"I am fully converse in the English language, Miss Bishop-Price. I studied at Cambridge and Duntroon for many years."

"Did your conscience suddenly get the better of you?" Abigail asked in a patronising tone.

"The man that is about to join us, do you think that he and I are so different? Be careful when you cast that first stone, ladies." The Jindeugi stood and walked over to a window. "Excuse me. I think our last guest is about to arrive."

Stone jumped the short distance from the marina to the open deck and landed on the balls of his feet with a hushed *thud*. He noticed a tub full of crabs lying on their backs looking like they might be working on a suntan and thought that was a little weird while sliding the glass galley door open. The Jindeugi stepped out from behind the fridge with his gun arm raised. "It's nice to see you without your helmet, Mr Stone. The others await your arrival upstairs." He waved the silencer to indicate he wanted Stone to lead the way. Stone walked the final stair and looked on in astonishment.

"Any chance of a refund, Jack ...?"

Chapter·30

THE MINUTE TANYA and Narley arrived back at the Carnarvon Hotel, Tanya placed a call to Clancy Thornton.

His mobile rang while he was stripping down an old windmill that still supplied water to the two main water tanks on Boolathana Station. Clancy couldn't believe what his ears were hearing, as Tanya gave him a blow-by-blow description explaining the bizarre chain of events.

"Are they boat people, is that what the cops are saying? Crikey, they must have been hammered during that storm that swept through the other night. Lucky to be alive. And Colin—what would they want with him?"

"None of us can figure this out, Clancy."

"Don't worry, Tanya. We'll find the bastards. Leave it with me, and I'll call you back."

"Clancy, can you send a couple of vehicles to pick up all our gear at Bush Bay? It's strewn all over the place," Tanya asked.

"I'll do better than that, Tanya. I'll organise a rig travelling down from Karratha to stop in and grab the lot. How are you getting home?"

"I want to stay and keep an eye on, Cooley. And I don't think Narley wants to leave me alone, so we're fine for now. But thanks for asking, Clancy."

Clancy hung up his mobile and walked into the kitchen. He looked at the big wall-mounted clock and noted the time was only 5:00 P.M. Still bolted on the opposite wall was the old Bell party line phone that was all you had when his parents worked the station property. The primitive Bell multi-party line was a communal service line. A local loop telephone circuit shared by multiple telephone service subscribers in a continuous line that connects every farmhouse, station property and whatever else is built in the outback. You can pick up the single earpiece, give the old handle a few cranks and have a conversation with anything from one, to over twenty neighbours at the same time. Clancy blew the dust from the small speaker attached to the main unit and gave the handle a couple of solid turns.

Macy Parker was already talking to her closest neighbour, Bronwyn, and she was waiting for Lisa to finish making a cuppa. Tom Hawkins listened in and rang his two brothers on Gnarloo Station, and they relayed the details to the Munyard twins, who were talking with Rosey and Helen, in Monkey Mia. The bush telegraph came to life and within the hour, just about every person from Geraldton in the south to Carnarvon in the north, was now fully aware of Colin's kidnapping, and things started to happen very quickly.

Sheik Aris was seated in the passenger's front with Aditya Sukato currently on drive duties while Waluyo Mayadi slept across the width of the back seat. Colin was in the only spot he could be, with his wheelchair strapped on to the two rails that extended to the electric hoist at the rear. His role was to be a guide and offer directions first back to the main road and then the long haul to Perth along the North West Coastal Highway. Colin's functioning brain was working feverishly, and his track record as a bushman to think his way out of a sticky situation was part of his character. His very life would now surely rest with his ability to turn things in his favour. His best weapon was he was a local lad, born and bred, and he knew the lay of the land better than most.

Sheik Aris' first instructions were to his two accomplices, who were hand-picked for this very assignment because of their English-speaking skills. All future conversations were to be in the infidel's native language as a precaution to be ready. If the time arrived, they would need to order fuel, food and water. Most of their worldly possessions were lost at sea when they were battered by the tail end of an Indian Ocean storm.

Colin leaned to one side and checked the speedo. The Toyota *Land Cruiser* was equipped with a V8, but they were crawling along at just over 70 kph whereas the speed limit was 110 kph, which basically meant you add another 20 k's to that. That was both good and bad. The good being if a local cop passed by, he would notice the slow speed and maybe pull the vehicle over to tell them to keep up with the traffic flow, and the other bad reason was fast approaching from their rear at about 120 kph. "You might want to speed up, pal," Colin advised the driver.

The Sheik turned and faced Colin, smiling through his stained teeth. "So we can attract the attention of your highway patrol units? I don't think so." He wanted it known that he was no fool. "Keep driving, Aditya."

A bright light started to appear in the rear vision mirror like a Jumbo Jet was about to land. Aditya bent his head and was almost blinded by the glare that filled his large driver's side mirror. The Sheik turned and gazed out the rear window with his mouth wide open. "What in God's name is that?"

"You're about to find out real soon, and it's a hell of a lot quicker than any camel you've ever ridden, mate," Colin enjoyed explaining.

Across the front of an incoming Big Mack prime mover was a blue-tinted stone deflector with the CB radio call sign, 'Rocket Rod', scrolled in bright gold lettering. The two trailing bogeys were meandering like a gargantuan grinding metal snake as Rocket Rod thundered down Highway One listening to the classical sounds of Kenny Rogers reverberating through his surround sound Pioneer stereo. He was singing along to *The Gambler*, tapping the wheel with his fingers and imagining Dolly Parton sharing his cabin on this lonely stretch of highway. Suddenly a slow-moving vehicle appeared from the shimmering haze of his spotlights. He lowered his high beam connected to the four quartz halogen driving lights attached to the cast alloy bull-bar that's designed to knock a stray emu or any misguided wild donkeys to the side of the road like a bowling pin and pulled hard right on the wheel.

The driver's side front wheel left the hard bitumen surface and was soon followed by the remaining eighteen, 20-inch duel-axle dolly wheels spitting rocks and gravel like an erupting volcano. A thick dust cloud formed and blocked what little light there was from the waning moon to the west. The long-wheelbase *Land Cruiser* started to shake and shift sideways like it was caught in a wind tunnel. The driver was blinded and white-knuckled the wheel while offering a solitary prayer to Allah. The noise of rubber, steel and the turbocharged V8 diesel engine, rambling past at lightning speed, drowned out any further conversation, and red dust started spewing in through the open front windows.

Colin knew enough to close his eyes and mouth. The man in the rear wasn't sleeping anymore. He sprang up like he'd just been jabbed in the arse with a cattle prod and thought they were under attack. He watched in horror as seemingly endless rows of red and orange trailer lights slowly pulled past and continued down Highway One like a motorised tornado. The Toyota had slowed to under 40 kph and was heading straight for a ditch on the opposite side of the road.

"Sweet mother of God, what was that?" the Sheik screamed while the 4wd veered sharply to the left to stay on the hard surface.

"May Allah protect us from this devil," Mayadi prayed from behind.

"He won't do you much good against one of those, mate. Lucky for you, the real big road-trains only work the inland roads. Those buggers can be a real hand-full to get around sometimes," Colin thought they should all know.

Mayadi then asked, "Sheik Aris, why do they have trains on the road in this country?"

"Aditya, quickly, speed up to 110 kph for Allah's sake before we are all killed, and someone, please hand me a bottle of water," the Sheik ordered, visibly shaken. The three new arrivals to the Land Down Under began clearing the thick film of northwest dust that covered them like a bad suntan.

The Sheik took some time to settle his nerves while attempting to locate a signal on his cell phone. Colin laughed from the rear.

"Why do you laugh? You think this funny?" the Sheik grumbled. He was still on edge.

"I laugh watching you trying to get a signal out here in the middle of the W.A. scrub. You ever heard of Telstra?"

"You have a charger, I need a GPS." The Sheik opened the glove compartment and started to rummage through the contents. He pulled out a pair of small binoculars and a wallet. He flipped it open, then asked, "Who is this pretty lady—your wife? Perhaps you need to consider her welfare, Mr Colin Gibson from Sunset Beach in Geraldton. Her future may be determined on our safe arrival in Perth," the Sheik smirked over his shoulder.

The lights of the Overlander Roadhouse could be seen illuminating over the shortened horizon. The Sheik asked Colin, "What are these lights?"

"It's a fuel stop. Toilets, food and many people," Colin answered, truthfully.

Three Irish back-packers, Liam, Riddock and Kean, had previously decided to hire a car on the W.A. leg of their trip of a lifetime, to travel around Australia after reading the travel advice issued by the Australian Government website. Only recently an English couple had been abducted on the road between Adelaide and Alice Springs. She somehow managed to escape and hide before being picked up by a passing road train. The boyfriend's body, to this day, has never been found.

After just passing through a police roadblock, fifty kilometres south at the Billabong Roadhouse and Tavern, the whole place was bubbling with curious travellers stopping for fuel while they gawked in curious fascination from the small tavern next door at the hub of heightened activity as the police numbers began swelling. And now the Department of Immigration had just arrived to join in the circus. Kean pulled into the quieter Overlander Roadhouse, farther up the highway and stopped at a fuel bowser next to a long-wheelbase 4wd.

"You fill up the tank, while Riddock and I go take a piss, then we'll see you inside." Liam then asked, "Are you hungry?"

"I'll order my own bloody food, thanks all the same. Go on then," Kean answered in his almost undecipherable native Irish accent.

"Have it your own way. You need to lighten up a wee bit, Kean."

"Faawk me, Evan. Those bloody cops thought it would be okay to sift through all of our backpacks and throw our shit about. Do we look like three bloody refugees who just arrived by boat? I mean—come on, seriously?"

"Don't forget to ask for a receipt. Tomorrow we'll be in Coral Bay and all will be forgotten," Evan assured his angry university roommate, as he headed for the cafeteria.

The Sheik's eyes narrowed. He knew a roadblock was a distinct possibility, and now it was time to make good use of their kidnap victim. He rattled off some instructions in his native tongue. While Aditya Sukato was refuelling, Waluyo Mayadi slid out the rear door and leant against the *Land Cruiser*'s spare tyre, pretending to study a map. Kean tightened the fuel cap and made his way inside to pay for the fuel. Mayadi folded his map and opened the rear door to the Hertz rental. Inside was an army-green backpack. He leaned inside the driver's window and flipped the boot release. Within thirty seconds, three backpacks were now hidden from plain sight behind Colin's wheelchair. The Sheik turned his head to face Colin. "How do we bypass this roadblock?" He was waving the picture of Tanya as a gentle reminder of the consequences if he attempted to deceive them.

Colin was already one chess move ahead of the game. "The only way around is through the station roads. Tamala, and then the Murchison. Turn around and head back up the highway and then chuck a left, following the Useless Loop Road, west."

The Sheik followed Colin's instructions. As soon as they were far enough away from the main highway, he ordered the 4wd to pull over at a rest stop where the large federal government-sponsored sign stated that Shark Bay was now recognised as a World Heritage area. They removed their long white robes including the faleela vest worn under the kandura and discarded the loose-fitting sirwals then re-dressed in the stolen jeans and T-shirts with a waist-cut denim or leather jacket each before stuffing their old Arab clothing tightly into the three backpacks and stashing them behind some low-lying mulga bushes.

"Where does this road lead to? I know we are heading west. These stations you talk about, I want to head for Perth, and that is south," the Sheik demanded of Colin.

"West first, then south along the coastal track through Kalbarri," Colin answered again, truthfully.

The sound of a small single-engine plane could be heard buzzing from the north-east. Soon Colin would need to power up his wheelchair and set the wheels in motion to lead these three terrorists into what was hopefully his well-planned trap.

Chapter-31

THE JINDEUGI stepped past Kelly, who was still sitting with his arse on the deck as Stone surveyed the saloon for a way out of this predicament. The North Korean emptied the loaded chamber and thumbed the lever of his weapon to safety mode, then placed the barrel into the palm of his hand and handed it to Stone—butt first. Five sets of eyes looked on in total bewilderment.

"My name is Duckhwan Toa. I am a North Korean national and a retired major general in the North Korean People's Army. I wish to hand you my weapon, and I seek political asylum within Australia. I have but one condition, and that is you guarantee my sister's safety and fast-track her refugee status to full Australian citizenship." Then he sat back down in the big chair.

Stone dropped the magazine into his open hand to check it was still full. He reinserted the clip and flipped the safety off. He raised the barrel end and pointed it at the Jindeugi. "Stand up and turn around. Place both hands above your head." Stone padded him down from head to toe and pulled from the Korean's rear pocket the remaining ties. "Lower your hands and place them out in front, fully extended, then turn around slowly." Stone slipped on a tie and closed the zip-lock, tight. He shouldered Toe back into the skipper's chair, then turned and sliced the plastic restraints from each person's hands and feet.

Kelly stood straight up. "Get out of my chair, you prick." He grabbed the Jindeugi by the scruff of his neck and was about to dump him unceremoniously onto the deck.

Evina's head was still coming to grips with what just happened. With thoughts of Barnacle Bob reverberating inside her current angered state of mind, she leapt up, clenched her fist into a tight ball and punched the Jindeugi in the face. "You bastard, that's for shooting an innocent old man and for trying to do the same to my sister and me," she vented in a threatening tone.

Duckhwan Toa was startled. He dipped his head and licked his bleeding lip. "I ended a man's life that was already taken. He side-stepped a slow and painful death from mesothelioma, and his family will be the beneficiaries of an insurance policy that did not cover a pre-existing illness. I did him a favour."

Stone stepped between Evina and the retreating North Korean. Evina was feeling the pain of the lusty blow on her hand while shaking it as she turned to face Abigail. "Good bloody job, Evina. I didn't know you had it in you."

"He had it coming," she answered her twin.

Till raced back down the stairs yelling in a slightly distressed state, "*Poo* die for sure."

Abigail was now picturing herself accepting the position of lead editor at The Daily Telegraph. *What a story this will be. Maybe even syndication? Oh, yeah, baby*, she silently rejoiced.

Stone addressed the retired major general, "You'll be taken aboard the Navy frigate anchored out there in the bay. After that, you're not my problem."

"You and I, Stone, we tread water in the same shit-filled pool—and for what? So the next president or prime minister can repeat the mistakes of his predecessors. It never ends until each man decides one day to pull the pin—finished. My sister's safety is a deal-breaker. I have intimate knowledge of the North Korean military capabilities, but I want asylum in Australia. I don't trust the Americans."

"Well, I've got news for you. Your sister is no longer being held in Australian custody. Yesterday, she was transferred to a private facility. You might want to rethink your strategy about trusting the Australian Government. They all paddle in the same river of shit, I can assure you," Stone answered.

"I don't believe you. I spoke with Mi-sun via a webcam only two days ago."

Stone unfolded the Federal Order and waved it in front of the Jindeugi's face. "Read it for yourself."

Duckhwan Toe's zygomatic arched-shaped eyes widened under his flattened nose bridge. The confidence he'd previously displayed seemed to slowly sap from his drawn facial expression.

"Lucky for you, I know where she's being held," Stone taunted his adversary.

"The Geulaendeu Maseuteo and his e'prentis." The words slid from the Jindeugi's mouth like a foul taste.

"The who?" Stone asked.

"The Grandmaster and the Doje; his half-brother. This facility you say my sister is being held, do you mean the casino?"

"What do you know about the old casino?"

"That's their headquarters, the base of the entire Anomura operation."

"What is there operation? What do these people actually do, apart from hiring you to assassinate innocent people?"

"What Western democracy fails to comprehend is you plan ahead using a timeline that is directly related to the term of an elected government or leader, perhaps four or five years. These people, together with their Islamic fanatics, work in decades and centuries. This casino, their HQ—I have been inside, I know the layout. We need to find my sister."

"What's this, *we*?" Stone reiterated.

"Stone, the enemy of *my* enemy is my ally. Today we find ourselves in an unusual situation." The Jindeugi then asked, "Do you have a family?"

Tobias immediately thought of Felicity. She was the closest person he had to a living relative. His life didn't include a wife, kids, and a house on a quarter-acre block. The great Australian dream was not meant for the likes of his kind. "You're not going anywhere, Toa, except to spend some time inside the brig on board the frigate anchored up in the bay."

"You need me more than you think, Stone," the Jindeugi replied with renewed confidence.

"I work alone. Give me a hand Jack to remove this traitor from your yacht, will you?" Stone answered.

"I can help you reveal the leak within your organisation," Toa quickly offered.

Stone propped, he looked over towards Kelly, "Give us a minute, will you?" He turned and faced the twins. "That also includes you two. This man and I need to talk alone."

"Fine by me," Evina replied gruffly. "Things are a bit on the nose around here, anyway. I think I'll take a shower."

"I'm bored shitless already," Kelly spoke next. "I've got a boat to run, and a couple of thousand kilometres of dangerous ocean to navigate safely plus the sisters' welfare to consider. Good riddance to both of you." He glanced out his port-side window and could see the fuel boat about to pull alongside. At the same moment, Ed was strutting up the pier in his Sunday best, and a Navy tender was also heading towards the marina with four men and an officer on board.

"I think it's time to leave you two alone to discuss your differing ideologies together. I'll be down below. Tobias, time to cough up that special Visa Card, old mate," Kelly reminded his paying guest while he followed the twins down the stairs.

Stone waited until the saloon was clear and turned to face the North Korean. "All right, speak. You have my full attention, Toa. What do you know about a mole?" Stone asked with more than a curious interest.

"What is it you Westerners like to say—you scratch my back, and I'll scratch yours? My sister first, Stone, and only then will I reveal who this traitor is in your midst. A person, we are both acquainted with, I can assure you."

Ed jumped on board *Thin Lizzy* and leant a hand to secure the fuel boat. Kelly filled the starboard tank first, then reeled out the hose to reach the port cap. Then after pumping 3,600 litres, and with an amount of $2088.00 appearing on the rusted meter, Kelly passed over Stone's black ops, ASIO-supplied Visa Card.

The fuel boat skipper swiped the card and waited. "Sorry, mate, this says it's declined," the old salt informed Kelly while chewing on a toothpick.

"Swipe it one more time, will you?"

The boat captain ran the card a second time and looked at Kelly with an expression that needed no confirmation.

"Hang on a minute, and I'll get my own card." *Stone, I'm going to throttle that bastard.* Kelly called out up the stairwell as he grabbed his MasterCard from Till. "Tobias, get your arse down here now, we seem to have a small monetary issue to deal with."

The Jindeugi finished his proposal. Stone looked at him and shook his head, "Well, that's all well and good, Toa, except, personally I think you're full of shit. I don't need you now or anytime soon. The commander of the *Ballarat* is pulling up as we speak."

"What about my sister?" he pleaded in a last-ditch effort to sway Stone's mind.

"If she turns up, your sister will be safe. I'm an Australian, Toa. We don't read the same handbook as you bloody North Koreans."

The Navy tender berthed and two sailors dropped a large canvas bag down onto the marina. The commander formally introduced himself to Kelly, "Lieutenant Commander Scott Larson." He and Kelly exchanged a firm handshake. "I'm looking for, Tobias Stone. I believe he may be on board."

"You're not the only one, Commander. He's on his way down, now—or he'd better be." Kelly was less than impressed.

297

Stone appeared on the rear deck. "Jack, what's up? Hang on a minute while I speak with, Commander Larson."

Two minutes later, Ed was walking back to his marine business, counting the cash after settling his bill with Kelly when Stone caught him up. "Hey, Ed, you got a minute? I need a favour," Stone asked.

"Always got time for an old Navy man. What is it you need?"

Kelly was waving the Visa Card when Stone finally made his way back to the berthed yacht. The Navy tender was heading back to the HMAS *Ballarat* with the Jindeugi under armed guard sporting a set of handcuffs.

"This is useless, Tobias, declined two times. Someone doesn't like you."

"Fucking, Jones, that double-crossing son of a bitch. This is not going to end well for him. You know I'm good for it, old mate." Stone lifted one end of the Navy bag. He looked at Kelly, "Are you just gonna stand there, give us a bloody hand? Then we need to talk—in private."

"I must be getting soft with age," Kelly said.

"Time to harden the fuck up again. You owe me one if I remember—Cambodia—ring any bells, Special Warfare Officer Phil Kelly? You're not MIA right now, and from where I'm standing, you don't look like your KIA either, so, time to go to work."

Chapter-32

THE MERCEDES-BUILT Evo-31 was a front-lift loading refuse truck, built to collect waste from large commercial sites. As it rolled down Golf Course Road, Ed was at the wheel, and the only other two occupants were hidden from view in the collection bin. Ed had been kind enough to hose it out before Stone and Kelly took up their positions, armed with standard SASR small arms and in full combat dress. Both men were cradling the AuSteyr F88 IW assault rifle. This weapon boasted a fixed barrel and bolt catch release with the 1.5 magnified optical sights inside the carry handle. The air-cooled, gas-operated magazine-fed assault rifle was capable of both, semi-automatic—short three to four bullet bursts or full-auto if you needed to deal with multiple targets.

Stone always carried his Browning 9mm, but Kelly grabbed from the Navy kitbag a Heckler & Koch USB with the mechanical recoil reduction system. It was lightweight and easier to handle in close combat.

Stone's phone vibrated as he pulled it from his top pocket and looked at the caller ID: Emma Peel. Kelly looked on and just shook his head.

Stone placed it to his ear.

"Is that you, John Steed?" Felicity opened with.

"Jesus, Felicity, just give me an update."

"Do you want the whole shooting match or just a quick revision?"

"Anomura, what did you find out?"

"They're very nasty people, and their tentacles reach out to a host of dodgy dealings. It's headed by two half-brothers;

one from North and the other from South Korea. That Federal Order the detention centre received, came from the Russell Offices, in Canberra. That is HQ for the Admiralty and . . ."

"I know who else shares that building, Miss Peel. Go on," Stone interrupted.

"Well, it seems they have been financing the arrival of certain refugees and fast-tracking their due-process to the release point into the Australian community. I have found over thirty-seven anomalies, so far—and I'm sure there'll be more. It seems to me, they're waiting for a final person to head the entire operation. All I have is they refer to this man as, the Sheik. They talk about a 'last brick in the wall', but I have no idea what that is."

"All right, Felicity. We may have access to more intel on that shortly."

"You sound like you're in a 44-gallon drum, I can hear an echo. Emma Peel, over and out."

Stone cast a look over at the shadowy outline of Kelly.

"Who is, Felicity?" Kelly murmured.

"The closest thing I have to a daughter. We need to deal with these men with extreme prejudice, Jack. Do you get the picture?" Stone emphasised.

Kelly nodded his head and checked the safety was off. "I still can't believe I let you talk me into this."

"Jack, you're still a serving member of the ADF, a part of an elite team, don't fucking forget the Tiger Force. Stop your crying and get your shit together. Just like old times."

The sound of the air brakes slowing the Mercedes truck caused the spitting gravel under the dual rear wheels to quieten. Ed pulled up to the front gate, lowered his driver's side window and entered the four-digit pin number. A CCTV camera turned slowly on its mount and stopped. Ed smiled. A voice sounded from a small speaker. "You were here earlier today, why do you need to return?"

"Arr, the front forks on the lifter blew a hydraulic hose, and we had to cancel emptying the bins. Don't want all those food scraps starting to stink out the place. I'll be in and out in no time flat," Ed answered like he was reading from a script.

"Make it snappy then, there'll be someone waiting at the rear of the building."

"Roger that."

The gate slid open, and Ed drove through, then turned left and followed the building perimeter to the side of the plant room. An armed guard was unlocking the padlock when Ed arrived. He watched as the guard swung the two pressed steel doors open then took up his spot, leaning against a six-course fast-brick-wall that housed the two skip bins. The two front forks slid into each side sleeve, and the bin lifted into the air above the roof of the cabin. The rear refuse lid slid open to swallow its incoming load. Stone and Kelly pressed their bodies hard against the rear of the compressor wall while the dozen or so commercial-strength kitchen waste bags were emptied. Ed gave the control a few shakes, then paused. Stone and Kelly moved like grease lightning and crawled inside the empty suspended bin.

Ed eased the controls and replaced the skip back to its original position, then slowly reversed the truck. The guard shouldered his semi-automatic and stubbed out his half-smoked cigarette while he shut both doors with the padlock still in his hand. A yellow muzzle flash was all Ed saw from the end of Kelly's silenced Heckler & Koch as the guard slid to the ground.

Ed's last job was to provide cover for the hundred metres of open ground to reach the staff quarters. Both men ran alongside the slow-moving garbage truck, then peeled off and took up their positions. Stone glanced inside through an open window and was shocked. It resembled a scene from a sick movie. A few half-dressed and some other naked women were systematically being sexually abused by the four off-duty guards. Open bottles of liquor were scattered about the room. Two young girls were sobbing and crying in the corner, dreading their turn with the Korean rapists. *Their friggin' refugees.* Stone then looked at Kelly and indicated four fingers:

two right, two left. He followed that with a friendlies sign. Kelly nodded. Stone silently counted down with his raised hand, three-two-one. Kelly eased the door open while crouching and fired off two perfect shots. Stone stood at the open window and tapped his first guy in the middle of his forehead and the other with two to the heart. It was all over in a matter of seconds.

"All of you get dressed, now," Stone conveyed in controlled anger hoping the women understood then ran back outside. Ed was reversing the truck back up to make his three-point-turn before heading back out the way he'd arrived. Stone tapped the driver's door twice with his open hand. "Stop here a second, Ed, and open up the passenger door. We've got some outgoing friendlies."

Ed swept the crap lying on his front seat to the floor to make way for the three, scared out of their minds, battered and bruised Asian women. Within a minute, Ed was on his way back towards the main gate with three new arrivals to the shores of Christmas Island. "Welcome to the bloody lucky country," Stone hushed angrily under his breath.

Stone indicated for Kelly to follow him. They stopped at a reinforced rear fire door that looked like it hadn't been opened in years. "You're up, Jack." Kelly unfolded a strip of primed detonating cord filled with pentaerythritol tetranitrate which acts like an exothermic torch to vaporise a hole large enough to access the door from inside. He secured it around the bronze lock, then fired the fuse. The white-hot strip ignited, reaching a temperature of 140 degrees Celsius as both men stood to one side. The smoke trail blew away on the breeze, and Kelly pushed his gloved clenched fist through the burnt-out hole and opened the door-wide fire exit handle from inside.

Two sets of concrete emergency exit stairs with a tubed metal railing greeted them on the other side; one went up, the other down to the basement and loading bay. Stone had studied the blueprints and indicated up first with his thumb. He eased a side exit door open enough to get eyes on two guards seated inside the main entry doors. Together, they both looked like they were about to nod off. Another two guards occupied the space behind the old reception area with both eyes glued to a flat-screen TV with their backs facing a row of smaller CCTV monitors. The buzzing noise of the intercom sounded as Ed approached the exit. A single guard leant over and pressed the gate control.

Stone unclipped a stun grenade, while Kelly did the same with a smoker. Stone locked eyes with his ex-Tiger Force sniper. With fingers and hand movements, he indicated two bad guys at three o'clock and the same at nine o'clock. He held three fingers up and counted back a second time. Stone pushed the door open, and both men entered in crouching positions. Stone released the pin, counted to four, stood and lobbed the grenade into the generous reception space. Kelly rolled his smoker like a lawn bowl towards the front doors then moved to his left.

The reception area lit up like a giant flashbulb for a couple of seconds. The percussion wave lifted both guards from their seats, slamming their bodies hard against a row of waist-high filing cabinets. Stone edged his way towards the countertop, then leaned over and fired two rounds, one into each body that now resembled a pair of unloved rag dolls. Then the smoker started spinning thick, acrid smoke in a 360-degree circle. Before Kelly could find some cover behind a set of three comfortable cushioned chairs, suddenly he felt like he'd been hit by a golf ball. First one, then a second pounding *thump* to his chest. His body was propelled backwards, and he stumbled before sliding along the polished floor, cracking his head against a clay flowerpot. A second and third round of fire whistled past above his head. *Fuck, not again*, was his first thought.

Stone was the first to return some covering fire into the haze of thick smoke. Kelly was sucking in some deep breaths as he felt for his kevlar vest. Still seated, he raised his AuSteyr and let rip, emptying half his clip in short bursts. Two men came stumbling out of the thickening haze, bleeding and very pissed-off. Stone fired two more short rounds and watched both guards drop. He looked over at Kelly, "You okay?"

Kelly replied while looking at the two holes under the right side pocket of his disruptive pattern combat uniform, "I don't fucking know. Do these things actually work?"

"You're alive, aren't you?"

"You make a good point."

"You'll feel it tomorrow. It hurts like hell for a day or two. It's been a while, Jack. You want to sit on my six, just in case?"

"I can deal with a bit of discomfort, but please, no comedy." Then Kelly asked while in a world of brain-numbing pain, "Where to now?"

Stone led the way to what was once a set of private lift doors. He pressed the *up* button. The lift stopped, and the doors opened. "We going up?" Kelly gestured.

"Not the way you might think," Stone answered. He stepped inside. "Give me a leg up."

Kelly interlocked his hands and hoisted Stone above waist height to the suspended ceiling where he pushed open a panel and crawled through, head first. Seconds later, his head popped back out. "Press the button marked *Admin* and then why don't you join me?" he smirked back with his arm outstretched. Both men felt the elevator car rising as they remained perched alongside the lift's sheave while the steel cabling wound itself towards the mechanical lifting drum above with the counterweight moving in the opposite direction. The lift stopped, and both doors slid open. Both the two Sumo wrestlers Stone had seen earlier that day stepped inside and pressed *Foyer.* The lift descended one level, and the doors opened a second time. The two men were presented with a scene of total devastation. They both instinctively positioned their weapons ready to fire and cautiously stepped out. The lift doors closed. Kelly and Stone dropped silently through the removable panelling to the floor and pressed *open doors* with their gun arms raised. Sumo one and two didn't even get to see who fired the two shots into the back of their thick necks as they fell heavily to the floor. "Now we're going back up," Stone suggested casually.

"How many more?" Kelly asked.

"Maybe four, don't know for sure, but we're bound to find out." Stone stepped back inside the elevator. He slid out his seven-inch-long KA-BAR knife, then pried the control panel from the wall. The top button was marked *Private*, with a security keyhole positioned to one side. He firstly isolated and then cut both wires before telling Kelly to hold the button down while he made sweeping contact with both the red and brown wires. "Get ready to hightail it back inside that false ceiling," he told Kelly. A couple of sparks flew, and the lift jolted, then moved. "Let's go." Kelly slid the ceiling panel back in place as the lift ascended to the top floor before coming to a final stop. The sound of the doors opening for the third time was instantly followed by a deafening spread of semi-automatic fire from two waiting guards. Stone ushered Kelly to follow him through a small service door located in the wall of the elevator well. Crawling on all fours, they followed a single file gantry to a point that would place them above and behind the lift doors. The rear of the elevator wall was being pulverised under the relentless fire as it shook on its cables. After emptying their entire clips, the guards looked on in amazement as the smoke cleared. There were no bullet-ridden bodies as expected.

Kelly and Stone dropped through a manhole simultaneously, then body rolled and lay in a prone position. The two guards were still trying to figure out why the lift car was empty. Two shots arrived from behind with a muted body *thud*. Both men keeled-over while collapsing to the floor. Kelly unclipped then checked his magazine while Stone went about confirming both men were indisposed.

"The plans show we follow this corridor to the high rollers room," Stone explained while pointing to his right.

"Only one way to find out." Kelly shouldered his rifle and slid out his Heckler & Koch while approaching another pair of fancy-looking hand-carved wooden doors. He crouched down with his back against the wall while extending his hand towards the centre-mounted doorknob. He looked up at Stone and whispered, "I'm Heckle, and you're Jeckle. Do you remember?"

Stone nodded. *Just like old times*, he smiled back. Now realising how much he'd missed his old Tiger Force teammate.

Kelly fingered the ball-shaped knob anticlockwise while feeling for any resistance. He raised three fingers. Stone stepped out into the corridor, facing the closed doors while standing over Kelly's right shoulder with his rifle poised. Kelly counted down, then swung the door open.

Stone entered first in full commando mode, and what he and Kelly stumbled onto next almost defied belief. The high rollers room was huge and had been converted into a private den of debauchery for personal sexual self-indulgence. There were chains with padded handcuffs hanging off one wall, and a choice of exotic-looking leather whips was self-explanatory. A wooden custom built pleasure chair was placed in the centre of the room with a neat circle cut from the seat, ready for that special moment, fully equipped with wrist and ankle straps.

"Bloody hell," Stone cried out in controlled horror. Kelly stood rigid while trying to absorb the macabre scene he was facing. A mattress big enough to accommodate eight people covered with an oiled-up plastic liner sat on the floor behind a raised Roman bath. Stone dipped his hand in the water. It was still tepid. A camera on a tripod accompanied by some well-placed lighting with reflective umbrellas was set-up on a raised stage next to a small bar lined with half-finished drinks still sitting on the glass top. The whole room reeked of cigar smoke and incense. Stone walked the inside perimeter when a reddish discolouration on the floor caught his eye. He crouched to his haunches and flashed his light. "Dried blood, and lots of it."

Kelly made his way over to where Stone was still crouching. He followed the droplets that ended at the base of a freestanding floor-to-ceiling glass-shelved cabinet full of ornamental pots, jugs and other Asian collectables. He gave it a nudge with his shoulder to see if it might shift. Two large egg-shaped decorative pieces rocked and shattered as they rolled off and hit the floor. "Somehow, I think this whole unit is designed to move."

Stone stepped in closer while Kelly was moving vases and small sculptures attempting to clear some space. "I think there may be a false wall built in behind."

"Here, let me give you a hand with that." Stone shouldered his semi-automatic and stepped to the corner of the antique-style cabinet. "Grab the other end, Jack." Together they both tried to lever it from the wall. A length of steel matching the length of the cabinet supported a set of rubber wheels bolted to the wall above head height. The plaster behind started to crack and peel away. Some electrical wiring became exposed. "Put your back into it. I think it's starting to move." Together, Kelly and Stone took a firm grip with two hands, then heaved with all their combined strength, toppling its entire contents before the complete structure crashed to the floor. "Is that what you're looking for?" Stone was pointing at what looked like a half-sized door with no handle.

Kelly gave it a couple of decent knocks with the back of his knuckles. It felt and sounded like it was made of solid timber. Then he stepped back and booted it with his heel, and it didn't look like budging an inch.

"Fuck this, step back and let the expert take over." Stone let rip with a solid spray from his AuSteyr F88, splintering the wood in a peppering of point-blank fire at a spot where the door handle should have been. Stone lowered his rifle, placed a hand inside the hole and felt for an inside handle. He looked back at Kelly with a blank look on his face.

"Okay, my turn. Now you step back." Kelly ran another length of detcord from top to bottom where he hoped the hinges would be located. "Find a spot behind that Roman bath because this is gonna pop." Kelly tripped the fuse and dived for cover. The resulting crackle and pop of intense white light filled the room with the smell of burning wood as a gaping hole started to appear down one side. The two men waited while the smoke settled. One whole side of the door had just disintegrated. Stone

307

was first to stand while wiping his face clear. After kicking the remains of the door clear, he fired up his Mag-Lite and ventured inside, following a short hallway to another steel-plated reinforced door with no visible external handle.

Kelly looked over Stone's shoulder. "Fuck me. What is it with these people? Give us one of your grenades, Tobias." Kelly taped it to the outside door skin. He pulled the pin, and he and Stone bolted back down the short passageway. Kelly went left while Stone headed for the right side of the room with their backs pressed up hard against the wall. An ear shuddering explosion sucked the air from the short corridor in a reversing vacuum. Kelly counted to ten, then with arms fanning he reentered the short corridor. The door was sort of still intact from the outward-facing blast radius, but severely damaged. The smell that any serving soldier knows only too well started to sift through the shifting cloud of dust and smoke.

Kelly steadied himself and sent the heel of his boot into the centre of the internal locking mechanism. Two more times he needed to apply his best directed Muay Thai foot-fighting skills, to eventually bash it clear until he heard it fall to the floor inside. That smell was becoming more and more obnoxious. Kelly and Stone swapped awkward glances, each reading the other's private thoughts. Kelly pulled his Mag-Lite out and bent down to gain first eyes on what was on the other side of the door. "You're not going to believe this." Kelly addressed Stone, in a tone that suggested he wasn't quite prepared for what he was confronted with. He fought back the urge to dry retch, then reeled backwards.

"Try me." Stone pointed his torch and followed Kelly's lead. "Fuck me, is there no end to the suffering and misery? This is inhumane. What sort of a mongrel person being can do this? Who in God's name are these sick people? They're just bloody kids, for fuck's sake."

"Maybe the reason Duckhwan Toa wants to seek asylum in Australia," Kelly answered with a forlorn look on his scowled face. He was still struggling not to gag. "I can't deal with this shit. I need some clean air. These bastards aren't gonna get away with this. Not on our watch, Tobias. I'm fucking angry now, and that spells big trouble for whoever is responsible for these crimes against humanity." Kelly pushed past. "Come on, we need to get out of here. These bastards have to be long gone by now."

Stone didn't agree. "This place is like a giant maze. This Anomura mob has to be here somewhere—trust me. It's an island. And we need to locate the North Korean's sister."

Kelly was a bit thrown by that last comment. "Sister? You mean, Toa? The same man who tried to eliminate the twins and me—twice?"

"I'm looking at the bigger picture, Kelly. Remember, I'm still on the job. Blue Skies is unfinished. Unlike you, old mate, not all of us have the luxury of deciding when to bail out and go feet up while enjoying the sun and surf in tropical South East Asia."

"You're just pissed off, Tobias, that I had the balls and the moral compass to know the difference between right and wrong. And if what is stacked up inside that bloody room isn't a stark reminder, well then, maybe you just don't get it. Anyway, now is not the time for that conversation. So, why do you think this sister is inside this old casino?"

"Good fucking question. But more importantly, I need the sister to use as leverage to convince Toa he needs to play ball. And don't ask me why."

"I wasn't about to. This is your show, Tobias. I'm just Santa's little helper. I'll meet you at ground level. I mean, this was once a fully operational casino. Maybe there's something down there. Just so you know, I'm using the stairs this time. That lift is a health hazard now."

Stone cleared the air with a waving arm and entered with his own torch reflecting off the cloud of smoke and dust inside. The room looked to be an old prep kitchen with the remnants of what was now an empty cool room with the sliding door lying in two pieces on the floor to his right. Stone noticed a pile of discarded clothes, some cheap imitation children's jewellery together with some shoes, sandals and hair ties. Above that was an angled cast-iron door at waist height. He forced it open to see a trailing wash of blood disappearing down a long chute to a furnace located in the basement. *Jesus bloody Christ.*

He retrieved his mobile and powered it back up, then tapped the camera icon. He reeled off six quick photos of the piled-up mess of disfigured human corpses. Some were only young girls, no more than 12 or 13 years of age, with slice and dice marks covering their entire frail petite-looking bodies. A few of the teenage girls were missing their breasts, carved and hacked clean off, leaving the exposed wounds to fester now full with crawling maggots. The penises of a few of the young boys showed obvious signs of mutilation. *These bastards have been making snuff movies.* Stone fought back his own urge to vomit, remembering not to breathe through his nose. He had a job to do. *Someone is going to pay for this, I guarantee that.*

Stone closed the mangled door as best he could and left the scene of decaying human destruction. For the first time in a very long time, he thought of his Christian upbringing and was angry he couldn't even remember a short, simple prayer to recite. He met Kelly still standing, now looking towards the rear of the high rollers room. He was surveying the wall opposite to where they entered. "Something looks skew-if to me, Tobias. From the lift doors to the end of the building is thirty-four paces. This room is only twenty-eight. I know because I just checked."

Occupying the entire space was the larger than life photographic portrait of the North Korean General Secretary Kim Jong-il, laser-etched onto a mirrored glass backdrop all the while casting his evil eyes over the entire room built for personal pleasure, bondage, human enslavement and cold-blooded murder. Kelly was feeling, with his open palm, the giant-size image of the supreme leader of the Democratic People's Republic of North Korea. He placed a fingertip against the reflective surface and watched as the reflection of his fingernail touched his actual nail. Kelly stepped back towards the pleasure chair and turned slowly. "Stand back." He removed his sidearm and raised his weapon, then fired a single round into the receding sloped head of the North Korean leader. A slight crack appeared above the left eye. He fired another two rounds in rapid succession. Suddenly the entire showpiece shattered and fell to the floor in a shower of mirrored glass shards. Behind was a hidden room with a woman lying on a single bed in a disarranged state. Kelly re-holstered his weapon and stepped his way across a pile of what was the remains of a one-way window and held the woman's head in his hands. Stone looked on in hope while Kelly felt for a pulse. He splashed some water from a water bottle lying on the floor over Mi-sun's face while he gently placed his arms under her frail body and lifted her like she was made of wilting rose petals.

They arrived back in the predominately tinted glass foyer. The smell of cordite hung low in the cool, temperature-controlled air. The four bodies' lay where they fell, bleeding out on the polished floor. Kelly was about to suggest now might be a good time to retrace their steps back to the casino's main entrance where those two cars were parked. Then Mi-sun started to stir with an awakening groan. She shifted her body weight and opened her eyes while still safe in Kelly's arms. "Who are you?" Mi-sun struggled through the dried blood from her swollen lips.

"Australians," Kelly answered. "You're safe now. Your brother, Duckhwan, is waiting for you."

She started sobbing, "They forced me to watch everything... through that window. Those young children, it was pure evil, I don't think I will ever be able to forget." She burst into a full-blown howl and curled into Kelly's awkward embrace. She began to lift her head as Kelly eased her back to the floor with her back supported by the bullet-ridden wall next to the damaged lift doors.

Stone felt he could have almost shed a tear if it wasn't for the morbid images filling his mind of the human toll of stacked bodies, discarded like kitchen waste, still playing havoc with his inner-most emotions.

"Come on, we need to get her back to the *Ballarat*. We're done here," Kelly voiced angrily. He just wanted to get out of this hell hole.

"No—no," Mi-sun summoned the strength. "This way, I'll show you." She pressed the *down* button. The lift creaked and groaned as it slowly descended in what was more than likely going to be its last ride.

Kelly wanted to say, "I for one am definitely not getting inside that death trap."

Mi-sun allowed a knowing smirk to wash over her rounded face. The doors struggled to extend to their fully open position. Mi-sun squeezed her way in. The inside silver aluminium panelling resembled a slice of Swiss cheese. Mi-sun held the emergency stop button down and with her free hand pressed floors one, two and three simultaneously. The back wall of the lift swung open to reveal another small foyer. Kelly forced the front lift door open wide enough for him and Stone to make their way through to the opposite side. "After you, maestro."

Both of them stepped through the awkwardly angled elevator, one at a time as it swayed on an uneven angle. They were now looking at a pair of twelve-foot-high, double glassed doors with another laser-etched image of a red crab stretched across the entire width of each door. Stone checked the clip in his rifle and pushed through first. A large six-sided boardroom table was positioned inside a sunken floor, two steps down. It looked like it was made for the seven dwarfs and was conspicuous under a hanging bronze and purplish-blue-coloured re-creation of a Christmas Island robber crab, with the word Anomura, written in raised gold lettering across the underside of its carapace.

Stone started photographing the entire room in a circular motion. There were white-boards with handwritten graphs and projected financial profits. An aerial photo of the detention centre was on full display, pinned to a corkboard with an assemblage of photos of both young girls and boys with corresponding names alongside. Some had a tick next to their name; others had a big X plastered across the entire photograph.

There might be others? The lucky ones, Stone considered briefly.

A map of Australia with large tracts of land shaded in different colours was pinned on the opposite side. Stone read with a gathering interest the familiar historical name: Sidney Kidman, with all the family's property holdings all highlighted throughout Queensland, the Northern Territory and Western Australia. He ripped it down and folded it into his small pack.

Kelly noticed an enlarged black-and-white photo of a full military parade, with the customary fake, inter-ballistic missiles being towed on their self-loading launchers through the packed, flag-waving streets of the North Korean capital of Pyongyang. It looked like it was slightly askew as it hung from the wall. He walked over and backhanded it off its hook. A safe sat behind in a walled recess. "Anyone know how to crack one of these?" Kelly directed the question towards the only other two people in the room.

Mi-sun answered by walking over to study the make and model. She placed her ear to the safe and slowly turned the tumbler, anti-clockwise.

Stone crossed the room and stood beside Kelly. "What are you looking at?"

He was pointing to a small screen and intercom built into the wall. Kelly grinned. He pressed the power button, and a CCTV camera mounted inside a safe room came to life. The Geulaendeu Maseuteo and his e'prentis, Doje, were seated on a comfortable sofa sipping champagne from a bottle sitting in a free-standing ice bucket. Four other men from what looked to be diverse ethnic backgrounds shared the room off to their immediate right. They didn't look quite as confident as the two smirking Koreans.

"Well, I'll be fucked. Who might you six people be, then?" Stone asked, mixed with sarcasm and pent-up anger. He then asked Kelly, "Can we get them out of there or not?"

The Grandmaster answered the question with unwavering confidence via the intercom. "I am happy to share with you that the casino's old titanium walk-in safe has been converted into a non-penetrable panic room. We have taken the liberty of destroying all incriminating documents, computer hard drives, and any other connection to alleged crimes committed while on Australian soil. We now wait for the arrival and the corresponding protection from the Australian authorities. We are more than willing to be taken into custody and will answer all charges through the Australian legal system." The Doje raised his glass and smiled smugly, "We can afford the best lawyers, and it seems we were right in not laying our trust with, Duckhwan Toa. He is a disgrace to our Supreme Leader and all of North Korea."

"Smart man," Stone commented. "I wouldn't trust any of us, either." Inside, Stone was fuming.

Kelly eye-balled the two Koreans locked in the safe room before addressing the Grandmaster. "We Australians have a tradition called 'cracker night'. Soon you're going to get a first chance to witness what that is—up close and personal, you condescending pricks. This room gets its air from somewhere. You might want to think about that for a few seconds, then, BOOM!" Kelly smirked back.

Stone added, "Actually, it's more like a slow burn before the final explosion. The X-50 Air Grenades are bloody awesome. They just suck all that oxygen right out in a matter of seconds. I used one only last month in Afghanistan—dropped it straight down a cave chimney—fuck—what a mess."

The Geulaendeu Maseuteo and his half-brother swapped unknowing glances before topping up their glasses and raising them into the air. "*Geonbae*," they gestured with the sublime arrogance of somebody in total control. Suddenly the American jumped to his feet and ran towards the camera, yelling, "I want out. I'm an American, you are Australians—we are allies. Get me out of here. I'll take my chances alone. I want some sort of guarantee I will be safe. I am an important businessman with powerful friends in high places. Plus, I have money. More money than you can ever imagine. You might want to think about that for a second or two."

Kelly and Stone swapped glances. "What do ya reckon, Jack?"

"This ain't NATO, you sick bastard. You're on your own, pal. Sometimes, karma is a beautiful thing."

"Couldn't agree with you more, Jack. Sorry, Mr Money Bags, but my old mate here controls the moral compass. You can spend these last minutes countin' your cash."

Stone retrieved a DASALS seeker optic with infrared-guided laser capability. He attached it to the strengthened bulletproof glass and offered a patronising smile towards the six occupants. "Just in case, boys, remember, bunger night, it will be a real hoot. Should go off with a big bang," Stone returned with his own cocksure look.

"Oh-my-God," Mi-sun almost screamed in madcap hysterics from the opposite side of the room. Both Stone and Kelly turned their heads. She was struggling to hold a 375-troy-ounce, 99.5% pure, gold cast bullion in her slender arms. Stone crossed the room and looked inside the open safe. He pulled out three other identical gold bars, each cast with a different country's minting signature on the face. Russia, Japan and Germany.

"I know exactly how I can put these to good use," Stone enjoyed saying before advising everyone, "we need to get the hell out of here." He was about to leave the room protecting the people responsible for so much sadness and human suffering when the flashing red and green diodes from a router sitting on a small ledge high up on a wall caught his attention. A yellow Ethernet cable was connected and the other end disappeared into the featured brickwork. He dropped his weighted pack and shifted an antique Elizabethan cushioned chair, steadied himself and stretched high to disconnect the cable.

Soon Stone was hot on the heels of Mi-sun, while he struggled with the extra weight of the four gold bars as she led the two men through a myriad of underground tunnels. Suddenly she stopped and placed her finger on both lips. "Shoosh, quiet. Do you hear that?" A slight *tap-tap-tap* noise could be heard pinging through the underground plumbing. Stone lay his free hand on the old cast-iron pipe, *dot-dot-dot, dash-dash-dash.* "It's an SOS call. Shit, where does this tunnel lead to?" he asked.

Mi-sun answered, "I only know this is how I arrived here in the middle of the night."

Stone handed Kelly his backpack and told him to wait at the front of the casino. Kelly and Mi-sun kept moving. He threw the backpack into the boot of the limo, then told Mi-sun to stay with the two parked cars and went off in the other direction. Kelly knew what he wanted to do. All he needed to do was find where it was.

Stone reversed and ran back along the tunnel, looking for another exit. It was dimly lit with just a row of 25-watt bulbs hanging every fifty or so feet. He could see the small door they entered through just minutes before.

There's nothing down there, he knew already.

He turned around and slowly started retracing his steps while scanning both sides of the tight tunnel. He stopped when he noticed some soiled boot prints that seemed to be pointing left. Stone climbed over the knee-high plumbing until the beam of his torch highlighted something that looked out of place. He ran both open hands against the rough cement walls. "Bingo! That feels like wood to me." The tapping sound was becoming clearer. Stone crouched down and forced open a small trap door. His light beam caught the reflection of young eyes in a state of frozen fear. Inside were the cringing figures of another eight young Asian girls, huddled tight in the far corner of a dirt-walled room no higher than a man's waist. "English, does anyone speak any English?" Stone's voice was laced with the inner desperation he felt.

A slight crackle from a young voice holding a small screwdriver in her soiled hand answered with a petrified whimper. "Yes, a little."

"My name is, Tobias. I won't harm you. You're all safe now."

Stone's voice was showing the first signs of cracking. He wiped a tear from the corner of his eye with the back of his sleeve. The room remained silent, and no one was game to move. *This isn't working.* "I'm Australian, you know; Crocodile Dundee, throw another shrimp on the barbie . . . Kenny, the koala bear." He was willing to try anything to gain a slither of trust.

"Huh, koala bear?" the timid voice replied. "You Australian?"

"Yep, born and bred, please come now. I want to take you away from the bad people. We need to hurry," Stone pressed.

The shifting sounds of bodies sliding on the dampened soil was a welcome relief. The room was musty, just breathing was a struggle in itself. The first face appeared with the screwdriver still held in the frightened girl's small shaking hand. In a slow shuffle, the remaining girls crawled out of the small space where they had been held for who knows how long with no water and nowhere to relieve themselves. *The mind boggles,* Stone thought.

The SUV and the black stretch limousine were both still parked under the main entrance awning. Stone piled all eight girls into the rear opposite facing seats and pointed to the small fridge with cool bottles of drinking water and a couple of packets of nuts and chips. They shared the meagre offering without dispute.

He turned towards Mi-sun, "Where's Kelly?"

She pointed with her finger, "That way."

Kelly had found exactly what he was looking for. A yellow electrical conduit that exited the plant room was clipped down the eastern wall, then fed into a subterranean two-inch-wide PVC pipe. Kelly placed his back to the wall and lifted his arm like pointing a compass. He followed the imaginary line towards a small cliff edge that overlooked the ocean. He walked over a hundred metres until a slight whirring sound from a set of tired bearings could be heard to his immediate right. He flashed his light until he identified a slight bump in the landscape. Kelly allowed his ears to zero in on the source. Ten metres farther on, two, four-foot-wide exhaust fans were spinning inside their own tubed housing behind a steel-meshed safety screen. One was expelling carbon dioxide while the other was inhaling Co2.

"The air that I breathe," Kelly sang to himself.

Stone arrived then asked, "What the fuck are ya doing? The *Ballarat* can take out the whole casino with one Sea Sparrow."

"Subtle as a sledgehammer like normal, Tobias, plus you'll destroy all the evidence. My idea is much better. Help me find something to stop these two fans."

Stone went searching for a tree or something strong enough to do the job. Kelly could see a small jetty below that was once used by the high-flyers who flocked to the casino resort from the non-gambling Asian countries. Kelly slid down the small incline to the jetty. Tucked away and hidden from view was a small boatshed built on the rock wall side of the beach. Two railway tracks exited a pair of closed doors that followed a direct line into the water. Kelly shouldered his way through a wooden side door, ripping both hinges off, sending the door flying to the ground inside. Staring Kelly in the face, sitting on a slipway with four dolly wheels, was a decent-looking half-cabin 24-foot-long fibreglass boat with two pedestal seats up-front and a fairly new big four-stroke outboard attached. He leaned over the rear transom and shook the two tanks of fuel. They were both full, and the key float was still dangling from the ignition.

He heard Stone come sliding down the hill. Kelly turned to face him, "This is a getaway boat either to Flying Fish Cove or a stashed car that will take a person or persons to the airport."

Stone flashed his light and then walked to the rear of the shed. A steel reinforced door was bolted shut from the inside.

Kelly then said, "These arseholes have a ready-made escape plan." He paused for a moment. "Not anymore, here grab this, Tobias." Kelly handed Stone one of the red plastic 25-litre fuel tanks, then he grabbed the other and started tipping the fuel through the gap in the floorboards. Kelly grabbed a funnel tucked away in the stern of the boat. He placed it inside the tank's open cap, then unzipped his fly and started to take a leak, careful not to miss. Stone caught on real quick and joined in the pissing contest. They placed both tanks back inside and reconnected the fuel line. Kelly looked at Stone. "There, that should do it. They want to take the piss out of us; I think it's only fair we return the favour. Should be just enough fuel to reach deep water."

Stone looked up and to his right, then reached out and pulled an oar down from a roof rafter. He juggled the weight in his open hands. "This should be able to sort those fans out easy enough."

They both scrambled back up the small incline and propped in front of the two extractor fans. Stone counted, "One – two – three," and rammed it into the intake fan with instant results. For good measure, Kelly snapped kicked the oar in two and did the same on the outtake side. "Where did you learn that?" Stone asked.

"The President of God's Garbage bike gang. Him and I are drinking partners now." Then with his best baseball pitch, Kelly unclipped his last smoke grenade, pulled the pin and hurled it down the corrugated iron shaft. The *rattle-rattle* sound slowly faded as it picked up speed and bounced its way to home base. He looked at his watch, "I give 'em two minutes, what do ya' reckon, Tobias?"

"Maybe less, they didn't look to be in peak physical condition."

Both men retreated and prepared for the wait. In less than two minutes, one by one, six men came scurrying out the secured door at the back of the boatshed. The two sea doors suddenly flew open. The Doje was last to step inside the boat, then he pressed a handheld remote, and the four dolly wheels started to reverse down the slipway into the water. A white light came on above the wheel, then the red port and green starboard navigation lights lit up as the motor kicked over the first time. The boat reversed then turned towards the north with the Doje behind the wheel, his Grandmaster seated by his side and the other four passengers were facing one another on the two rear cushioned bench seats.

Stone asked, "What happens next? They might still make it back to land—with or without fuel."

Kelly laughed, "Are you sure you're in the Navy?" Kelly pointed to his left, "That headland reaches out a good two kilometres forming a natural seawall protecting the cove inside. To negotiate that safely at night without radar, they'll need to make a wide berth staying clear of the rocky shoreline. The outgoing tide will do the rest."

Stone and Kelly made their way back to the parked cars with the fading sound of the outboard beginning to misfire in the distance.

Kelly and Mi-sun squeezed into the front bucket seat. Stone turned in the driver's seat and addressed all eight occupants, "Hang on girls. We're all going for a boat ride on a big grey-coloured frigate, VIP all the way to the real Australia." Stone stepped on the accelerator pedal and smoked the rear tyres on the way out, and then he pulled out his phone and pressed redial.

The HMAS *Ballarat* swung gently on her anchor chain as the fast-moving tide turned once again. Commander Scott Larson stood from his chair and answered the incoming call. He faced his XO, "Ready the SASR unit. I will accompany the landing party ashore personally. You have your orders. XO has the bridge."

"Yes, sir. XO has the bridge."

The twin blackened outboards from each of the two rubber landing crafts could be heard skimming over the flat waters as Stone emptied the parked limousine. Ed was patiently waiting by the pier, and he looked like a cat on a hot tin roof. His three passengers were seated on the dock edge with a bucket of River Rooster fried chicken and a two-litre water container. "Ed, you ever consider going into the limo business?" Stone asked, tongue in cheek.

Ed was already eyeing off the all-wheel-drive, stretch Cadillac XTS Epsilon II, four-door sedan with a renewed glint in his business eye. "Mmm, very nice. Why do you ask?"

"Because I think the Navy Special Forces unit about to arrive might appreciate a lift to the detention centre," Stone explained.

Lieutenant Commander Scott Larson, launched himself from the snub bow onto the cement surface and crouched to his haunches to meet the eyes of the tightly packed ring of eight young girls. He turned his attention to Stone, standing to one side and just shook his head in silent disbelief.

"Stone, I have my orders from Admiral Peterson. The North Korean's sister will need to be taken into custody and confined to quarters until we arrive in Fremantle. Chief, escort this woman to the second landing craft."

Stone replied, "Commander. Before we pull anchor, you'll need to send a complete recovery and medical team to the old casino. It's now a crime scene, and will need to be photographed, evidence recorded, bagged and tagged. And I mean everything."

Commander Larson stood and singled out his Chief Petty Officer. "You heard, Chief, let's get a move on, shall we? And advise sickbay we will have eleven patients arriving for urgent medical assistance and tell the cook to prepare some of those Asian rice and noodles he loves to serve so often. We've got some hungry mouths to feed. "

"Yes, sir."

Kelly jumped back aboard *Thin Lizzy*. The twins looked at him sideways, still dressed in his blackened, night combat fatigues.

Evina was first to speak, "We thought you and Tobias were at the pub getting pissed."

"If only. Finish up whatever you're both doing. Stow all your gear, ladies." Kelly looked over at Till, "Grab the bowline, I'll get the stern. We're outa' here. Let's go and find you a good book to read, shall we, Evina?" She returned an acknowledging smile and gave a double thumbs up.

The *Thin Lizzy* crept out of Flying Fish Cove at under 10 knots. Kelly waited until the twins were inside their staterooms, then made a slight course change to the south-east. He expanded his radar sweep to a ten-kilometre-radius. A blip appeared on a heading of 65°. Kelly turned the wheel slightly to the north-west while increasing his speed to 15 knots. Within a couple of minutes, a set of green and red nav lights could be seen bobbing up and down on the small swell about 500 metres to the north. He switched on his roof-mounted halogen searchlight. Two men were standing on the deck while waving their arms in the air.

Kelly slowed and scribbled something down on a blank sheet of paper. He grabbed a litre bottle of water and dropped both items into a plastic bag and tied it off.

He could hear voices screaming for help over the wind and waves. Kelly slipped both engines into neutral and allowed the yacht to drift on an approaching course with the stranded boat. The Grandmaster and his e'prentis were both showing the happiness and relief of their impending rescue. The other four men were huddled together in a shivering ball of fear.

Kelly leaned over the side, and the Doje's jaw dropped. "You?"

"Yes—me," Kelly replied, then threw the bag onto the deck.

The Doje then directed his increasing inner rage at one man, "You are obliged to offer us safe passage back to Christmas Island. I demand that you fulfil your maritime obligations as the captain of a passing vessel."

The Grandmaster snatched the bag off the swaying deck and pulled out the short note. He held it under the fading white light. "I can recommend a good lawyer, his name is, MR WHO FUK YOU NOW?" It was signed, Jack Shit.

The Grandmaster turned his head and looked up. Kelly raised his middle finger in a one-finger salute, and then slowly shifted it to face north-east. "I'm obliged to give you sweet fuck all. North Korea is six thousand kilometres that-a-way. Watch out for the big white pointers. Enjoy the trip."

Part-IV

The Archipedious Key

Chapter - 3 3

KELLY SAT in his skipper's chair while thumbing through the 3,000 songs on his iPod and stopped on Chicago before scrolling down to his favourite track, 25 Or 6 to 4, remembering his promise to the twins when they came within view of the West Australian coastline. He turned the volume up to seven and made sure the two Bose speakers mounted in both staterooms were online and then pressed play. The sounds of the bass guitar and the crisp, sharp crack of the snare drum beat through all three decks of the *Thin Lizzy.*

Abigail arrived first, while her sister grabbed a shower. "Is that your alarm clock, or are you just pure evil?"

"Maybe a bit of both," Kelly smiled.

After the 880 nm journey across the Indian Ocean, the first false mirage of the land-based horizon started to form a shimmering heatwave. Evina arrived while still towel-drying her hair, and both ladies stood as mirror images on the flybridge to witness the sunrise over the Earth's curvature of mainland Australia in a rising giant orange inferno with Exmouth Gulf in the foreground. Exmouth was well known for its prawns and a stepping stone to some big-game fishing plus the famous whale sharks that can weigh as much as twenty tonnes and grow to twelve metres in length, attracting divers from all over the world for the chance to share the ocean with these leviathans of the sea. A pod of southern right whales could be seen breaching off the starboard beam as they surfaced in a rising fountain of spray while on their annual returning migration to the food-rich Southern Ocean.

Abigail excused herself and headed for the shower. Kelly shifted downstairs to the main bridge and gazed over his left shoulder at Evina's open laptop and a scattering of papers occupying almost the entire floor and coffee table. "I can see you've been hard at it now you have access to the Internet again."

"I was up half the night working on my theory regarding that latitude and the strange markings on Wouter Loos' tombstone."

"And—what did ya come up with? I'm interested to know," Kelly asked.

"I need a map of the Abrolhos Islands."

"In my quarters, there's a printed satellite map hanging on the wall, go grab that."

Evina entered the skipper's room for the first time, not sure what to expect. It was clean and tidy thanks to Till. Two pictures were hanging on the wall opposite the bed-end. She gently lifted the aerial view of the island group clear off its hook while glancing at the other framed photo. There were three separate images. The first was of a stark-looking hospital ward full of newborn babies. The second was of a small group of children, maybe no more than five or six, scavenging a rubbish tip, and the last was a classroom of school-age children all in uniform. The caption read: 'every kid deserves a chance' with a web address below to donate money.

Of course—now I remember where I've heard that name before—Jack Kelly and The Buddhas Tooth?

Evina closed the door behind her and laid the glass frame on the bridge console. She turned her head and looked hard at Kelly while he checked the updated weather data. He tried to focus his attention on the map. "Didn't your mother ever tell you it was rude to stare?"

"I just put two and two together. That children's fund . . . every kid deserves a chance, that's the brainchild of you and your partner, Tiaan?"

"There's no secret about that. The more people that *do* know, the more money we raise for the abandoned babies in Thailand," Kelly explained.

"What about 'The Buddha's Tooth', Jack? The shrine returned to its eternal and historical resting place on the mountain hideaway in the Khao Khitchakut National Park in Chanthaburi, alongside the Buddha's Footprint. You wouldn't know anything about that either, I suppose?"

"Nothing slips through to the keeper when you're at the crease, does it?" Kelly quickly changed the subject. "Now, let's look at this map, shall we?"

Evina removed a ruler and a non-permanent marker from her carry bag. "I've been looking at the markings Jan Pelgrom de Bye inscribed on Loos' tombstone."

The satellite image showed the archipelago of coral atoll's that had been the demise of many a fine ship. North Island was the starting point of the Abrolhos Islands, one of the few that have any sand. The Wallabi, followed by the Easter and Pelsaert groups, ran in a southerly direction. Evina circled Beacon Island on the eastern perimeter of the Wallabi group and then drew a straight line to the mainland on latitude 27 degrees.

Evina concentrated on the map. "On Pelsaert's return journey to Batavia on the *Sardam*, he says he saw smoke and anchored up in twenty-one fathoms on what he says was clean and safe ground. Many people have argued the point, whether Pelsaert cast adrift his two prisoners at Wittecarra Creek, just south of the Murchison River mouth where the small seaside town of Kalbarri sits, or the Hutt River, seventy kilometres farther to the south."

"Latitude twenty-seven fits in with Kalbarri, and obviously the locals follow the same theory," Kelly verified.

"Why is that?" Evina asked.

"The actual creek is mostly a dry sandy 4wd-only track allowing access to a left-hand surf break called Jake's. There's a boulder-shaped plaque erected to acknowledge the historical reference to Australia's first European settlers."

Evina had another theory about that as well. "Why would have Pelsaert not include a longitude?" she asked with a shrug of the shoulders.

"Well, all he had was a mariner's astrolabe. It wasn't possible to accurately determine longitude at sea in the early days of transoceanic navigation. How far to the east or west they had travelled was more of an approximation by measuring the average speed of a boat at sea. This was achieved by checking the last six watch records and then chart their estimated progress on a map. To do this, each four-hour watch would use the time-honoured method of dropping a triangular piece of wood attached to a line overboard and having the sailor who dropped it count the knots that slid through his fingers in one precisely measured minute. Then each midday, the *Batavia*'s captain would complete a task known as 'shooting the sun' while standing steady, ensuring his astrolabe was absolutely level by pointing at the horizon and then measuring the angle of the sun above the horizon.

"To find the latitude of a ship at sea, the noon altitude of the sun was measured during the day, or the altitude of a star of known declination was measured when it was on the meridian; due north or south at night. The sun or a star's declination for the date was determined using an almanack. The latitude is then ninety degrees minus measured altitude plus declination. Combining their results would determine where their position was on the planet. Should I continue, because that is just the basics, there is plenty more?" Kelly boasted.

"Okay, I get the picture. Similar to a celestial globe. If Pelsaert was half as good a navigator as he was a businessman . . ." Evina let the words hang in the air before continuing. "He spoke of brackish water near the coast," Evina knew from his journals.

"That then fits in better with the Hutt River. The ground around Kalbarri is surrounded by fingers of coral reef, definitely not clean and safe, I can tell you from personal experience. To gain entry to the Murchison River, you need to negotiate Oyster Reef to your port side. The local rock-based fisherman usually just refer to this spot as 'Frustrations' because of the amount of gear you lose on the reef encrusted bottom. The Hutt River Lagoon definitely has discoloured water as it mixes with the salt from the sea on the inside of a sandy spit, depending on the weather."

"How do you know so much about the lay of the land, Jack?"

"Evina, I spent an entire season cray fishing between Geraldton and Steep Point." *Who can ever forget Big Bank?* "And the islands! We camped at Robinson Island in the Pelsaert Group for three months at a time. You need to toss a coin, Evina. Heads the Hutt River, tails for Kalbarri," Kelly offered to break the deadlock.

Evina remembered Barnacle Bob's own theories regarding Pelsaert's return journey to Batavia, and that coin he slipped into her bag. *Prince Leonard?*

"Well, my money is on Hutt River," Evina stated, wanting to sound confident.

"Either way, it's Kalbarri first and then a 4wd," Kelly explained.

After passing the southern tip of Dorre Island, the first signs of Inscription Point came into view as the northern tip of Dirk Hartog Island slowly transformed into something solid. Kelly turned to face Evina then made the comment, "Wouldn't it be nice if the historians could, and should, rewrite the history books so the kids at school were actually taught the truth about the first Europeans to make landfall in Australia?"

"I don't follow?" Evina asked.

"Wow! Do you mean a professor of the Smithsonian doesn't know the real history? Inscription Point was the first ever recorded landing in Australia where Dirk Hartog nailed to an upright post the oldest known artefact of European exploration while sailing on the *Eendracht* on October 25, 1616. And then eighty-one years later, Captain Willem de Vlamingh found and then replaced the pewter plate, including the original inscription while adding a list of his own senior crew before also replacing the original rotting post inside a fissure with a length of cypress pine he removed from Rottnest Island. I mean, Dirk Hartog's Plate is still on display at the Rijksmuseum in Amsterdam. How bloody hard can it be?"

"Like I've always said, Jack. History doesn't give up its secrets easily."

"Except this is no secret. They reckon the English never wanted to acknowledge Dirk Hartog's Plate as it may have allowed the Dutch to claim Australia for itself. Bloody politics, greed and corruption were games perfected a long time ago."

The yacht continued south past Turtle Bay, then Withnell Point until reaching Louisa Point located just north of the only homestead on the island. Kelly wanted to make use of three half-decent moorings he knew were on the leeward side of the island where they could escape the swell and wind and moor up for the night.

Before the first ocean albatross could be seen in the dawning sky, they were passing the southern island point of Dirk Hartog Island, and the first high cliffs of Steep Point towered high in the distance dwarfing the 72-foot-long yacht as it cruised past in its imposing shadow. Kelly steered a wide berth around the half-dozen balloons dancing on the white caps from a handful of land-based rod fishermen. Then he headed due west to place some distance between *Thin Lizzy* and the mainland to avoid the constant backwash as the incoming swells roll in from the south-west until his GPS alarm pinged before he made a slight course adjustment back towards the south.

Within a couple of hours, Kelly checked his GPS one more time, and it showed they were approaching latitude 26° 14' 45" S, longitude 111° 12' 55" E. He slowed *Thin Lizzy* and placed the twin Man engines into neutral. Kelly glided down the stairs and met Evina in the galley, busy pouring coffee. "Leave that and go grab your sister, then meet Till and me on the rear deck."

Till had set up an ice bucket with a bottle of 1992-Veuve Clicquot Grande dame, first released in 1972 to celebrate Madame Clicquot: nee Ponsardin, known as the 'Grande dame' of Champagne who took over her husband's empire when widowed at 27 years of age. Abigail and Evina arrived with surprised looks on their identical faces.

"Why are we slowing?" Evina asked.

Soon to be followed by Abigail, "What's the celebration? I love Champagne," she declared excitedly.

Kelly popped the cork and filled the four flutes. He raised his glass first. "Evina . . . Abigail, and you too, Till. Somewhere out there below our keel in the deep dark expanses of the Indian Ocean rests the HMAS *Sydney* in about 2,500 metres of water. On November 19, 1941, six hundred forty-five officers and sailors laid down their lives, including your Uncle Callum, whose final resting place is not far from here. I ask you to join me in raising your glasses to remember these brave Australian men. Cheers."

The moment was lost on Till, as he struggled to come to grips with the bubbles dancing inside his nose, but the two sisters both stood immersed in family memories and started to tear up.

"So much history and so many lives lost. Both Australian and Germans," Evina spoke first, through her cracked voice.

Kelly passed the twins a very basic wood-carved replica of a boat with a plastic-stemmed daffodil poking from a funnel. "To Uncle Callum," Abigail announced, as the ladies placed the small offering into the sea from the rear swim platform.

"To Uncle Callum," they all replied like a church choir and emptied their glasses. The twins showered and ate, then met Kelly back on the flybridge.

"I can see why you love the sea so much, Jack. This really is quite beautiful, up here—looking out across the expanses of the ocean."

"It's nice to have the weather in our favour, trust me. But, yes, you're right. I do love it. Soon we'll be passing the northern boundary of the Zuytdorp National Park, and the wrecksite is farther south. Evina, when we arrive in Kalbarri, hopefully, we can hire a decent 4wd. I want to know what your plans are regarding this globe? There's a lot of nothing out there, my girl. Talk about the needle in the haystack. You don't even know where the hay is yet? After Kalbarri, we can head to Murchison House then introduce both Abigail and yourself to the owners and seek permission to cross their property to find this gravesite," Kelly wanted to point out.

Evina started to explain, "To make sense of these eight signs Jan Pelgrom de Bye scratched out, first you need to understand that he was still just a young boy. He had no schooling, no other skills other than what his own father taught him, and what he learnt from the Vereenigde Oost-Indische Compagnie."

"The Oost, what?" Abigail replied with a look.

"The VOC. Dutch East India Company," Kelly answered.

"Yes, the VOC," Evina confirmed with an underlying tone of cynicism in her voice. "The VOC was more than just *a* company, they were the first to issue bonds and stock certificates, and the first-ever publicly listed company. They wielded enormous influence with quasi-governmental powers. The right to wage war and imprison and execute convicts. Negotiate treaties and strike their own coins; even establish their own colonies. The golden age of Dutch exploration between 1590 and 1720 put enormous pressures on the VOC to provide capable captains' and crews to take command of these ships that travelled to Jayakarto, which the VOC renamed Batavia. Voyages of the likes of Willem Janszoon on the *Duyfken* and Abel Tasman on both the *Heemskerck* and the *Zeehaen* were all financed by VOC.

"Have you ever heard of a game called the Mansion of Happiness?" Evina questioned.

"Sounds like my home on Koh Chang when I surprise Tiaan with some gold jewellery," Kelly laughed.

"I can't wait to eventually meet with, Tiaan. I bet she is nothing like you describe," Abigail replied.

"Yeah, right? When I was due to arrive back in Thailand, we were both supposed to be spending a week on Koh Samui for what was to be a first-time holiday. I even had a suite booked—with one *king-size* bed. They call it the honeymoon island. Do you get where I'm going with this scenario, girls?" Jack looked into both women's eyes with the look of a frustrated man.

Abigail cottoned-on first, "Oh, I think I understand now."

Evina asked, "Understand what?" Then she almost shouted, "Oh, now I get it. You and Tiaan haven't had sex yet?"

"Right, and now we're all travelling down the west coast of Australia. Maybe I can tell her I decided to pop in and say hello to my brother in Perth. Don't worry, ladies—this little side excursion *is* going to cost me big time," Kelly joked. "Sorry, go on, Evina."

"Well, the game was based on a Puritan worldview that Christian virtues and good deeds were assurances of happiness and success in life. It was a board game inspired by Christian morality, devised around a board with sixty-six spaces to be filled with an eternal pathway to the pearly gates of heaven awaiting the eventual winner. So, the VOC came up with its very own version, with the grand prize a position as a cabin boy on one of its boats."

"Like a sort of seamans' scholarship?" Kelly asked.

"I suppose so," Evina replied. "This game was played out over six months with the young twelve- to sixteen-year-old participants needing to find certain items, locations and other nautical paraphernalia to fulfil thirty obligations. They would be given instructions and told to go assure their futures. An example would be to demonstrate evidence to the administrator of the game, with no prior warning, each participant would need to display the ability to tie off a bowline or a figure of eight knot, a reef or a sheet bend, a rolling hitch, a cleat hitch or a round turn and two half hitches. These were a minimum requirement when going to sea, and so it went on."

"Sounds like a bloody good idea, if you ask me," Kelly wanted to add.

"The game included following a map to locate certain objects that would then be given to each boy as an incentive. Like a boy's first compass, or a set of all-weather gear, even things like an oak sailor's fid, for braiding ropes. These were all there to be found if you could follow the legend. The competition was fierce to the point that fathers' would blindfold their sons' and drop them into the middle of a thickly forested area or plantation with just a compass and a terrain map to find their own way home, just to hone their skills. Jan Pelgrom de Bye won the VOC game in 1627, which put him on the *Batavia* two years later."

"I'm sensing that these signs and numerals are somehow connected," Jack assumed.

Evina laid out her copied inscription on the fibreglass console.

≈≈≈ ß-m ζ ◊ γ bel uil ↓

"We can see seven symbols plus eight letters. I think we would all agree the downward-pointing arrow is self-explanatory. The letters b, e and l is simply how the Dutch spelt 'bell', and the last three letters translate to the word 'owl'. The first thing we need to understand is that *all* words in the treasure sign system have a specific numerical value. If we look at 'bel', the letter b is the second letter in the alphabet, so it represents a value of two. The e is five, and l equals twelve, which adds up to nineteen. If we follow the same sequence for owl, we come up with fifty—or do we? Remembering that Jan is trying to lead us to a specific destination using his own limited knowledge base. When the words 'bel' and 'owl' are used together on a Mansion of Happiness map, bel means 'bank', an accumulation of treasures, and the owl relates to the owl of Minerva, which refers to knowledge, wisdom, perspicacity or erudition. But concerning, Jan, we just need to look at the letter m, which has a value of thirteen. Now, look at the first group of three symbols. I think this represents a large body of running water, but not the ocean; more than likely a river. The next symbol looks like a capital B, but if you look closely, the bottom of the ß doesn't connect to the straight line." Evina placed her magnifying glass over the letter to highlight what she meant. Then she turned her open laptop around to show each person an image of a Budweiser can. "Here is a prime example of what I mean."

Kelly spotted the anomaly first. "When you look at it in that context, it now looks like the number thirteen."

"Yes, thirteen m. And the Dutch word for 'mile' is mijlen." Evina turned to face Kelly, "So, what's thirteen miles north of the Murchison River?"

Kelly punched in some numbers on a calculator, "That's roughly twenty-one kilometres north, which puts you somewhere near the southern end of the Zuytdorp Cliffs."

"That's right," Evina acknowledged with an increasing look of excitement. "Now, it wasn't until we came across that pod of whales that it suddenly dawned upon me. The sixth sign could very well be exactly that, a whale spout, and for Jan to be able to see this from the land, he would have needed to be elevated; like on top of some cliffs."

"That fifth symbol looks like a diamond," Abigail pointed out.

Evina finished the conversation by saying, "But I am none the wiser to what that fourth symbol means, which is the reason why we need to trace these steps and see if something, might match up with the local terrain. I know it's a long-shot, but it's the only shot we have."

"A three-hundred-ninety-year-old long-shot, to boot," Kelly threw in.

"These cliffs are tens of thousands of years old, and they've stood the test of time. Let's all hope that rings true." Evina folded the inscription and stood to allow the wind to fill her long flowing brunette hair while she sucked in a lungful of fresh ocean air and absorbed the ruggedness mixed with the natural beauty that was the Zuytdorp Cliffs.

Jack passed Abigail a set of binoculars and asked her to stand on the port side.

"Scan the tops of the cliffs from left to right, when you come across a scree slope, where the cliff has given way, you can just make out the final remains of the huge A-frame, or quadruped. Prince Jah built it as a means of giving the salvage divers access beyond the swell so they could work on the *Zuytdorp*'s recovery. A good idea in theory, but it failed miserably."

"Oh, wow, this is incredible, I can see it. Look, Evina, follow the shoreline. That's where Uncle Callum is buried, somewhere."

"Prince Jah?" Evina questioned.

"Yeah, the Nazim of Hyperabad, reportedly the richest man in the world. He purchased Murchison Station after being exiled from India. He also owned a boat called the *Kalbarri*. They reckon it was as good as Cousteau's *Calypso*."

"Right... and the same man, Bob's brother, completed all that legal work for. I can see the flat rocks near where the swell is washing over. Bob says the site is a short distance to the south." Evina looked on in rekindled family-link fascination before asking, "Are they goats to the right?"

"Probably," Kelly answered before adding. "Imagine those poor bastards, smashing into the cliff face in the dead of night—unbelievable really to think that anyone could have survived."

The last of the cliffs faded into the distance to be replaced by the red and white tumblagooda sandstone and the high sandhills with Kalbarri catspaw, the spider orchid and Murchison hammer orchid, all in abundance. Gantheaume Bay was dead ahead with Oyster Reef less than a kilometre away on their port quarter. Kelly slowed *Thin Lizzy* and started counting the incoming swells.

"Should we have cause for concern here, Jack? That's not much of a gap to the river mouth," Abigail expressed with a look of concern.

"That's the least of our problems. When we make the blind turn to port, I hope we don't bump into some tourist on a rent-a-catamaran. Powered vessels have the right of way in these small passages of confined water—try explaining that when these smaller boats are diving out of the way. It's happened before. Hang on, ladies—here we go."

Kelly throttled the twin Man diesel's and placed the bow in front of an incoming two-and-a-half metre swell. Like a surfer hitching a ride on a wave, the 72-foot yacht glided and picked up speed. He turned hard to starboard and was soon behind the scant protection offered by a small rocky outcrop opposite the mouth of the Murchison River to their immediate right. Then a second hard turn to port saw them enter the calm mixture of fresh and salt water with an upside-down, L-shaped sand-bar that was so close, you could almost lean over the side rail and sign your name in the wet sand.

The twins both smiled. "I see what you mean, Jack, this place is truly beautiful," as Abigail returned a wave from some envious beachgoers.

"Yep, one of the best-kept secrets along the entire West Australian coastline, but more importantly—it has a pub," Kelly needed no reminding.

Chapter-34

THE KALBARRI WHARF was located at the northern end of town. Kelly reversed *Thin Lizzy* in stern-first. After securing all lines, he connected his three-phase extension cord to the jetty power supply before shutting down both engines and a single generator. The ensuing quiet was only interrupted by a pair of kookaburras laughing away in a nearby tree. Kelly grabbed his wallet and then hauled himself up and on to the wharf. He needed to side-step three young boys with fishing rods lined up on the opposite side, right under a sign that read: '*Strictly no fishing – penalties apply*'. He privately pictured in his mind, the same three boys, lounging around at home with a smartphone each in their hands, tapping away at some mind-numbing game or texting friends with useless information no one is really interested in reading.

Too many bloody rules in this country these days.

Kelly's first job was to visit the local copper, only a short fifteen-minute walk away and a man he was well acquainted with after he'd previously lent a helping hand removing a group of four drunken Polish tourists from the pub, some years back. These idiots had decided it was okay to start harassing some local teenagers, half their size while minding their own business playing a game of pool at the family-friendly Kalbarri Hotel.

He remembered driving the young, Constable Shillings, the 120 kilometres to Northampton Hospital that night, which resulted in seven stitches and a mild concussion. From that moment on, the two men became good friends.

Kelly was about to pass the crowd of tourists gathered to witness and participate in the daily feeding of the pod of pelicans currently in full eating mode when the sound of a car horn sounded, and he heard a familiar voice yell from the driver's seat. "You still remember my face stranger, do you need a lift?"

Kelly turned his head and bent down to see who was driving. "Bloody hell, Dixie. I don't believe it," he replied, absolutely rapt to see his old deckhand mate.

"Jump in. Terri told me you were still alive and well. When did you turn up and where you off to?" Dixie asked. He hadn't seen or heard from his old workmate in years.

"We arrived today, and now I'm on my way to see, Ryan. Is he still the long arm of the law around these parts?"

"He sure is, but no longer in uniform. He's the District Detective Inspector for the Murchison and parts of the Lower Gascoyne, now. If you're trying to track him down, we'll need to chuck a U-turn."

"Huh?"

"He *was* on holidays for another week, but because of those three refugees kidnapping some guy in a wheelchair, he's been called back to duty as of tomorrow. He's at the pub right now," Dixie explained.

"Shit, I hadn't heard about that—crazy bastards. Well, what are we waiting for? We can kill two birds with one stone now. Lead the way please, driver," Jack sprouted, still excited at bumping into his old friend after a long unplanned absence.

Dixie parked his Nissan *Patrol* in the rear car park, and they both strode in with money in their pockets and a thirst that needed quenching.

"Any chance a man can get a bloody drink in this place, Detective Inspector?" Kelly announced for all to hear.

Without turning his head, Ryan took a swig of his pint. "Not likely for a dodgy character like you. Maybe I need to run you out of town before you start causing trouble again," he answered, knowing who had just entered the front bar.

Kelly pulled up a stool. "How's your head these days? Maybe you've had a bit of sense knocked into you since I saw you last. And now a detective, very impressive," Kelly nodded.

"Good to see you, Lucky Phil. What brings you to Kalbarri?"

"Just call me, Jack. The old Lucky Phil has been retired for now."

"The less I know about that, the better I think," Ryan replied, not sure what Kelly meant.

"I need a favour—well, two actually?" Kelly asked while ordering a round for everyone.

"Fire away," Ryan replied. "I probably owe you one, anyway."

"I need a seventy-two-hour visitor's visa for a Thai national, and where can I hire a 4wd from?"

"Thai national? You didn't actually find someone gullible enough to finally say yes—did you?"

"Funny you say that. I do have someone on the radar, but this person is on my boat berthed at the wharf, and he's not nearly as pretty as, Tiaan."

"I can help you out with the car, Jack," Dixie offered. "Take mine. We're back out to sea tomorrow for a three-day turnaround. It's just going to gather cobwebs. I'll drop it off tomorrow at the wharf. What's the name of your boat?"

"Trust me, Dixie. You won't miss it, mate. It's always a bit of a crowd favourite," Jack wanted to boast a little.

"Has he got a passport, your Thai friend?" Ryan questioned.

"Yeah, his name is, Till. He works for me, but he is more like family. I just want him to be able to walk the streets, maybe do a spot of fishing while I'll be out of town for a few days."

"Okay, I'll make a call, and someone will come and see him later. Should be fine. Where you off to?"

"Looking for something that may never be found and I'll also need to cross Murchison Station. Do I still need permission to access the old coast track?"

"You're in luck, Jack. I'll be talking to Jock McKlintoff tonight for the very same reason. The Perth cops want me to backtrack from Kalbarri to Shark Bay. Looks like these three jokers on the loose may have taken a back road to side-step a roadblock on the main highway."

The barman delivered the round. Kelly raised his pint. "Cheers everyone."

"Good to see you're still all in one piece, old mate," Dixie wanted to share before taking his first mouthful.

"Apparently I owe you some money?" Kelly posed the question.

Dixie shifted on his stool. "How so?"

"The North Sydney Bears, my annual membership."

"Old habits die hard."

Ryan was slowly turning on his barstool to face Kelly. "You're not still following the...? " He stopped mid-sentence while both his eyes were now locked onto the front swinging doors. "Hunk-a-hunk of burning love," he whispered while almost spilling his beer. "Check out what's about to walk into our little pub. You've gotta be kidding me. I've never seen these two before. They must have come up from Perth in the past day or two. You don't get to see a couple of classy ladies like that walking the streets of Kalbarri very often."

"Listen up everyone, ten bucks in," Kelly challenged all comers. "I'll bet the lot of you that the still—somewhat handsome, Jack Kelly, can have both those ladies sitting right here, on these two empty stools, with a drink in their hands and paid for by me. I still reckon I've got the magic touch."

"You're on." Dixie was the first to oblige and slammed his ten dollars hard down on the bar. Soon after there were five other notes stacked on top. Kelly brushed the front of his T-shirt down and asked each man to wish him good luck, then went to introduce himself to the two exquisite-looking women about to enter. All eyes from the bar were glued to Kelly's back.

"He's actually having a conversation, that's further than I thought he'd get," Ryan spoke first.

"Shit," Dixie hushed, "they're heading this way. I don't believe that cheeky bastard."

Kelly arrived with one lady on each arm. "Guys, I would like to introduce to the twin roses without thorns. This is Evina and her sister, Abigail. They think I am a very handsome man, don't you ladies?"

Evina and Abigail leaned in, and both planted a gentle kiss on each of Kelly's cheeks.

"Oh, no, this is too much. How does he pull it off?" Ryan couldn't believe his eyes, wishing he had the nous to do the same.

Dixie gazed awkwardly at the dazzling blonde woman standing in the front bar of his local pub. *That is one fine looking lady*, all the while wishing, *'if only'*.

Dixie blushed and thought to himself, if he had to choose from a thousand photos of the type of woman he could see himself settling down with, this would be close to the top of the pile, no doubt about it. His stomach was being slowly tied in knots from what was probably nothing more than just a polite return smile from Abigail. He visualised what their children would look like and then realised he needed to calm down, so he headed for the men's room to throw some water on his blushed cheeks.

Kelly leaned in and cradled the cash winnings in his open hand, "Ladies, can I buy you both a drink?"

As the cray fishing boats prepared to go to work under the emerging dawn sky, the sounds of marine diesel engines at idle were all the wake-up call Kelly needed. Dixie's Nissan was already parked at the Co-op end of the wharf with the key under the visor. The gang on board had enough time for a cooked breakfast before meeting with Ryan, to follow him as far as the Murchison Station homestead.

Ryan's police Toyota *Hilux* pulled up, and he sounded his horn, twice.

"Time to go, everyone," Kelly announced. He turned to address Till. "Here's some Australian dollars. Everything you'll need is within walking distance, that's the great thing about Kalbarri."

"Okay, Boss. I clean the boat tip top and then go fishing."

Jack, Abigail and Evina all stepped off *Thin Lizzy* and marched towards the parked Nissan. Detective Ryan Shillings looked like a man who'd just lost the pot to five aces when he recognised the same two ladies from the pub.

"You owe me ten bucks, Jack Kelly—you cunning bastard."

"I'll split the cash if you can keep a secret," he replied, with a cheeky grin.

The fully customised police 4wd pulled away with Kelly close behind before turning right into the Ajana-Kalbarri Road, then headed east. "You can close your mouth now, Constable. Someone might think you've never seen a couple of pretty ladies before," Shillings smiled at his young junior officer still visualising himself in his own testosterone-fuelled mind, marooned on a lonely Pacific island being fed grapes by both the twins.

Chapter-35

JOCK McLINTOFF'S WIFE was waiting under the bull-nose awning on the expansive wooden verandah that surrounded the circa 1890s refurbished Murchison House. Kelly and the twins exited the Nissan *Patrol* to stretch their legs and formally introduce themselves to Janette. She extended the hand of friendship and asked Evina, "You are the Bishop twins, is that correct?"

"Yes, I'm, Evina. And this is the baby of the family, Abigail," she loved to point out.

"I've taken the opportunity to prepare this for both of you. My father-in-law was also a close friend of Tom Pepper and both Robert and Richard's father."

"Barnacle Bob and his brother?" Evina quizzed.

Janette resisted the urge to smile at the reference to Robert's pet name, "Yes. He will be sorely missed around these parts." She then handed over a beautifully hand-crafted wreath of native wildflowers with a small wooden-carved figurine of the HMAS *Sydney*, woven in as a centre-piece. "I knew you wouldn't have the time to prepare anything yourselves, so please take this with our blessing."

The twins were both caught off-guard at the thoughtful gesture and reached for a tissue each. Janette offered Kelly a hand-drawn map showing exactly how to gain access, passing through the myriad of gates and key locations to the padlocks they'd need to access the location of the *Zuytdorp* wreck.

"Good luck and I hope you can both find what you are searching for," Janette added.

Kelly bid farewell to Ryan. He was heading due north to Tamala Station.

After three hours of bumping their way over the rain eroded wash-outs and dry creek gulleys, Kelly's handheld GPS signalled they were approaching the 15-kilometre mark north of the Murchison River. He stopped and manually engaged the front hubs, giving power to all four wheels and moved the short stick into the four-wheel-drive position. The coastal road was more of a track than a gazetted road. Right on cue, a pod of humpbacks could be seen making their way back south.

"Why are they so close to the shoreline?" Evina asked Kelly.

"The northernmost point of the Abrolhos lines up east-west with Port Gregory just south of here. The islands offer natural protection against the incoming swells, and they take advantage of that as they pass through. When they migrate north, a mother with a newborn calf might rest within the island group for up to a week at a time while the main pod just hang around and wait for the calf to gain enough strength to continue."

"Just imagine, Loos and Jan may have stood right here, on this very spot, and witnessed the very same," Evina wanted to share while absorbed in her own thoughts.

"Come on, we've got a lot of hard ground to cover to find your lost book." Kelly looked up at the warming sun and estimated midday within three hours. He hated wearing watches.

The 4wd crawled along at a steady 10-15 kph as close to the cliffs as was humanly possible. Each kilometre ticked off, Kelly would count it out loud to Evina. "Coming up to the twenty-kilometre-mark north of the Murchison River now, Evina."

"Can we walk for a while?" Evina was hoping to see any sign of a rock formation that might resemble the shape of a diamond. The twins each grabbed a small backpack and started to follow what looked like a worn path.

"Probably a goat track," Kelly explained. "I'll take the Nissan another five kilometres north, then backtrack and meet you in the middle." He handed each of them a four-pronged snake killer, "Just in case."

Both Evina and Abigail looked a bit startled. The twins, under the shade of their Akubra rabbit-skin hats, battled their way under the escalating warmth of the day and the thousands of flies that needed to be constantly brushed away with any small leafy branch.

"Jack was right about there being a lot of nothing out here, Evina, and the heat is becoming almost unbearable. A shady tree would be a welcome sight right about now," Abigail let fly with her first whinge of the day.

"Come on, Abby. Let's push on. Only another kilometre or so and we should bump into Jack soon enough." They needed to make a slight detour back inland to pass a deep crag where the swell was pummelling the open void below with each mountain of water that rolled off the Indian Ocean. They pushed their way through some waist-high scrub for a couple of hundred metres until it was clear again to find the hard ground of the rocky cliff edge.

"There's Jack now, Evina, and look, he's found what must be the only shade for miles." Evina looked up to see the bent trunk of an old-growth red river gumtree. It looked like someone had tied a rope and pulled it over like a catapult ready to slingshot a ball of Greek fire. The blazing sun was now directly overhead, and Jack was taking his fill of water. Suddenly Evina noticed the rays of the sun reflecting against a vertical limestone ridge to her right. The Pleistocene aged Tamala limestone formed by the ancient calcareous sand dunes accumulated near the coast during the last ice-age suddenly danced to life, with a sprinkling of glittering white and golden specks of light that sparkled like the stars under a clear night sky, rebounding off the limestone and granite flecks embedded into the igneous rock.

"Will you look at that, Evina?" Abigail shouted to her sister. "It resembles the shopfront to a jeweller's window—full of a girl's best friend."

"You're referring to diamonds? Yes, of course—a girl's best friend. *Diamonds,*" Evina almost screamed while raising both hands above her head.

Evina pulled the inscription from her jeans pocket while Kelly turned his head to see what all the fuss was about. From his vantage point under the tree, all looked as it should, which it never is.

"That fourth symbol may be the bent-over tree. I mean, what else could it be? There's nothing else out here. And the reflection off those rocks has to be what Jan was referring to as diamonds. But how does a whale spout fit into the equation?" Evina directed her question to anyone listening.

Abigail sat down on a sizable ball-shaped boulder and unscrewed the lid of her canteen. With her head tilted back, for a moment she thought she could feel the ground shudder under her backside. She swallowed a mouthful of water and then felt the inside of her left leg as a gentle spray of seawater soaked the inner seam of her pants. She jumped up and looked at the small space around the base of the unusually shaped rock. It reminded her of a giant cork. "Jack . . . Evina—help me shift this boulder."

"What for, Abigail?" Evina asked.

"Just trust me. Come on, give us a hand, will you?"

Jack ambled over, curious about what the twins were up to. He joined in the futile task of trying to shift something that probably weighed at least a couple of hundred kilos.

"Okay, now I need to ask, Abigail. Why?" Kelly looked on like he might be the one wearing the dunce's cap.

"The fountain of water may not be from a whale. Don't just stand there, make yourself useful. Surely it can't be that heavy?" Shortly after, with a renewed vigour, all three were leaning into this small mountain of rock that didn't look like it was going anywhere.

"Hang on, I've got an idea. Wait here." Kelly started a slow jog back to the parked Nissan. Almost an hour passed before he returned to find the twins crouched on either side of the rock listening to the rising roar as the incoming tide together with the increasing swells were colliding against the cliff face then funnelling all that combined water into what looked like an almost perfectly drilled hole before surging upwards only to be halted by the huge sandstone stopper. Kelly had seen hundreds of these blowholes dotted along the coast from Pepper Point south of Steep Point, right down to Red Bluff at Kalbarri. Nature's own saltwater geysers. He reversed the Nissan and pulled out a snatch strap, wrapping it around the rock twice, then connected the other end to the tow hitch.

"Right then, stand back, you two." He closed the door and shifted into low second and gave the accelerator some stick. The one and a half tonne 4wd lurched forward, then stopped like it just hit an invisible wall. The boulder shifted slightly but rolled back to its parked position. "Okay, this time I'm just going to flatten it and let the strap do its work," Kelly explained to the crowd of two.

Like a giant rubberband, the snatch strap is designed to do just that, expand under force, then contract; sling-shotting free a bogged car. The sound of the 4.2-litre turbo diesel engine revved hard as Kelly dropped the clutch and took off. The snatch strap stretched and then rolled the rock away from the hole like a giant free-wheeling marble. Both the girls jumped for joy and were applauding their own combined efforts.

"All right, time to sit back and wait to see if your theory is right, Abigail?" Kelly said.

Abigail dangled the inside of her wet leg. "I didn't spill this from my canteen, mister," she answered.

Like a badly laid piece of wrinkled carpet, a set of six, three-metre-swells were about to end their journey across the 4,500 miles of open ocean and meet with destiny in a long-awaited marriage as they kissed the vertical cliff face below. The sound of the rising water and the fast-escaping air mixed with a venting spray hissed from the small rounded entrance, then a surging funnel of salt water sky-rocketed into the air like an oil gusher, soaking the only three people within a 100-kilometre radius. Abigail rejoiced in a scream of excitement and grabbed her sister; they were both jumping up and down in a disjointed disco jive that belonged back in the '80s. Kelly looked down at the size of the hole and then placed his open hands on each of Evina's shoulders. "Yep, you should fit through just fine."

Abigail immediately stood still, then pointed towards the hole. "No way, surely you're not thinking of going down there?"

Evina tapped the downward-facing arrow on her map, "Just try to stop me, sister."

"All right, let's just hang on a minute and take stock before we rush into something fraught with danger, Evina," Kelly quickly interrupted.

"Jack's right, Evina." Abigail was starting to picture her byline under the story of the missing artefact recovered after three centuries, hidden along the already famous Zuytdorp Cliffs. This was a career-maker. Evina had spent the last ten years of her life to reach this point. No force on this planet would stop her from searching what might lie below their feet only a matter of metres away. She was considering this could be a defining moment in her scientific career—at last.

Kelly removed the Esky from the back of the Nissan and set up a makeshift table under the bent tree. "Let's knock off these sandwiches first, count out the swells for twenty minutes and discuss how I'm going to explain exactly what to do, and no ifs or buts. That means the both of you . . . Got it?" The twins looked at Kelly, like two teenagers caught puffing away on a cigarette.

Twenty minutes later, Evina now stood with a roped harness around her shoulders and waist with a length of nylon cord tied off to the front bull bar. The winch hook was extended from its drum and was now hanging vertically down into the dark space.

"It's only about five or six feet to the floor of the cave. I can see it clearly with the torch. As soon as we lower you in, move off to your left as you're standing now. It seems to head in that direction. Now, remember, don't panic if you hear the water rising, which it will inevitably do. Find a dry spot and brace yourself, just in case. When you make your exit, stop and wait for the next water spout, then head for the hole. If you need to be hauled out, give three solid tugs on the rope, is that clear?" Kelly explained slowly and methodically, like talking with a kindergarten group.

Abigail held her sister in a tight embrace. "Evina, please be careful. You don't know what may be down there."

"That's exactly right, Abigail, and now it's time to find out. I'm ready. Lower away," she hollered.

They waited for the next geyser to run its course, and Evina slowly disappeared into the ten-thousand-year-old cave. She was pumped, and her heart rate was proof of that.

Control your breathing, like Jack said, she remembered.

Her boots touched the wet surface, and she stepped to her right now because she'd swivelled on the short drop down. Evina pointed her torch and turned a full 180 degrees in both directions and moved the only way she could. The surface was unevenly filled with small cracks with salt water still seeping in a uniformed gravitational flow. Some fine green weed covered most of the floor and some of the walls. She arrived at a slight bend and pulled some more slackened rope to give her room to turn the corner. The next thundering roar filled the confined space as the next gusher rose from below. She pushed into the wall and held tight, but she barely felt much more than a gentle hazing. It looked relatively dry as she moved on with her light beam sweeping from left to right.

Evina's light flashed over a strange-looking object that seemed to be out of character with the surrounding formations. At first glance, Evina could make out a spherical shaped rock that looked like a bowling ball wedged into a small crevice with a full covering of dark seaweed and black-shelled crustaceans almost concealing its presence. She moved the light to a rocky ledge above shoulder height, and her heart skipped a beat. "What is that?" It wasn't seaweed, but it could have been as it hung from the ledge in strands. Evina stepped in closer, mindful of her footing. She raised both arms above her head then ran a hand across the surface, and if she didn't know any better, it felt like the crusted hide of an animal, or what was left of it. *Maybe the remains of a dead feral goat?* Evina then found a firm grip and tugged at it slowly. The noise of something dragging across the rock surface was backed up by the weight of resistance. She kept pulling it ever so closer to the edge, with her eyes peeled for what may reveal itself in a matter of seconds.

"Oh, my God," Evina's heart almost burst from her well-endowed chest. She reached up with both hands and eased out a small wooden and brass chest. It didn't feel empty, and the weight caught her by surprise. She needed to step back quickly to stop herself from falling forward, face first. In the process, she knocked the strange, round-looking rock with the back of her heel, forcing it to roll a couple of turns. Evina looked on and was spellbound.

"That has to be man made."

It looked like somehow a handle had been humanly attached to the outer surface. Evina gazed like she was in fairyland at the chest held in both her outstretched arms. "This first, then I'll come back for whatever that may be," Evina panted while trying to succour herself. She needed to clinch the base of the torch in her open mouth to manage the chest and retrace her steps.

Evina was perspiring, and her arms started to ache as she waited for the next fountain to pass, then she started her count. "One crocodile, two crocodile—oh bugger this. Jack... Abigail," she screamed in a state of unrestrained furore. "I have something, please help me." Kelly leaned over the edge of the hole and poked his torch down into the dark space. "Shit, you weren't kidding, were you?" He raised his head from the hole and faced Abigail, "Go grab the smaller Esky."

Kelly tied off a length of slack rope between the plastic icebox handles and lowered it down with the winch, using the remote. Evina placed the chest inside, and Kelly pressed reverse.

"There's something else. Hang on, and I'll be back," Evina was almost hyperventilating now. Abigail grabbed one end of the Esky, and together she and Kelly hoisted it clear of the cave entrance. They swapped glances that suggested this surely couldn't actually be happening. Both their combined attention was drawn to a second echoed demand to be pulled back to the surface. Kelly worked the winch, and Evina's two extended arms appeared first concealing something inside an old animal hide. She rolled it away until she was clear enough to boost the rest of her body clear.

Abigail was snapping away with her iPhone as Evina discarded the hide and let it drop to the ground. Kelly pointed to some strange markings on the inside of the skin. The only thing he could decipher was a possible date: 629 and the part word, avia.

"Jesus Christ, Evina, take a look at this. You've done it. This is proof that Loos and de Byes were here. This is unbelievable." Kelly was almost shell-shocked at the magnitude of such a significant find. His Special Forces training instinctively forced him to check their surroundings, even though the closest possible intruder was more likely to be at sea and not land-based.

Evina placed what looked like an old spent cannonball on the rear open tailgate and just stared in riveting hypnotic enthrallment. Then she picked up the chest and carefully placed it down with a wavering hand. "God, what have we just achieved here today? I'm almost too nervous to open it. Abby, please—for prosperity and the history books," as Evina showed off her best associate professor pose.

Kelly had already removed a toolbox and had at the ready a small screwdriver and a bigger one with a hammer if necessary. Evina looked on in dismay. "I don't think attacking a three-hundred-ninety-year-old historical artefact with a hammer is quite how this is going to happen, I'm sorry to say, Jack."

Evina started fiddling with the two locked clasps like they were made with wet tissue paper. "Come on, Evina, get on with it. We all want to see what's inside," Abigail pressed.

"All right, hand me that small screwdriver." Kelly obliged. Evina placed it behind the closed clasp and gently eased it forward. A welcome *click* sounded, and it separated from the lock. The other lock popped open, and three sets of eyes were glued to this small chest as Evina pried the lid open. Coins, both gold and silver, all dated 1628 and 1629 accompanied by a collection of an assortment of coloured gemstones lay inside. In her rush to get a closer look, Abigail knocked the shell-encrusted ball off the tailgate, and it fell to the hard rock, rolled on for a bit before tumbling down a trench-like fracture, disappearing from sight. Everybody froze as a cracking noise was all they heard, maybe expecting some ancient toxin to suddenly be released into the atmosphere. Instead, the ball-shaped object was parted like a split coconut. Evina sprinted over to the edge and gazed down into the chasm. And that was it for her. She burst into tears, trying to explain to both Abigail and Jack through an uncontrolled howl what it was she was looking at, now lying idle on the bottom of the shallow crevice.

Abigail looked over at Jack with clouded eyes. "I think she's trying to explain to the both of us, that it may well be the third celestial sphere."

Kelly crawled down the crevice and retrieved the cracked wooden casing that looked like a broken macadamia nut and lifted the celestial globe clear, gently placing it into Evina's open arms. "I'm guessing this is what you've been searching for all this time? Congratulations, Mrs Bishop-Joiner," Kelly offered, as a genuine token of his respect for this woman's unrelenting resolve.

Evina just starred in abstract disbelief at what had taken ten years of her life to locate, and finally, she held it in the palms of her hands. Abby was still filling the storage memory of her iPhone with more photos.

"It looks like a metal basketball," Kelly observed.

"I need to get busy on my laptop in the car," Evina managed to dribble through her quivering lips.

"So, you don't want to visit your uncle's gravesite, then?" Kelly questioned, knowing the answer.

"Shit. I forgot about that. Yes, of course. Let's get moving. We haven't got a second to lose," Evina rejoiced.

Kelly repacked the Nissan and marked their location on his GPS, then followed the map through three more locked gates. They were now heading slightly to the north-east before a turn to the west again would guide them back to the cliff edge. The welcoming ocean breezes soon could be felt cooling the heated landscape as the temperature dropped by ten degrees. The site of the *Zuytdorp* wreck itself was relatively simple to find, and within a matter of minutes, Kelly was able to scramble down the face of the broken escarpment and snake his way along the rock-strewn coral edge while being caressed with a fine mist of ocean spray from the breaking swells on an incoming tide. Evina was next to ease herself down and soon caught up.

"Give us another look at that mud map Barnacle Bob gave you." Evina passed it over, and Kelly followed the lay of the land, estimating their distance from the flat rocks to be about twenty-five metres. "Here comes, Abigail. We need to follow this line farther south and keep our eyes peeled for some collapsed rock along the higher point of the cliff face. Keep an eye on the swell."

Kelly moved on with the twins in hot pursuit. Black crabs were in abundance, all scurrying to find cover as the noise of three people clambering over the piled rocks mixed with the rumble of the breaking waves. Abigail stopped and pointed to a large slab that was like a natural ceiling jutting out from the vertical face. "Jack, look up there. What do you think? It looks different from the surrounding landscape."

"That's because it is. It's been sheared off, and look over there, you can see where it has collapsed. Wait here, and I'll take a closer look."

Kelly scrambled his way up the uneven surface. He moved a few loose boulders to one side and stopped. "This looks interesting," he shouted below.

"What is it, Jack?" Evina's anxiety was becoming impossible to conceal.

Kelly crouched down on all fours, then pointed his Mag-Lite towards an opening. "You might want to head back to the car and grab that wreath, girls. This is it, the gravesite is right here."

Abigail squeezed her smaller body size inside the natural crypt and take some photos of the bones and headstone. The twins laid the flowered wreath a metre inside and offered The Lord's Prayer as a final farewell to Acting Sub Lieutenant Callum Bishop - HMAS *Sydney*, 1941. Jack captured a couple of photos of the sisters standing in front of the final burial site of both their Uncle Callum and Wouter Loos. Together, they all sat down and allowed the moment to engulf them like a historical cloud of enlightenment. Evina removed a necklace from under her shirt. She unclasped the small gold cast of Jesus Christ as he appeared on the cross. She crawled in as far as she could and stretched her arm to place the offering on top of the headstone. Her hand felt something loose. She fumbled blindly with her fingers and grasped three items in her clutched hand. She eased her way back out and down, then stood next to Abigail and Jack, while she opened her soiled palm. All three people looked on in astonishment at the three coins Jan Pelgrom had left as a final memento to his only friend, 390 years ago.

Kelly cast his eyes upwards to see the sun begin its lazy transition towards the ocean horizon. He motioned towards the twins. It was time to leave as they made their way back to the parked vehicle. He addressed the twins together, "It's going to be farther in overall distance travelled but much quicker in time if we head back to Kalbarri via Tamala Station, then we can travel along the graded Useless Loop Road and follow the sealed North West Coastal Highway back south to the Kalbarri turnoff."

Both girls nodded in unknown agreement while the events of the day finally caught up with Abigail, as the moving vehicle enticed her to a window bouncing slumber. Evina was busy studying her new toy while tapping away on her laptop from the rear bench seat.

"You're not going to believe this, Jack," Evina broke the long silence of the 50-kilometre run to Tamala. "This globe is exactly as I thought. It's both signed by Muhammad Salih Thattvi, and completed, with no errors. There's no doubt about it. The date is right here. January 26, 1606."

"Is that important?" Kelly asked.

"Oh yeah, it certainly is. As I explained before, this is basically a map, but to read where it points to, you need a starting point, and that is the date. The Zodiac is a band which extends to either side of the ecliptic and is divided into the twelve Zodiacal signs. It contains the course of all the planets known to the Ancients. The Tropic of Cancer is a circle parallel to the celestial equator which touches the ecliptic at its northernmost point. When the sun is at this point, just about to enter the Zodiacal sign of Cancer, it is the summer solstice. The Tropic of Capricorn holds the same position concerning the point on the ecliptic corresponding to the winter solstice. The solstitial colure is a great circle which passes through the celestial poles and these two solstitial points. The equinoctial colure is another circle which passes through the celestial poles and the ecliptic at the two equinoxes."

"You're losing me, Professor. Give me the cereal box version," Kelly answered her detailed explanation.

"By forming a triangle between the Zodiac sign inscribed on each globe, the position of the sun and either the Tropic of Cancer or Capricorn, depending on which hemisphere you are looking at, I can pinpoint a location on the planet. And maybe— just maybe, this might tell us where Emperor Jahangir; Conqueror of the World, ordered his *Book of Remedies* to be safely stashed away waiting for me to locate it—I can only hope."

"Can you do that now?"

"Yes, I have all the necessary signs, and now I have the all-important date with the positions of the Zodiac on this given day."

Abigail's head bounced off the window as the Nissan negotiated yet another wash-out while Evina could be heard tapping away feverishly. She reviewed all her data and the coordinates a final time and then hit enter. "There it is, Peppers Seven Spirit Bay?" Evina gasped. "Do you know where Arnhem Land is, Jack?" Evina asked, almost unable to conceal her verve.

"That's in the Garig Gunak Barlu National Park up on the Coburg Peninsula. Due east from Melville Island off the coast of Darwin. It's all Aboriginal-owned land. Why?"

"That's where the map points to."

"How accurate is it? Does it actually say go to the third palm tree on the right with a shovel in one hand?" Kelly asked, thinking this was far from being solved. "There's a lot of unchartered country up that-away, Evina. I'm pretty sure someone built an Eco Resort somewhere on the northern peninsula, bloody hell, Evina, do you even...?" Kelly stopped mid-sentence and slowed the Nissan to a baby's crawl. "Did you hear that?" Kelly's words hung in the air for the next few seconds of silence.

"Hear what?" Evina replied.

"It sounded like a gunshot coming from over the next rise," Kelly replied.

Then a second *crack* sound reverberated over the landscape, instantly alerting Kelly to danger ahead. "Hold on, Evina." He shifted back into second gear and flattened the accelerator.

Chapter-36

THE HMAS *BALLARAT* was currently anchored two kilometres west of Carnarvon, close to the mouth of the Gascoyne River. At 865 kilometres in length, it was the longest-running river in Western Australia.

The Sikorsky S-70B-2 Seahawk helicopter on board the *Ballarat* was designed to offer the ANZAC-class frigate, both anti-submarine and anti-surface warfare capabilities with the ability to fly search and rescue missions plus the added bonus of delivering air-launched torpedoes, if necessary. Right now, Stone was being strapped into the rear seat as the engine warmed to operating temperature. The pilot went through his pre-flight checks and turned to eye-ball his only passenger. Stone gave the two-thumbs-up signal, and the twin turbo-shaft, General Electric – T-700 engines roared to life, lifting the helicopter clear of the rear-deck launchpad, soon reaching its optimum cruising speed of 160 knots.

Stone had requested that he personally interview both the remaining witnesses of these so-called 'refugees' landing at Bush Bay. His instincts were telling him that this was the last man on his list. Operation Blue Skies was still live and ongoing. The co-pilot indicated through his earphones that a satellite call to the *Ballarat* was being diverted. Stone lowered his mouthpiece and heard the voice of Felicity, loud and clear.

"You're a busy man, Tobias, but Emma Peel tracked you down."

"I'm hoping you could find something on that router's memory we uploaded from the *Ballarat*," Stone prompted.

Felicity fell straight into her next spiel to explain the intricacies of the working Internet. "Through a modem, the router is the link to the world of cyberspace, so any communications to a PC or a laptop for the web, e-mails, social media and so forth would be logged into one of four types of non-volatile router memory. D-RAM is erased when you power off, non-volatile memory holds its data indefinitely through the use of a small battery. ROM, Flash and NX-RAM retain data when powered off. The data is transferred between the RAM and the CPU, such as the paging in and out of operating data, packet buffers, ARP cache, the running-config and routing tables. For the CCNA, only the config needs to be considered. Upon the bootup, info from the NV-RAM and the IOS is copied into the D-RAM for the duration. As you enter commands and make changes to the config stored in the D-RAM, this is called the running-config to the start-up config in the permanent storage so that if you need to reboot your changes are not lost."

Stone had drifted off to another place in time. "Felicity, I must have missed that class while I was busy learning how to survive in the jungle on a Sao biscuit and half a cup of muddy water. I didn't understand a single word you just said, so let's try again. This time in plain simple English."

"A facsimile transmission was received to a laptop connected to that router. It came from a password-protected, government listed fax number, and that number, Tobias, is yours and my boss at the Russell Offices, in Canberra... or at least the fax registered to his office."

"That's ASIO's old address. All ASIO personnel have been relocated to the Jurlique Centre, or so I'm led to believe," Stone replied.

"Yes, but we already know the director has retained his old office. The official reason was its close proximity to both the Army and Navy HQ."

The co-pilot's voice cut in, "Sir, you're a popular man today. You have another incoming call from, Bradley Monarsh. What do you want me to do?"

"Patch it through. Great work, Miss Peel. Keep turning over rocks Felicity and try to trace the money trail. I'll talk later.

Over and out." Stone waited a few seconds. "Brad, I'm hoping for some good news today." Stone needed some answers.

"Tobias, since our last conversation, I took the liberty of running a live trace on all HABIT cell phones registered to the Australian Government. This consists of enabling the chipped mobile to sit in an idle mode, then..."

"Brad, spare me the prawn cocktail and let's just get to the part where I eat the steak."

"Right'eo then, old chap. The problem is that all mobile phone communications are transmitted via radio waves, so if anyone from inside Parliament House received or sent a text message by phone, well that would be virtually impossible to track, without involving the CIA. But we got lucky."

"You see, Brad—there's always a but."

"It was just three alpha-numerals, six four and three. And the reason we got lucky is that HABIT detected a hack and initiated a trace on the sender. That particular text message was actually sent by a third party."

"What the fuck?" Stone asked, a little stunned. "How is that even possible, Brad?"

"This is the new world, Tobias. We have an exact time the text was received. Now, what I did was worked backwards. Instead of tracking who *was* using a HABIT protected mobile at that moment, and from that cell tower, we eliminated all the other encrypted cell phones that were idle during that interval. We came up with four probabilities, and they were all in the New Parliament House on that precise date and time."

"Give me the details," Stone then asked.

"Tuesday at ten A.M. The connection to the tower finished exactly three minutes later. Tobias, are you still there? Hello..."

Stone was already redialling Felicity.

"Emma Peel, here."

"Listen up, when was the last JNSC meeting and who was in attendance?"

"Actually, I already know that," Felicity answered, a little chuffed.

"Why?"

"Because the director-general of ASIO was ordered to attend by the attorney-general. The complete list was all in attendance on that Tuesday meeting in the Menzies Room."

Darcy Jones, I would never have believed it. Stone contemplated the ramifications of a man in his position committing treason. *Blue Skies—finish the job at hand and then front, Jones.*

Each time those images of dismembered bodies flashed through his perturbed mind, he forced himself to remember the smiles on the faces of the eight young girls when they sat down to their first decent meal in the mess hall on the *Ballarat* and the crew of 141 sailors, all playing the role of the doting uncle. *Someone still has to pay the ferryman,* he promised himself.

Stone left the Carnarvon police interview room with the mindset that this Narley character seemed like a credible witness, but under their own admission, they'd all been drinking that night. Detective Neil Hoosan had updated Stone on the failed roadblock. Stone needed to get inside this Colin guy's head, and for that, he needed to speak with Tanya, but in a more comfortable setting. *Not here, surrounded by a room full of cops.*

Tanya stirred two teaspoons of sugar into her flat white coffee while Narley took advantage of Stone's free breakfast offer.

"Tanya, I work for a different part of the Australian Federal Government, the part that gets to the truth without any of the bullshit, if you'll forgive my language, but my job is to track down these three refugees and find your husband. Timing is crucial. Look around, there are no cops here today, just us. You need to trust me. Tell me about your husband, Tanya. We know your 4wd was heading towards Perth, or maybe the closest domestic airport, which in this case would be Geraldton. Somehow they skipped the road-block at the Billabong

Roadhouse. How well does Colin know his way around this part of the outback?"

Narley almost choked on a piece of crispy bacon. "Are you kidding me?" he replied with his mouth still half full, "Colin knows all this country like the back of his bloody hand. His team had the shearing contract at the Murch."

"The Murch?" Stone questioned.

"Tamala and Murchison Stations, plus he fished all that area before his accident," Narley added.

Tanya and Narley spent the next ten to fifteen minutes filling Stone in on what type of man Colin Gibson was.

"Jeez, maybe I should be working for him!" Stone joked. They all shared a nervous laugh. Tanya thought she might have felt a slight vibration from the inside of her bag.

Chapter-37

AFTER THE CYCLONE SEASON finishes in late March each year, the Shark Bay Shire sends out a scheduled road crew to re-grade the first 150 kilometres of gravel road, repair any potholes and check the culverts are still in working order along the isolated Useless Loop Road. It was still late in the year, and for the last 100 kilometres, the long-wheelbase 4wd had been rattled senseless by the road corrugations. Colin leaned forward to gain the Sheik's attention, who looked like his bottom jaw was about to separate from the rest of his bearded face.

"We need to slow down," Colin voiced from the constraints of his wheelchair. The skeletal head of a Brahman cow with corkscrew-shaped horns was attached to a steel swinging gate with the words: Tamala Station burnt with a branding iron on a piece of driftwood, indicating the start of the five-kilometre winding incline to the main homestead.

Colin shifted his upper body and unbuttoned his AFL premiership-winning-edition West Coast Eagles jacket, then pulled his shirt clear from his belt. On his shaved stomach, fixed by some wax over the stoma was his colostomy bag made from surgical-strength plastic. He unclasped the double clip-lock and prepared for the inevitable.

The driver was first to react, winding down his window, and was soon followed by the Sheik. The smell of human excrement filled the interior of the car. Both men in front shared a look, the one that poses that question no person wants to answer truthfully. The disgruntled passenger in the back leant forward and was the first to ask, "What is that smell, Aris?"

That was Colin's cue. "It's my bag, mate. Full to the brim. A koala bear might shit in the woods, but when you're confined to a wheelchair, this is what happens." Then Colin lifted his shirt.

"Praise to be Allah, what is that?" the Sheik exasperated while placing a hand over his mouth and nose. Waluya Mayadi stuck his head out the window and spilt his guts down the side of the door, heaving and dry retching into the wind. "We need to stop—*NOW*," he screamed. His chin was dripping with his own disgorge.

"The station house is not far. I can empty the bag there. They get a lot of fishermen dropping in unexpected to pay the camping fees and put a deposit on the key to the padlock that gives access to the bay area, north of here," Colin needed to explain.

"Please, Aris. Can we pull over soon?" Mayadi pleaded.

"All right, but we'll be watching you closely. No funny business—quick, quick," the Sheik threatened.

The majestic old homestead came into view, and the 4wd slowed. The Sheik ordered Sukato to pull over near an old discarded out-house. He turned in his seat and faced Colin while pointing. "You can use this to deal with that bag?"

"I need power to the chair. Can't push it by hand," Colin explained.

The rear door swung open, and the noise of the hydraulic lift sounded. Colin was unclasped and rolled out backwards. Sukato reconnected his battery power cable, and Colin was back in business. He closed the hinged wooden door of the outdoor thunderbox and flicked on the red switch to enable his GPS locator.

Tanya finished her second cup of coffee. She glanced over at Stone, seated across the table and felt a second vibration from the inside of her bag, and then a series of loud beeping noises alerted her to what was happening.

Stone looked on and asked, "What's that?"

Tanya unzipped her leather knock-off and pulled out a small hand-held device. "It's a global positioning satellite locator. Colin has a GPS attached to his wheelchair in case he breaks down somewhere or is in distress. It's just been activated," she explained.

"That's bloody brilliant, Tanya," Stone replied. "Where's it showing his current position?"

"You see, I told you Colin would know what to do. Those poor bastards have no idea who they're up against," Narley enjoyed explaining.

"The homestead at Tamala," Tanya answered Stone's question.

Stone unfolded a map of Western Australia. "Show me where they could track their way to Perth through this station property, then?"

Within thirty minutes, Stone was securing his harness on the Seahawk with the map marking the gates and possible routes along the coast road to Kalbarri.

"Where we headed, sir?" the pilot needed to know.

"Tamala Station and let's blow a bit of aviation fuel in getting there as quick as you can, Lieutenant," Stone answered.

Waluya Mayadi made a running mad-dash towards a tap located on the side of the main building to wash away the effects of his ordeal. The rear house door was open, and there was no sign of anyone inside. He decided to chance his luck in finding some fresh drinking water to rinse the foul taste in the back of his throat. He stepped up to the porch and swung open the fly screen door, which led straight to the country-style kitchen. Mayadi found three one-litre plastic bottles of Kalbarri Spring Water in the door of the fridge. He filled his mouth, gargled, then spat out his fill into the sink. He turned to leave when he noticed an old rifle above the mantle of a stone hearth.

He lifted the World War I, bolt action, Lee-Enfield .303 off its holder and returned to the vehicle with a bullet belt slung over one shoulder while proudly displaying his prize to the Sheik.

Sharyn Tomlinson was a widow and managed Tamala Station with the help of her two daughters, Patricia and Katelyn. They were returning from a fence check along the eastern boundary and were only a couple of kilometres from home. She noticed a dust trail over the Old Cemetery Hill that lead to the Kalbarri Road.

"Take a left, Trish. Let's see who our visitors are?" she instructed her youngest, wondering why they didn't see the chalkboard advising any new arrivals of her expected return. In the distance was the back-end of a 4wd. "Pass me the binoculars, Katelyn?" Sharyn asked before raising them to eye level. "I know that number plate," she called out to her daughters. "That's Colin Gibson's vehicle. Quick, head back to the house, right now. We need to ring the Denham police and reload your father's old shotgun."

The Sheik also noticed a dust trail from his higher vantage point heading their way from the south. He opened the glove box, snatched Colin's binoculars and zoomed in on the approaching vehicle. "The police!" he yelled at Colin. "You said no police." The Sheik swung the binoculars while holding the strap and collected Colin clean across the side of his face, leaving an open cut which soon started to leach a small blood trail down one cheek.

"Stop the car, Aditya. Waluya, pass me that rifle," the Sheik screamed. He launched himself out of the front passenger door, checked the spring-loaded magazine before loading ten bullets. He tapped it on the rifle's wooden butt, then inserted it under the breach before he adjusted the sliding rear ramp sights to the 500-yard setting and leant his upper body across the warm bonnet. With the stock of the .303 firmly embedded into his shoulder, he prepared for a short wait.

Detective Inspector Ryan Shillings shifted back a gear to negotiate what he knew to be the last set of rolling hills that would lead to the rear entrance of the homestead. As he approached the next summit, his windshield shattered into a thousand pieces. His initial reaction was maybe a stone chip, but that was an impossibility, then a second bullet entered the passenger's side, and his junior officer rocketed back into his seat with an over-powering body slap as the bullet ripped a hole in his chest cavity, forcing his head to slump forward, colliding hard against the dash. Instinctively, Ryan pulled hard on the wheel as another shot rang loud. "Some bastard is shooting at us," he realised too late.

The *Hilux* suddenly swerved off the side of the road and headed down an embankment, stopping only when the bull bar collided head-on into the opposite side of the small gorge. The airbag exploded and momentarily stunned Ryan while the radiator started spewing water and green coolant through a split down one side. He checked for a pulse on his now-dead constable then opened the driver's side door, slid out and unclipped his police Glock 22 .40 calibre while taking cover behind a natural mound of red dirt. Another bullet ricocheted off the bonnet before he could duck for cover. Ryan stood and returned some covering fire, then retreated back down the gully. He needed to negotiate the small ridge top and attempt to backtrack his way to the homestead past the airstrip. He fired off another three rounds and made a scrambling run up and over the incline. The Sheik followed the moving man with the fixed-post front sights, following his every move. He squeezed the trigger and watched with a relieved satisfaction as the body fell backwards and out of view.

"Are you people crazy?" Colin yelled from the back of the Toyota. "You just shot a cop—a W.A. cop at that. You're all dead men walking, you morons. They'll hunt you down and execute you all—legally."

The Sheik turned to Aditya, "Drive down to the police car. We need to check both men are dead, then we can turn around and head back to the house. The time has come to organise a plane. This country is too big to drive by car. They must have a land-based phone inside." Colin watched on in utter dismay. This had all just gone to complete shit, and now he felt remorseful and ashamed at being responsible for the possible deaths of two police officers.

The sight of the police *Hilux* angle parked down a steep gully filled Kelly's head with uneasy thoughts. He pulled hard on the handbrake, leapt from the vehicle and slid down to the trough of the windswept sandstone on his backside. The radiator was still steaming, and the driver's door was swung wide open, but there was no sign of Ryan. He bent his head and was greeted by the young constable slumped to one side of the passenger's seat. A pool of cajoled blood on the seat and floor needed no explanation. Kelly felt for a pulse. He raised his bloodied fingers and ordered the yawning Abigail to get back inside the car. The blood on his hand told her he wasn't kidding. Evina packed away her laptop.

Kelly searched the dead officer's holster for his weapon. It was empty. He opened the glove compartment in more hope than expectation, again, nothing. Then he remembered. He opened the back door and ripped the rear bench seat out and discarded it behind him. Underneath, still clipped into its holder, was Ryan's personal Colt AR-15 semi-auto rifle with a full 30-round staggered-column detachable magazine. Kelly recalled how proud Ryan was the day he pointed out his secret hiding spot. *You never can be too sure out here in the wild outback*, he remembered Ryan explaining.

The Nissan's four off-road Bridgestone all-terrain tyres barely touched the rough gravel and sand-based surface in Kelly's haste to arrive at the homestead. He rolled to a stop behind the shearing sheds. "Stay here, both of you. I want to see what we might be up against." Kelly was in no mood for any arguments from the twins. He ran the short distance using the two 5,000-litre corrugated iron water tanks as cover, ending up near a tool shed that gave a clear view of the back door and verandah. There he laid-first-eyes on a long-wheelbase Toyota *Land Cruiser* pulled up under the shade of a tall gum. A small plane came buzzing in at low altitude from the east, then banked hard right, almost skimming the gabled roof.

Who the hell is that? Kelly pondered.

Clancy Thornton jumped on his two-way and selected the open channel. "I've got him. It's Colin—I flew right over the homestead, and it's his 4wd for sure. How far you boys away? Over."

"This is Rocket Rod on-channel, Clanc'. Our ETA is about twenty minutes. I gotta warn you though, me two brothers are getting itchy trigger fingers. Over."

"This is Roy on-channel, Clancy. Johnno's just closing the last gate now, near the abandoned ram yards. We should be coming up to the old Karkaru burial site shortly. Maybe twenty to twenty-five minutes away. Can you see Colin anywhere? Over."

"Bob and Leroy Clements on-channel, Clancy. We're coming in from Carrarang Station along the western boundary, and nobody is getting past us. You can count on that. Over." The Penneman brothers who were both ex-army were currently sitting on 145 kph in their souped-up V8 Range Rover on their way from Nanga Station.

Over three hundred people throughout the Murchison region were glued to their two-ways, hanging off every word spoken as the avalanche of help was zeroing in on the bullseye that was Tamala Station. We take care of our own, was their call to action.

Stone was busy reloading two spare clips from the back of the Seahawk. He was still over seventeen minutes away with no idea what to expect on his arrival.

Inside the homestead, Katelyn lay on the lounge room floor with a broken jaw from the butt-end of the .303 and was being cared for by her sister. Sharyn stood resolute, between her daughters and the three deranged foreigners who now occupied her lounge room. One was screaming in another language at someone on the phone. Sharyn thought he may have been trying to order a plane to come pick up him and his two accomplices. The Sheik interrupted his heated conversation and told Mayadi to see if the plane that just flew by was the police. He waved both his arms towards Sharyn, "Can this plane land? Do you have an airstrip on your property?" he screamed in perspiring desperation.

She took her time and thought about her answer, then just pointed to an aerial photograph that hung on the wall above the stone fireplace. The station airstrip was located behind the Billie Cythera well, about two kilometres south of the homestead.

She knew Henry's old 12-gauge Browning was still leaning against the wall behind the kitchen door, but it was unloaded, at her own insistence. The beady eyes of the smaller Arab never left her for a second as he held the dead constable's Glock 22 at arm's length. Aditya Sukato was becoming nervous as beads of sweat dripped from his hooked-shaped nose.

Mayadi pushed through the rear door and turned right along the wooden porch. Kelly ducked his head just in time. Mayadi walked within ten feet of his position, then followed the house back out to the front and searched the skies. Kelly grabbed the only opportunity he would have to reach the side window and get some eyes on what might be happening inside. The curtains were made from sheer white lace and allowed a distorted view into an empty bedroom. He moved down to the next window. *Bingo! Ground zero.* He counted five people and two weapons. *Not good odds.* He pressed his back up against the Tamala limestone wall and quietly actioned a single round into the empty breach.

Just then a thundering roar could be heard from the distance, causing the windows to vibrate. Kelly propped with his back hard-pressed against the side of the house and turned to his left in time to see an airborne Big Mack prime mover come flying over the last rise along the gravel road in a cloud of dust with the name Rocket Rod, emblazoned on the front stone guard.

"Who the hell is this bloke?" he asked again. "He looks like he's late for his own funeral."

The Sheik snatched the Glock from Sukato's hand and passed him the old Lee-Enfield. "Go . . . Go now, Aditya. Shoot the infidels. God is great . . . God is with you. *Hurry*," he shouted. Aditya followed the orders of his religious leader without question. He ran through the front door, yelling, "Allah is great, Allah is great. Come, Waluya, destiny awaits us in heaven." Sukato fired two rounds at the inbound Mack truck. Mayadi pulled out a machete and started to wave it around above his head while running towards the parked *Land Cruiser*. Colin could only watch on as the distance between this crazed, machete-wielding Muslim closed with each stride. "Kill the infidels, Allah is our prophet—death to you all," the disillusioned Arab chanted.

The Sheik smashed down the phone. He was reaching the point of no return, and he knew it. The wagons were circling, and he was being corralled into an inescapable corner. He walked over and back-handed Sharyn, sending her sprawling to the floor. Patricia jumped to her feet to remonstrate and was kneed hard below the stomach, knocking the wind from her lungs. The Sheik ran from the house with the Glock pointed out in front. He spotted another parked car and ran towards it. Only then did he realise there were two more infidels, both women, still seated inside. He opened the passenger door and used the barrel end of the Glock to muzzle Abigail to the driver's seat. "You—drive now," and then he half-turned and pushed the barrel into Evina's forehead. "You—crawl into the back where I can keep a close eye on you." He waved the gun in her face until she complied. "Drive, now. This way," he was pointing back down the road they'd just travelled.

Kelly couldn't see Colin through the side window tinting of the parked *Land Cruiser*. He crouched to one knee and took aim with the AR-15 at the man carrying what looked like an old World War I rifle. Another shot echoed from the .303 and ricocheted off the alloy bull bar. Kelly placed the crosshairs of the scope in front of the running man, still randomly firing at the incoming Rocket Rod. Through the optical lens, Kelly could only watch on as the man's body suddenly lifted into the air in the opposite direction and crashed hard against the dried red clay. The rifle bounced from his grasp and came to rest next to a clay tum full of water. His body shook for a moment and then went still. Kelly turned again to see the under-over blue metal barrel of a Winchester .44 lever action poking out from the open passenger's window of Rocket Rod's truck.

"What the f...? Who are these guys, the Earp family?" He was totally confused. He could see the other man opening the rear door of the Toyota with a machete held high in his hand. A second cannon shot sounded from the cabin of the Big Mack. A hole the size of an orange suddenly appeared and started spilling blood from the Arab's back as his head bounced off the rear-mounted spare tyre, forcing him to spiral backwards in a slow pirouetting twirl. Kelly grabbed another look inside the house and was shocked to see all three women lying flat on the floor with no sign of the third man. He opened the window and jumped through. Just then, the unmistakable sound of a helicopter landing disturbed the dry heat outside as the rotors started shifting dust and flies in every direction.

"A helicopter, why not? Am I the only bastard without an invitation to this little get-together? This is getting ridiculous," Kelly was still trying to make sense out of this whole ludicrous setting unfolding like a Wild Bill Hickok western show.

He raced into the kitchen and wet down a tea-towel for the mother's head. It was painfully obvious that the youngest daughter was nursing a broken jaw, and her sister was still gasping for air while pointing to the rear door. It took a good couple of minutes before she could gather her breath to speak. "The other man, he's got a gun and ran out the back. I think I heard the sound of a car driving off." Kelly suddenly went rigid, every sensory receptor in his body spiked and his adrenalin level peaked like a shot of morphine. *The twins?*

He raced out the door, almost ripping it off its hinges. Dixie's Nissan was nowhere to be seen. He heard the sound of a familiar voice.

"Bloody hell, Jack, what have you and these boys been up to here? Honestly, I leave you alone for..."

"Tobias, the third man, he's taken off in our 4wd—with the girls," Kelly interrupted.

"Shit, quick, follow me. Come on, old man, shake a leg— let's go. The twins are counting on the two of us now. Which way are they headed?" Stone shouted as they ducked and made a desperate sprint towards the idling Seahawk.

"They must have backtracked. There is no way on this planet they could have got past old, Wyatt Earp," Kelly explained.

"Who . . . ?" Stone's frown was that of bafflement.

Kelly tapped the pilot on the shoulder and pointed south as the metal bird lifted into the air while he and Stone harnessed up. With his earphones now secured, the voice of the co-pilot came bubbling through. "What are we looking for?"

"A silver Nissan *Patrol,*" Kelly replied.

"The ground radar will pick it up as soon as we get some altitude. What sort of head start do they have?"

"Not much, so, let's step on it," Kelly anxiously replied.

"OK, hang on." The co-pilot completed his first sweep with the Seahawk's An/Aps-124 Raytheon radar. "Nothing yet, but we're still climbing."

Kelly looked over at Stone. "Why are you even here anyway, Tobias? Or maybe I shouldn't ask."

"Maybe we are looking for the same man, Jack. Just like the good old days."

"All right," the co-pilot interrupted. "There's the contact now. Travelling west- by south-west sixteen kilometres away. We'll have a visual in less than three minutes."

"Jack, you might need to take this guy out, he's a real nasty piece of work, and he won't hesitate to take the twins with him."

"Who are these clowns, anyway?"

"His name is, Aris Munander: a.k.a. the Sheik. He's a wanted terrorist and is connected to the Bali bombings. He and his two dead buddies were trying to sneak into the country through the back door."

"Not a difficult thing to pull off in a State the size of W.A. What do you want *me* to do, throw rocks at this shithead?" Inside, he was cursing the fact he'd left Ryan's rifle back at the homestead.

Stone unbuckled his harness, leaned over the seat and dragged a canvas bag closer. He unzipped it and pulled out another rifle. "This should do the trick, just nicely." Stone placed it on his old partner's lap. Kelly held the American-designed Barrett M82 semi-automatic anti-material rifle and struggled to suppress a grin.

"You can see they've made a few improvements since the last time you fired a shot in anger. You're the man, Jack. It's up to you now. No one else up here has a chance in hell of getting off a kill shot at a moving target while bouncing around in this helicopter. Make it happen, Jack, make your country proud and at the same time take out the last of the scum who ordered the deaths of two hundred two innocent people in Bali."

"The scary thing about that load of crap you just fed to me, Tobias—is it's all true."

"Approaching the vehicle now," the co-pilot advised.

"Engage the blue pulse," the pilot casually ordered. The vortex interaction would now almost be entirely eliminated with just three added flaps to the rotor blades that move up and down at 15-40-times-per-second, using piezoelectric motors. The Seahawk was now a silent bird of prey.

Stone raised his binoculars and could clearly see Abigail driving, with the gun-toting Sheik waving a handgun in her general direction. Evina looked to be in the back storage compartment. "Here, take a look," Stone offered.

"I only need to see through this lens, Tobias, and hopefully just the one time," Kelly replied, a little apprehensive about what lay ahead.

"They seem to be heading for the coast. Radar says it's only four kilometres away," the co-pilot announced.

"The cliff face? A final blaze of glory as this terrorist goes to meet his seventy vestal virgins—with Abigail and Evina," Stone advised. The mere thought sent shock waves of horror through Kelly's entire body and prompted him into action.

"Manoeuvre the bird around to the passenger's side. This Sheik bloke is facing Abigail and won't spot us from that angle," Kelly instructed the pilot.

"Roger that."

"Two k's to go, and their history, Jack," Stone reminded him.

Kelly didn't need to be told the obvious. "I got it, okay. Now just shut up for a second, will you," he shouted back.

He pushed his shoulder into the open window frame then counted down and squeezed the trigger which was followed by a sharp *crack* just as a wind shift jostled the Seahawk sideways. The front quarter-panel window on the Nissan shattered. Abigail screamed while the Sheik turned his head and gawked in denial at the silent airborne metal monster.

"Don't stop, keep driving," Aris Munandar roared while waving his handgun at the distraught female driver. The anguish in his voice was that of a man fast running out of options. He was becoming irrational and struggled with the futility of his dissolution that was becoming more and more apparent as each second ticked by. Evina shifted her weight and prepared to launch herself over the rear seat. The hollow end of the barrel pointing directly in her line of sight stopped her in mid-flight. The deranged Arab leader turned 180 degrees in his seat, wound down the window and started firing wildly at the hovering Navy Seahawk.

The pilot pulled back hard on the twist-grip-stick mounted on the collective control to change the pitch angle of the main rotor. The Seahawk responded in an instant and gained altitude.

A spark flew from the starboard skid, and Kelly instinctively lifted his leg. "Fuck, I missed." He steadied himself a second time. "Get me back down," Kelly demanded, as a matter of urgency. He steadied his body as the Seahawk buffeted. "That's good, hold it right there." *All right, you prick, this one is for the eighty-eight.*

The Seahawk was now shadowing the moving vehicle like chewing gum sticks to a shoe. Their airspeed was just 37 knots. Kelly completed a quick mental calculation. He calmly rolled back the clock to his sniper training days and murmured, "Bullet speed nine hundred m.p.s. Distance; approx two hundred fifty metres. Okay, Lucky Phil, aim for where his head is going to be—not where it is."

Kelly's breathing slowed. He expelled the last scintilla of carbon dioxide from both lungs and leaned into the Seahawk's rigid frame. "Three – two – one . . ."

He squeezed the trigger a second time. The 50 BMG-416 Barrett cartridge left the 29-inch-long-barrel at a muzzle velocity of 853 metres per second and punched a neat hole above the neck into the base of the Sheik's skull causing a showering spray of blood splatter to cover the left side of Abigail's face like she was inflicted with some sort of pox. Aris Munandar was dead—killed instantly, and his lifeless impetus propelled him forward in a sprawling action. Abigail squealed as his head landed on her lap before sliding sideways down both her legs onto the floor. His upper torso and backside were jammed under the steering wheel.

Evina yelled from the rear, "Abby, stop the car or turn, do something!" The watery horizon of the Indian Ocean loomed larger than life beyond the fast-approaching cliff edge.

"I can't, what's left of his head is jammed in front of the accelerator and brake pedals, and his backside is pushed up hard against the wheel. I can't turn in either direction," Abigail shouted. She frantically tried to free the dead weight by pulling at the Sheik's stolen belt and pants with her free hand, causing his ill-fitting trousers to slide down his buttocks.

"Whoa—don't look now, but I can see this man's arse, Evina. Yuk, that's disgusting. Oh look, he has a birthmark in the shape of a crescent moon," Abigail shared.

"A bloody what? Abigail, jump for God's sake—NOW! Before we go over the edge," Evina screamed and pleaded at the same time as she opened the rear tailgate and firstly rolled out the celestial globe, wrapped in a towel and then that was soon followed by the Esky with the chest full of coins and jewels inside. Abigail was still fighting with the door handle. She gained a firm grip and pulled it hard. The door flew open, but her seatbelt was still secured, and the clasp was buried under the dead weight of the bleeding Sheik. Evina threw herself over the rear bench seat and landed headfirst between the two front bucket seats with her face inches away from the moon-shaped birthmark, now clearly visible against the sun-deprived hairy rear-end of the dead Arab. She placed both hands on his belt and yanked frenziedly in an attempt to slide the corpse towards the passenger door. Evina slid her hand down between the body and the centre console and fumbled for the clasp with her fingers.

"Whatever you're trying to do, Evina—please hurry." The panic in her sister's voice was crystal-clear. Evina dug deeper and flipped her thumb and index finger forward. Both girls heard the sound of the clasp releasing. Abigail's belt loosened as she wiggled her legs free of the Arab's final death grasp. Evina launched herself over the back seat, grabbed the strap of her shoulder bag and remembered the one-hour ground training the one and only time she parachuted from a perfectly good aeroplane as she dived from the rear luggage bay onto the hard sun-parched landscape in a rolling action.

Abby had little choice but to jettison herself sideways as the edge of the Zuytdorp Cliffs were only a matter of metres away. She landed hard on her shoulder and started bouncing uncontrollably towards the steep bluff. Abigail could feel bits of skin being peeled off different body parts, and her head was being pounded against the hard ground until her momentum slowed and she came to a sudden halt in a seated position with both legs dangling over the precipice. From this position she got a bird's-eye view as Dixie's Nissan *Patrol*, his pride and joy, nosedived over the two-hundred-foot drop-off, landing bonnet first and imploding, before erupting like a plummeting earthbound meteorite. A thick black cloud of smoke and proliferating diesel flames erupted in a scene that resembled a World War II Spitfire colliding with the White Cliffs of Dover.

Evina jumped to her feet and dusted herself down, then hobbled over like a drunken emu in full stride to her sister who looked like she was just sitting there while enjoying the view. She grabbed Abigail by both her shoulders and dragged her back to a safe distance. She held her tight in both arms. Tears flowed in a slow trickle, then each twin started crying, which soon turned into a full-blown howl as they both eventually realised their precarious situation. Abigail was the first to switch to a slow laugh. Evina met her sister's hazel eyes and soon followed. Seconds later both twins were in unabated raptures of side-splitting laughter. "So, Evina," Abigail spilled out, "where do you think we should spend our next vacation? I hear Paris is lovely in the spring."

"I managed to save the globe *and* the chest," Evina blurted out, without even knowing why.

"Well, that *is* a relief. Don't worry about your twin sister. I think I'm okay, and thanks for asking, by the way." Abigail couldn't resist the jab under the bizarre circumstances.

The four occupants of the Navy Seahawk had all bear witness to the whole ordeal from their stationary flight position less than a hundred metres away. They all sat in stunned silence. Kelly broke the reticence first. "I owe Dixie a new car now. Do you believe that? Why—why would she just drive it off the cliff like that?" Kelly was dumbfounded.

"Women drivers, Jack. They're all the same, mate," Stone answered.

A combined laugh from the two front seats could be heard through the earphones. "Well, we better go and pick 'em up and then you can ask that same question in person, Jack. Put her down, boys. Oh, and one other thing, Jack. This mate of yours, Dixie, he owns a cray fishing boat, is that right?" Stone asked.

"Yeah, why?"

"I'm going to need a water taxi from the *Ballarat* into Kalbarri. I'll leave it up to you to make the call, okay."

Operation Blue Skies is now complete—well, almost, Stone silently surmised. He walked over to the edge of the Zuytdorp Cliff face then retrieved from his top pocket the third wooden figurine of a goanna standing tall with a blue-tongue lizard dangling from the corners of his mouth. "Here, you can have the honours, Jack. It was your shot that got the bastard."

Kelly cast an inquisitive eye over the carved figure and smiled while he thought of the real Thin Lizzy back at his home on Koh Chang. He stepped back and threw it towards the burning wreckage and smiled at the irony.

Chapter-38

THE NAVY SEAHAWK put down a short distance from Rocket Rod's stationary Big Mack. Stone and Abigail ducked under the rotors and headed for the increasing crowd of spectators who were gathered on the front bull-nosed porch as the helicopter immediately lifted back into the air on a return run.

Sharyn Tomlinson raced out to meet Abigail and, while holding her bleeding and bruised arm, directed her to the dining room where she had already put together a makeshift infirmary to deal with both her injured daughters. The St John's first aid kit supplied by the hospital in Northampton was neatly laid out across the twelve-seat marri wood dining table. Ray and Johnno's black dust-covered Holden Ute came to a skidding stop, and the Penneman brothers also arrived while Clancy's Cessna was preparing to land over the ridge to the south.

Jack and Evina were still staring at the unrecognisable remains of Dixie's Nissan *Patrol*. The sudden realisation that her laptop was now somewhere amongst the burning wreckage was like being slapped with a feathered pillow.

"All my work, my research—was in my notebook," Evina cried out.

"Surely, you have a backup somewhere?" Kelly hesitated while waiting for her answer.

"Yes, of course. I'll need to access the Smithsonian's website and buy another laptop. Bloody hell, what a contradiction of events today turned out to be. Who were those people anyway?" Evina's anger was palpable.

"Tobias said they were terrorists, on the run."

"Well, they're not running anymore, that's for sure," Evina answered, with a satisfied look imprinted on her dirt-covered face. She ran four fingers through her matted hair. "Bloody hell, I must look a right old mess," as she wiped her face with the sleeve of her ripped shirt.

"It's just you and me standing here right now, Evina. Trust me, you still scrub up okay."

Evina cast a womanly glance over towards where Kelly stood, still in a state of shock at what happened to Dixie's Nissan. "All of a sudden, Jack, I'm feeling really horny right now. If we had the time, we could tear off a quickie."

Kelly turned his head and cursed at the sound of the Seahawk returning. Evina picked up her precious celestial globe while Kelly scoured the red scorched earth for the 17th-century coins and gemstones scattered around the place.

By the time the Seahawk landed again, the crowd had grown to over fifteen people. Clancy Thornton then arrived driving the abandoned police *Hilux*, still spewing green coolant with a wounded and thirsty, but relieved Detective Ryan Shillings occupying the passenger's seat with two more men named Geoff and Leroy following close behind. Together they removed the body of the young constable from the back of the pickup, wrapped him in a blanket, then placed the corpse inside the meat cooler located in the shearing shed opposite the windmill and water tanks.

Stone stepped out the front door of the homestead with Katelyn following close behind and gestured for Ryan to follow him to the waiting Seahawk. The co-pilot strapped both the injured into their harnesses and prepared for an immediate medical evacuation to the Carnarvon Hospital before heading back to the HMAS *Ballarat*, now steaming down the inside of Dorre Island and about to head past Cape Inscription at the northernmost point of Dirk Hartog Island as they chartered a course back to their home port on Garden Island.

The twins accepted Sharyn's offer to shower and were both given a change of clothes, courtesy of Sharyn's two daughters' wardrobe. They both could have passed muster as a couple of station hands in their jeans, flannelette shirts and riding boots.

Evina sat under the shade of the front verandah with her cup of tea in hand. Now firmly immersed in the quagmire that was her celestial globe and contemplated the next link in her never-ending chain that now pointed to Seven Spirit Bay in the Northern Territory. She knew she was close to something, but the hand of fate kept reaching into her quest for answers and shifting the goalposts. She was well aware she was close to what some may refer to as, reaching a fork in her road journey, an impasse to unravel a 17th-century manuscript that would reverberate throughout the modern world.

Evina stood and made her way to the kitchen to rinse her cup in the sink. She looked out through the window that cast a wide-angled view of the rolling landscape that was Tamala. A hazy reflection from the polished glass window caused her to turn. A row of three elongated framed old black & white photos hung on the opposite wall as a backdrop to the six-seater kitchen table. She pushed a chair back under the ornately carved wooden setting and ran her eye over the first frame. A picture of the larger-than-life Tom Pepper beamed back with his Aboriginal wife, Lurleen, and her sister, Ada, all standing on the cliff face that was the site of the *Zuytdorp* discovery. It was dated 1954 and captured by Philip Playford.

The second photo was of two smiling faces portraying a pair of women from obviously different cultures. One was Aboriginal while the second was of European ancestry. The caption read: Great Aunties Edna and Jan. Upper reaches Murchison River - 1964.

Aunties—how can that be? Evina silently questioned the validity. The third in the set of three photos was titled - 'Family Art' in someone's own handwriting and the image that was staring back at her almost caused Evina to stumble backwards and trip over the table. She stood in a state of frozen paralysis and anticipated fervour at the photo taken inside a cave of a hand-painted twin-masted ship with square rigging under full sail, and the other sent Evina racing to gather her bag. She almost bowled over Abigail in her haste to recover Barnacle Bob's old coin. Both Sharyn and Patricia were startled by the sudden rush of movement inside the house and went to investigate the reason why.

Evina viewed the worn image on the back of the coin, and then she compared it to the photo of the second cave painting. The rising sun in the background was easily discernible, but it was the image of a strangely dressed man, seated cross-legged with both his palms facing out that sent her into a complete tailspin.

Could it be—it has to be, who else could it possibly be? She mulled this over for a while when a shadow appeared over her bruised shoulder. Sharyn stood next to Evina. "That's Robert's old coin. How did you come to have that in your possession?"

"Robert? Sorry, I only knew him as, Barnacle Bob, and our one and only meeting was, unfortunately, cut short. I was with him in Bali when he was murdered."

"I read about that in *The West Australian*. That must have been terrifying." Sharyn strolled over to a Queen Anne dresser and slid open a drawer. She retrieved a leather-bound photo album and placed it open on the table. "These are the actual original photos." She pointed to the three frames hanging on the wall. "All those are enlarged reprints for show only."

Evina's heartbeat was increasing with each page she turned. She stopped at the photo of the two aunties and met Sharyn's gaze with a look that screamed—*please explain.*

"Oh, boy," Patricia interrupted. "Here we go again. Once Mum starts talking about the old times, Evina, she gets on a roll, and you can't stop her. Foretold is forewarned. I'll put the kettle on again, shall I?"

Evina hardly heard a word spoken. She was totally captivated, trying to absorb the snippets of information her scientific brain was attempting to analyse in a matter of just milliseconds.

"You're not the first to question our two aunties, Evina. It often stirs up an interesting conversation and sometimes heated debate with those that don't quite understand the history."

Evina was studying the rock art of the yacht. "This is unbelievable. Where was this photo taken?" she managed to verbal through her escalating excitement.

"Walga Rock," Sharyn answered in a matter-of-fact tone. "And now you're wondering how two sisters can be both black and white, aren't you? And it's a fair question, Evina. Just look at me. Would you believe both my parents were of full Aboriginal blood? Of course not—and why would you—unless . . . ?" Sharyn let the question linger. Both the twins swapped an unknowing glance as Kelly entered the kitchen and joined in the ensuing history lesson.

"Your skin is fair, you have predominately blonde-coloured hair plus you have freckles," Abigail pointed out the obvious.

"The White Tribe," Sharyn answered, clearly passionate about this topic.

Evina could not hold back anymore. "This image of the seated man with the sun over his shoulder, who painted this, and how old is it?" Her desperation for answers was equally matched by Sharyn's willingness to share her family's history.

"In our Aboriginal culture, stories are passed down the ancestry line through corroboree, an event where the Dreamtime interacts with dance, music and costume. There is no doubt whatsoever that the interaction of Dutch shipwrecked survivors interspersed with the Aboriginal people, probably as a pure survival mechanism. We truly believe it was Jan Pelgrom de Bye van Bemmel who painted the early Dutch ship on that rock. He was more than likely the earliest proponent of the White Tribe from the north."

"How could you possibly come to that conclusion without evidence?" Evina needed to clear the path of reason to intervene. A nice sentiment that might lighten the mood around a campfire conversation, but the undeniable proof was the way of science, not hand-me-down stories through the generations of families, however romantic they might seem.

Sharyn gestured towards where Patricia was standing over the sink filling the kettle. "Darling, go fetch the trumpet, will you?"

Patricia returned and unwrapped from a velvet cloth a stained brass trumpet. Evina knew immediately it was old—very old. She put on her reading glasses and read a small inscription along the exterior of the flared bell, "Cornelis de Dikke Trumpeter".

"Do you recognise the name, Evina?" Sharyn was almost challenging her scientific and historical knowledge base.

"No, I can't say that I do," she replied honestly.

"Cornelis was his given name, and the pet name of the Fat Trumpeter was a reference to his bulbous wide girth and the fact he kept the sailors on the *Batavia* amused for hours with the tunes from this very trumpet. This was found close to Walga Rock."

The Batavia—*what am I hearing?* Evina wanted to ask. *What else does this family have conveniently hidden away?*

She knew from her own experiences that this was not a time to spook anyone. Tread very carefully. The sense of nostalgic history was not lost on Kelly. He left the room and returned with the small wooden chest, and the withered hide, then plonked them in the centre of the table. Patricia was first to walk over and read the barely decipherable carved markings on the inside of what was left of the hide. "This looks interesting, avia – six-two-nine," she read out. Now it was both Sharyn and Patricia's turn to look on in shared amazement.

Sharyn was floored, "It seems we were destined to meet, Evina. The last time these objects would have shared the same space was more than likely on the *Batavia* three hundred ninety years ago." It was turning out to be a wistful moment.

Evina wanted more answers, and she was prepared to beg, borrow or steal. "But this likeness of what I believe to be,

Emperor Jahangir, how could of someone copied that unless they saw this very same image depicted elsewhere? This is of the utmost importance, Sharyn. Do you have any idea?" She felt like she was balancing on a see-saw; a push one way spelt another dead end, but the alternative was giving her goosebumps. The consternation of where this may lead to was almost unbearable.

Sharyn was on a roll now. "This dates back to the White Tribe who once thrived amongst the Spirit Bays, a settlement of over three hundred people that survived for over one hundred fifty years and then mysteriously disappeared—almost overnight from the face of the earth in the late Seventeen Hundreds. Our ancestors talk about an invading force that resulted in the people fleeing inland and trekking over fifteen hundred miles through the desert and the hinterland of Australia's harsh interior. A few survivors made it to a place known as Palm Springs, and these are just two of the many examples of rock art that still survive today and will continue to endure as long as they remain hidden from prying eyes. I have been privileged to have witnessed them with my own eyes while my aunties were both still alive."

"The Spirit Bays?" Evina questioned. "Are you referring to Seven Spirit Bay, Sharyn?"

"There are more than just seven spirits. Throughout Arnhem Land alone there are roaming ogres, bogeymen and bogeywomen, sorcerers, cannibal babies, giant baby-guzzlers and feather-slippered spirit beings able to dispatch victims with a single fatal garrotte. Lustful old men wishing to satiate their unbridled sexual appetites who relentlessly pursue beautiful nubile young girls through the night sky, and on land. Plus, there are many other monstrous beings, as well." Sharyn explained like she was reading poetry from a book.

"Australia's north is the abode of malevolent shades and vampire-like wind and shooting star spirit beings. There is also the murderous flesh-eating bunyip, a humanoid lizard-like devil who lurks in the deep rocky crevices and waterholes, biding his time to rise up, grab and drown unsuspecting human children or adults who stray close to the water's edge. Certain sorcerers gleefully dismember their victim's limb-by-limb, and there are other monstrous entities as well, living parallel lives to the human beings residing in the same places. You need to talk with Leonard. He's the keeper of *kaartdijin* or knowledge from the *kura*, our cultural past. I remember him sharing a story about how the *bulyits* worshipped an altarpiece that was left by the invading forces. That may be a clue to the Emperor Jahangir you refer to, Evina?"

"The bulyits, I don't quite follow?" Evina wanted to clarify.

"The white-skinned, smelly people with hair over their entire bodies," Sharyn explained. "At the risk of sounding rather crass, Evina, all white people have a certain odour about them that is easily identified by any blackfella. Just as you might be offended by the body odour of a black man, the reverse is also true in our culture."

Suddenly Evina was very aware of her self-being, wishing now she still had her *Chanel Eau de Parfum* spray.

"How would I find this man called, Leonard? Is he a family friend?" Evina's face felt flushed as she allowed her thoughts to drift to what the *Book of Remedies* might actually look like. *Stop dreaming, Evina, and stay on point.*

"Leonard Casley is his full name. You hold the answer to that question in your very hand this minute. Look, and all shall be revealed," Sharyn almost prophesied.

Evina opened the palm of her hand. Barnacle Bob's coin was still firmly in her grasp. *Prince Leonard?* "You mean this Prince Leonard actually exists? He is real—is that what you're telling me?" Evina asked, slightly aghast.

"Oh, he is more than real. He is my uncle," Sharyn walked over to view the coin closely in Evina's hand.

"Robert's older brother Richard did a mountain of legal work for Leonard back in the 1970s and gave the two brothers a commemorative coin each as a token of his goodwill.

"A country within a country without a king," Abigail remembered Dixie's explanation of Prince Leonard when they shared a few cold beers together back at the Kalbarri Hotel.

Evina's head was reeling. An hour ago her quest to uncover her ancient manuscript lay in ruins at the base of the Zuytdorp Cliffs. And now the trail was hot again.

Who would ever want to be a research scientist? I would, that's who. Her investigative juices were about to start churning once more.

Chapter·39

STONE WAS BACK ON BOARD on board the HMAS *Ballarat* steaming down the West Australian coast towards the Port of Fremantle. The Carnarvon police together with a full team from the Perth-based forensics unit converged on Tamala Station like a swarm of awakened carpenter bees. Firstly, they needed to deal with both the murdered police officer and the two very dead terrorists masquerading as refugees, then with the logistics of recovering the Sheik's cindered remains.

Dixie shifted on his barstool while seated at the front bar of the Kalbarri Hotel. Barry—the big bad bustling barman, set up a round of drinks at the insistence of the twins who still held the pool table, beating the last challengers by seven balls. The girls weren't half-bad at doubles.

Dixie slowly turned to face his old mate, before he asked the burning question. "So, Jack, just so I fully understand what it is you're trying to explain to me? You say my 4wd is now at the bottom of the Zuytdorp Cliffs. But that's okay because *why...?*" A look of anguish stretched across Dixie's face.

"Well, just think about how many crayfish and crabs might decide to make the old Nissan their home. You like eating lobster thermidor, don't you, Dixie? A couple of egg yolks, a splash of brandy—beautiful." Kelly was still working out a way to repay Dixie without hurting the bank balance. He pictured himself explaining the wrecked Nissan to Tiaan back home who could still account where he'd spent his first dollar and what for. Like all Thai women, she was a genius when it came to money.

Dixie asked in a last-ditch effort to understand why. "I can't believe it. Why did she just drive it off the cliff, then—did you even ask her?"

"Be my guest." Kelly waved his arm towards Abigail, who was about to pot the black in the middle pocket. "Go for your life, Dixie. Just be prepared to duck and run while she's holding a pool cue in her hand. Abigail is still a bit sensitive about the whole episode. You understand—don't you?" Kelly answered, tongue in cheek.

"Someone owes me a car, Jack, and that ball, old mate, has squarely landed in your court."

"All under control, Dixie. Leave it with me."

"Yeah, right? Like that last job in Darwin, heh, Jack?"

A young man with an Avis rent-a-car logo emblazoned on the pocket of his bright red shirt had just entered through the public bar's swinging front doors. Evina racked her cue and almost burnt a hole in the carpet to part with her AMEX card and sign the insurance forms before she was handed the keys to a sparkling near-new bronze Ford *Ranger*.

Kelly drove the rental down the one and the only main street of Kalbarri. Grey Street leads into Red Bluff Road and then heads south, past the Rainbow Jungle and over Wittecarra Creek. The scenic drive passes the Red Bluff Lookout, Mushroom Rock, Pot Alley and Eagle Gorge Lookout and then continues on to become the sealed coastal drive named after George Grey, an early explorer tasked with mapping the Western Australia coastline and beyond for the purposes of possible colonisation. His boat, the *Russel,* was reported wrecked in the vicinity of Shark Bay back in 1839.

The coastal town of Port Gregory was a farther 40 kilometres to the south and home of the not so famous Pink Lake. Hutt Lagoon is fed by a series of underground natural freshwater springs that run parallel to the ocean behind a barrier of sand dunes and is one of two possibilities concerning the brackish water Commander Pelsaert noted on his return trip to Jakarta. The lakeboasts a strange phenomenon where a pink hue created by the presence of carotenoid-producing algae called *Dunaliella salina*, which is a source of B-carotene, a food-colouring agent and a form of vitamin A, causing changes in the colour of the water. Depending on the time of day, the season and the amount of cloud cover, the lake changes through the spectrum of red to bubble-gum pink to a lilac purple.

The Batavia Coast soon gives way to the agricultural heartlands of the Mid West region with its rich volcanic soils supporting a myriad of cereal crops, including wheat, barley, canola and some lupins. Jack turned the Ford *Ranger* left onto Ogilvie West Road and continued driving until the first road-side mileage post indicated they were close to their destination.

Hutt River Province or the Principality of Hutt River, as it was now titled, is located about 70 kilometres south of Kalbarri. It is a micro-nation within Australia and was declared an independent province in 1970 after a dispute with the W.A. State Government over what the Casley family called draconian wheat production quotas. The Casley farm consisted of 4,000 hectares of farmable land. After their quotas were drastically reduced to just 1,647 bushels of wheat, which equated to about forty hectares of his total property holdings, the Casleys', together with five other farming families banded together to lodge a formal protest to the Governor of Western Australia Sir Douglas Kendrew.

Leonard George Casley believed that because the governor acted as the Queen's representative, this made Her Majesty liable, in tort, for applying an unlawful imposition as the reduced quota had not yet been passed into law. Casley lodged a claim under the Law of Tort for fifty-two million dollars in the belief the court action would force a revision of the quota. He also used the Law of Unjust Enrichment to successfully seize government-owned land surrounding his farm, which he hoped would increase his quota. Weeks later, he then claimed the State Government introduced a Bill into Parliament to resume his and other families' lands under compulsory acquisition laws. At this point, he and his associates claimed that international law allowed them to secede and from this moment on, Leonard Casley had declared the principality successfully seceded from the Commonwealth of Australia.

At about this time, Casley styled himself, His Majesty Prince Leonard I of Hutt. He did this because he believed it would enable him to take advantage of the *British Treason Act 1495*. This provides that the de facto king of a nation cannot be found guilty of treason due to an act of Parliament against the lawful king, and that anyone who interfered with that monarch's duties could be charged with treason themselves. Casley argued and continued to sell his wheat in open defiance of the quota. He believed that under Australian law, the Australian Federal Government had two years to respond to his bold declaration of sovereignty. Their failure to do just that gave the province 'de facto autonomy' on April 21, 1972.

Kelly slowed down as the bricked front entrance came into view. An old clapped-out EH Holden was parked to the side of the skinny road. Three Aboriginal boys, probably no older than 16 or 17, were in the process of loading up their boot. Kelly shifted back to second, and crawled past, which prompted Abigail to ask, "What are they up to?"

Kelly answered, "Poaching marron, freshwater crayfish, and they taste great."

"Won't they get into trouble?"

"Abigail, this is their country. As far as I'm concerned, forty thousand years' head start gives them the right to do what they bloody-well like."

"I see your point."

A swinging gate was hitched open under the shade of an enormous paperbark tree with a sign welcoming all visitors to the Principality of Hutt River.

Abigail checked her mobile for a signal then said, "Sharyn was right about no cell tower reception anywhere around here. I just hope this Prince Leonard is holding Court today, for your sake, Evina."

The self-proclaimed capital of Nain was a short drive up a winding dirt road. Kelly parked near the entrance to the administration building and government offices.

The first order of the day was to either present your passport or just simply apply and be issued a visa-on-arrival—for a $5.00 fee, of course. A well-displayed sign advertised there was no arrival or departure tax. A man in his early forties introduced himself as, Prince Ian The Grand Duke of Hutt and The Earl of Fairvale, then went about dispatching with the visa formalities like a well-honed bureaucrat. A Red Earth Safari Tour bus pulled up, and eight overseas visitors started jostling for a front position while forming a line behind the twins, eager to boast a stamp on their respective countries passports.

Evina wanted to introduce herself, explaining Sharyn's offer that her Uncle Leonard may be willing to share some information. She opened her phone and displayed her own photo of the cave painting and also offered Barnacle Bob's old coin, as proof of her well-intentioned request. Prince Ian directed her to the Royal Art Collection and then had to add, "We have over three hundred works available for viewing. If Dad's not there, try the Royal College of Advanced Research which unravels the discovery of the mathematical formula revealing, nature's basic construction code, and if that fails, he might be at the Stone of Light. Enjoy your stay at the Principality of Hutt River." Prince Ian was a natural at self-promotion.

Evina led the way like she was marching into battle. This mountain she had been trying to scale for the past ten years was suddenly looking like it may actually have a summit. An elderly man of slight build and stature with hunched shoulders was busy explaining the story behind the Stone of Light to a group of interested school-age excursionists. Kelly and Abigail sidled up to a glass cabinet filled with an array of rocks and crystals while Evina busied herself in perusing some of the other unusual exhibitions on offer.

Abigail listened with a growing interest while Prince Leonard stood slightly arched over another glass display and was obviously enjoying imparting the pearls of his wisdom and profound knowledge on a subject matter he was passionate about.

The enthusiastic Prince Leonard explained to the enthralled gathering, "The latest area of study embarked upon by the Royal College of Advanced Research using the ancient mathematics involved in gematria is the discovery made of nature's spirit code and its relationship and identification of every living being. World-leading discoveries in this area have led to further expansion on the subject, and an edifice is presently under construction in which we will endeavour to open as part of our thirty-fifth-anniversary celebrations to be held in 2007.

"This construction will be named as Princess Shirley's Sacred Educational Shrine. Gateway to Nature's Spirit World, and will contain the Stone of Light, which will reveal a never seen before newly discovered mineral. This stone has revealed great historical factors after the royal sons gathered it from a place in the Ashburton Ranges. You will also find the identical nature's spirit codes of both Jesus and Muhammad, as well as the spirit codes for Jerusalem and the Kaaba which was taken from Jerusalem. Hence you will also see that nature's spirit code for the Kaaba is reversed to that of Jerusalem. The equations for the universe at rest and the universe then creating are also to be found within this shrine," Prince Leonard concluded.

The teacher in charge thanked the prince for his wise words of wisdom in such interesting matters and led her students to the next attraction in the adjacent building.

Prince Leonard stepped forward and spoke in a voice that resounded with some authority. "Mrs Bishop-Joiner, I believe? It's so good of you to finally visit our country. Robert and I have discussed you in fond terms many a time." The prince extended his hand towards Evina, who was still preoccupied with a hand-stacked replica of a gateway built from what she was pretty sure resembled ballast bricks similar to other VOC ships. She turned to meet face-to-face with the self-appointed sovereign, trying to size up whether this frail, balding man standing in front of her with a lazy eye was enjoying the fruits of a thirty-year-old scam or was some reincarnated prophet. The two exchanged a soft handshake.

Evina extended the introduction. "This is my twin sister, Abigail, and our friend and boat captain, Jack Kelly."

"I was disturbed to find out about the death of Robert. He was truly a guiding light to so many of the younger generation. He will be sadly missed. You were present, then? Simply dreadful," Prince Leonard offered a heartfelt apology.

"I'm at a loss how I should address you. Your Royal Highness—Prince Leonard...?" Evina wanted to clarify.

"Just call me, Leonard. As you can see, I am neither crowned nor robed and seated on my throne. Right now, I am just another civilian—until three P.M." Abigail was sure she caught a disguised wry smile.

Evina asked, "Are you aware of my research, Leonard—is that what Bob and you discussed in private?"

"Yes, and no. Bob was a family friend, and we shared many interests, but you were a fascinating topic. I'll grant you that."

Evina opened up her photo gallery and displayed the image of who she thought maybe Emperor Jahangir. "Do you know how this rock painting came to be in existence?" Evina thought she was about to become very excited or start pounding her head against the ballast bricks, only a few feet to her right.

"The only honest way that question can be answered is by the true custodians of these lands. I have arranged for you all to accompany me tonight to witness something only a handful of white people will ever venture to see, in person. And the only reason this request was granted is that your research will have a direct bearing on the very people that may offer you an answer—for the betterment of humanity, or in this case; the

Aboriginal people. Tonight—eight o'clock at Murchison Station. Bring your toothbrushes and wear something warm that covers both your arms and legs, please."

The prince meandered off and instantly started up another conversation with the next group of tourists, wondering if this visit to another country was for real or a story to be shared with friends and family back home, wherever that may be.

Kelly and the twins spent a confusing hour visiting the many displays and different paraphernalia that was on offer throughout the principality before heading back to the rental and commenced the return trip back towards Kalbarri.

Chapter-40

TWO BONFIRES, the size of an Indian tepee, burnt brightly at either end of a red-earth natural amphitheatre. There looked to be over two hundred Aboriginal people in attendance, mostly seated cross-legged, forming a Bora Ring made from a raised platform of earth. All the children were herded into one tight group with some of the older women in control of proceedings.

Jack and the twins were ushered to a piece of vacant ground near the smaller of the two open fires. A tarp had been laid out with an icebox close by, stocked with bottled water and some soft drinks. Sharyn Tomlinson was in attendance with her eldest daughter, so was Jock and Janette McKlintoff. Leonard introduced Evina to an indigenous man who could have been anywhere from 50 to over 80 years old. He wore the clothes of a stockman with a face that was the keeper of a thousand stories. His creased eyes were a steely grey, but they portrayed calming friendliness diluted by the hardship of his life on the land he loved.

"This is, Apari. He will be your interpreter tonight to guide you through the ceremonial significance and keep you informed of the mythical history and interpretations. It will occupy about two hours of your time," Leonard wanted to explain.

Abigail leaned in close to her sister and whispered, "I think we might be three of only a handful of non-Aboriginal people here tonight. It feels a bit weird, but also enlightening. Why do *you* think we were invited, Jack?"

"I have no idea, but if I were to hazard a guess, I would say these people want to share with you a story. So listen up girls, we all might learn a thing or two tonight," Kelly could only guess.

Four men dressed in animal-skin loincloths with leafy twigs and shells tied around their ankles arrived with their otherwise naked bodies adorned with hand-painted white and a burnt orange dots the colour of a setting sun sinking behind a shroud of fine dust with streaks of clay-coloured reddish browns covering most parts of their upper bodies. They all stood at the ready, in individual positions of halcyon poses. A group of blackfellas held clap sticks, and the sound of seed rattles in the shaking hands of some women could be heard over the quietening crowd.

Apari broke his silence and spoke in a quiet but deliberate tone. "This first part of the corroboree is called the smoking ceremony and involves smouldering various native plants to produce smoke, which we believe to possess cleansing properties and the ability to ward off bad spirits. Tonight is the coming together of many tribes for the first time since the last big floods. This only happens when something of the utmost importance needs to be discussed amongst the elders.

"We all know what the white woman searches for; we have seen it in our Dreamtime. Our children are sick, our old die too young, and we have limited access to the white man's medicine. This is for you as much as it is for all of us as one nation, working together for the greater good of both cultures."

Evina was rendered speechless. At that precise moment, it all became perfectly clear why she had embarked on this journey. Apari just summed it up in one short sentence. She was totally captivated by the moment—she was immersed, and she wanted to find that bloody book.

Apari ran his extended arm in a clockwise motion. "You see that mob over there? They are the Tiwi and the Mikapiti tribes from the Spirit Bays near Bathurst Island. The Gamberre and the Ngarinyin tribes are both from the east and west Arnhem Land. Then there are the Balgo, Kunawarritji plus the

Parnngurr and the Kutkabubba from the Kimberleys. The others, like the Yulga, the Yamatji and the Nhanda are mostly from the Mid West and the Murchison regions. They are all here and all chasing the same thing. Good health and happy life in sync with the land and nature."

A deep throaty drone resonated from the two didgeridoos, and fifteen sets of rhythm sticks started to beat in mesmerising time—an ancient time. A lone voice mimicked the call of a laughing kookaburra. A squawk from a perched currawong pierced the night air. Two boys covered in emu feathers pranced in a high knee lifting action, moving their necks forward and back in a chicken-like, straddle. Another blackfella was covered head to toe with a white paste wearing a mask in the shape of a stunted dugong's trunk. It was time for the corroboree to begin.

The dancing men lifted their legs high and stomped the dusty ground, waving their arms and craning their necks. They all held painted sticks, boomerangs and woomera's while dressed with leaves and feathers to mimic the roles of Australian native animals. The mob became silent and watched as one in a captivating entrancement. Evina and Abigail were transfixed, bewitched as they were about to enter a night of fulfilment and hypnotic ceremony, timeless as the land they sat on.

Apari commenced his low murmuring narrative to the waiting ears of Evina while Abigail jotted down some shorthand notes at the insistence of her neurotic sister.

"The blackfella," Apari whispered, with his hand pointing to the centre of the Bora Ring, "his name is, Pindari, and he's talking with the water serpent. Pindari follows a dugong with a starfish and an eel in his dugout canoe. Together they search for the *marnamnyan;* the barramundi have disappeared, and the tribe is hungry. A storm is brewing—a real big bugger, stripping bare the leaves of many a tree. Pindari can sense *balangurrk;* black magic, the land is unbalanced. Then he stumbles across a floating wooden lion serpent with a broken timber spine. White pillows filled with wind push it up the flooded creek. The white men with coloured *laberri*; body hair, swarm the spirit islands like *bull-jar* ants, the water serpent is angry. The bulyits bring with them their god and carry an altar ashore. Pindari flees while the starfish hides in a rock pool and the eel searches for an underwater cave. The dugong is *ngotjje-ma*. He's frightened and heads for the shallow seagrass. Pindari has been chased away and throws his boomerang, then he hears a loud *crack* like a tree trunk splitting, and his shoulder starts to bleed. The river gods are angry, and the creeks stay dry.

"For two thousand *geletj-ja*; new moons, the bulyits live, eat and offer a prayer to their altar. More half-casts are born; boys and girls, black and white skin with fair hair. Lubra's, gins and bulyits sharing the earth. The blackfellas want the *mamin*, bulyits—the smelly devil's to be banished. A group of Aboriginal elders led by a holy man named, Akama, meaning a whale decides to steal the altarpiece, but the ironwood is heavy with the white man's sun god staring back at him. Akama becomes frightened. He covers the image and then the fighting starts."

Ironwood, a sun god? Evina sensed she was being gifted a sneak preview into a time that had since passed on by. A history lesson, but not from any book. This was real and part of Aboriginal culture—it was magical and swept through her body like persuasive schooling. She was totally entranced.

A group of young Aboriginal boys entered the Bora Ring. Another man laid some dry timber to stoke both the fires. The music and the rhythm changed to a slower beat. The mood of the mob seemed to shift as the corroboree continued its chronological call of events from a time long forgotten.

Apari took a swig of water and rolled another smoke before he continued his rendering. "The tribe splits, and some go walkabout, across the *gumuny*. The desert is hot and dry, many black and whitefellas die together until a handful reach paradise. A *gorlondin* is a hinterland rainforest with a *billabong* and tall trees for shade. Together they live in peace, grow strange new food, make canals, then the floods come. Akama's first-born son, Yarran, decides to return the altar. It has brought bad luck to the

White Tribe. When he returns to the spirit islands, the white men have disappeared. The yellow and red lion serpent has vanished. He follows some tracks towards the setting sun. Bleached bones and skeletons scatter across the scorched earth and hills. The bronze lights shine from inside the earth. Yarran decides to *ngordok-ga*. He wants to look inside the altar, to destroy the black magic—but he cannot.

"It's hot, and there are tall termite mounds. A willy-willy blows for many days. Pindari is *ngotjje-ma*; frightened and hungry. He is chased and bitten by a *yakba*, a freshwater crocodile and the sun god becomes a burden. He finds a hole in the *wolok* to hide the ironwood. The high country is a dangerous place. Pindari follows a *diwana*. The eagle flies high in the sky and shows Yarran the way back to the tall palms—back to paradise. The White Tribe has also vanished, and now he is alone. The altar and the bad magic have taken their vengeance. He paints the caves to warn others of the devilish ironwood and the lion-serpent with the white pillows. The sun is scorching, and Yarran is forced to leave. He sets off on another walkabout and follows the *diwana* back to the Malkana tribe near the breathing rocks and the home of the baby sea cows."

Evina was rendered speechless. Jack was totally enthralled, and Abigail just snapped the led in her pencil.

Apari rolled another smoke. He shook the twins' hands in a two-handed clasp. His smile came from deep within, and his perfectly lined teeth were as white as the natural Tamala limestone. He placed his dingo skin hat on his dusted, greying, tightly curled hair and looked deep into Evina's eyes. "The rest is up to you now, *biyakgin*. Take care, *mangells.*"

The long tail feather of a wedge-tailed eagle fluttered above the peak of his hat from the heat of the fire as he turned and walked back to be with his people.

The corroboree had come to its ceremonial end, and now it was time for the elders to meet and discuss secret men's business. Sharyn McKlintoff stood side by side with the twins and walked with them back to the parked cars. Sharyn then said, "Apari paid you the ultimate compliment, Evina."

"I don't follow," a slightly bemused Evina replied, "a compliment?"

"Yes. Apari referred to you as a sister, and that is the highest accolade an Aboriginal man can bestow upon a non-Aboriginal person. He also advised you to be *mangells*; to stay safe. He senses danger."

The silence on the return trip to the Murchison homestead was in direct contradiction to what was grinding away inside Evina's scientific mind. Her brain was still beating to the rhythm sticks as she attempted to absorb the story she and others were privileged to play a small role in—even as just invited spectators. Abigail looked down at her notes, and without realising, she had three full pages of shorthand scribble to decipher.

Evina eventually asked, "Jack, can we just head back to the *Thin Lizzy*, I don't want to sound ungrateful, but I need some alone time to attempt to make heads or tails of what we witnessed tonight."

"I'll stop and pass on our apologies to the, McLintoff's. Then we can head straight off. You two can stay in the car."

No person spoke until the turn onto George Gray Road, then Evina suddenly sat upright and asked Abigail, "Read out your notes, Abby. Somewhere in amongst that story is the answer . . . I can just feel it."

Abigail felt inside her bag, "Okay, it starts off with Pindari canoeing to search for barramundi."

"Yes, and later they referred to this place as the Spirit Islands, so let's assume this may be Seven Spirit Bay. Go on," Evina urged.

"He sees a yellow and red lion serpent, made from wood, carrying many white men," Abigail continued.

"Right, the VOC figurehead on many of its ships was a yellow lion mounted against a red-coloured beakhead. Maybe a ship was damaged in a storm and sought sanctuary in the safety of a river or creek?" Her hands were becoming moist, and Evina took a deep breath.

"Not to mention, if it had a broken mast, they would need to replace it to sail home," Kelly added.

"Then Apari talked about this altar and a sun god. He mentioned a thousand something, but I didn't quite catch what he said."

"*Geletj-ja*; new moons, he called it. Two thousand new moons. That's over one hundred fifty years. Organised colonisation," Evina stated, and then posed the question. "Where's the evidence of that?"

"I saw your eyes light up when he mentioned ironwood, Evina. Just remember it grows wild all throughout the north of Australia. Anyway, then he talks about the tribes splitting after a fight. They seemed to then cross a desert."

"No shortage of them in the north of Australia," Kelly interrupted, as he slowed for a kangaroo grazing on the wild lucerne.

Abigail continued, "Then Akama returns with the altar. He finds tracks, skeletons and some high country, where he says he was attacked by a crocodile and hides the ironwood altarpiece in a hole."

"And he also mentions the bronze lights from within the earth. What could that be?" Evina questioned.

Kelly wanted to say, "Maybe a reflection, the red earth. The landscape has many colours as the sun rises and sets every day. They discovered gold in the early eighteen hundreds plus copper, zinc and of course, iron ore."

"The final telling was of Yarran returning to the breathing rocks and the baby sea cows," Abigail added as a finish to her notes.

"Well, I can answer that one," Kelly sprouted from the driver's seat.

Before he could offer his own explanation, Evina broke in with another scientific spiel. "They are layered bio-chemical accretionary structures formed in shallow water by the trapping, binding and cementation of sedimentary grains by biofilms or microorganisms, especially cyanobacteria. Fossilised stromatolites provide ancient records of life on Earth by these remains, some of which may date to be three to four billion years old. Lichen stromatolites are a proposed mechanism of formation of some kinds of layered rock structure that are formed above water, where rock meets air, by repeated colonisation of the rock by endolithic lichens."

What the f..., Kelly thought alone. "Well, that's all very interesting, Mrs Smarty Pants. I'm talking about sea cows, not the breathing rocks. They're talking about the dugongs, and how the saline waters offer an ideal breeding ground for the calves to be raised as the high salt content in the water gives them extra ballast and cannot be accessed by the schools of black-tipped sharks—the salt damages their eyes."

"What about the reference to Akama attempting to search inside the altar to destroy the black magic? Obviously, it was able to be opened, so maybe it wasn't an altar, but something of equal significance," Evina continued before sucking in her next breath.

"You're clutching at straws, Evina," Abigail said. "We don't know what it was or where that hole is. Okay, I'll admit there is a distinct possibility that a ship landed with your mysterious ironwood casket, and may have even been moved to another unknown location, but what happens next? Where to now, I ask?" Abigail waved her hands in a gesture of hopelessness.

Kelly was already considering winding down this charter. He and Till still had 2,700 nautical miles of dangerous waters to navigate on the return trip back to Thailand. He'd been away from home for almost nine weeks now. First, he planned a quick detour to Singapore to visit Starindo Boat Builders and repair the bullet holes to the hull and deck before Tiaan lays her inquisitive eyes on the evidence and then starts asking questions he would prefer not to answer. He had a life, and he missed his two tail-wagging dogs.

The car rental agency's holding yard was a short distance from the wharf. Kelly decided he would park the Ford *Ranger* and slide the keys through the 24-hour lockbox on the inside of the front door, then walk the last five hundred metres back to the berthed *Thin Lizzy*. Abigail stepped onto the wood-planked wharf first, to see Till, casting and retrieving a squid jig into the reflection of an overhead fluorescent light directly under the *strictly no fishing* sign. A second seated person—a stranger, sprang to his feet like he'd just been caught wagging school.

Fair dinkum, I'm sure Till would start up a conversation with Jack the bloody Ripper if the chance presented itself, Kelly silently considered. Then he asked himself who this person might be?

Till looked up at Kelly, "We catch *plahmuk,* Boss. Graeme show me how. He very good." Till's excitement was catching. Abigail bent down to see inside the bucket. It was half-full of squid.

"Mrs Bishop-Joiner...?" Evina stopped and turned towards the young man's apologetic face. "As Till says, my name is, Graeme—Graeme Casley. I am the youngest son of..."

"I know who you are. I saw the photo of the Casley family tree back at the giant clay bust of your father," Evina cut in. "You're, Prince Graeme, and due to succeed your father after his forthcoming abdication. What do we owe the pleasure at this late hour?" Evina asked. Her interest was waning behind a cloak of some much-needed sleep.

"Can we talk in private somewhere?" Graeme asked.

"We have no secrets on this yacht, Graeme. You have permission to come aboard. I need a drink, anyway." Evina led the way.

The young man looked to be less than 30 years old. His shirt was buttoned to his neck like he'd forgotten to put on a tie. His hairstyle was old-fashioned, short with a long fringe brushed to the side. Very Sixties. His manners were impeccable, as he motioned for both ladies to lead the way to the upstairs saloon. From below, Till let out another excited cheer as tomorrow night's dinner started to take shape. Kelly helped himself to a stubby of cider while Abigail opened a bottle of white wine. "What can I offer you to drink, Graeme?" Kelly filled his own glass.

"A pot of tea would be nice, sorry but I don't drink the tea dust they put inside those dangling bags," Graeme replied.

"Tea it is then. I'll be right back." Kelly half-shouted from the rear mezzanine deck. "Till... a pot of tea for our guest."

"Please, have a seat, Graeme," Abigail smiled, thinking if he was just a little less nerdy-looking?

Graeme surveyed the inside of the yacht. His eyes immediately stopped when he locked-on to what he knew had to be the celestial globe his auntie had spoken about. All eyes were now on the nervous-looking last-born Casley son. Some polite conversation was exchanged between the twins and the handsome young prince. He looked very anxious. Till arrived with a silver tray. He placed the pot of tea with a cup and saucer on the glass table. Graeme leaned forward and began to pour. The gurgled croak sound from the satellite phone slightly startled him, causing the young man to spill some drops of piping hot tea.

"Do you have a girlfriend, Graeme?" Kelly asked.

"Arr... no, I don't, sir."

"Well, that noise you hear is the sound of a Thai woman wondering where a certain boat captain might be. Excuse me." Kelly stepped to the bridge cubicle and eased himself into the skipper's chair. "Sàwàt dii khràp, thii rak."

Graeme sipped his tea and placed his cup neatly back onto his saucer. "I suppose you're both wondering why I'm here, then?"

"Well... yes," Abigail answered first.

"My Auntie Sharyn explained to all of us about your recent ordeal at Tamala Station. Quite an adventure. She also took the time to point out to me personally about you, Mrs Bishop-Joiner, and your position as associate professor in Islamic Sciences at the Smithsonian. I Googled you, and I think I understand what it is you seek."

"Do you now?" Evina pondered. "What is it I seek then, young man?" Evina's preoccupation in where she considered this conversation was heading was circumspect. Her level of interest was at DEFCON 5.

"I was very close to both, Richard and Robert. In fact, it was I who gave Barnacle Bob his name. I grew up with his children *and* grandchildren," Graeme replied. His tone exuded a type of raw honesty. He was like the boy next door, a mother-in-law's dream come true.

DEFCON 4. Evina sipped on her wine. She was still sceptical but remained upright. She felt a little tense in the shoulders. Her internal radar was sensing an incoming informational rocket.

Graeme's eyes shifted to the three-seater couch. "Is that the celestial sphere you uncovered—absolutely amazing? Do you mind if I take a closer look?"

Abigail slid off her stool, lifted the globe and handed it to Graeme. He studied the surface while slowly turning it on its axis. "An ancient mapping device. Is this what pointed you towards the Spirit Bays, then?"

DEFCON 3. *Who is this man?*

Graeme continued, "You search for a casket made from ironwood with the image of the Emperor Jahangir emblazoned on the surface. Your search for the ultimate prize—the gift of knowledge and natures wonderments."

Abigail was sitting on a barstool and drew a long breath. Evina spilt her wine; she brushed the front of her shirt dry. She then swallowed, her mouth felt parched. DEFCON 2.

"You have my full attention, Graeme. Let it be known that my quest for answers is no secret, and *that* information can be readily sourced from any person who wishes to dig around a little. It's no mystery that we search for history's answers. What are you actually getting at?" Evina challenged. "This is no time for innuendo, or he said - she said scenarios. This is serious science and not some wild goose chase."

"And I totally agree with you, Mrs Bishop-Joiner," Graeme answered, almost in a conciliatory manner. "Maybe it is I who might be able to help you locate that golden egg."

Evina shifted in her chair. "Forgive me for sounding doubtful, but I'm in no mood for practical jokes. Please enlighten all of us how you might pull that one off?"

"Well, since it was actually I who ultimately found what I think you search for, buried in our old copper mine, and again, it was me who needed to find an equally safe place to store it again—I can assure you this is not a practical joke, Mrs Bishop-Joiner."

Evina turned to face Kelly, who had just finished his call. "Jack, open another bottle of wine, would you please?" she asked in an almost trance-like voice.

DEFCON 1.

Chapter - 41

HMAS *BALLARAT* eased her 380-foot metal-grey-hull into the protection of Careening Bay and made final preparations to berth. Fleet Base West was located on Garden Island, separated by a single man made service bridge. Dampier Road was the only connection to the mainland at Point Peron, where the main Naval Base was housed. Two uniformed Navy police were standing at arms alongside a parked unmarked car with red federal government plates as the gangplank was swung into place.

Lieutenant Commander Scott Larson negotiated the angled gangway, stood to attention, and returned the salute from the two standing guards. The passenger's rear door opened, and a man stepped out sporting a Tom Ford suit, complete with a Burberry Heritage trench coat. The commander did not recognise the man standing in front of him. "My name, Commander, is Kimball Boyd Deputy Director of Security and Operations for ASIO."

Scott Larson offered a nondescript return blank stare. "That's nice. What can I do for ASIO today?" he replied, a little bemused why the cloak and dagger approach.

"I have in my possession an official order for you to hand over your special passenger. Where is this person of interest right now?" Boyd questioned in a semi non-threatening tone.

"Well, Mr Boyd, we are currently taking care of eight very frightened young Asian girls plus three terrorised teenage Vietnamese, a couple of North Koreans, and one Arab masquerading as a refugee. They're all on board right now. So, which one, in particular, are you referring to?"

"Tobias Stone, Commander," Boyd responded with a terse tone. "Stone . . . Where is he at this very moment? He is to be placed under house arrest and accompany me back to Canberra. Guards, search the ship," Boyd barked the order to the two nervous Navy police. They fixed eyes on the stony-faced lieutenant commander, wanting a verbal okay before they boarded the Navy frigate.

"Oh, you Navy boys sure do stick together, don't you?" Kimball Boyd was about to repeat the order.

"Let me save you the time, Kimball Boyd Deputy Director of Security and Operations. Stone is no longer on board the *Ballarat*. He is MIA. Be my guest, you have permission to go aboard, but rest assured—he is not there." The lieutenant commander struggled to conceal a satisfied grin.

"Really, Commander, he just jumped overboard and swam away then, did he? At what point was he reported missing?"

"The *Ballarat* needed to make an unscheduled stop eight kilometres off the coast of Kalbarri to deal with an electrical issue in the main generator. He failed to arrive at the mess hall for the evening meal."

"How convenient? What about your other prisoner, did you also manage to misplace him, Commander?"

"Mr Duckhwan Toa is being held in the brig and his sister Mi-sun is under guard and will be escorted off the ship by Immigration officials. They should be here to meet with the *Ballarat* at 1400 hours."

"This won't look good on your record, Commander Larson," Boyd replied curtly.

"I have no authority to detain, Mr Stone. I suggest if you have any further questions regarding this matter, you take it up with, Admiral Peterson. Good day to you, sir."

Kimball Boyd pulled his cell phone from the side pocket of his coat and dialled Darcy Jones.

Stone was currently on Skywest Airlines flight no XR-102 from Kalbarri on board the twin-turboprop Fokker F50 due to land at Perth domestic airport to connect with the 9:10 A.M. flight to Canberra. He used the 70-minute flight-time to scroll through the two mobile phones he sequestered from the Jindeugi as they shared some interesting conversation while travelling down the coast on the *Ballarat*. The first prepaid was useless for the exact reasons Stone would purchase the same, the minute he landed in Perth. The second mobile showed two outgoing calls with an answered text, titled 6-4-3 from a private caller.

What I wouldn't give to have that number, Stone contemplated for a brief moment.

He replayed in his head the conversations with both Felicity and Monarsh. Stone needed to form an understanding of the motives behind Darcy Jones, and what possible involvement he had with the detention centre and the North Koreans back on Christmas Island.

None of it made any sense. Stone privately considered. *What did Jones have to gain—money? Maybe, but I doubt it. What am I missing here?*

Stone deplaned through the rear cabin door and made his way down the mobile stairs. It was a short walk across the open tarmac, negotiating a construction zone while passing under some scaffolding as part of an upgrade to terminal 2. He found a newsagent and purchased a prepaid, then headed for the Jet Star check-in counter. He emptied his pockets and slid his carry-on down the steel rollers through the X-ray and strode through the body scanner. An airport security officer stepped forward and waved his mobile hand wand up and down Stone's body while a sniffer dog went to town on his carry bag. Stone found a secluded seat at the far end of the departure lounge and sent a text to Bradley Monarsh's second mobile number. Three minutes later, his prepaid cell phone vibrated.

"You certainly lead an eventful life, Tobias. The news is just filtering through about the demise of your unwelcome guests in Western Australia."

"Never a dull moment, Brad. Did you receive my secured e-mail from the *Ballarat?*"

"No problems there. Everything is in place. Just give me the nod, and we're ready to roll the dice from this end."

Stone ended the call and dialled Felicity's number. She answered while puffing and panting. "Did I get you at a bad time?" Stone already regretted asking and didn't really want to hear the answer. His paternal instincts imagined some disturbing images.

"It's all right, *Daddy.* A group of us are abseiling down a rock face in the Belanglo State Forest for the weekend. It's called rest and recreation, you should try it sometime."

"Can you talk?"

"Just hang on a minute while I clear my tent of the four hunky-looking guys, all wanting to take advantage of a lonely and vulnerable woman. You know I'm no longer a virgin, Tobias, so you can calm down." Felicity loved to play on Stone's emotions. He was so old-fashioned it was cute. "Fire away, I'm all alone now."

"Can you access historical CCTV footage in the old Russell Offices?"

"How historical?"

"Like the day that fax was somehow sent from Darcy Jones' old office."

"I won't have clearance for that. You would need a secure password to access those archives. That building is almost empty now."

"Use this password to gain admission to the historical footage. This is to your memory only—are you ready?"

Felicity cleared her thoughts and recited the nine alpha-numerical password three times. "I'm not even going to ask how you managed to get your hands on that. This is a level-nine security clearance."

"We all have our skeletons rattling away in the closet. Find a public Internet café and don't be online for more than four minutes. Move locations if you have to—understand? Be good and stay away from slick-talking, good-looking men. I'll be home for dinner tomorrow tonight, your shout. Love you." *Click.*

Chapter-42

DARCY JONES slammed the phone down in its cradle. "Damn that sneaky bastard. I knew Stone was up to something." He picked up the phone a second time and pressed 1 to talk with his front office receptionist. "Miss White, isn't it?"

"Yes, sir, I've been stationed here..."

"Get me Admiral Peterson on the phone," Jones snapped.

Sheila White searched her list of secured numbers and found the admiral's private office line. She punched in the digits with a shaking hand. A minute later, the director's secured phone buzzed.

"Darcy Jones," Boomer sighed with a condescending edge.

"Where have you stashed, Stone? I know he was on board HMAS *Ballarat*. And what the hell did you get up to on Christmas Island? Why am I receiving reports from MI6 about a possible attack on an abandoned casino? May I remind you I am still the director-general of ASIO."

"I know who—and what you are, Jones. You should be asking yourself—why is Stone side-stepping you? Is there something you want to share with me, Darcy? Because when this shit hits the proverbial fan, you might just want to check if you're facing up or downwind. You know which way shit travels, Darcy—downhill, and straight towards you?" Boomer wanted to plant the seed of unknown thought into the director's mind. *What was Jones not telling the JNSC—and why?*

"In my position, Admiral, it's not a simple task to know who you can trust."

"That's a load of horse-wallop, Darcy, and you know it. The wagons are circling, and you'll need to figure out real soon which side of that fence you want to find yourself sitting on. Stone won't stop until he gets to the bottom of this mess, and he won't give a rat's arse who or what gets in his way. He's pretty fired up about what he found on Christmas Island... *old mate*." Boomer was enjoying turning the screws on the director. Everybody has to be accountable, eventually, the admiral knew from personal experience. "Meet me at the foreshore to Captain Cook's Memorial Jet in one hour—alone."

The admiral hung up and turned his chair to face the same spot he would entice the director-general of ASIO into the broadening web of deception proposed by Stone.

Stone's mobile rang. He ignored the call momentarily while he gazed through his binoculars from his current location at Patrick White Terrace, directly opposite where Admiral Peterson was standing alone. This offered an unobstructed view past the National Exhibition Centre down to the skeleton globe sculpture at Regatta Point, showing the paths of Captain James Cook's ocean expeditions, which made up the viewing platform on Lake Burley Griffin.

The Cook Memorial Water Jet is powered by two 560-kilowatt electric motors driving four centrifugal pumps capable of pumping up to 250 litres of water per second to a height of over 145 metres which made for a spectacular sight under a rainbow of changing lights at night.

Stone plucked his phone from a left side pocket with his free hand. "Felicity, speak my dear."

"This is turning out to be like a Russian Matryoshka doll, layer upon layer of shrewd deceitfulness designed to mislead, I kid you not, Tobias."

"I'm still listening."

"You told me to follow the money trail, so that's what I did. At first, it was just mundane, boring wire transfers between the Anomura Group and its debtors. Then I expanded the search to include all transfers between Australia and Korea that turned out to be another dead end. I changed the transfer destination to Indonesia. It's unbelievable, do you realise how much money is actually...?"

"Emma Peel, you're doing it again. Stay focused."

"Sorry, I'm new at all this spy stuff. Something popped up on the grid that was a little strange in that the amount of money in question was so small and exact. Just twenty-five thousand dollars wired in Australian currency. It's too high for personal needs as it's above the daily limit of ten thousand."

"And...?" Stone posed the question. He knew there was something else—there always is.

"This company's head office is in Jakarta. So I asked myself, why would an Indonesian-based company send funds to its own country via Australia? It doesn't make sense. So then I searched the websites of the local papers and found an interesting article in a place called Makassar on South Sulawesi—and bingo! There was a report of a female foreign national being arrested and held without bail to await trial on some pretty flimsy evidence suspecting her of trafficking in illegal narcotics. I rang our embassy in Jakarta and was directed to an Australian foreign correspondent based in Timor-Leste. This journalist who covers the entire region told me the whole thing was a setup, a sting orchestrated by the local police. But get this—the woman at the centre of the controversy was an Australian citizen. Her name was quoted as, Miss Anna Wilkinson. But there was never an exit visa issued to a person with that name, I checked."

"How did she leave the country, then?" Stone could sense something brewing.

"Good question. The charges were dropped after an Australian-based law firm with offices in Indonesia were engaged in dealing with her eventual release. This person of interest arrived back in Australia on a Garuda A-320 Airbus last Wednesday, thanks to a twenty-five thousand dollar donation from a company with a registered Australian Business Number called Final Productions. But Tobias, there's more, like I said Matryoshka dolls. The law firm in question is named, Crean, Sandhurst and Toll." Felicity let the three named partners swing in the breeze for a few seconds while it alerted a first alarm bell in Stone's head.

"Hello, is anyone home?" Felicity joked

"Do you mean the attorney-general's brother?" Stone wanted to clarify.

"Yes. Miles Sandhurst is a named partner, and as his brother, he virtually walked straight into a full-firm partnership agreement with all the bells and whistles already attached," Felicity shot back.

"That was Sandhurst's old firm before he gained office if I remember right?" Stone wanted to confirm mentally.

"But wait, because there's more. The name, Crean, does that ring any bells, Tobias?"

"Crean, the current treasurer and the man who holds great aspirations to be the next prime minister," Stone answered with a picture forming in his head.

"Exactly. The rumour mill in the corridors of the old Parliament House will tell you he was promised the 'top job' in a 'behind closed doors' deal with the previous PM before he became ill and retired from politics. That was up until Jeremy Collins was asked to nominate and won the Party leadership ballot in a landslide. Simon Crean and Franklin Sandhurst shared a room while attending Sydney University together. They were, and still are, close friends to this day."

"This Final Productions, what do they do?" Stone felt he might already know the answer to this quandary.

"This obscure company's only business interests is exporting X-rated DVD's, out of all places—Canberra."

"The Australian Capital Territory?" Stone questioned. "Now we're getting somewhere."

"Yes, the ACT. To outsiders, Canberra seems a soulless, grey city populated by politicians and bureaucrats. But to those in the know, the Australian capital was – until only recently – referred to as 'Pornberra', the throbbing heart of the nations' sex industry.

"For about fifteen years, the capital was one of only two places in Australia where it was legal to produce, sell and distribute sexually explicit videos. Business boomed. That was until the Internet arrived, hammering its first nail in Final Production's coffin as early as 2000. Some say X-rated movies were Canberra's second-largest export after timber products. Pine then porn was a common saying, apparently.

"The federal government legalised X-rated material in 1984, but it was up to each individual state to decide whether it could be sold locally. The Reverend Fred Nile, a Christian Minister and self-appointed guardian of Australian morals, toured the country with Britain's, Mary Whitehouse, and the pair persuaded each State Government to ban the films.

"That left only the liberal-minded Australian Capital Territory, comprising Canberra and its surrounds, plus the Northern Territory, both of which remained subject to federal law. The ACT thus became a little haven for the porn industry," Felicity finished explaining.

"Shit. This is getting really messy now." Stone's exacting memory instantly recalled the gruesome images from the casino. "What about the historical CCTV footage at ASIO's old offices?" Stone asked. His resolve to unravel this entangled list of law firms, listed companies and politicians was becoming a single-minded obsession.

"That was a dead end. The surveillance equipment was removed once the building was decommissioned. ASIO don't make a habit of leaving anything behind. I'm waiting for you to say, *and* or *but*, like you usually do."

"And or but?" Stone had to smile.

"I checked the New Parliament House car-pool logs on the day that fax was sent. Helena Wilks has a full-time chauffeur on hand twenty-four-seven, but this day she requested a government vehicle and was recorded entering the

Russell Offices main gate just after midday. All federal vehicles available for use by both the Senate and front bench ministers are GPS enabled in case of a kidnapping. I hacked in and followed her movements after she exited at 12:47 P.M. Then I matched this to available Department of Main Roads metropolitan CCTV. They've got cameras everywhere these days. The car stopped off at a bar called Honky-Tonks on Garema Place. It's a well-known gay and lesbian hangout in the entertainment precinct."

"I don't quite get the connection? Are you saying the deputy PM prefers same-sex relationships? Nobody cares."

"Yes, I know that. I matched the face of the second woman leaving her vehicle to the face of the woman charged in Makassar. It's her older sister, Anna Wilks: a.k.a.- Anna Wilkinson, and the money wired from that shelf company was coincidentally also listed as the largest contributor to the deputy prime minister's election campaign when she first ran for office in the seat of Bowman, over four years ago."

Stone was dissecting all this new information while watching the Cook Memorial like a hawk. The unmistakably large frame of Admiral Peterson stood out like a granite boulder—unmovable and unshakable. Now the second man to attend this clandestine meeting could be seen striding across the grassed area between Parkes Way and the Molonglo Riverfront. He needed to end this call and text Monarsh.

"By the way, what are you cooking for dinner tonight?" Stone asked, before hanging up.

"It will be a surprise, don't be late, and you bring the wine—okay." Felicity heard a *click*. The call had ended.

The admiral stood resolutely with both hands entrenched into his knee-length Australian-Navy-issued trench coat while he watched the purposeful stride of Darcy Jones approach his position at breakneck speed.

"What's this all about, Admiral? I don't have time to be playing silly buggers with the Navy at this moment," he responded slightly angered.

"Shut up and just listen. Hand me your phone," the admiral demanded.

"My phone, why? I don't need to put up with..."

Boomer cut Jones off mid-sentence. "Like I said, Darcy, the shit trail runs down Capital Hill, and right now, it's about to knock you out of the park for six."

Jones' steely gaze was interrupted. He bent his head to see two red laser dots dancing over his suit jacket. He immediately turned and searched for the source.

"Your phone, please," the admiral repeated.

Jones pulled out his federal government supplied mobile. "Not that one," Boomer demanded, "the other one."

"You better have a bloody good explanation for this, Admiral," Jones snapped back as he retrieved a second cell phone and placed it into the admiral's open palm.

"Flushing the sewerage pipes, Darcy. Now, where is my number, I'm sure you have it on speed dial?" He pressed *call* and held the phone up in the air with one hand while his pants pocket vibrated. He slipped his own phone out and answered the incoming call.

Stone phoned Bradley Monarsh's mobile. "Go, the number is in play now." The line remained open while he watched with interest in what was unofficially soon to be his ex-boss. One minute passed, then three. Soon a full five minutes had ticked by.

Monarsh's voice broke the silence. "Is everything all okay at your end because I have nothing?" was his only reply. Jones' phone was not the source of the 6-4-3 text message.

"What the f...?" Stone was startled and now slightly confused.

"I can assure you, Tobias," Monarsh continued, "there's no digital footprint pinpointing the source of the six-four-three message. One down, four to go old boy. Russian roulette. This was always going to be a long shot," Monarsh finished.

The admiral and Jones were locked in a silent battle of wits. Admiral Peterson pressed *end call* and handed the director-general of ASIO his phone and redialled Stone. "Give me something, Stone, because the man standing opposite is going to need some answers, and real quick. He is looking less than impressed right at this moment."

"Go to Plan B, Admiral," Stone replied.

"I hope you know what you're doing, Stone? This could backfire and end badly for you," Boomer warned.

"No choice, Admiral. We need to shake the rug and watch which fleas try to run for cover." *Click.*

The admiral and Jones could be seen walking back to the Russell Offices in deep conversation.

Stone looked at his watch. He needed to get to the airport.

Chapter-43

ABIGAIL ALMOST fell off her stool. Jack needed to launch himself from the skipper's chair to intervene as Evina almost became airborne while she also sprung to her feet. The tension in the saloon was ostensible. Evina took the time to breathe deeply before she spoke. "Let's just all take stock for a minute—or two. Pour me another wine, will you, Abby?"

Evina stopped pacing the room like a caged lioness and returned a dagger-like stare towards the young man who looked like butter wouldn't melt in his mouth. "It's the wrong time of the month to be playing games with me, young man," Evina threatened. "I've spent a good part of my life scavenging for information in dusty, decrepit museums. I have travelled to three continents, chasing an ideal that may or may not exist. It has cost me a shitty marriage and aged me more than the ten years it has taken to get to this pivotal point, and now, sitting right here in front of me, a man I've just met is trying to tell me he knows the location of Jahangir's golden leafed casket."

"Yeah, pretty much exactly that, except it's not golden. Just a chunk of old petrified wood. But the Jahangir connection is definitely there. I Googled that as well," the brash and innocent man replied.

"Oh, he Googled it! Shit, why didn't I think of that?" Evina circled the room, meeting each person's gaze. "Just think of all the time and effort I could have saved." Evina looked like she wanted to throttle this guy. She was still in a state of unravelling cynicism regarding his wild and so far, unsubstantiated claims.

"All right, let's all just settle and listen to Graeme's explanation why he *thinks* he may have what you have dedicated a large part of your life pursuing. Evina, take a seat, and I'll open another bottle," Kelly wanted to offer a truce before Evina threw this guy overboard. Young Graeme had no idea about the monthly cycle of women. "Graeme, I hope for your sake, mate, it's a bloody good story," Kelly warned.

"It's okay, Jack. The truth is the truth and can't be distorted. Did you take the Stone of Light tour when you met my father?"

"We only heard the tail end of that one," Abigail was first to answer. Again, trying to remain straight-faced.

"Well, the Stone of Light was named after our father instructed the three royal sons—Ian, Wayne and myself, to go to our copper mine located high up in the Ashburton Ranges in what is sometimes referred to as the Capricorn Coast. It took us two days to get there and a further day to find the actual mine site at Bali High, which was home for a particular type of crystal he wanted us to bring back to Hutt River.

"After three days searching, Wayne, who had been to the site previously, well none of us could locate this particular rock. I mean, this thing was supposed to be pretty big, but now it was gone. We retreated back to camp and that night the sky put on its own spectacular iridescent show. There were strange streaks of coloured lights traversing the night sky in unusual directions and patterns that were anything but natural. This one strange phenomenon seemed at one stage to arc around a star and then return on its original path of trajectory. It was both extraordinary and frightening. There was no alcohol, and certainly, no drugs were involved. This spectacular light show spanned over fifteen minutes, easy.

"The very next day, we resumed our search at the exact spot, but now a three-foot-high rock with a huge crystal embedded inside had miraculously decided to mysteriously reappear. It was just sitting there amongst our own boot tracks. It was too big and heavy to move, so we chipped off enough of the crystal to take home and left. Only two kilometres from our campsite, Wayne explained both our parents always liked to stop at the Koonong Natural Spring for a swim and a scrub before the long trip home. This day, with no warning, all the birds and other native animals taking water around the pool started to become flighty. The birds were cawing, and the dingoes, with some wild brumbies, started becoming spooked. Fish began to jump and then there was a great rumbling sound, like an earthquake that came from the direction of the mine site. The ground beneath shook, and the pool created waves big enough that Wayne made the comment they were good enough to surf. It was all very weird. After lunch, Ian and I took the 4wd to check on the mine. There was clear evidence of a rockfall, and soon we realised a great vertical crag had split away from the main precipice. Inside was this wooden box with the unusual emblem carved on the top."

"Are you still breathing, Evina?" Kelly wanted to make sure she was still okay and not hyperventilating.

She nodded and took some more wine. "For God's sake, Graeme, go on," Evina wanted to scream.

"Well, we had this thing propping up the front-end of an old tractor for years..."

"You can't be serious—a tractor?" Evina thought nothing would surprise her these days—she was wrong.

"Yeah, the old Massey Ferguson. That old chunk of wood was like steel, solid as a rock. Then the run of bad luck started. First with the state and federal governments. That was soon followed by two bad harvests. Then that tractor, which was only a spare anyway, refused to start and to add insult to injury, Ian tripped over the bloody thing and broke a leg. The final straw was when my mother was struck down with cancer. I knew then I had to get rid of this strange wooden box that was bringing bad luck to our family, so that's exactly what I did." Graeme finished his tea and began to pour a second cup. "Do you have any biscuits? I often like a Milk Arrowroot biscuit with my tea."

Evina looked like she was about to pop a couple of blood vessels. She was playing seven-card stud with a short deck. Kelly asked Till to grab a packet of Milk Coffees, which he did.

"Yes, go on. You were about to say where you got rid of this old chunk of wood." Evina could hardly believe she may have just referred to Emperor Jahangir's final resting place for what could be the most important reference book for the last three centuries as an old chunk of wood.

"Bob took it to the islands for us. Kill two birds with one stone, he said. He wanted a new anchor, and I, for one, was just thankful to have the bloody thing gone, to be totally honest."

Oh, my God, I think I am going to strangle this country bumpkin any minute now. "These islands," Evina had to ask, "— and of course, you mean the Abrolhos Islands?"

"Absolutely. After the West Australian Maritime Museum removed the old *Batavia*'s anchor, Bob needed something solid to hold the bottom when he was bait fishing around the old wreck. We found an old 44-gallon fuel drum, dropped it inside, then welded the lid back on with a couple of half-size star pickets attached to the outside of the drum to stop it rolling around on the bottom. It made a real flash anchor, it was ideal."

"Well, of course, it did," Evina gasped. "And Bob is no other than *the,* Barnacle Bob, I assume? And now this chunk of wood is rolling around in a drum on the bottom of the ocean. Please tell me a rope and float shows its current whereabouts?"

"It was the last time I laid eyes on it. How else would old Bob find it? Beacon Island is where I last saw it, two floats painted in red and white, South Fremantle colours. Bob was a lifetime member," Graeme answered enthusiastically.

Evina looked at Jack. "And you *do* know where this Beacon Island is located . . . ?"

"Never heard of it." There was a difficult pause in the room. "I'm joking. Yeah, of course I know where it is. Dixie took me diving on the wreck a couple of times. Not much to see now, I might add," Kelly replied, knowing now where *Thin Lizzy* will be headed at first light. "I better give Dixie a call, just in case I can't locate it straight away. Don't want another mutiny on our hands, isn't that right, Evina?"

She was still pacing the floor in a shell-shocked state as her mind passed from thinking this man who was the son of a self-proclaimed prince from a farm that had ceded from the Commonwealth of Australia could be a possible nut case, to actually believing that no one could contrive that much bullshit, surely?

What if he is telling the truth?

Kelly retrieved the satellite image of the Abrolhos Islands, still lying on the dash console. He passed it to Graeme and asked him to point out the anchor's precise last known location. He placed his finger on a spot east of Traitors Island.

Evina slumped back into her cushioned lounge chair and let out a prolonged sigh. She contemplated the irony in Emperor Jahangir's golden casket possibly sitting in a 44-gallon drum on the ocean floor at the very wrecksite that the celestial globe ended its original journey from Texel. The loading port for all VOC ships and the point of entry to the North Sea, due to the shallow Amsterdam harbour. Then sailing across over ten thousand nautical miles of unchartered ocean just to end up wrecked on a small coral atoll, later to be named Morning Reef, situated a short distance off the coast of the great unknown southern continent that was Australia.

Life just wasn't meant to be easy, Evina was learning the hard way.

Chapter-44

FELICITY ALWAYS USED Stone's penthouse located on the Lower North Shore of Sydney in the suburb of Milsons Point to cook the two of them dinner, at his own request. Stone's taxi from Charles Kingsford Smith Airport pulled up to the address in Dind Street, which was almost shadowed by the big grey coat hanger better known as the Sydney Harbour Bridge. He wanted to sleep in his own bed tonight, and there were some things he needed for tomorrow, which was shaping up to be a bad day for a growing list of powerful people.

The smell of garlic, cloves, bay leaves and mozzarella cheese filled the kitchen as Stone entered. Even though he enjoyed the quiet solitude of his own privacy, he loved it when he could stroll in through his front door, like any one of the other thousands of fathers, and smell the home fires burning. It was a simple distraction from what was his otherwise chaotic life. He opened up the bottle of Pinot Noir and placed it on the IKEA-purchased table with matching chairs that belonged on the set of *Happy Days*.

Felicity was turning 21 next month, and it had been playing on Stone's mind now for some time. None of them had any family, except each other. Stone had no idea about the responsibilities of fatherhood, but still, he felt the paternal pull from inside. The little green fella whispering in his ear that he needed to stop looking for excuses and get his act together—and soon was ever present. He pondered while he washed for dinner. How does a man in his line of work take time out to go shopping for gifts and organise a 21st birthday party? He wasn't even aware of who or what type of friends Felicity associated with. The guilt trip was coming in on the crest of a big wave and about to crash over his sorry self—again.

"Dinner's ready," Felicity's excitement resonated through her voice.

Oh, boy, Stone sighed.

The prodigal father and the young woman who at one stage wanted to end her life, both got stuck into their tacos like two hungry Mexicans. Made up of lean minced beef, diced tomatoes, thinly cut lettuce, sour cream, hot sweet chilli sauce and mountains of cheese. Stone loved the simple food; finger food that was messy to eat but tasted bloody great. The conversation flowed in its normal easy style, and the wine was welcomed. They never usually talked shop while sharing these cherished times together. This was a time-out from the outside world and belonged to just the two of them.

"So tell me about your abseiling, which sounds like fun?" Stone wanted to steer the conversation in another direction.

"You mean who was I with and did they have good intentions?"

"No... no, not at all." *Shit.* "Is it that obvious? I'm just trying to..."

"Tobias. Stop trying so hard. Just be yourself. I know what you do for a living. I admire and respect the job you do. How many of my friends have a father figure that is a secret agent with an adopted daughter as your trusty side-kick? We make a good team—you and me. Granted, it's a bit left-field, but we're good, Tobias. Oh, and by the way—I don't have a boyfriend."

"I wanted to talk to you about your twenty-first coming up in a few months' time. Have you made any plans yet?"

"Have you?" Felicity was quick to reply.

"Well... no. I mean... I've given it plenty of thought, but nothing concrete yet."

"Is that when you're dodging bullets, flying in helicopters or sailing the seven seas? I don't want you to be distracted, Tobias. You just remember to duck and come home after each assignment. That's your gift to me."

"This will be the last dance. Darcy Jones and I will be well and truly finished after tomorrow." Stone was adamant.

"Anyway, I have already organised a surprise for my birthday," Felicity shared with a mischievous look. "I'll give you the details closer to the date, but clear your calendar for two weeks after that."

"Under normal circumstances, I wouldn't bring work home, but together we need to piece together what we know so far, and I'll update you on what my contact in MI6 is telling me. Somehow we need to figure out who is behind these terrorists masquerading as refugees and how that links into the detention centre and ultimately a traitor masquerading as another one of the political slimeballs."

"I thought you would never ask. Emma Peel has been busy, and I think I may have found something."

Felicity stood to clear the table. Stone filled the sink with hot water and washed. She grabbed her laptop, opened up her work bag and began spreading a series of satellite images of northern Australia, from the channel county in Queensland, across the Northern Territory, including the Victoria River Downs Station property to the Carlton Hill Station in the north of Western Australia in that order on the cleared tabletop. "You've heard of the late, Sidney Kidman, haven't you?" Felicity asked.

Stone's eidetic memory immediately recalled the name written on the whiteboard at the casino. "I know he was the largest single landowner back in the early Nineteen Hundreds. Why?"

"The entire Kidman property holdings are currently all up for sale. Under the *Foreign Investment Act,* the treasurer has the authority to block the sale by invoking the National Interest Clause which would eliminate any overseas buyers—but only his office has the authority to veto the purchase, and is under enormous public pressure to do just that," Felicity continued.

"Go on, you have my full attention now," Stone replied.

"Well, I'll give you one guess who the deputy PM shared her fully funded penthouse suite with while holidaying in Indonesia?"

"Certainly not, Darcy Jones. He probably hasn't enjoyed a holiday since taking over the top job."

"No. This man is known as the playboy of Canberra. A devoted husband and father who currently has a couple of kids attending university: Simon Crean!" Felicity spoke like she'd just swallowed something foul-tasting.

"The bloody treasurer?" Stone gasped. "You think Wilks may be exerting her womanly influences to sway his impending decision?"

"It's something to consider," Felicity questioned before adding. "That would open up a Pandora's box as far as foreign ownership of property is concerned within Australia's borders."

"Are you talking about the Chinese? I've read the papers reporting they already own vast tracts of farming land to feed their own population," Stone added.

"Considering what the Chinese currently own, this will be a drop in the ocean if this deal goes through," Felicity answered with a worrying glare.

Two hours later, the clock on the wall ticked over to midnight. Both Stone and Felicity were preoccupied with their own thoughts.

"So, that's the plan," Stone gestured, as he helped to gather up the evidence Felicity had painstakingly pieced together. "Are you okay with this? There might be repercussions." Stone was apprehensive about Felicity's involvement. He knew it would be an exercise in futility trying to convince her otherwise.

Felicity stood and gave Stone a hug. "Stop freaking out, Tobias. This will work—trust me?"

Stone locked the door and watched Felicity drive away while he stood on his balcony. He poured himself a Rutherglen

Tawny Port into his favourite port sipper; an old Vegemite glass and allowed himself the pleasure of a rare cigarette.

Tomorrow—the tangled web of lies and untruths. Someone has to pay—and pay they will.

He picked up his phone and placed a call to a personal ex-Navy contact he previously served with who was now a big-wig with the Department of Immigration.

The Canberra suburb of Belconnen was only a short jog from Lake Ginninderra, where the interim holding cells of the Department of Immigration were located. The cell numbering sequence of F-I translated to foreign illegal, and the reinforced iron bar door to cell no-107 was almost indiscernible as it slid along its well-oiled tracks to its open position.

Inside was a single detainee dressed in purple overalls, waiting patiently on his made bed. The sound of a bag being dropped to the walkway outside his cell prompted him to stand. He stretched his tall, lean body, stepped from his place of incarceration for the last few days and leant down to grab the sports bag. The walk from the holding cell to the front door was a lonely one. He opened up the end zipper and felt inside for what he already knew to be two sets of keys. One was for a Ford *Telstar* parked in the Immigration staff car park and the second was to a one-bedroom apartment in the exclusive suburb of Forrest which was within walking distance of Capital Hill and home of the New Parliament House.

The driver turned the ignition and entered the street address on the dash-mounted Garmen drive-assist. He felt the warmth of the heater at this early hour against his legs and hands. He searched the bag for the only other important piece of equipment he will need to carry out his specific instructions the following day. His hand felt the familiar cold metal barrel of a handgun. He pulled it clear and smiled as he recognised his old 9mm Precision K5. The scar on his chin stretched with deep satisfaction, knowing the end was near to a meticulously planned job that was reaching its inevitable outcome. The Jindeugi was truly the master strategist.

Chapter-45

EVINA DID NOT SLEEP a wink all night and was the first in the shower, the first to eat her breakfast and almost dragged Dixie from the passenger's seat of his sister's car as she pulled up to drop him off at the wharf with his dive gear in the back of her ute. Till cast off the bow and stern lines and *Thin Lizzy* set a course for Batavia's Graveyard, now renamed Beacon Island, 48 nautical miles to the south-west with an ETA of just over two-and-a-half hours.

Dixie parked himself next to Kelly on the upper flybridge. He was just itching to take the controls. "Here, grab the wheel, will you, Dixie. You're the skipper on this trip. You do still remember how to get there—don't you? I'll go rustle up some Thai grub you won't be able to pronounce and a couple of real bean coffees."

Dixie's smile was sincere, and he was in his element. Once the ocean becomes your life, it also evolves into the soothing voice of reason—the reason for life itself. The creator, the master and the almighty conqueror. The complete spectrum. The good days needed to be enjoyed for what they were—far and few between and the bad days you needed to prepare to meet the hand of God—in a very bad mood. That was the deal, and there was no shirking a captain's responsibility to his boat, the crew and the all-important passengers. It was a choice not many get or need to make, but a choice it was. Some men are born for it, and Dixie was at the front of that line.

"Whatever this is, Jack, it tastes great anyway," Dixie shared. "On another note, what's the deal with the sisters, then? Is it worth a shot? I was thinking, Abigail, she seems really nice.

The other sister looks to be a bit highly strung at the moment. What do you reckon?" Dixie asked, then hesitated. ". . . You seem to have a pretty good handle on both of 'em now."

"Go hard or go home, I always say. You never know if you don't have a go, Dixie. Considering Evina has just given her husband the flick—Abigail would also be my choice." Kelly was only too happy to offer some sound advice about the complexities that make up a woman. A topic no man ever really knew much about but considered themselves experts.

Evina was in the dive-bay just aft of the stairs to the engine room. Till was busy fitting her out in a wetsuit and some other gear. Without knowing where this precious anchor is and working out the depth, currents and the swell plus the water clarity, it was all a waste of time at this early stage, but dare anyone that tried to explain that to the associate professor who was about to become the female version of Jules Verne. She wanted underwater photos, video of this thing being winched on board, photos of Evina cuddling it like a lost child. Abigail wasn't far behind. As a reporter, this could be a huge story. Jack and Dixie sat back and just enjoyed the quiet solitude, together.

"Which way you thinking of heading in, Dixie?" Kelly asked.

"We'll head towards the south-east end of East Wallabi Island and anchor up there. Safe from the swells and a natural windbreak. Then we'll drop the tender in the water and go and take a first look. Not many calm days at the bottom part of Morning Reef, so we'll just have to see where this Barnacle Bob actually dropped this thing. I think it will be farther north up inside the deeper channel to the east of Long Island." Dixie knew his stuff, and Kelly was in total agreement.

A lone voice from behind sounded above the hum of the twin diesel engines and the whipping ocean spray. "That's the same route Pelsaert took on his return to the Abrolhos all those years ago. So you're not alone there, are you, Captain Dixie," Abigail was duly impressed.

Kelly gave Dixie a quick jab in the ribs. "Abigail, take my seat. I need to go check your sister hasn't tried to re-arrange the entire dive-bay and all the gear with it. Plus Till might need rescuing by now."

Abigail was more than happy to oblige. Dixie was a good-looking guy. Abigail moved in close with her tighter than usual T-shirt and her hair clipped back. Her long tanned legs were hard to ignore as she edged her way into the now-vacant seat. Dixie suddenly felt slightly fazed.

Evina was fully suited up. Tanks, buoyancy vest, weight belt and even had on a pair of flippers. Till shrugged his shoulders in defeat. Kelly entered and wasn't surprised. "Evina, we may not even need tanks for this dive. Let's just see first, shall we? Give her a hand removing her gear will you, Till."

"You can never be too prepared, Jack Kelly." Evina's voice slowly became louder to keep pace with his retreating exit. "You of all people should know that, Jack," she shouted. "Sorry, Till. I am just so excited, that's all."

"Okay, *khràp*. We are there soon, I think for sure," Till hoped.

The first breaking white water could be heard thundering in the distance as the mid-morning Fremantle Doctor arrived early from the south-west and began its time in perpetuity role of slowly gathering momentum with its land-cooling sea breeze. Both the sisters were absolutely awestruck as the low-lying islands started to take shape. The sounds of the swell crashing over the exposed spiked rocks increased with each sea mile covered. Morning Reef itself was still a farther four kilometres to the south as Dixie turned to starboard and headed to the safe anchorage. The mood on the *Thin Lizzy* was un-curtained. Evina's nervous Nelly demeanour was affecting everybody—well, all except Till, who was already rigging up some handlines.

Kelly started to prepare the tender for launching. He'd already decided to stay on the yacht and send Till with Dixie and the twins to run the first sortie. Within thirty minutes the rooster tail from the 50-hp Yamaha four-stroke could be seen disappearing into the pristine clear blue waters of the Houtman

Abrolhos Islands. The twins were seated against the rear transom, Till stood at the bow hanging onto the anchor rope, and Dixie had the wheel. He headed almost due east for about four and a half k's then hooked a hard right around the northern tip of Long Island that led to a deep, eight-hundred-metre-wide, north-south running channel. Beacon Island or Batavia's Graveyard came up on the port side as the channel took shape in front. Traitors Island was another kilometre farther south as Dixie gave a full running commentary and the very reason Kelly wanted both women to experience this with someone that actually knew what they were talking about.

Dixie continued, "Seals' Island is about a kilometre and a half due west of where we are now, and the actual site of the wreck is just around the corner on Morning Reef. I won't take the tender past the protection of Long and Dick Island, but you'll get a sense of what it's all about from our vantage point. Then we'll retrace our steps back along the east side of this channel to search for the red and white striped float. What did Graeme say—this Barnacle Bob was a South Fremantle supporter?"

Dixie slowed the 14-foot plate-aluminium tender and allowed the bow to drift within fifty feet of the breaking giants as they plundered the reef with the full weight of their watery load. Even as a cray fisherman with fifteen years under his belt, Dixie's mind still boggled at the drama and confusion that must have wreaked havoc for those poor souls on board the pride of the VOC fleet that fateful night in 1629. In the middle of a winter sea with the swells at their most dangerous, it's a wonder so many survived the wreck only to be met by the premeditated deranged bloodbath that followed. That very same outcrop of reef *Batavia* met on a moonlit night, under full sail, was there for all to see and then—and only then would the average person perhaps fully understand the power of the Indian Ocean.

The twins were both captivated and remained speechless, enthralled while imagining what played out on the decks of the *Batavia* all that time ago. Dixie had seen it many times before.

"It's almost too incredible to believe that it could have actually happened—right here on this lonely coral atoll in the middle of pretty much nowhere," Dixie continued his commentary. "Another five hundred metres to his right, Captain Ariaen Jacobsz, would have sailed right past the danger and probably would have been totally unaware of how close they came to running aground. Sadly, history tells us that was not the case."

Dixie handed Evina and Till a set of binoculars and advised them to follow a left-to-right sweep pattern to spot the float if, in fact, it was still attached at all. Kelly told Dixie not to share that snippet of information with a certain woman whose name began with the letter E. Dixie figured the anchor will be inside the shallows that would be accessible between a middling to high tide, which was due at 1300 hours; still three hours away.

"The baitfish like to ball up where there is always some shelter and calmer waters. Away from the pelagic predators and the thousands of different species of sharks that call this home," Dixie explained. He gave Abigail a thorough once-over as she stood next to Till and forward of Dixie's position behind the wheel.

Evina slowly turned. "Which way you looking, Captain? You see something you like in your line of sight?" Evina chuckled.

Dixie's face turned bright red.

"I see - I see the little buoy in the water. Look, look," Till was animated, as he lowered his binoculars and pointed out the spot to Dixie.

"This way Till you reckon?" Dixie questioned, as he snaked his way through the myriad of blue holes, sand bottom channels and coral bombies that could shred a propeller in a couple of seconds.

Till looked a second time, "Gone now, I can't see."

"Over there. I see it now. Red and white. Follow my arm, Dixie." Abigail was almost jumping up and down.

"Do you mean right into that reef just in front?" Dixie forced her glasses down to waist level.

"Oh, wow! I see what you mean. Can we get in closer though? I can still see something floating, and it looks red and white."

Dixie turned to face Evina, who looked like she was about to walk the plank. "I'll mark it on the GPS and drop another float over the side. We can pick it up after the tide peaks. Just a bit longer, Evina."

Chapter-46

STONE CAUGHT the six A.M. flight and landed at Fairbairn Airport. Formally a Royal Australian Air Force Military Base, the land that occupied an area north and east of the Canberra Airport runways was sold to Capital Airport Pty Ltd to advance civil aviation and the development of a business park with its close proximity to Capital Hill.

He had spent the best part of the previous night revising his plan. After the epic failure with the meeting between Darcy Jones and Admiral Peterson the previous day, his major obstacle was rounding up all the players and placing them in the same place—at the same time. The bait for that to happen appeared on each of the JNSC members secured e-mail servers in full graphic colour at this very moment.

Helena Wilks was first to enter her parliamentary office at seven A.M. She scanned over the assemblage of media releases on her desk due to be fed to the waiting hyena's that go by the name of the Canberra Press Club. Each morning they all needed to be scrutinised before being redirected to the media hungry wolves. A short text message on her phone provoked an immediate response. She placed her Gloria Jeans latte next to the photo of her parents and read the short message. *Secured e-mail: Access - Ministers Eyes Only - Level-7 password required.*

Wilks sat down and turned on her desk PC. She entered her office password and clicked on the icon that would open the JNSC-only secured e-mail server. She then entered her memorised seven-digit access code and opened up the *.jpg* attachment. Within seconds she placed her hand over her gaping mouth, then made a distraught scramble towards her private bathroom and emptied the contents of her stomach. Still gagging and dry retching, she turned on the tap and rinsed her mouth while trying not to heave again. The reflection in the mirror was that of a pale and deeply disturbed woman.

Darcy Jones was met by the smiling face of Sheila White. She followed him into his office and placed the day's agenda in order of importance to the left side of his huge desk, as per his instructions. Jones offered a polite acknowledgement and waited for the door to close. His computer screen flickered and settled on the desktop image the day the U.S. Embassy fell in Saigon. A North Vietnamese tank was pushing over the main gate as the last Sikorsky CH-34 Choctaw was airlifting the remaining terrorised embassy staff from the rooftop.

Jones remembered the day well as he witnessed firsthand a U.S. Marine hanging out the open helicopter door with his Sterling submachine gun at the ready.

The secured e-mail icon was flashing red in the top right corner of his monitor. He double-clicked his mouse and waited. It prompted him for a security code. He punched in his Level-9 ASIO password, then opened the attachment.

Darcy Jones was accustomed to death. He'd tasted and fought it in two theatres of war. He wasn't prepared for the vivid images of mutilated bodies piled on top of one another with intimate body parts missing. Jones swallowed hard and closed the attachment. *Fucking, Stone!* Jones pressed his intercom, "Miss White, get me the attorney-general on the phone—NOW."

Franklin Sandhurst was in the back seat of his chauffeur-driven *Statesman* when his mobile rang. He looked at the caller ID and pressed *talk*. "Jones, a bit early for you, isn't it?" For the next two minutes, the attorney-general's ears were burning as he listened to the director-general of ASIO, a man that answered directly to him, fire off a series of random questions he wasn't prepared to answer, and he knew Jones knew that to be the case. It was a fishing exercise with only one outcome in mind. The morning was still frigid in Canberra, but the first droplets of perspiration beaded off Sandhurst's forehead. He tapped the dividing window and instructed his chauffeur to drive to Capital Hill.

Prime Minister Jeremy Collins was still seated in the ministers-only section of the dining room, enjoying his second cup of coffee with a freshly baked croissant after his morning ritual in the parliamentary pool. The private door that led directly to the ministerial wing and the Office of the Prime Minister glided open. Collins turned in his chair, interested in who else might be seizing the opportunity to enjoy some quiet time alone before the grind of another day dawned upon the elected members of Parliament who were tasked with running the country and protecting the citizens of Australia.

The heavy footsteps of hard-soled boots bounded off the freshly polished tiled floor as Admiral Peterson strode towards the only occupied seat, while a second man, unknown to Collins, sat down alone on the opposite side of the room. Collins knew from the scowl on the admiral's face that all was not well on the front lines.

Admiral Peterson sat down and matched eyes with Collins. "This stops today." He searched the room to confirm they were alone and placed a photo on the table that made Collins gasp in disbelief.

"Is this someone's idea of a sick joke?" Collins animated loudly, barely able to control his disgust while picking up the print to confirm what he was looking at was, in fact, real. "My God—I feel ill inside." He slammed the gruesome photo onto the table, face down, spilling the remains of his coffee into his saucer.

"I want to introduce you to the man that snapped this, and others just like it. He was there—on Christmas Island."

"Christmas Island? What the *hell* is going on here—is this connected to the detention centre?" Collins was almost hesitant to ask.

Boomer turned and motioned for the stranger to come forward. "Prime Minister, I would like to introduce, Tobias Stone. He works for, Darcy Jones—off the record."

Collins stood and sized up Stone as he approached, with his hand outstretched. The man's bouncing full head of curly black hair told him he wasn't regular Army or Navy. The glint in his eyes suggested he was a man that wasn't to be jerked around. His handshake was firm and only substantiated what Collins had already mentally established. "You're Jones' man on the ground—on second thought's don't answer that? Admiral, follow me if you would, and please ask Mr Stone to join us."

The three men stood in silence as the private lift stopped at the PM's office. With his customary loud holler, Collins ignored the closed door and issued instructions to his personal PA. Mary had been at the prime minister's side since the first days he became an opposition backbencher representing the seat of Eden-Monaro, back in 1980. "Mary, I need you in here right away."

The door pushed open, and Mary breezed in. She knew from the tone of her boss's voice that something was seriously askew.

"Yes, Prime Minister," Mary acknowledged the admiral and wondered who the third man was.

"Organise a temporary level-seven security pass for the Menzies Room on my written authority and send out a mayday call to *ALL* the other JNSC members. I expect each one of them to be in this building and seated in *that* room within the hour—no excuses." His hand was pointing towards the lift that only had one destination—down three floors.

"Do you want me to draft the authority *and* sign it as well, sir?" Only Mary could have got away with the insider's joke. Collins returned an understanding glare as she left the office.

The intercom buzzed on Collins' desk. "Yes."

"It's the attorney-general on the phone. He sounds agitated. What do you want me to tell him?"

"Tell him he has under an hour to get his arse over here to Capital Hill."

Three tense minutes passed. Mary entered a second time with the printed authority and a security badge with a unique bar-code impregnated electronically onto the black magstripe. "The attorney-general was already on his way, he should be here in twenty minutes. Sign here, Prime Minister."

Collins passed the card to Stone. "It's just on loan. I want it back when this is all over. I'm hoping that's going to happen today, Stone."

"It will if you leave it up to me," Stone returned the barb. He wanted the PM to understand that he was in control of events from here on.

"Have the remaining three JNSC members responded as yet, Mary?" Collins asked.

"General Connelly is in the building, and the director-general has come back with the confirmation code," Mary replied.

"And, Wilks? What about the deputy PM?"

"Nothing yet, sir."

"Maybe you should ring her hairstylist," the admiral enjoyed sharing.

Just then, Stone's phone vibrated inside his jacket pocket. He pulled it out to see a 6-4-3 text message, then an attachment appeared, it was a *.jpg* image. A photo began to appear on Stone's screen. He turned his phone sideways and expanded the image with his forefinger and thumb. "What the fuck?" Stone let slip. Three sets of eyes turned and glared. The barrel of a handgun with a silencer attached was pressed to the right temple of the deputy prime minister.

Stone's phone rang again. "Sorry, but we *all* need to listen to this call." His scowl changed to confusion as he put the caller on speaker.

Chapter-47

DIXIE FINALLY CONVINCED a very sceptical-looking Kelly, that there was more than enough room to anchor *Thin Lizzy* up in the channel. It did at least chew up another hour while setting the anchor to the skipper's exacting requirements. Kelly was definitely not leaving his yacht now. If the anchor were to shift, the fibreglass and kevlar hull would be the next shipwreck to be welcomed into the jaws of the hungry Abrolhos. *These guys are on their own when the tide reaches its highest peak.*

The mood on board was slightly more relaxed now as each person made last-minute preparations for the final hurdle which was hopefully only a matter of half a kilometre to the east in the calm, aquarium-like-waters off the back of Traitors Island, which was smaller than the average football oval.

The inside shallows were like a lagoon of sand-bunker-shaped blue holes crisscrossed by sandy coral-based channels that followed no map. The float was another six hundred metres inside, slightly to the south where the *Batavia* would have slowly disgorged her contents along a northerly flow spreading throughout the atoll with the wind and tides pushing it towards Batavia's Graveyard. Dixie nodded towards the exuberant Evina. It was time to collect her prize.

Evina and Abigail were both kitted out in full-length neoprene 5mm-thick wetsuits while Dixie donned a pair of boardshorts in the temperate 22-degree ocean water. Abigail was familiarising herself with Kelly's Olympus T-50 underwater camera and working out the inbuilt Wi-Fi capabilities to allow her to send digital photos directly to her laptop. Till bought the centre console runabout alongside and the four marine treasure hunters set off towards the float Dixie laid down earlier. With the high tide, the only major worry was the coral bombies, named-so as they resemble the mushroom cloud from a nuclear explosion with a thin trunk topped by a cauliflower-shaped coral head that was as sharp as a razor's edge. The depth of water ranged from half to over five metres deep.

Till picked up the marker float with the long gaff. The clarity of the water was glass-like. What looked to be about a foot of water was, in fact, over ten feet deep. You could easily make out the curling sand trails of the sea snails with retreating hermit crabs backing up to hide amongst the many forms of coral. A pair of shovelnose sharks meandered past, sending up a tail swish of disturbed sand. Two cow tail stingrays scurried away from the shadow of the tender as it pushed closer to the red and white buoy, gently bobbing in the distance. The whole ocean resembled a giant over-sized personal fishbowl. Blue-bone groper, coral trout, small trumpeter fish and a hundred other species thrived in these unspoilt waters.

Till motioned with his arm to slow. Dixie placed the outboard into neutral and used the hydraulics to raise the leg. The bottom was changing to a darker colour as the seaweed became thicker and the brain coral heads changed to a greying spectrum of speckled intertwined greens, reds and yellows. The buoy was only fifty metres away now. Dixie moved the stick back into gear and idled in closer, then killed the engine. Till lowered the coral pick over the side and fed enough rope out to bring the tender alongside the algae-covered floats. He set the anchor and dropped a blue and white dive flag over the side, then slid the boarding ladder over the port-side rail.

Dixie firstly wanted to lay down the order of the dive. "I'll head over the side first. Evina, you can follow me, and Abigail, I think until we identify what's on the end of this line, you might as well float around near the tender and snap away." With flippers, mask and snorkel, Dixie stepped off the ladder then spat and adjusted his mask. Evina and Abigail soon followed. While still treading water, Dixie explained to his dive partners. "Just take it easy, remember slow and deliberate breathing. It's not deep, and the water clarity is over forty feet, so we shouldn't have a problem identifying the drum."

Evina returned the single thumbs-up signal, and they set off in the same direction as the vanishing anchor rope.

Dixie soon felt a tap on his back leg. Evina was pointing up. He raised his head above the water and spat out his snorkel, "Are you all right?"

"Did you see those crayfish? Oh, my God, they're everywhere. This place is unbelievable. C'mon, what are we waiting for? Let's go," Evina shouted like she was rousing the troops to battle. She was still pumped.

Dixie shook his head and swam on. He grasped the rope that was covered in fine green weed and slimy algae, then dived under, pulling himself along its path. It disappeared into a kelp bed. He let go and parted the giant kelp leaves, hoping to be greeted by the drum. The rope fed through a thin crevice and then was lost from sight. He resurfaced, filled his lungs and dived a second time. Dixie swam past the first section of kelp and followed the coral ridge. He stroked his arms and kicked with both feet to go deeper. A small drop-off fell away to a depth of about twenty-five feet, which was a deep hole for this mostly shallow inner water. The first thing he saw was a three-metre-long tiger shark rear its big ugly boofhead and then watched it casually swim away.

People were not usually on the menu with the ocean floor scattered with tasty rock lobsters like saltwater cockroaches. Evina arrived back at the surface like an Adelaide penguin. Dixie soon joined her to offer some calming words.

Dixie dived a third time and picked up the trailing rope again as it followed a thin divide along the uneven seabed, then reappeared with the fading image of a large yellow and red Pecten seashell emblem with the words: Go well - Go Shell. He had found the drum. Evina was still floating above when Dixie surfaced one more time. He raised his arm, and Till started pulling on the anchor rope to move the tender closer.

Dixie was last to scramble up the ladder. "I'll try to shift the drum from the ledge it's wedged against with the outboard. Then we'll need to attach some floats using the scuba gear and bring it to the surface slowly. After that, we can tow it back to the Hiab and hoist it on board Jack's yacht."

Evina just kept nodding. It took another forty minutes to drag the drum far enough from the jagged ledge for Dixie and Till to secure two flotation devices to either end of the 44-gallon drum. Till hooked the hose to a small 3-hp Onan pump and flipped the switch. The hose quickly filled with air and started to inflate both the salvage balloons. Abigail was snapping photos. Evina was trying to control her heart rate while Dixie watched the rate of accent and made sure both balloons cleared the sharp coral edges. Kelly watched on through his binoculars and readied the hoist. Both balloons surfaced simultaneously. Dixie tightened all the knots and placed a safety line with two long white torpedo floats attached.

With the drum floating like a submerged sea container, Dixie put the tender into gear and eased the throttle. The drum was cumbersome and parted with a good-sized bow wave as it lumbered its way behind the outboard, back to the waiting yacht. Till dived back into the water as the tender pulled alongside *Thin Lizzy*. He slowed the drum's forward momentum while Kelly lowered the freight net. Till reached up and grabbed the loose end. He swam under the drum and slipped the braided loop over the hook secured to the Hiab's webbed winch cord.

"Okay, Boss. You good now," Till shouted from below. He raised his thumb, not really knowing what that meant, but he'd seen Evina and Dixie both do it. The twins stripped their dive gear off in near-record time. Abigail continued snapping away. Right now, Evina would have been happy to have in her possession a diamond blade angle grinder.

From the rear of the mezzanine deck, Kelly manoeuvred the controls and lowered the drum onto a folded silver tarpaulin. A steady trickle of seawater slowly seeped through a couple of rust holes. Dixie unhooked the net and stood the drum on its bottom plate before grabbing a length of nylon rope.

"How's your heart beating, Evina?" Kelly yelled from above. "First things first, and that means we need to vacate this channel. Dixie, you take the wheel. Till and I will retrieve our anchor, and then we'll secure the drum on the rear deck."

"Don't you want to open it first—I mean, just in case it's not... " Evina started to say.

"How many drums do you think are hanging off the end of a float with South Fremantle colours? This is our drum—with or without your precious book."

Dixie had already decided to head straight back to his own camp on Robinson Island. It was a good 55-kilometre run, but with *Thin Lizzy*'s top speed of 28 knots, they would be there in no time flat with the added bonus of access to an oxy-acetylene kit, a safe berth plus the wind was picking up. It was the smart thing to do and a safety-first decision.

Like the great boat handler he was, Dixie swept around the north marker in a wide sliding semi-circle, still pushing 22 knots, then straightened up for the two-kilometre-run through the gap between Robinson Island and the southern point of Iris Refuge Island. Then he turned hard to port to ease the 72-foot yacht against the protective rubber tractor tyres of his old boss's private wharf.

"Not hard to see you're trying to make a memorable first impression, Dixie. Not bad, not bad at all." Even Kelly was impressed, and he hoped for Dixie's sake, Abigail was the same.

Till secured the bow and stern ropes, then tightened both stringers. Kelly negotiated the outside stairs and powered the Hiab back up, then swung the drum over onto the wooden-planked wharf. Dixie undid the padlock on his storage shed at the wharf end and rolled out on a hard wheeled trolley, the dual tanks and cutting nozzle of his Cigweld oxy set. With his goggles on, he fired up the nozzle and went to work on the old weld marks. Abigail stood shoulder to shoulder next to her sister while Dixie completed the first quarter. Both girls held hands in a tight squeeze as half the top plate was now separated and beginning to slowly reveal its first secret. The sparks flew in all directions; all eyes were turned away from the intense, white-hot particles of carbon. The noise of the cutting nozzle ceased, and Evina was first to turn and face the drum. Smoke and the smell of burning metal drifted away on the south-westerly breeze. Dixie lifted his goggles and parked the Cigweld to one side.

"I think you've well and truly earned the right, Evina." Dixie offered his welding gloves. She slipped both hands into the elbow-length protection then gathered a firm grip on the smouldering serrated top and like peeling a can of tuna, she pulled back on the lid. More smoke billowed from inside, the red glow from a couple of cooling hot pieces of metal dags still glowed from the bottom of the drum.

Evina waved her hands to clear the smoke and cast first eyes on what had consumed her life for the past ten years. It took a few seconds for her eyesight to adjust. She circled to the opposite side and removed a single glove then leaned over and touched the surface, feeling with the palm of her hand as she caressed the uneven grooved surface. It didn't look like anything wooden, but the feeling was unmistakable. She raised her head and beamed back an anxious glower, still unsure what it was.

Together, Kelly and Dixie grabbed each side of the drum. They laid it down on the wharf, then shifted to the base and lifted it at an angle while shaking it from side to side. Whatever was inside started to slide out until what resembled an over-sized inflated charcoal pillowslip of coal spilt out. Each person stood and gazed. A series of shallow creek-like channels meandered over the surface with the ground-in red dirt, highlighting the inevitable evidence of burrowing teredo worms.

"Well, at least it's still in one piece," Evina was the first to break the trance-like state that existed. "We need fresh water and some clean rags." She didn't have the luxury of a

Smithsonian standard equipped laboratory. Dixie came back from his shanty two-room fishing camp with a five-litre bottle and an old towel. Evina ripped it into equal pieces and passed them around. Each person started rubbing and scrubbing away at the blackened surface. Gradually a hand-chiselled image started to take shape under the grime and built-up film of green slime.

"Have you any old brushes lying around anywhere, Dixie?" Evina anxiously asked.

Dixie was back in a flash with two paintbrushes. One brand new—the other not so much; its bristles were crusted firm. Evina brushed away the dried and cracked grime from around the centre surface as the casket gave up its first clue. Kelly was the first to stand and retire, Dixie soon followed, and they cracked their first beer together. Till kept rubbing away while the twins continued brushing the surface clean.

"I think this is an outer protective casing," Evina pointed out while brushing away feverishly. "Oh, boy—will you look at this? It's the Dynastic Seal." Evina stopped and stared at the carved image, slowly morphing into a beaded circle shape. The seal contained eight smaller circles, numbered from I to VIII in a counter-clockwise design and another larger circle at its centre with the number IX. Each surrounding circle listed the royal ancestry tree in order of birth.

Evina immediately recognised two names. "This one in position eight reads: *Aben Acabar Pad Shah*, Jahangir's father, Akbar, and the ninth says: *Aben Almozaphar Nur Din*. This is absolute confirmation of Emperor Jahangir's affiliation. Incredible—will you just look at me—my hands are trembling. This distinctive design, consisting of the ruling emperor's name in the centre and surrounded by his Timurid ancestors, became an important symbol of Moghul imperial authority and was noted by several contemporary European travellers, including, Sir Thomas Roe. It was used on official orders known as *farmans* and differed from the smaller personal ownership seals which are sometimes found in manuscripts."

"There looks to be a seam along the entire circumference," Kelly pointed out. "Maybe the top half lifts off?" Kelly leapt off a wharf pylon and knelt down. "Till, pass me that piece of towel." He wiped away at a coin-sized cylindrical deviation on one end. "These two smaller end sections are made from a different grain. Look, you can see the variation in the colour. Hang on a sec." Kelly raced down to his workshop in the engine room and came back with a wooden mallet with a flat-nosed centre punch. "I think this may secure the two halves together. If we can tap them clear, I reckon it might just come apart." He looked at Evina for confirmation. She nodded in agreement. Kelly then placed the end of the centre punch over the first cylinder-shaped length of dowel. "Dixie, hang on to it with your hands to stop it shifting." Kelly eased the mallet back and gave it a soft tap. The mood was likened to disarming the timer on a ticking bomb. Nobody dared to usher a sound.

Bang. Evina flinched: nothing happened. "All right, I'll gradually increase power." *Bang* again, still no movement. Evina's face told the tale. She looked jittery. Kelly stood and straddled the casket, then bent over and wielded the heaviest blow. "It moved. Look, Evina, you can see the inside of the sleeve hole." *Whack - Whack*, he belted it harder with each blow. A wooden dowel pin popped out the other end and fell to the ground. Kelly swapped sides and from the silence of the moment, able to hear a pin drop, a second dowel slowly eased its way clear. He then tapped the upper section lightly, following the seam in a clockwise direction. Crumbling dirt and some sea grime fell away to the wharf below, and the seal was broken.

Kelly and Dixie reached down and placed their hands on either end, then shifted it back and forth. More built-up grime and muck settled at the base of the ironwood casing. "You ready Dixie? On the count of three, we'll lift it clear. One - two - three." Five sets of eyes stared downward in construed allurement while Kelly and Dixie held the sealed lid at waist height.

A polished parquetry wooden box sat inside. An inscription of a small key, followed by a line of Persian text was surrounded with what resembled a dawning sun, with its extended rays beaming in a 360-degree rotation, encompassing the image of a highborn man bent over the neck of a charging elephant with a long menacing spear held out in front. He looked resplendent, adorned in a jewelled kafsh atop his head, only worn by nobles and kings and a knee-length jama. The Yaktahi jama originated in Persia and Central Asia. It was worn both short and long, over a pai-jama to form an outfit known as the bast agag. The garment was dazzling with gold and silver thread matching a side-fastening frock-coat with a nipped-in-the-waist bodice and a flared skirt covering his knees. A pair of ornamented Persian jhuti, with turned-up toes, covered his feet and a complexly designed pátka, handwoven and embroidered with a silk sash made for royalty showcasing the textile craftsmanship of the era, ran around the waist of his chogha or hip-length gown with a jewelled-handled sword hanging to one side.

Evina was taken aback, unsure of whom this person of royal blood might represent. The entire scene was surrounded by what resembled a raised spoke wheel, with flecks of blue still visible. She bent down and gently eased the rectangular-shaped case from its protective home for the last three centuries. "We need to get this inside, Jack. I have an uneasy feeling I may know what this is." She handed the weighted protective box to Kelly as he stood and waited for an explanation.

Abigail then asked, "Would you like to expand on that last statement, Evina?" Abigail's facial expression was like a small child asking why the sky was blue.

Evina sat down on her backside and let out a long, drawn-out breath. Kelly could see her interpretive brain trying to deliberate with what she was confronted with. "Do you remember me explaining what a Himitsu-Bako was, well, that's what this is?" Evina sighed.

Kelly and Dixie looked on with a total mental blackout. "Okay, so remind all of us what a himsu-baku is again or whatever it was you just said?" Both men felt like they were mentally challenged.

"Hakone-Yosegi-Zaiku." Evina continued.

"Your turn to ask," Kelly motioned towards his good mate.

"I'll save you the trouble, Dixie. It's a Japanese puzzle box," Evina explained.

Evina spoke softly, only this time slowly and speculatively. "Traditionally these lockboxes were constructed with an inbuilt failsafe mechanism. The Chinese were known to have used eggshells to carry inside an acid that would crack and disperse, destroying what lay inside after either tampering or a third failed attempt to follow the exacting sequence, in solving the riddle. The last one found in Madagascar was similar, and it took over nine-months to unlock. It wasn't until a Tibetan monk came forward and recognised the signature on the underside, right-side corner. Not a specific name, more-so a reference to the style and to which line of builders the design could be attributed to. He explained that when the Chinese ransacked Tibet and the Dalai Lama was forced to seek exile, all their prized written history was stored and hidden in similar style locking devices. On the monk's second attempt, the seal cracked open to reveal four cannonballs and a small jade effigy of Mirza Nur-ud-din Beig Mohammad Khan Salim, or as we know him: Emperor Jahangir. It was a decoy," Evina went on to explain.

"We have to follow a precise set of unknown instructions in the exact order to open the seal," Evina conceded. "Plus, I'll need to access the Smithsonian website to download my research. Abby, where's your notebook? I just remembered something I read years ago that may have some relevance to solving the puzzle, and I need to talk with the curator, Byron."

"Evina," Kelly called out as she leapt onto the yacht like a bull at a gate. "Before you go racing off to share with your work colleagues this good fortune, remember, mum's the word about what we dragged up off the floor of the ocean today.

Better to be safe than sorry." Kelly touched his finger to his nose. "Nobody knows like Jack's nose—get it?

If Evina's brain was a cash register, it was showing 'No Sale', but eventually, the $ sign appeared inside her confused head.

Chapter·48

THE MENZIES ROOM was named after what a majority of older Australians would regard as the country's greatest ever prime minister. Sir Robert Gordon Menzies was the longest-serving PM from 1939 to 1941, encompassing the end of the Second World War and a further second term from 1949 to 1966: a total of twenty years.

The current prime minister was seated at the head of the Tasmanian blackwood boardroom table. To his right was Admiral Peterson and next to him was General Connelly, still kitted out in full ceremonial dress uniform due to attend a vice-regal event to support the governor-general, being held within the grounds of Government House before he was summoned by the prime minister, back to Capital Hill. Directly opposite him sat Franklin Sandhurst, who was desperately trying to portray a cool, calm and collected mindset. Nothing could be further from the truth. To his immediate left was Darcy Jones, replaying in his mind what was about to be played out in a few short minutes from now, with his piercing eyes throwing daggers into Stone's heart, seated at the opposite bookend of the table. The room became deathly quiet as each person contemplated the disentanglement that was about to unfold.

A high-pitched alarm sounded from the low dose of non-ionising electromagnetic radiation used by the Backscatter X-ray scanner, causing all but one set of eyes to turn and gaze with arrant nihilism. A wall-mounted flat-screen monitor behind the plexiglass divide showed the reverse black-and-white image of a man holding a handgun to the back of Helena Wilks' head, as she was forcibly escorted into the secured room.

The last member of the Joint National Security Committee entered with a look of dread firmly entrenched across what normally would have been a perfectly manicured face. That was until the retired Major General Duckhwan Toa of the North Korean People's Army rounded her up in the underground car park and placed a gun to her pretty little head. Helena Wilks eyes were swollen, and mascara ran down both cheeks. She looked defeated, and probably for a very good reason.

The tall figure of the Jindeugi forced Wilks into one of only two spare chairs. He waved his 9mm K5 at the man seated at the opposite end to the prime minister. "You don't seem surprised to see me, Stone? Get up... slowly and then walk through the scanner."

The Jindeugi stepped around the table and tapped the admiral on the shoulder with the tip of his silencer. "You— Admiral Peterson and General Connelly—please, if you would be so kind?" Both men followed Stone, while the Jindeugi eyeballed the monitor. "Hand it over, Stone. Left hand first. This is no time for any more of your heroics." Stone leant down to ankle-height and ripped open the velcro of his calf glove. His 11.5 ounce, 'two in one policy' was a .380 calibre Glock 42. He slid it towards Toa, where it was quickly dispatched with the flick of his boot to the other side of the room.

"Director, now it's your turn, move it," Toa snapped. There was no love lost between the Jindeugi and Darcy Jones. Their paths had crossed once before. Each person returned to their allocated seats, unsure of what may transpire, next.

"Prime Minister Collins, I believe?" the Jindeugi addressed the elected leader with disdain. He then shifted his sadistic, cold-blooded eyes towards the only remaining man seated "I haven't had the pleasure of a formal introduction. Who might you be, then?"

Franklin Sandhurst stood up in a show of defiance. "I'm the attorney-general, and how dare you . . ."

The sound of broken glass stopped him mid-sentence as a bullet whisked past his right temple and shattered a photo of

Sir Robert Menzies, hanging next to a portrait of Queen Elizabeth II. "You'll get your ten seconds in due course, sit down and do not interrupt me again," Toa demanded. "When will you politicians ever learn, democracy is dead? Greed and corruption are the new modern politics. Every man, or in this case, every woman, lining their grubby little pockets with the people's gold."

The Jindeugi enjoyed taunting the leader of a country who referred to his own birthplace as 'the axis of evil'. He surveyed the seven faces staring back at him, then stopped while viewing the man seated at the opposite end to where he currently stood. "How are you, Stone? As you may well have worked out already, that cesspool we swim in is alive and still filled with a few of us old-time snakes." His scar stretched to match his broad grin.

Darcy Jones cast an evil eye towards the man he previously had named the Tick. "For a snivelling dirty two-time double-crossing retired North Korean major general—or should we just call a spade a spade? The word I'm looking for is an assassin, yes—for a cold-blooded killer you speak pretty good English, Toa," Jones rolled off his tongue with a distasteful slur.

"That's ironic coming from a man who himself plays the role of a traitor with such benevolence, Director." The Jindeugi slid a copy of a Federal Order onto the polished table surface. Jones picked it up and read the two paragraphs. "What's this? I know nothing of this order." Jones cast it aside. It floated towards Admiral Peterson. He read it and handed it to General Connelly. Wilks didn't need to see the document for the second time. She remained tight-lipped, still clinging to the last ray of hope that she may see a way out of this dilemma—of her own doing.

"This order came into my possession while I was on Christmas Island, courtesy of your own paid assassin. Thank you, Stone. You should really be more careful where you leave such important documents."

"I thought we had an understanding? A common cause—your own sister, if you remember, you prick," Stone responded.

Collins snatched the order with the Australian Coat of Arms pictured at the top of the page. Staring him in the face was the formal symbol of the Commonwealth of Australia. A shield enclosed in a border by two native Australian animals, a kangaroo to the left and an emu to the right which represented the Federation in 1901, when the six States and two Territories united to form one Nation.

"Perhaps you recognise the ten-digit code in the upper right-hand corner? Why don't you share with your colleagues what that might be?" the Jindeugi further prodded the elected leader.

Collins found his glasses and confirmed the prefix was, in fact, the code assigned to ASIO. He lowered his gaze and locked eyes on Darcy Jones. "Would you like to explain to me what's going on here?"

The Jindeugi turned and faced Jones. "I never liked you from the first time we met at Check Point Charlie in 74, Jones." His infamous scar shifted with his condescending smirk. A few seconds passed, and then he fired a single shot into the left shoulder of the director-general of ASIO. "That's for allowing my innocent sister to be taken captive by Geulaendeu Maseuteo and his e'prentis." A piece of his jacket tore open, and a trickle of blood oozed out. Jones' upper body shuddered while recoiling to one side. But with teeth gritted, not wanting to break his steely gaze, he stared down the evil eyes of a natural-born killer. He pulled a handkerchief from his top pocket and held it over the wound without missing a beat. Wilks screamed and started sobbing.

Collins stood and took exception to the unfolding events. "Now look here," he started to cry out.

The Jindeugi placed the barrel-end of his Daewoo K5 into his forehead and pressed hard, Collins was forced back into his chair.

"All right, Toe. We all know you're a tough son of a bitch. What do you want, or would you like *me* to fill in the blanks?" Stone was about to cast the first lure into the shark-filled waters of modern-day politics and its financial marriage with the big end of town.

"Through some weird twist of fate, Stone," the Jindeugi challenged, "our two objectives clashed in Bali. We were both acting on the orders from a higher power. Your own Government sought revenge for the eighty-eight dead Australians, and I wanted to assure the future of the only surviving member of my family. Be my guest—let's see what you *think* you know so far since you're so smart?"

Stone leaned forward in his chair. "Let's start with the reason you came here today—you want an ace up your sleeve to guarantee your sister's safe passage into this country, and to do that you need to find out who double-crossed you. Because you're not sure now, and it's eating you away inside. I can read you like Mao's little red handbook on how to be the perfect communist. No imagination, Toa. After your own Korean buddies tried in vain to cancel your contract, you decided to cut another deal. And from your contacts in Jakarta, you knew our own misguided, Miss Wilks, was on their payroll. A stooge who was set up from the beginning to occupy a position of power in the seat of a democratically elected Parliament, but when she suddenly rocketed to the second top job, it was like all their Christmas's had come at once. Sometimes you get lucky, I suppose." Stone leaned back in his chair to let it all sink in.

Wilks grimaced but stood her ground. "These accusations carry little weight from a man that makes his living from deception and murder. You have no proof of these wild allegations."

"Miss Wilks," Stone continued. "At best, you are naïve. At worst, you have committed treason, fraud and lied to the Australian people. You are going to jail for a very long time. The time has arrived to come clean. I know about your sister, Anna. I have also followed the money trail that flooded into your election campaign, which leads straight back to Indonesia. You chaired the standing committee which presided over the SEA-1444 agreements to build the eight Armidale-class patrol boats, destined for a foreign navy. You might be a victim of your own ignorance, but this has escalated to a point where innocent people—children as young as twelve, have suffered horrendous cruelty and acts of prolonged sexually explicit enslavement." Stone glided a photo of the mutilated bodies towards the deputy prime minister. "You make me sick. You can shoot *her* anytime you like, Toa."

"These photos, and that e-mail I received this morning? How can you possibly entertain the thought that I would choose to be a willing party to anything as abhorrent as that? You're sick in the head, and if that's all you have, well then, you've got nothing?" Wilks vehemently denied.

"These kids, Miss Wilks, were the children and wives of the refugees who paid these people smugglers with their life savings, the same people that you're in bed with. The same Indonesians that greased the wheels of your election campaign. The same Indonesians that paid for your last four holidays and the same fucking North Koreans who profit out of the business of people trafficking. These kids were sex toys to be used and abused and then killed, all the while being filmed just so they could play a starring role on some sick bastard's DVD player. These movies are produced and copied right here in Canberra and then sent back to South East Asia for resale. Big money, Miss Wilks—blood money."

Collins was reeling. He searched for a sign, anything that would convince him all these accusations were unfounded. Wilks sat in cold silence with her head buried in both palms. The admiral and General Connelly were in a state of unimaginable disturbing paralysis. As the truth started to unfold, their confusion slowly shifted to total bewilderment. Boomer was outraged. He sized up the prime minister with a look of contempt. "What did I tell you about this woman. She is a disgrace to the flag of this country."

Wilks was clearly distressed at the final sledge. She reacted vociferously by placing her finger on the photo. "I am not responsible for this. These children—what happened to these poor kids?" She turned the photo over and burst into tears, "Oh, my God—what have I done?"

The attorney-general squirmed in his seat as the first signs of Wilks cracking were there for all to see.

The Jindeugi moved and stood behind Wilks. "If you don't stop that infernal racket, you might end up just like those young girls you sentenced to death at the casino. Shut up—and do it *now*." The Jindeugi squeezed her shoulder with his free hand.

Stone showed no mercy. "Three enemies of this country have been eliminated under Article-289. The third was on Australian soil because we were lucky that a RAN Special Forces trained sniper just happened to be around when we needed him most. That, plus the quick thinking of a man whose life suffered a terrible tragedy and is now a paraplegic. How many more of these, so-called refugees are running around the country, Miss Wilks? My sources say the number maybe seventy. I'll bet it's more... much more, in fact. Who's responsible for that?" Stone's words resonated throughout the Menzies Room.

"Even one is too bloody many for my liking," the admiral threw in. General Connelly nodded in agreement.

Stone addressed the Jindeugi. "I'm going to pull something from my jacket pocket, so easy on the trigger finger, Duckman." He unfolded three printed satellite maps and laid them out neatly on the table for all to see. Stone was particularly interested in the reflex actions of one person. He waited for a response, but he wasn't looking at Wilks anymore. Stone glanced to his left for a reaction. Body language is its own vocabulary and difficult to disguise. A slight shift in posture, the almost unnoticed tightening of an obscure facial muscle or a subtle swallow, a quivering lip or shifting of the eyes—up, down or sideways. All problematic for a trained operative to conceal—for the inexperienced novice—practically an impossibility.

General Connelly was first to react. "What are all these shaded areas?" He asked while placing his index finger on each image.

"That, General, are the future land holdings for the North Korean owned Anomura Corporation," Stone spat out.

"How can that even be possible? Australia has laws to protect against such a large purchase of any privately owned property. The Department of Treasury has the final say on all foreign investment in this country," the general so kindly pointed out.

"Yes, they do," Stone replied while shifting his focus to the deputy PM, and then he locked eyes with Collins. "Prime Minister, you might want to consider appointing a new treasurer. The current one has more than likely been compromised."

Collins looked confused, "The treasurer? What does he have to do with all this?"

"Miss Wilks, would you like to add anything at this point?" Stone asked in a condescending tone. "Yes, the treasurer. The same man that cannot distinguish what is in the best interests of the country or the dick in his pants." Stone considered each person sitting in this room today should be made aware of the intimate relationship.

Wilks raised her head to be met with Stone's glare and knew that moment her fall from grace was complete, and she was privately relieved it would now be finished. She contemplated her ensuing legal defence. All eyes shifted to the already disgraced Miss Helena Wilks.

"Is this true, Helena? Is there any substance to these wild accusations?" Collins demanded.

Through her shaking and sobbing, she cried out with her only pathetic answer, "I'M BEING BLACKMAILED," she shrieked through her painted lips. "God, I'm glad it will be finally over," she added.

"Aris Munandar was the final linchpin, but not just in some well-planned terrorist plot," Stone continued. He was on a roll now. "With the help of the detention centre under your portfolio as Immigration Minister, Miss Wilks, he was also being groomed to take control of setting up a farming network on behalf of Anomura. This ancient book that the Smithsonian Institution has spent huge resources uncovering if at all it turns out to be more than just a myth, well then, it presents a huge risk to the legal drug-peddling pharmaceutical industry. They were hedging their bets while backing both sides; a win-win situation. They needed vast tracts of land to grow the natural herbs and medicinal remedies if necessary to protect their own financial interests."

Franklin Sandhurst considered his position. He knew he needed to take the initiative and shift the focus back to Jones and this Stone character. His best defence was to attack and continue to incriminate the director. It was time to drive the final nail in his coffin and sink him once and for all.

"Jones—why was I not informed of this operation continuing on Australian soil? As the director-general of ASIO, you are under the direct control of the attorney-general's office. In case you have forgotten, I currently hold that office, and your actions are in direct contradiction to the terms of your appointment. You do not have the authority to enact Article-289 within the borders of Australia. You have participated in and assisted in the murder of a foreign national. I expect your resignation—on my desk tomorrow. Your immunity might save you from facing an Australian court, but I'm afraid that does not extend to you, Mr Stone, or your old RAN cohort you referred to earlier."

Stone eyed off the Jindeugi for confirmation. It was time to roll the final dice. "This proposed purchase of the Kidman station properties was being funded through an Australian-based law firm using an off-shore Indonesian account. I bet if we dig a little deeper, we will find this same firm represents the company that has been high-rolling you all this time—what do you reckon about that, Miss Wilks?" Stone had learnt the hard way, never to ask a question without knowing the answer.

And there it was. We have a winner. Body language, the eyes never lie. The Jindeugi really does know his shit, Stone had to admit.

Wilks was all but done. She had been deceived, lied to and become a victim of her own greed and perception that she would be the bastion of women's rights. She was now bound by the golden handcuffs.

Stone continued unopposed. "The other thing I want to know, Toa? You told me you spoke to your sister while she was in custody at the detention centre. How was that even possible? The number is not listed in the Yellow Pages."

"I received a coded text message from the only other man that knew the significance of three numbers. The very same man that graced me with the title of, the Tick, while in East Berlin." The Jindeugi was going to enjoy his moment in the sun. He walked slowly past the prime minister, at the head of the table, then continued and paused behind the broad shoulders of Admiral Peterson. Boomer turned his thick neck to follow his steps. General Connelly was amused by the theatrics as Toa kept a methodical pace. He stopped and placed his hand on the shoulder of Darcy Jones. "You remember that day, don't you, Jones?"

"What are you dribbling on about now? What text message?" The Jindeugi placed his open mobile in front of Jones. "Read it for yourself. Six For Three was the name of that operation in Berlin. Six North Korean agents in exchange for three British spies held captive, which you ended up reneging on the deal. You tried to retire me that day, and I don't take kindly to that."

"Don't you mean the three British tourists you replaced the real spies with?" Jones fired back. "I can't read that tiny little screen. Is this the best your Government can afford in North Korea? Tight budget these days?" Jones only needed a small distraction. The Jindeugi leaned over and pointed to the 6-4-3 message. "Look—right there. Are you blind?"

Stone shifted his lower body slightly to his right. He fumbled under his chair and searched with his fingers. Jones seized his only possible opportunity and chopped down hard on the extended arm of the Jindeugi, then pushed back suddenly with the force of both his legs, sending his chair into the North Korean's midriff. Jones wanted to stand and continue the premeditated attack on the Jindeugi, even *with* his bleeding and painful shoulder. It was all unnecessary.

Stone rushed his hand out from underneath his chair, raised his arm and fired two shots. *Thud! – Thud!* One in the left side chest, right where the Jindeugi's heart was, and the second was slightly lower and would penetrate at least one lung. The Jindeugi was punched hard by the force of the two 9mm slugs. He stumbled back once, then again. He coughed up his first mouthful of blood and fell to one knee. The Jindeugi tried to raise his weapon. He just wanted to get one clean shot at that arrogant prick, Jones, before he knew he would die. Mi-sun's image flashed through his mind. "Please don't let me die in vain. I do not wish to fail my sister's trust," he almost cried. The gun fell from his failing fingers, and in a pathetic attempt to stem the flow of blood, he tried to place his open palm over both holes. It was sickening to watch, even after what he'd just put these seven people through. It was like watching a dying dog after being been hit by a speeding car.

"Show some mercy and stop this man's suffering. Someone help him. Call an ambulance or something..." Wilks cried out. She was horrified, having never witnessed someone actually being shot, let alone a person die right in front of her own eyes. She wanted to turn away, but she couldn't. It was a morbid fascination, and both eyes remained glued. The Jindeugi let out a blood-curdling gurgle. A deep red crimson bubbled from his open mouth in a futile attempt to inhale his last breath. He slumped to one side, and his head struck the hardwood floor. Wilks baulked and looked away—briefly.

General Connelly pushed his chair clear and strode over to the trembling corpse as it went through the final throes of death. He picked up the handgun with a pencil pushed down the silencer and placed it on the table. The admiral looked at the now-lifeless corpse and wondered why this individual's bowels had not released. Collins stood and placed his hand on the scanner to disable the security. The red light illuminated to show the room was now unsecured. The bombproof door hissed open. There was an overall feeling of relief in the Menzies Room soured by what had just been divulged, regarding the deputy prime minister, and possibly the treasurer.

Darcy Jones dropped his blood-soaked handkerchief on top of the corpse's face and then asked Franklin Sandhurst if he could lend him his own. "I think I may need to find a hospital. Can you give me a lift, Franklin? I don't want to attract any media attention. No ambulances. You can call the Federal Police if you wish while I'm being attended to by a doctor. I agree with you, Franklin, we need to sort this mess out. If you still want my resignation, you will have it in the morning."

Stone listened on with interest and watched the attorney-general nod in agreement. Sandhurst seemed to relax as he and Jones prepared to leave. Stone then casually stepped over to the corner of the room and picked up his Glock 42 off the floor. He brushed past Jones and slid the six-inch handgun into Jones' side jacket pocket.

"Hang on a bloody minute," Collins barked out loud. "What about all this? Shouldn't we be notifying the police?"

"Our own Military Police will handle this from here on. This is a time for cool heads, Prime Minister. No knee-jerk reactions are needed now," Admiral Peterson reassured the prime minister.

"I'm losing blood here, can we get a move on?" Jones reminded everyone.

"Yes, of course," the attorney-general was only too happy to oblige. He and Jones exited the Menzies Room. All were under the tight control of the ADF now, and soon Sandhurst's own attorney-general's office will be tasked with the impending investigation and the follow-up prosecutions. Or so he assumed.

Collins followed both men as far as his office doors when he heard a banging noise coming from his private bathroom. He turned to see a chair wedged under the handle. He kicked it out of the way and opened the door. "Prime Minister, are you all right? What happened?" His personal assistant for the last twenty years was startled.

"It's okay, Mary. Please take the remainder of the day off. This office will be off-limits until further notice. Someone will be in touch with you tomorrow." He ushered her from his office, closed the door and reentered the Menzies Room. What he saw next was beyond comprehension, not in his wildest imagination could he have prepared himself for this. The man who he witnessed being shot twice, a person he saw with his own eyes draw his last breath, was now standing with a towel in his hand wiping the blood from his face and chest. Stone was handing him a glass of water. "What is going on here?" The prime minister felt like a duped fool. He was being hoodwinked by the very people he trusted—without question. His face reflected a look of utter dismay.

The Jindeugi continued to wipe away the trail of blood dripping down his chin. "They should make suicide pills out of this crap." Toa rinsed his mouth and spat his discoloured fill into a nearby sink. "If the cyanide doesn't kill you, the foul taste of this special effects blood will do the trick. It tastes like Senegal of Ammonia."

"You should seriously consider an acting career, Toa. A Gold Logie awaits you. Bloody hell mate, you poured it on a bit thick, didn't you?" Stone said.

Collins tried to comprehend the anomalous scene. "Someone needs to brief me on proceedings. I mean—I am the bloody prime minister." He looked over towards General Connelly for some back-up.

"Prime Minister, I can assure you, you are not alone," the general replied. He looked for some form of endorsement from Admiral Peterson. Instead, he was greeted with a wide beaming grin, which was soon followed by a knowing wink. "The plan is still in motion. Don't look at me, this was all his idea." The admiral's finger was pointed squarely at Stone, who was already on his phone.

"Bradley, are you ready to go? The fox has left the henhouse." Stone met Collins' stare. "Patience, sir. We're about to go fishing. Keep her on ice until we get back." Helena Wilks was still slumped in her chair attempting to reapply her smudged makeup.

The Jindeugi snatched his phone off the table and followed Stone out the door. Waiting in the underground car park was an unmarked ASIO pursuit vehicle. Stone and the Jindeugi slid into the rear seat.

"Long-time-no-see, Tobias," the driver greeted Stone while introducing his junior partner "This is, Agent Davide Lippmeier, fresh out of the academy."

"They're just entering State Circle now. The Canberra Hospital is about six kilometres south," Lippmeier called out, keen to impress.

"Good to see you again, Mack. How's the wife and kids?" Stone asked as he redialled Monarsh.

"Have a first grandchild now. A little boy," Mack replied.

"Congratulations. We're all getting too old for this shit, Macca. I need to find another profession," Stone joked.

"You and me both, Tobias." Mack turned the wheel hard right, "Buckle up, boys." The sound of the V8 350-hp HSV roared as it flew over the ripple strip and straight through the open boom gate, then turned onto the loop road that circles Capital Hill. Mack headed towards Adelaide Avenue at speed. The memory of his teenage hero, Peter Brock, flying down Conrod Straight at the famous Mt Panorama circuit spurred him on.

Stone and the Jindeugi were pressed hard up against the back seat. The white *Statesman* came into view. Lippmeier checked the government plate. "That's the attorney-general's car on the outer lane, sir," he called out as Mack shifted back to third gear, slowed and kept a safe, two-car distance behind. The

Jindeugi was wondering why this man's parents would name their son after a hamburger.

"Brad, we're ready to make the connection. Is HABIT ready to go?" Stone's voice reflected the tension he felt. This was a big play, and if he stuffed this up, he would be spending the rest of his days in a Federal Penitentiary.

"Rock-'n-roll, Tobias," Monarsh answered.

Stone looked to his left. "You're on, Toa. Make the call." The Jindeugi scrolled through his history logs and stopped at the number he received that text from when in Bali.

Darcy Jones was still nursing his shoulder. He felt the inside of his jacket pocket a second time for the weight of Stone's insurance policy. Franklin Sandhurst was gazing out his window as the vehicle drove past the Royal Australian Mint with his briefcase lying at his feet. The familiar sound of a muffled Apple ring-tone sounded from the floor. Sandhurst cast nothing more than a casual glance at his luxury Edmond leather attaché case and ignored the call.

"That's your phone, Franklin. Don't you want to answer it?" Jones asked.

"It can wait, it won't be important. That's a private phone I use for personal calls only."

"How do you know if you don't answer it?" Jones prompted.

"I think your injury takes precedence over a simple call, Jones. There will be some agents waiting for our arrival. You are history."

"Really, Franklin—I insist. Take the call." Sandhurst noticed the change in tone. He sensed an indifference in Jones' demeanour. He turned to face his disgraced director to offer a sharp rebuttal, now looking down the barrel of the Glock 42.

"What's the meaning of this? Surely you're not attempting to weasel your way out of this with *that*? Accept the consequences of your deceit, Jones—it's over—just deal with it," the attorney-general offered.

The chauffeur chanced a passing glance in his rear-view mirror, not sure what was happening in the back seat.

"We're going to deal with this all right, Sandhurst. Now—one more time—open the bloody case." Jones was at the far reaches of his strained patience. He picked up the case and laid it squarely on the attorney-general's lap. "Do it NOW!" Jones roared.

Sandhurst fumbled with the two combination locks. He was looking increasingly agitated. The locks snapped open. Sandhurst eased the case open as the annoying ringtone filled the interior of the vehicle.

"Is everything all right, sir?" the driver asked.

"Just drive," Jones answered with malice in his tone. "Answer the call, Franklin. I think you may recognise the caller." Jones was becoming prickly. He lifted the barrel and prodded Sandhurst's right side.

Sandhurst was becoming desperate, "Driver, this man is in my custody. Drive to the nearest police station." He fidgeted with the phone, reluctant to answer the incoming call. The sound of that stupid ringtone was stampeding through his lawyer's brain as he contemplated his next move. His body started to shake, beads of perspiration dripped from his brow. His armpits were moist and felt hot.

Jones shifted forward in his seat, "Driver, look behind you. You see that HSV pursuit vehicle following? Three armed ASIO agents are inside with a very pissed-off North Korean assassin. You make a wrong move and your driving days will come to an abrupt end. Drive on," Jones replied. "Now, answer the *fucking* call, Franklin." Darcy Jones wanted to rip the head off his skinny-looking neck. He knew he had him, and the time for squirming behind the facade of his title was over.

The attorney-general looked doomed. Sandhurst placed his shaking index finger on the answer button. "Hello, Franklin Sandhurst speaking." His eyes dropped, and his neck became limp as both shoulders sagged.

The Jindeugi repeated the words Stone had recited while waiting for the call to be answered. "Mr Sandhurst, this is a past employee of the Anomura Corporation. We were hoping Crean, Sandhurst and Toll, may be available to act as a negotiator in purchasing a piece of land in the Alexander Maconochie Remand Centre, located right here in the suburb of Hume in Canberra? It's not even large enough to swing a cat, or so I've been told," then he laid the phone down on his lap.

Stone placed his phone back to his ear. "Give me some good news, Brad."

"That's the phone. The same cell that instigated the hack on the mobile registered to the director-general of ASIO. It's the identical unique ten-digit MSIN. You've got the bastard, Tobias. Who is it?" Monarsh waited with bated breath.

Stone simply said, "A lawyer buried under six feet of concrete, Brad, just means someone didn't order enough cement. Thanks, and I'll be in touch. My shout next time we're in London together."

"I'll hold you to that. Take care."

Stone rang the admiral. Boomer answered, "Give me an update, Stone. Jerry looks like he's about to have a coronary."

"Send in the troops, Admiral. Pick up the brother and the other partners. Even if they're not guilty, it won't hurt to harass a few lawyers for a while—don't you agree?"

"Consider it done." *Click.*

Sandhurst searched for the switch on his door panelling to activate the glass divider that soundproofs the rear of the vehicle. "How did you find out, I think I'm at least owed that much?"

"You're owed what Paddy shot at—sweet fuck all. You know, Sandhurst, it's always the little things you can never plan for that bring the best-laid plans unstuck. The one per centers. And yours was that single text message answered by the only person who could do something about it. You got down and dirty with the wrong people. Wilks got played by you, and you and your brother got screwed by your own greed and the

Indonesians. They were being led along the garden path by the North Koreans and in the middle of all that great big pile of crap was a bunch of desperate people willing to risk everything for the slim chance of offering their kids a better life in a country that doesn't persecute its own citizens. You remember what that is? A country with an elected government and an honest legal system. The fucking lucky country. Not when there are arseholes like you in charge, you piece of shit."

"Jones, you are a small pawn in a game of political chess that is far beyond even your scope. You still have to prove all this. I am a barrister, and I have a lot of powerful friends. This will take years to go to court, and even if that happens, I'll cut a deal. This is above and beyond your limit of understanding."

"Yes, both Admiral Peterson and I have discussed that very subject. The slime at the top of the legal juggernaut sticks together like a smelly glue. The scales of justice do not weigh evenly for people in your position, I know that. Shit—you probably share a tee-time with the very judge that will preside over your case, so we both considered it our civic duty to save the taxpayer all that time and money. But, you're right about one thing, it *will* never make it to a courtroom." The director-general of ASIO was willing to stake his career on that. He pressed the intercom. "Driver, we have a new destination. Turn around and cross over the Waterloo Bridge then take the second exit onto Parkes Way, drive past the Casino Canberra, then follow Constitution Avenue to the end."

"You want to go back to the ASIO offices?" the chauffeur questioned.

Not the same offices you're thinking of, young man.

"Where are you taking me?" Sandhurst demanded, looking more and more unheaved, as the *Statesman* completed a U-turn. "I want to meet with the prime minister. Why are we turning? I demand you answer me." He resisted the overwhelming urge to vomit.

Jones remained silent. The time for talk was over. *Actions speak louder than words.*

The attorney-general's car stopped next to the parked HSV in an underground car park under the old vacant ASIO building. Jones exited and motioned for the driver to accompany him through a door that led to a service elevator. Sandhurst sat in the back seat alone, wondering why? He even considered if he should just step out and walk away.

I could make the airport in less than thirty minutes.

The Jindeugi stepped out from the rear seat of the parked HSV pursuit vehicle. He approached the attorney-general's vehicle, slid into the driver's seat and then placed the chauffeur's cap on his head with a pair of dark Ray-Ban sunglasses. Stone was next to leave the scene. He leaned over the Jindeugi's right shoulder and flipped a photo towards the cringing Franklyn Sandhurst. "Enjoy the ride, you sick fuck."

The new chauffeur turned the ignition key and enabled the total-security option that seals all the doors and windows, including the plexiglass divider. The vehicle reversed out from the building and exited the grounds from an unmanned rear gate that had just been snapped open. Stone waved as the vehicle sped past. The white *Statesman* left Constitution Avenue, which leads into Marshead Drive. They entered the A-23 and followed that for a farther five kilometres.

"What's this all about?" Sandhurst tried unlocking the rear door, and then he pressed down on the *open-glass* button—still no response. He thumbed the intercom, "Take me to the airport immediately. Do you understand me? I am the attorney-general," he wailed in a desperate attempt to salvage some control over the ensuing wrecking ball that was heading his way. The vehicle turned off at the sign that read, Jerrabomberra Wetlands Nature Reserve. The bullet-resistant, self-inflating tyres crunched over the loose gravel surface as they edged their way to a secluded sloping corner of the isolated marshlands. The Jindeugi placed the T-bar auto into neutral with the handbrake off and stepped from the car.

Sandhurst started beating at the rear window with his bare fists, his mouth was screaming in noisy, desperate silence, and his eyeballs were consumed with raw and unknown fear as the only sounds to be heard were the frogs croaking along the murky water's edge. The Jindeugi placed both hands on the boot, bent his back and felt the four wheels edge forward. The vehicle slowly started an easy, sluggish crawl, then inch-by-inch it gathered some tortoise-like momentum until the front wheels found the start of a slight incline. The chrome radiator grill created a small bow wave as it was swallowed by the nebulous of stagnated, blackened swamp water. Then the bonnet disappeared, followed by the roof slowly being devoured until only the rear taillights were visible before they also vanished in a bubbling mass of bespattered quagmire of putrefying green slime.

"A snake should never be far from his cesspool, Mr Attorney-General," Stone voiced from behind as he closed the door of the HSV. Some small reparation could now be salvaged on behalf of the families who have suffered under the flag of freedom and a fair go for all. "That's the rough Australian justice these men in power deserve. Quick and with no fanfare. The genuine refugees who arrive on the white sandy shores of this country, the same people who only ask for a chance to start over, a better life for their children, that's the real Australia you and your sister seek."

The Jindeugi faced Stone and extended his open hand. The two men shared a firm handshake.

"You're still gonna have to do some time, Toa."

"Time spent inside an Australian Federal Prison will be a breeze. Like I said, it's all about, Mi-sun."

Darcy Jones and Stone were being escorted back to the Menzies Room by two uniformed Military Police, who stopped at the lift entrance before returning to their stations. Jones punched in his code and turned to face Stone. "Let me do the talking. Even if you're asked a direct question, do not answer unless I say it's okay—you got that?" Jones wanted to explain the rules.

"Not really, but this is your show, so... be my guest. One thing, Director, before we all start roasting marsh-mellows and singing Kumbaya. Access to my operational account was terminated while on Christmas Island—I want to know who and why?" Stone asked.

Jones laughed. "If I told you that was an innocent administrative error, where a recently sacked misguided personal assistant, appointed to manage the affairs of my old office, unknowingly placed a two thousand dollar limit on that card; would you believe me?"

"The bigger the lie, the easier it is to sell."

"You don't trust anybody, do you, Stone?"

"The fact I'm standing here right now should attest to that."

The prime minister was pacing the carpet like an expectant father. Helena Wilks was still seated in her chair, and she resembled anything *but* the glamorous centrefold for women in politics. Collins strode towards Jones and shifted his jacket lapel to one side. "You *also* seem to have superhuman healing powers. You'd better start explaining what transpired here—in this boardroom today, Jones?"

"Operation Blue Skies is what happened, Prime Minister."

"Don't give me that bullshit, I want answers," Collins fired back.

"No, you need to make some decisions now on how you want to proceed from this point, onwards. I *can* tell you that a statement advising of the unexpected disappearance of the attorney-general, due to his suspicion of illegal activities, will need to be released to the media. Then a decision on the deputy PM and the treasurer needs to be made."

"Should she be placed under arrest? Do we have a case against her—proof?" Collins was trying to line up his ducks.

"Franklin Sandhurst set her up for pre-selection in a safe seat with the financial backing of the Jemaah Islamiyah infiltrated Indonesian Government, funding her election campaign—orchestrated via his own brother, through his old law firm. Their intentions, under the charade of 'boat people', was to place a steady influx of sympathisers to the Islamic cause, in creating three Australian-based eco-terrorist cells, using the North Korean managed detention centre as a means to be vetted and pass the 'refugee status' test. That contract was handled by the deputy PM's office.

"Sandhurst didn't bargain on HABIT tracking the hack he made on my own ASIO encrypted cell phone. That threw a spanner in his plans. He set up Wilks' sister for a bullshit drug bust and then blackmailed her into helping him to set me up by sending that falsified Federal Order from my secured office fax with the carrot of previously organising her sister's release and dodging some serious jail time in an Indonesian prison cell. Helena Wilks should be stripped of her office, resign as a sitting member and prepare for a long stint inside a federal prison, and I will personally see to it that is exactly what happens," Jones promised.

"These North Koreans on Christmas Island, do we know who they are? Is this Government still compromised?" Collins was trying to stay one step ahead of the political fall-out.

Admiral Peterson thought it best he answer that. "Prime Minister Collins, the Koreans have been dealt with under the *Criminal Code Act 1995*. They decided to abandon ship and go shark fishing—or maybe shark bait—who knows and who cares?" Boomer enjoyed his answer while glaring at the discredited Helena Wilks.

Jones continued, "Sandhurst's brother had squandered the family's wealth through some bad real estate deals, overseas investments, gambling debts and a taste for the ladies—the really expensive ones. He was a liability and acting as an agent in setting up the treasurer, and the proposed purchase of the Kidman property portfolio was the attorney-general's get-out-of-jail-free-card until Stone stumbled on the Christmas Island connection, and from that moment on, it all went south. We should be pinning a medal on this guy," Jones turned and faced the tight-lipped Stone, standing alone.

Stone considered silently. *So, this is what happens. The PM searches for a means to sweep it all under the rug. The political monkey, hear no evil, see no evil and bullshit your way through the rest. They had their scapegoat, and that was all that mattered now, and these people actually run the country. God help us all.*

"What about this Duckhwan Toa character, what will happen to him?" Collins, at the very least, wanted to look like he was part of the solution.

"We have plans for him, Prime Minister. It would be best if you weren't privy to those details," Jones answered.

"What about this other man—the sniper; where does he fit into all of this?"

"Arr, yes. Well, Prime Minister, he is officially listed as MIA. Let me deal with that. It may cost the Australian Navy a few dollars in back pay, but I think I can find a hole in the budget to hide that. We may also have plans for him," the admiral went on to explain.

"And this man, Stone... ?" Collins knew only too well who he was.

"What man, Prime Minister, I don't see anyone—do you?" Jones asked while turning.

That was Stone's cue to leave, so he did.

Chapter·49

THE LAST of the available sun was fast fading, as Dixie finished his beer and headed off in the direction of his camp. Evina was still busy researching her database and talking to her scientific colleagues back in the U.S. Till finally decided it was time for tools-down when he noticed a yellowtail kingfish the size of a dolphin casually swim past the shallow waters in front of their jetty and Kelly was mucking around in the engine room.

Abigail stood and stretched her arms high above her head. She needed some time alone to clear her thoughts as the endgame to her sister's final push to unravel the mystery of Jahangir's *Book of Remedies* neared. She decided to walk off the tightening cramp in her calves from crouching for so long and headed off for a thinking stroll around the small island camp.

Robinson Island was shared with two other fishing camps and was the southernmost seasonally inhabited atoll as part of the Pelsaert Island group. From where she stood on the wharf, the view faced west, towards the natural breakwater that was Half Moon Reef, with a clear view of the unnatural silhouette of a rusted boiler that was all that remained of the iron steamer, the *Windsor*, after running aground in 1908. The relentless thundering roar of the swell breaking in a spectacular sierra of white water was a constant reminder of the perils that awaited any seafarer while navigating these dangerous windswept seas.

Abigail followed the jetty that was long enough to berth two cray fishing boats, end-to-end. She passed by Till, who was preparing to match his fishing skills with the schools of marauding Samson fish and the brutally strong yellowtail kingfish who are accustomed to being hand-fed as they dart in and out of the deeper channels protected by an outer reef. With a short-stroke boat rod and an overhead reel loaded with a mountain of monofilament line, the unsuspecting Thai man with the big smile was about to find out, firsthand, that it would be a one-sided battle.

A thinly covered crushed-shell footpath led up a slight incline past the plant room that housed the diesel generator with the inside walls covered in old eggshell cartons to muffle the endless throbbing knock from the power plant. A small area of land had long been cleared as a make-do helipad for Blue Juice Charters, who operated a twice-weekly passenger service during the three-month island rock lobster season. Abigail heard the sound of running water and turned from her raised vantage point at the island's small peak. The sight of Dixie's naked white buttocks showering under an aluminium bucket with a rose screwed into its base, hanging from the beam of the 'back to nature' outdoor shower prompted her to instinctively place a single hand over her wandering eyes. She parted a finger and chanced a quick second peak. *Mmm-hmm—nice bum.* She allowed her private thoughts to drift for a brief moment, trying to remember the last time she'd shared the affections of a man's squeeze. It had been more than a while.

The path wound its way around the rocky eastern corner, skirting the iceberg-blue waters that boasted a rich bounty of all kinds of sea life. She stopped to view an iridescent green and blue Maori wrasse, with its powerful buck-teeth crushing some wild oysters that were plentiful in the shallow waters, a mere few short feet away. The track continued towards a sand-covered, man made wooden walkway that would then journey Abigail back to the wharf, passing close-by the two fibro shacks. The soothing sounds of nature were a calming influence with the pollution-free ocean air invigorating in its re-nurturing effects with each breath inhaled.

Abigail noticed a coaxial cable extended through the eves that connected to a tall cell phone aerial located on the corrugated tin roof. As she approached, she could overhear a one-way conversation from inside. She knew it was Dixie and readied herself for her next move, a move that was effortless for a woman with the natural assets and magnetism that Abigail possessed in abundance. She rubbed both hands over her full breasts until both nipples became erect, then sauntered in through the half-open door. Dixie finished the call to his ageing, widowed mother and turned to see Abigail standing in an almost provocative stance. He was confused but equally excited. His second man-brain was delivering mixed messages as he struggled to keep his bulging eyes focused above shoulder height. Abigail eased herself onto the edge of the double bed with her open palms facing down on the mattress and bounced once or twice.

"Do you have someone special in your life, Dixie?"

"Just Mum at the moment."

"No, I mean a girlfriend. I don't mean to pry..."

"No, that's fine," Dixie interrupted. "I'm a single guy, mostly. It's a bit hard to meet that special woman when you're out at sea most of the time. What about you? They must be lining up like a Centrelink queue."

Abigail laughed. "What's your real name, surely it's not, Dixie? What does your dear old mum call you?"

"Pete, or Peter - same as my granddad."

"Pete, you may think it's easy to meet a nice guy—trust a woman that knows. It isn't. I get hit on by all sorts of creeps. Most men want to try their luck with the *attractive*-looking blonde woman. It gives you the absolute shits after a while."

"Really? Us blokes rarely have that problem," Dixie laughed. "I'll just go slip a T-shirt on. Do you want a drink?"

"Don't bother about the shirt, we're all friends here. Yeah, why not? Everyone is busy. It's just you and me. Sure— let's enjoy a drink together—just the two of us."

Dixie's heart was racing. *Am I reading this right? Bloody hell, Dixie. Don't stuff this up.*

An hour later, two empty six-packs of Corona spilt from a corner bin. Abigail steadied herself as she stood without warning, stumbled and half-fell into Dixie as he sat on an old FJ Holden vinyl rear bench seat located on the back landing that offered an unobstructed view of Long Island. Dixie braced himself and absorbed Abigail's weight, then slowly straightened her to a standing position. Their eyes met, Dixie could hear the sound of his heart thumping. The slight scent of Abigail's perfume hung in the air like an aura of sensual enlightenment.

Dixie made his move, and Abigail folded into his embrace. Their lips met, both tongues began a journey of passion as the gates of sexual bliss were about to be unlocked. Abigail ran her nails down Dixie's back and groaned in pleasure as he pressed hard against her moist, willing mouth. The final hurdle was cleared when she pushed closer, and he felt the firmness of her breasts rub against his exposed upper body. Dixie lifted Abigail under each arm; she wrapped both legs around his hips while they bumbled the short distance through the open door to his camp before falling onto the bed as one, lost in each other's personal desires, lustful, with only carnal thoughts filling their erotic—one-track minds.

Fifteen minutes is all it took. They both lay on the bed in a ball of soaked perspiration. Abigail huffed while catching her breath. "Never have I felt like I feel this minute," Abigail inhaled again deeply in a spasm of bodily pleasures. "That was unbelievable. *Wow!* I need to drink some water."

Dixie was off with the fairies. This was something totally unexpected for him. Never before had he scaled the heights of such yearning and exhilarated gratification from the opposite sex.

A woman like Abigail Bishop-Price doesn't just walk into a man's bedroom and start flirting like that—surely?

And yet that exact scenario had just walked in and sprinkled him with the magic dust of sexual satisfaction with no warning. *Is this how it happens, just like that?*

Dixie leaned over and placed both hands on either side of Abigail's perfect face. He embraced her in a long and passionate kiss, and they made love a second time. Dixie groaned with elation as the couple reached a combined orgasmic pinnacle like a full orchestra winding up the final act. Abigail squeezed him tight and felt the power of his strength. Dixie rolled away and closed his eyes, allowing the gentle quivering of his sexually satisfied body to take him away to another place—a place where dreams do come true. But he *wasn't* dreaming. This was *real* and happening in the now.

The moment of intensity and shared intimacy was suddenly torn away like a ripped-open shower curtain when an overly excited Evina came bounding in through the half-open door, completely oblivious to what she may inadvertently find on the other side. "Oh... oh dear. Whoops, I'm so sorry. I didn't even know this was a bedroom. Um, I'm still talking, aren't I? I need to go, shit, I'm so sorry."

"It's all right, Evina," Abigail shouted from a short distance, as her twin sister made her quick-fired exit. "We haven't just run away and eloped."

Dixie was mortified as the sound of Evina's hasty retreat could be heard. The vanishing sound of her voice slowly petered out as she scurried her way back towards her prize. "I think I may have found a way to solve the puzzle—that is, if *anyone* is still interested? It's okay. I can see you're *both* very busy."

"I *definitely* need that shower now." Abigail wanted to reassure Dixie that life will continue as usual. "Don't worry about, Evina. She'll calm down in a couple of years. She always gets a smidgen protective of her little sister."

"Little sister... but your twins," Dixie replied while hopping like a one-legged kangaroo as he slid his jeans back on.

"Three bloody minutes, that's all it was, and a day doesn't go by that I wish it were the reverse." Abigail waited until Dixie had completed his comical re-dressing routine, then pecked him on the lips. "Good job, lover boy. We need to do that again, are you up for that?" She liked Dixie but wanted to err on the side of discretion first by disguising her feelings behind a veiled attempt of humour.

Kelly was exiting the stairs from the engine room after changing out the air filters in both generators, the air purifiers on the two air-con systems and both desalination plants. He bumped into Abigail as she headed to her quarters. *She looks rather pleased with herself,* he pondered, and then walked over to wash his hands at the outdoor sink near the end of the wharf.

Dixie strolled past, pulling a T-shirt over his ruffled hair. Kelly looked up to see the same weird smile he witnessed a minute before. "You don't muck around, do you? When I said go for it, you certainly jumped straight in. Job well done, I say." He returned a satisfied, ear-to-ear grin, just as Evina exited the saloon with a pile of papers in her hand. She knew exactly what Kelly and Dixie were high-fiving about, but there were other pressing matters to be dealt with, like opening that Japanese puzzle box.

Evina entered the galley with Abigail's notebook under one arm. "Jack, can you lift the puzzle box onto the table? I want to scrutinise it further with the advantage of some better light. Careful." She looked over at Dixie. "And you can help. That *is,* if you *still* have the strength?" she expressed with a developing smirk. Dixie obliged without hesitation, slightly embarrassed.

Evina extended a tape measure and ran it along the length and breadth of the Himitsu-Bako. She scribbled down the dimensions on her notepad, 70cm long x 50cm wide x 40cm in height. Then she ran her keen eye over the entire surface with a magnifying glass. The emblazoned brightly coloured image beamed back as a personal mental challenge.

She typed into the Smithsonian website two words and hit enter. Abigail made a grand entrance after showering and pulled up a chair next to the other two interested onlookers.

"Must be your lucky day—*heh* Abigail? Pass me that torch, will you?" Evina had in her other hand a dentist's periodontal scaler. She scraped away the last remnants of dried wood and loose dust, then sprinkled some talcum powder to highlight the image against the faded surface. She looked at her screen, then back at the image and slowly straightened with a knowing look emerging on her face.

"I know who this is. It's Emperor Ashoka, and this raised background I originally thought may have been a sundial—it's actually the Ashoka Chakra. This wheel is a depiction of the Dharma Chakra or the Wheel of Dharma. The Buddha described the twenty-four qualities of ideal Buddhist followers as being represented by the twenty-four spokes of the Ashoka Chakra, which infers the twenty-four qualities of a Santani.

"The wheel has twenty-four spokes which map out the Twelve Laws of Dependent Origination and the Twelve Laws of Dependent Termination. The Ashoka Chakra has been widely inscribed on many relics of the Mauryan Emperor, most prominent among which is the Lion Capital of Sarnath and the Ashoka Pillar. The most visible use of the Ashoka Chakra today is at the centre of the national flag of the Republic of India, where it is rendered in a navy blue colour on a white background, which has been adopted as the national emblem of India. The Ashoka Chakra was created by King Ashoka during his reign. Chakra is a Sanskrit word which also means 'cycle' or 'self-repeating'. The process it signifies is the cycle of time—as in how the world changes over time."

Evina ran her magnifying glass over the entire image. "That's interesting. There's a slight gap around the circumference of the Chakra Wheel and a tiny black spear aimed upwards." She continued on methodically, stopping at the due-north position when a minuscule white dot, unseen by the naked eye, caught her attention. She followed the wheel in a clockwise direction, and another eleven colours were evident, displayed randomly on the face. "There are twenty-four spokes with twelve colours on the differing points of a twelve-hour clock face?" She racked her brain, trying to mentally summon the significance of this colour group. "Do they represent an indiscriminate order, or is there a hierarchy? God only knows. In my professional opinion, this wheel is like a dial that turns. Similar to a combination lock on a safe," Evina shared.

Evina recalled a short course she completed over one of the many summer breaks while she gave up a weekend away with friends in the pursuit of her studies. It was titled: Theosophy - Inward Dimension of Islamic Mysticism with Professor A. K. Sitarama Shastri.

Evina further studied the single line of Persian letters. She opened up a character map, then typed the text into a translation app and pressed enter. She read the results out loud. "It spells out lanif nwonknU?"

Abigail glanced over Evina's shoulder. "It looks *and* sounds like gobble gosh."

"What is this symbol of a key, I wonder?" Evina moved her mouse and typed the word 'key' in front of the text and looked back down at her screen. "Key lanif nwonknU."

"Still means nothing," Abigail said.

Then Evina retyped the short sentence a second time while explaining, "That's because we're reading it as written in English. Persian is read from right to left." She looked at it again, "Key final unknown." Then she remembered where she'd seen those ordered colours. "You've got to be kidding me?" she cheered in a buoyant voice. "Who would ever think that a short course would one day be worth the six hundred I parted with?"

Jack and Abigail shared a questionable glance and shrugged their shoulders. *Was Evina finally losing it?* Kelly thought.

"The rays, the divine evolutions of people and planets are represented by seven new age colours, and another five colours are known as new age gold or solar rays. The colours of the new age and solar rays are in a fixed order. Number one is blue: the power of faith. Two is yellow, which means obedience. Three is pink for beauty and geniality. The white is number four, meaning ascension, peace and light. Five is green, representing Mother Nature. Six is the red for true resurrection. Seven is violet. A New Age of Master Saint Germain. Eight is turquoise representing lucidity. Nine is for magenta. The divine wonder—justiciars. Ten is gold for the materialisation of wealth. Eleven is orange meaning sunshine, and the final number twelve is opaline for renewal. This has to be the combination to unlock the puzzle. What else could it be?" She searched the room for some kind of divine affirmation that she was right.

Kelly looked over at Dixie. "Did you know all that, mate?"

"Arr, shit yeah. I was just about to say the same until Evina rudely jumped in and stole the limelight."

Abigail just shook her head and wondered about these two men.

From outside, a high-pitched shrill sounded from the opposite end of the wharf. Each person turned as one to see the source of what surely must be someone being stabbed to death. Everyone rushed out to the rear deck to see Till, leaning back on his rod, bent like a reversed arrow man's bow, listening to the drag being stripped of metres of fishing line as each second passed. He was yelling and hollering something out in Thai with a look of sheer determination manifesting across his lit-up face.

"*Plā*, Boss, big *plā*. He is huge and swim very fast. BBQ fish tonight for sure," he yelled with excitement and adrenaline pumping through his winding arm and back muscles.

"It's all right guys. He's just hooked on to his first decent-sized kingy. I'll give anyone ten bucks if he even gets to turn its head," Kelly offered.

"What's a kingy?" Abigail asked.

"Dixie, do you want to do the honours?" Kelly gestured.

"A yellowtail kingfish, they're massive and pull like a freight train. Can't eat 'em, anyway. We call them neighbours fish, or sometimes we might use one or two for dhufish bait. He won't have a chance in hell of landing it. They grow to monster proportions in these protected waters."

"So, what next, Professor?" Kelly posed the obvious question.

"Well, the way I see it, these solar rays on the Chakra Wheel are definitely in the wrong order—but the question is—was that by design and is it part of the puzzle?"

"I don't follow," Dixie replied.

"What I'm referring to is simply—do we follow the exacting sequence from the first colour, which would be the blue, on spoke number one? We can see the colour yellow on the fourth spoke, does that mean the sixth spoke will then be pink and so forth? We have twenty-four spokes and twelve colours. Apart from the fact we know blue is the number one in the array, we don't have a precise starting point."

"The tumbler on a safe always starts from the top, and that's always zero," Dixie threw in.

"I wish it were that easy. We may only get two chances to nail this," Evina added.

"What about this translated text and that key, what's that all about, then?" Abigail questioned her sister. "It has to be relevant somehow."

"I'm not sure, Abby. Live by the sword—die by the sword. Let's do it," Evina spoke with a resolute tone.

"Even better, let's all watch you do it. You're the puppet master," Kelly suggested.

Abigail started to video the auspicious moment on her iPad.

"Here goes, then." Evina drew a long deep breath and placed her fingers firmly on the Chakra Wheel and attempted to turn it. The Earth did not move—and neither did the dial.

"May I?" Kelly tried again with some force, ending with the same result. "Maybe it's locked. Hang on a sec." He grabbed a torch and searched every inch of the puzzle box. Starting with the rear, he lifted it and viewed the base closely, followed by both the two sides. He ran his fingers along each polished end. The whole outer surface was covered with a brushed lacquer. He paused as his fingertip sensed the slightest deviation in the wood on the right-hand side. He tipped his head sideways for a second, closer inspection. "Bear with me, I have an idea." He picked up the wooden mallet and a length of dowel. "Grab the other end, Dixie." He tapped the dowel against the slight depression. The lacquer cracked and fell to the table.

Evina watched the proceedings like she was waiting for the second coming of Christ. Kelly hit it again. Dixie's eyes widened. "It's coming out this end, belt it harder, Jack."

Evina shuffled to her left and also noticed the dried lacquer flaking away as the cylinder-shaped locking device started to ease its way clear. Jack tapped away until a 25cm length of dowel, exactly half the length of the puzzle box, dropped to the table and rolled to the floor.

Kelly bent down and picked it up before suggesting, "Try the wheel again, Evina." She eased her grip and tried to rotate it clockwise. The muffled noise of two pieces of timber sliding could be heard from inside. Evina slowed and placed the black spear on the first colour of blue at ten o'clock. Each person exhaled.

"One down, eleven to go," Kelly spoke in hushed anguish as he nervously twirled the wooden locking rod in his fingers. Evina carried on with an urged repetition. The yellow dot was counterclockwise at two o'clock, then the pink and white. The last dot was the colour opaline at the five o'clock position.

"Are we all ready?" It was a rhetorical question that required no answer. Evina turned the dial back to the top position and held her shaking hand in the air while holding her breath. A slow-rolling sound resonated from inside, the final noise was like a ball bearing being dropped onto a wooden floor from waist height. Everyone stood frigid and waited for something to happen—anything.

Till suddenly burst onto the rear deck with his ticket booked to eternal fisherman's heaven while struggling to hold a yellowtail kingfish almost longer than he was tall. Four sets of eyes turned to face him, then immediately focused back on the puzzle box. The anti-climax was excruciating. Nothing moved, and the lockbox remained tightly sealed.

"Shit . . . What just happened?" Abigail broke the aphonic silence. Evina half expected a book-eating-acid to be released, destroying the contents. "I'm freaking out here, it's the wrong concatenation." She placed both hands on her ashen-looking face. Evina felt like she wanted to puke.

Kelly was tapping the wooden locking rod against his open hand in nervous dyspepsia when suddenly something caught his eye. "Evina, pass me that magnifying glass." There was a symbol burnt onto the cylindrical end. "It looks like a rose inside a cross inside a triangle or something. Here take a look at what I mean." Kelly passed it to the expert.

Evina raised the magnifying glass and immediately recognised the symbol. "You're an absolute genius, Jack, and I can't believe I didn't think of it earlier. I'm an idiot. It's the Rose Cross or *Rose Croix*, a symbol largely associated with the semi-mythical Christian Rosenkreuz, Qabbalist and Alchemist and founder of the Rosicrucian Order."

"Don't stop there, because none of us has a clue what you're talking about, but I'm guessing we will in a minute, Mrs Brainiac?" Kelly replied.

"A secret society—The Nine Unknown Men. The Persian text we translated—key final unknown. The U in the unknown is a capital letter... it's a proper noun! It means the key to the final Unknown. Jahangir is a bloody genius. That makes two of you now, Jack."

"Keep going, you're on a roll," Kelly agreed.

"The society of the Nine Unknown Men was formed shortly after 226 BC by Emperor Ashoka. After witnessing the aftermath of a great war where one hundred thousand Kalinga warriors lay dead, he converted to Buddhism. Then he renounced the idea of trying to integrate the rebellious people, declaring that the only true conquest was to win over the people's hearts and minds.

"Only by the observance of the Laws of Duty and Piety, because The Sacred Majesty desired that all living creatures should enjoy security, peace and happiness and be free to live as they pleased. So committed was the emperor to this mission that he sought to prevent his fellow man from putting their intelligence towards perpetrating evil, particularly the evil involved in warfare.

"The task of collecting, preserving, and containing all this knowledge was too great for one emperor to do alone, not the least because of the other duties required by ruling an empire. So Ashoka summoned nine of the most brilliant minds in India at that time. For security purposes, the identity of these men was never made public. Together, these geniuses formed a secret society that came to be known as the Nine Unknown Men.

"To better accomplish this daunting task, each of the nine was charged with a specific book that he was to update, revise, and ultimately perfect the knowledge therein. When one of the nine could no longer complete the task—whether from the wish to retire, fading health, or death—the obligation was passed to a chosen successor. The number of members of the society was always to remain at nine. Thus the society of the Nine Unknown Men has allegedly lived on for over two thousand years.

"Speculation about the contents of each of the nine books varies widely. Talbot Mundy, an English writer, published a book titled *The Nine Unknown Men* in 1923, which contained a list of the nine books. Most believers of the existence of this society accept this as being accurate.

"The first book was titled Propaganda. It dealt with techniques of propaganda and psychological warfare. The most dangerous of all sciences is that of moulding mass opinion because it would enable anyone to govern the whole world. The second book discussed the physiology and explains how to kill a person simply by touching their body, known as the 'the touch of death,' by basically reversing a nerve impulse. It is said that the martial art of judo is a result of 'leakages' from the second book. The third volume focused on microbiology and biotechnology. The fourth dealt with alchemy and transmutation of metals. According to another legend, in times of severe drought, temples and religious relief organisations received large quantities of gold from 'a secret source.' Communication: the fifth book contained a study of all means of communication, terrestrial and extraterrestrial. Alluding that the Nine Unknown Men were aware of an alien presence. Gravity, the sixth book, wrote about the secrets of gravitation and actual instructions on how to make the ancient *Vedic Vimana*, or to levitate."

"Like *My Favourite Martian*," Dixie threw in, "I used to love watching that show," he further added.

Evina frowned and continued, "Cosmogony was the seventh book which contained cosmogony and matters of the universe. Light, the eighth book dealt with the speed of light, including how to use it as a weapon. And lastly was Sociology. It included rules for the evolution of societies and the means of foretelling their decline."

"And—like Stone always says, there's always an and or a but," Kelly reminded each and every person.

"The Persian text alludes to the key to the final Unknown. Jahangir deemed his *Book of Remedies* with such importance he considered it as the tenth Unknown—the tenth solar colour is gold—and that is the key... the starting point." Evina was almost struggling to keep herself in check. She could feel the strain of the last few weeks taking its toll. Mentally she felt drained; emotionally, she was riding a wave of discovery. She was on the cusp of something so significant it was almost excruciating to absorb the enormity of what she could only hope rested inside the Himitsu-Bako.

Abigail held her iPad with a slightly shaking hand and started to record. "All right, here goes nothing," Evina voiced.

Abigail answered, "The moment has arrived. Either way, if your book is—or isn't inside, you've done an extraordinary job just to get to this stage. You should feel proud—and I want the exclusive—just so you know, *older* sister."

"I'll drink to that. You want another beer, Dixie?" Kelly asked.

"I need a bloody tranquilliser," he replied.

Evina stepped in and placed a nervous hand on the Chakra Wheel. She twisted the dial anticlockwise, bypassing three spokes and stopped the spear on the colour gold, and then clockwise two spokes to orange, she continued the sequence with exacting measure until she reached the final colour a second time—this time it was magenta. The tension was nail-biting.

The final turn was clockwise back to the twelve o'clock position. She felt increased pressure on the wheel—then stopped and waited with intuit divination. Two knocking noises sounded like wooden pins disengaging. At either end of the box, a slow trickle of sand flowed and started to form an ant mound on the table. Two wooden tongues slid free in perfect sync as the parquetry inlay slowly started to rise above its four borders. Evina's accelerated heart felt like it was going to explode from within her chest. She repeatedly swallowed to moisten the inside of her parched mouth.

Abigail's hands looked like they were shivering, fighting to keep the camera still.

Dixie sculled his beer, squeezed the can until it resembled a hockey puck, and lobbed it like a basketball into the yellow recycle bin.

Kelly drifted back to the time he and Till, on this same table, laid first eyes on The Buddhas Tooth. He considered the paradox while the leaking sand slowed to a halt. Till was busy dressing his own prize on the rear filleting table with Kelly's bone-handled knife.

Evina placed her fidgeting fingers on either end of the checkerboard lid and lifted it clear. There was a combined gasp at what greeted them from inside. You could hear a pin drop as each person's eyes bore down in a dazed realisation of what they had achieved. Evina's eyes glittered, struggling with the weight as she lifted out a gilded golden casket and gently eased the four turned legs onto the tabletop. It resembled an over-sized jewellery box with a casserole-style lid. The handle consisted of two opposing carved ivory elephant tusks balanced on top of two jade attacking Bengal tigers, raised on their hind legs. The lid edge was beaded with a dazzling parade of sapphires, rubies and emeralds along a pathway of garnet. It radiated its own aura in a glistening display of gold leaf and magnificent artistry engraved on all four sides.

The moment of truth had dawned. It was time to lift the lid and see firsthand if Evina's bestselling book was, in fact, real or a myth to be passed down the generations as, 'what could have been'.

"Look at my hands, I can't keep them still." Evina lifted the lid straight up—while holding it at shoulder height, and then almost fainted. Each person felt an emotional tug of the heart. Tears of joy rolled down Evina's reddened cheeks as the relieving intensity of ten years riding the unpredictable roller-coaster of discovery slowly dissipated like a deflating balloon. She handed the lid to Dixie and just stared in enthralled enrapturement. The moment felt saturated in the sense of unexplored surrealism. Protected by a richly decorative padded brocade inlay made from silk and woven fabric embellishing the base and sides was the face cover of a leather-bound book—and it was big, matching the size of a sheet of A2 paper. The centre of the cover displayed a glorious handcrafted painting with finite attention to detail, a tribute to the artist of that time.

"It's Emperor Jahangir, and he's holding the Asclepius Wand," Evina cheered loudly. She turned and hugged her sister, who was still awestruck in a frozen ice-like dress shop mannequin pose. Her open mouth was in fly-catching mode.

Both Jack and Dixie slapped hands in another high-five, then turned their heads as one, back towards the associate professor, who looked like she was performing some weird kind of fàràng Zulu dance.

"What's the Asclepius Wand?" Dixie braved.

"It's often confused with the Caduceus Wand of Hermes. The true symbol of the medical profession. It has long been seen by many people as a symbol of healing," Evina explained.

"And that's a good thing—*right*?" Dixie ventured further.

Evina gave him one of her 'looks' while he laid down the weighted gold lid to one side.

"Oh, my God," Evina was entering another stratosphere. "This is beautiful, absolutely unbelievable. He's holding in his other palm the Spiral Sun. Several Shamanic traditions consider the sun to be the first Shaman, that is, the first healer of people. The Spiral Sun comes from the Anasazi's petroglyphs as a symbol of healing. The symbol stands for the natural movements and rhythms of life, the constant motion of the universe. It is representative of the unique healing power that is being radiated all around the cosmos, which helps us recover from setbacks and fall back into a natural rhythm and healthy harmony of life. This is the solar symbolism of the Moghul Court. It embodies the accession of Jahangir to his position as the fourth emperor which coincided with the 'Great Light': the sun rising and shining onto the Earth, which allowed the emperor to assume the *'Layab of Nur ad-Din'*: meaning 'Light of the Earth'. This is simply breathtaking."

Till walked into the galley dangling two slabs of fillets that looked like they could have come from a small whale. "Boss, why everyone happy? You drink Lao khao?"

"Till, you remember, The Buddhas Tooth, well this is same-same, mate, and that fish you have is no good—taste like shit," Kelly needed to explain.

"I cook Thai style—spicy. Okay, *khràp*."

"All right, master chef. In the meantime, let's pack all this away. It's time to head back to the mainland."

Jack felt relieved it was all over, for him anyway. He wasn't sure what Evina's next step might be, and it didn't really matter. He was homesick and missed Tiaan and his two dogs, and he knew Till felt the same way. It was time to head home to Koh Chang.

His men-only thought's shifted to the possibility of welcome home sex when suddenly, his inner smile was interrupted by the croak of the sat phone. He made his way up the stairs and looked at the caller ID. *Private number, that's never good?*

"Hello . . ."

"Where are you right now?" The familiar voice of Tobias Stone resonated through the ear-piece.

"At a resort sharing a margarita with a pool full of beautiful bikini-clad women—why?" Kelly asked, not really wanting to hear the answer.

"You uncovered any decent books recently?" Stone added to his somewhat cryptic undertone.

"Reading one at the moment, it's about pain—financial pain. How's that Visa Card coming along, Tobias? You remember, don't you?"

"Jack, you may have a problem."

"You're my biggest problem. Seriously—what now?" Kelly was almost hesitant to ask.

Chapter·50

KELLY EASED *Thin Lizzy* from the wharf and headed for the channel, passing the northern tip of Robinson Island. With open ocean ahead and five fathoms of clear water under the keel, he opened up the twin Man diesel engines, and soon they were comfortably cruising at 24 knots, with a following sea that was more of an annoyance than anything else. He punched in the new coordinates on his GPS. This would lead them to a speck of ocean about the size of a football oval 25 nautical miles west of Kalbarri and outside Australia's Territorial Waters to meet up with Dixie's cray boat, the *C'Est la Vie*. The Contiguous Zone is a belt of water contiguous to the territorial sea that stretches to a distance of 24 nautical miles. In this zone, Australia has the legal backing to exercise the controls necessary to prevent and punish infringement of its customs, fiscal, immigration or sanitary laws and regulations within its land territories or territorial sea under the *Seas and Submerged Lands Act 1973*.

Stone's phone conversation was ambiguous without being evasive. The underlying tone was that Kelly should be on a 'watch and be prepared' state of readiness, which could mean just about anything, but he trusted this man's instincts unequivocally. Stone had alluded to the fact that while unravelling the contemptible acts of both the deputy PM and the attorney-general back in Canberra, Evina's best-selling book may still be compromised, by not only the private sector—but also at government level. Kelly recalled the conversation with the Jindeugi about the staggering monetary wealth and the resources available to the pharmaceutical industry and the roadblock Evina's discovery would create. Money means power, and power equates to corruption—something that was fast becoming almost a career choice of epidemic proportions for too many politicians, while a servant to the people.

Kelly's original plan was to offload the twins at Geraldton, where they could fly to Perth and continue on with their lives. He still had no real clue what Evina had in mind for her *Book of Remedies*, but as an associate professor, she was naïve about the ways of the world. That's when Kelly sat everyone down to explain his change of plans. It took some time to convince Evina, but eventually, the fog of her exposure lifted and cleared a pathway for logic and common sense to prevail, and she eventually came around. Maybe it was more like she was dragged, kicking and screaming.

Till was busy in the galley, while Abigail and Dixie were conspicuous in their combined absence. The sun's burning orange inferno had just dipped below the ocean horizon and the time was just after 6:27 P.M. At Kelly's own request, Evina had moved the new love of her life upstairs to the saloon and had about four hours to start the arduous task of documenting her findings.

With a pair of white gloves, she turned each page like it was her last Tally-ho paper, under a tripod-mounted digital camera, photographing each parchment while making notes on Abigail's laptop. Kelly wanted to stay in the big chair until they reached their rendezvous point. He would continually listen to the oo's, and arr's emanating from behind his captain's position like Evina was cuddling a baby panda bear. She was lost in her own medicinal, enchanted forest.

The book itself was really quite magnificent in its detailed descriptions, with a vast library of hand-drawn imagery highlighting different trees and roots, shrubs, flowers and herbs, all documented to relate to each inflicted part of the human body. Jahangir talked about the four dimensions of the therapeutic landscape: natural environment, built environment, symbolic environment and social environment. There were theories of environmental affordances, ecological psychology, the 'flow experience' and sensory stimulation theories. He discussed in detail the contagious nature of phthisis, distribution of diseases by water and soil, careful description of skin troubles; of sexual diseases and perversions and nervous ailments. He detailed how simple it would be for each household to nurture its own restorative gardens. He titled it the 'Healing Landscape', and its direct collation with the great outdoors and about the spreading of infection by noxious vapours.

The passage of infections by germs was beginning to be understood, and the lack of fresh air was felt to contribute to illness. Jahangir was at pains to explain the benefits of recovering patients to participate in grounds maintenance, gardening and farming as part of their therapy, utilising horticultural therapy to work with returning war veterans, the elderly, and various types of dementia. He discovered the simple exposure to nature causes heart rate, muscle tension, and blood pressure to decrease.

Evina estimated the *Book of Remedies* to be over 1,500 pages full with the miracles of natural healing, health remedies supplied free of charge by nature, and preventive measures to guard against influenza and common colds. It even laid out simple plans for each village to share the burden amongst its people in designing community-based natures own remedial clinics, including contemplative gardens, restorative gardens, healing gardens, enabling gardens and therapeutic gardens.

The *Book of Remedies* knowledge-base was light years ahead of its time. Its roll-on effects, in not just curing the sick, but more so on the prevention of illness for the masses was far-reaching and therefore represented a clear and present danger to the status quo—and that was sure to ruffle more than a few financial feathers. For the average modern family, it could mean a shift in their life choices. For a third world country, it would be mind-boggling in its everyday life-altering effects. Free medicine like nature's very own healthcare plan. The reality of the flip side was the justification by the captains of big business who prosper by a long-drawn-out recovery from the ravages of terminal illness, and profit by peddling pills to protect their business empires—anyway they saw fit. Like the man that boasted, he found a way to run an automobile using just six basic kitchen ingredients, *poof.* The oil industry made sure he was never heard of again. Trust no one.

The radar sweep beeped a low tonal alarm alerting Kelly the *C'est la Vie* was now three nautical miles away and approaching off their starboard quarter. He switched on the deck lights, and the main roof-mounted halogen searchlight, transforming the yacht into a floating lighthouse. Kelly eased back and shifted the gearbox into neutral to allow *Thin Lizzy* to drift to a rolling sway. He negotiated the stairs to rally the troops to prepare for a mid-ocean passenger transfer. The twins came out from their cabins with just the one suitcase and a carry on each. That was the deal. They could pick up the other five cases at another time as per the captain's orders.

Abigail approached Kelly first. She extended her arms around his neck and held on tight. "I can't believe this is going to end like this. I had hoped we could all share lunch at the most expensive and lavish restaurant in Perth and spend a lazy afternoon getting really drunk together while reliving our epic adventure. Never a dull moment with you, Jack—that's for sure."

Kelly looked over at Dixie. "Maybe it's just the beginning. Anyway, you're going to be a busy girl for a while—it should make a great read."

Abigail kissed him on the cheek and wiped her eyes clear. Evina was waiting for her sister to move. She strode up to face Jack, like a teacher about to scold a student. "I know we have discussed this at length, Jack, but it's not easy to just up and leave what has taken me ten years to locate. Are you sure you won't share with me where you intend to hide it? I will sleep better if I know," Evina pleaded.

"The hidey-hole on board is only temporary. The final resting place I've ear-marked has stood the test of time—trust me. Remember what we discussed. It's better that you *don't* know. You can breathe any time you like now, Evina."

The sound of an incoming outboard motor drew closer. Dixie threw out a line and hauled the tender alongside. Till started to load the two cases first. Dixie grabbed Jack's outstretched hand and shook it with a firm grip. "All the best, old mate. Maybe I'll come and visit you in Thailand, meet the missus? She must be someone special to put up with you, Jack."

"Yeah, I got lucky, maybe that's catching?" Dixie looked confused. Which wasn't a difficult thing for him when it came to the fairer sex? "Abigail? Good luck with that." The two men shared a shoulder-to-shoulder man bump.

Both women kissed Till on the cheek. "The Thai food we get served back in Australia doesn't come anywhere close to your culinary skills, Till," Abigail wanted him to know. Till nodded in agreement. Dixie helped the twins into the swaying runabout. The smell of exhaust fumes hung on the breeze as they disappeared into the trough of a lazy two-metre swell and made the mad dash to the stationary *C'est la Vie* before they would make port at Kalbarri and track their way back to Sydney.

"Till, how much diesel do we have in both tanks— enough to make it to Thevenard Island? I don't think it'd be a good idea to refuel in either mainland Australia *or* Bali—what do ya reckon?"

"Okay, *khràp*. We go back to Koh Chang now—very good. You want to eat now, Boss?"

"Maybe later, Till. Coffee and some sea miles under our belts first. Let's head for home, buddy."

Like a parallel universe, the *Thin Lizzy* berthed alongside the refuelling depot located within the Brani Terminal in Singapore Harbour. At precisely the same time, the midnight horror Jet Star flight landed at Charles Kingsford Smith Airport in Sydney, twenty minutes late at 6:40 A.M. Evina and Abigail disembarked through the rotunda, still half-asleep and stepped from the jet bridge into the domestic terminal. Waiting to greet them were two Customs officers, Immigration officials and a couple of disgruntled federal cops.

"Mrs Bishop-Joiner and Miss Bishop-Price, come this way, please." The taller of the two federal officers ushered the twins into a private interview room. They entered to find their luggage waiting, opened and strewn about on an inspection table.

"That was quick. You don't muck around—do you? What's the meaning of this?" Evina remonstrated.

"Its standard procedure, I'm afraid. Our embassy in Bali has been advised that two Australian nationals may have left Indonesia, illegally. Your passports, please."

"Passports? Why do you need to see our passports? We've only just this minute arrived from Perth."

"Mrs Bishop-Joiner, this process will move along with a lot less pain if you cooperate fully."

Abigail fired up. "What process are you referring to, then?"

The Immigration official was flipping through the last stamped page of her passport. "Well, to start with. How did you arrive on Christmas Island?"

"We swam while dodging bullets and bombs. Bugger this, Evina. I'm ringing my lawyer." Abigail reached for her mobile as the door opened and another person entered. Both women looked to their left, and Abigail was a little stunned at who had just entered. She recognised the face from a story she filed on her return from Kuwait.

"I'll take over from here, gentlemen." Darcy Jones flashed his director-general of ASIO credentials. He pointed to the clothes cluttering the collapsible tables. "Any chance one of you can repack these ladies' luggage? I think you would have to agree, there is nothing in there that concerns any of your departments."

Evina strode over and repacked her own clothing. Abigail smiled at the six men, looking like they'd just been caught with their hands in the cookie jar. "Excuse me." She pushed past and joined her sister, tossing her belongings inside and expertly slammed shut the locks. Each sister lifted their own suitcase and followed Jones back through the flight-staff-only exit gate.

"What was that all about?" Evina wasted no time in asking.

A Ford *Fairlane* was parked at the terminal exit. Jones loaded the boot and got behind the wheel.

"I can see now that your new best friend, Jack Kelly, took Stone's advice. Word travels fast," the director replied.

"Fast, we've been on an island in the middle of the bloody Indian Ocean—words can't travel underwater," Evina answered, still confused.

"Your friend—bonny Prince Graeme posted a blog on the Hutt River Province's Facebook page and announced to the world on their own website, sprouting his involvement in uncovering a lost treasure. Says the artefact will possibly be on display as part of the Stone of Light exhibition. He's a regular marketing guru, isn't he?" Jones' mind boggled at the naivety of some people.

The twins shifted and looked each other in the eye. "He was a nice kid, but a bit on the simple side. I never considered that happening," Evina mentioned from the back seat.

"What are your plans, Mrs Bishop-Joiner? Surely fame and fortune await you when you arrive back at the Smithsonian. You'll need to tread carefully. The forces of greed are a powerful aphrodisiac. The almighty dollar and the thirst for power, influential men with more than enough clout, will stop at nothing to stand in your way," Jones wanted to explain.

"The wheels are already in motion; some forces of nature cannot and should not be halted. Wait and see." Evina replied while smiling with thoughts of Jack and Till swimming through her mind.

Evina cast her eyes to the rear-vision mirror. "The director-general of ASIO picks us up personally from the airport? That can only mean one thing? Do you know where Tobias Stone is right now? I would like to thank him for all his help." She waited with more than a passing interest for an answer.

"Who is, Tobias Stone?" Darcy Jones finally replied.

"Bloody spooks," Evina murmured loud enough so Jones could hear.

Stone drove past Sydney Olympic Park, the venue for the Millennium Olympic Games in 2000. He continued down the Western Motorway and took the A-28 exit. The suburb of Westmead was a farther two kilometres away, at which point he chucked a right then slowed. A posted sign confirmed the park named Shannon's Paddock with Finlayson's Creek cutting a swathe down the middle. He glanced over at the pencilled address on his passenger's seat and laughed inside at the small nonsensical idiosyncrasies of life. Number 12-14 Darcy Road was a two-storey, nondescript block of four State Housing Commission units that looked like they belonged in a war zone.

A Korean woman was crouched on her haunches as only the Asians can do—all day long, tending to a small vegetable garden that backed on to the park on the other side of a leaning wooden-picketed fence. Stone dialled a number and waited for the woman to put down her gardening tools, then answer the call from the ringing landline inside.

He closed the driver's door behind him and pushed open the small steel swinging gate that hung lazily from a rusted, bent hinge. In his hand were an A4 manila-sized envelope and a zipped sports bag. Stone placed both packages down on the front doorstep, rang the bell and hurried back to his parked car. With the black tinting concealing his face, he watched as the front house door opened. The petite-framed jet-black-haired woman looked left and right, then down at her feet. She picked up the envelope first and noticed there was no name or address. Stone watched as she ripped the seal open and cast her eyes on the contents. Mi-sun pulled out a handwritten note:

There should be more than enough for you, your brother, and the eight girls from the casino to make a fresh start in life. Good luck, and welcome to the Land Down Under.

Mi-sun stumbled a few steps backwards, almost tripping over the bag. She crouched down and pulled the zipper open. Inside, the bag was bulging with wrapped bundles of Australian $100 notes that smelt like they were fresh from the mint. Mi-sun needed to find the floor before she thought she might faint. She sat down on the front porch, then cried. She raised her head and wiped away her tears when she heard the sound of an engine starting. Mi-sun looked out across the dried lawn, full of weeds to see the rear badge of a BMW driving off. She smiled and remembered.

Today is one of the few good days, Stone considered. He wanted to remind himself what it felt like to do some good. *And this is a great start.*

Chapter-51

JANUARY WAS SEASONALLY the coolest month on Koh Chang. The Thai people sometimes referred to this as the last part of their winter. Today the temperature was a simmering 32 degrees Celsius with the humidity dropping a whopping ten per cent. The time ticked over to five o'clock, which meant it was *that* time of the afternoon—the time Kelly liked to sit under the shade offered by a huge jackfruit tree and crack open his first Thatchers cider. Tiaan arrived with a handled frosted glass and a loaded ice bucket.

"Thanks." Kelly filled his glass, and then asked, "Tiaan... is your family coming over to eat tonight? I see both you and Till have been mucking around all morning cooking. And where did he go, by the way? I saw him drive off in the pickup over three hours ago."

"I think he went to see his brother. He should be back shortly," Tiaan lied, struggling to conceal her excitement.

The two Soi dogs, Kelly rescued from a sentence of death, were named Cilla and Tiga and were currently chasing a couple of chooks that ventured a bit too close to their morning dried food bowls. He leaned back into his deck chair and took in the panoramic views of the elephant lagoon, where *Thin Lizzy* was berthed while he relaxed into the sweeping 180-degree scene that was Baan-Salak-Phet Bay, with Phrao-Nai Island located a good drive with a one-iron out to sea.

Kelly turned his head at the sound of a motorbike entering his main gate, which was nothing unusual as every man and his dog owned one. What *was* out of the ordinary was both the rider and pillion wore tinted full-face helmets and the fact the bike was a Kawasaki-Z650 ABS. That's like the Rolls Royce of bikes around most provinces of Thailand. He swallowed another mouthful of his cider. The bike skidded to a stop, dropped to its side stand, and each person threw a leg over the seat and started to walk towards where he was seated. Kelly stood up, unsure of whom they might be. The strangers both unclipped their straps and removed their headgear.

"Well, well—do my eyes deceive me? Do I need glasses?" Kelly's facial expression was a mixture of un-curbed elation and perplexity.

"So, this is where you lock yourself away from the outside world. You can run, but you can't hide from an ASIO agent," Stone answered with a mischievous look.

"Tobias—bloody hell, mate, this *is* a surprise . . . Or is it?" Kelly glanced over at Tiaan, who was exuding an expression that fitted perfectly with Thailand's often preferred title as the 'land of smoke and mirrors'. Kelly asked, "You knew he was coming, didn't you, Tiaan?" She was almost beside herself with elation. The Thais just love to entertain, and Tiaan was the queen bee. "You are a resourceful man, that's for sure, Tobias. Come here and give your old partner a hug. Welcome to Thailand." Jack turned his head. "Tiaan, this is, Tobias. But I think you already know that. And who do we have here...? You pick up a hitchhiker on the way?"

"Jack and Tiaan, this is, Felicity, and I would never allow my adopted daughter to hitch alone. Felicity is turning twenty-one in two days, and she wanted to spend the time celebrating with some of *my* friends, so here we are. You're it, I'm afraid, Jack. Felicity didn't believe you actually existed."

"Well, we're real enough. Grab another two glasses, Tiaan, and that bottle of Ribena. Still drinking those snakebites, Tobias?"

"Only on days that end in y, Jack."

Kelly then asked, "And what about you, Felicity?"

"Felicity doesn't drink alcohol."

Kelly laughed then turned, "Great, we have a skipper then. Come on, let's go find you a comfortable seat with some decent shade. The only good thing about the sun anywhere near the equator is watching it disappear each night."

Each person's glass was filled. Kelly then lifted his own glass high into the air, "*Chai yoh*," he cheered loudly.

"Chow what?" Stone replied.

"Cheers, you clown."

Tiaan stepped around the opposite side of the table and greeted Stone and Felicity with the traditional Thailand bow with both hands clasped. "*Sàwàt dii khà*. This is the first time any of Jack's *fàràng* friends have visited us here in Thailand. This makes me very happy," she wanted to explain.

"Jack, this lady is well above your pay grade. Maybe that's the reason why, Tiaan? You are way too beautiful for Jack to trust with the friends he knocks around with—present company excluded, of course. Nice house, Jack. Bloody hell, check out the view. Doing it tough, old mate."

"Not my house. I'm working on a cosy little beach shack down closer to where the fish bite. Nice and quiet."

"Keep putting in the hard yards, Jack. Even Tiaan might come around one day," he laughed.

Jack looked over towards Tiaan one more time. "You can calm down now, it's just, Tobias." The sound of the pickup flying through the gate with a certain small Thai man behind the wheel caused Kelly to turn once again. "Well, now I am totally surprised. Let me be the first to say, I did not expect this. You guys are unbelievable. How the hell did you pull this off, Tiaan? I still can't believe it." Kelly stood in total shock.

The passenger door flew open, and a very animated blonde-haired woman launched herself from the front seat and sprinted over with a package in her hand to where Kelly stood, totally dumbfounded. He prepared himself for the incoming human missile. Abigail swept straight past and embraced Tiaan like they were long-lost friends.

"What is going on here?" Kelly asked. Evina was next, and like an Olympic sprinter, she joined the circle of friendship. The three women shared a group hug, dancing on the spot. Tiaan started to tear up. Kelly needed to get a grip on his own emotions. He reached for his cider and emptied the contents. "My shout," he whooped. "Margaritas for everyone."

"I have already taken care of that, Jack. Two jugs are made up in the bar fridge," Tiaan announced, above the rising commotion.

Then a lone voice shouted from behind the parked pickup. "About bloody time, you shouted. I hear there may be a party about to happen? I wasn't about to miss the show, Jack."

"No way, I don't believe it, Dixie, you sly dog. The troops are all here. Shit—I think I'm going to shed a tear myself, bloody hell!" Kelly was ecstatic. Till came back with six margarita glasses and filled each one to the brim. The finders of Evina's all-important book stood in a circle and raised their glasses once more.

"Cheers, everyone. On behalf of Tiaan and myself, welcome to the island of elephants. You are all more than welcome." Kelly sculled his margarita and one by one, each person followed.

Tiaan stepped towards Felicity and the twins. "*Ba*, we go now. I will show you to your rooms, maybe you want a shower, and then we can eat. Till, their bags, please. Follow me, *maa maa*."

Abigail turned, "Oh, I nearly forgot, Jack. When I saw that sad look on your face after you first pointed out to me the rubberised goanna riddled with bullet holes and now missing his tail, I thought there was only one thing to do, so, we all chipped in and bought you this. Here, take it as a gift from all of us."

Kelly opened up the bag and pulled out a rubberised replica of the old shot-to-pieces goanna version of Thin Lizzy. He smiled, "Now the planets are realigned. My first job tomorrow will be to replace this."

Kelly pulled two bottles of Leo beer and another cider from the icebox as the ladies left, chatting like only women can. "Sit down, guys. Today ends in y, so let's drink up."

The cider and beers flowed in what is a steeped Australian tradition. The champagne corks popped, and the mood was of jubilation, and if Evina's consternation was a guiding light, Kelly knew it would be only a matter of when, not if, before her inquisitive brain tackled head-on the mystery of where he may have stashed her ancient book.

Tiaan had prepared enough food to feed a small country, which is just as well as the word quickly spread throughout Baan-Salak-Khok. Having one fàràng living as a local was like sharing your daily life with near-celebrity-status, with the news of a further five Westerners arriving, this was a must-see event for the curious Thai people. Tiaan's two brothers arrived, soon followed by her cousin, Gideon. Within an hour, the numbers had swollen to over twenty. The Thais love a party and don't mind a drink. This was going to be a night to remember.

Kelly was always the first to rise with the sound of a resident Tokay gecko hollering in a high-pitched mating shrill from the inside of his ceiling. He was now munching on a piece of toast with Vegemite while on his front balcony. Evina poked her head around the half-length privacy screen with two fresh coffees in hand. "Can I join you?"

"Absolutely, I can't believe you waited this long, I mean you arrived yesterday afternoon, and the time is now six-thirty," Kelly replied.

"Is it that obvious?" Evina's expression was not fooling anyone. She was like a child the night before Christmas.

"So, tell me how you decided to tackle your small problem?" Kelly was genuinely interested.

"Well, I took some of your advice, and then indulged in some lengthy discussions with both the board of directors' who oversee the Smithsonian, plus the curator, Byron Clarkson. Good old-fashioned common sense still goes a long way."

"Go on," Kelly prompted between sips.

"I remember what you said when I asked all of you where each person thought the book should eventually be placed on display. You quite simply said it should be returned to its home—back to its original country, in India, and you were right. It will travel a world circuit for twelve months, starting just quietly, in Geraldton, then Perth, as part of the *Batavia* collection together with the celestial globe. Then it will be officially handed over to the National Museum of India, in New Delhi."

"One up for, old Jack. Well done, and...?"

"Do you know I was interviewed? Well, it felt more like an intrusive grilling to me, by both the Australian and American authorities, including the FBI and Homeland Security. What do they think this book is all about, how to build a bloody nuclear bomb or something? In the end, the Smithsonian attorneys got involved and brought the World Health Organisation into the mix. With knowledge comes a huge responsibility, Jack.

"I never considered the aftermath, only the discovery. There is a lot to consider in changing the way we harvest medicinal solutions and distribute these to the masses. It's jaw-dropping. I probably was a bit naïve in thinking I could wave a medical wand and change the world overnight, but we do have a plan, and that plan does involve the pharmaceutical industry. I mean, they have the wealth, the distribution network, and of course a vested interest in both future profits and protecting current markets. It's all about what you're willing to give up as a means of moving forward. The only deal-breaker that I have and will always stipulate is 'free access' to third world countries. That's my priority."

"I'm impressed, Evina. Shucks, you're all grown up now," Kelly poked a bit of fun. "What I mean is, you got smart. You can't expect to take on these huge corporations head-on—and end up with a favourable result. But by inviting them to be part of the process, not only publicly safeguards you but also guarantees a result. Just stay vigilant and keep a tight line on the shifty little bastards."

"So—Jack, where is it? It's been over two months now, and there is so much more work to be done. I bet you have your very own Aladdin's cave protected by herds of wild, untamed elephants or a secret dungeon inside a dormant volcano, maybe a hidden underwater cavern, guarded by a frenzy of man-eating sharks."

"Yeah, right? Follow me." *The vivid imagination of an associate professor?* Kelly thought.

They stepped off Jack's balcony. Then Evina followed him into Tiaan's recently completed home and entered the kitchen. Abigail was awake and waiting patiently for some of Gideon's poached eggs. Gideon handed Jack a freshly made toasted bacon and egg sandwich accompanied with a glass of some sort of Thai miracle jungle juice. Jack and Evina continued their journey of discovery through the double door entry back outside.

"Where are you two headed?" Abigail's inquisitive mind was alerted.

"Jump on the end of the line and find out," Evina replied, with an unchecked look of enthusiasm.

"Oh, hang on a minute, you have that look—I know where you're both off to. I'll be back in a minute, Gideon." Gideon turned off the gas knob. Both she and Abigail joined the end of the line. Kelly stepped back down the stairs and turned left. Stone was outside, playing with the dogs and Felicity was loosening up ready for a jog down to the beach. The line kept snaking longer.

Kelly circumnavigated the outside of the large home and headed towards what looked like a half-built wooden shed, surrounded by thin hexagonal wire. Evina's enthusiasm started to show signs of a reversal. "Jack, this is a chicken coop."

"Not just any chickens, these are specially bred angry chickens. Come on, we're almost there." He stopped and pointed to a shoulder-height shelf made from half-cut lengths of bamboo, and the shelves from a discarded IKEA table, all covered in piles of chicken poop.

"I'm not going in there, it stinks, and it's covered in crap." Evina was adamant.

"That's the least of your problems." Kelly ushered Evina through the first gate, the crowd swarmed and watched on with interest.

"Come on, keep going," Kelly urged Evina on with a friendly prod in the back. Suddenly a flapping, crazed chicken made a first bluffing run at Kelly. Evina jumped backwards with both arms raised and screamed.

"Quick, I'll draw them away, and you race inside that last door. There's a wooden vegetable crate on the middle shelf, grab it and run for your life back out here, where I'll be waiting," Kelly enjoyed offering instructions.

"Are you insane?" Evina shouted. "Why would I do that, these chickens actually *do* look angry?"

"Too bloody right. But if you want your precious book, that's where it is?" Kelly explained.

"Come on, Evina, get in there and claim your prize," Stone challenged.

Dixie couldn't resist jumping on the bandwagon, "It's just sitting there, Evina. All you have to do is deal with a couple of pissed-off chickens."

Abigail was almost beside herself with laughter. She knew the closest her sister ever got to a chicken was when she drove past a KFC store.

Kelly steadied. Evina looked determined and braced herself to run the gauntlet. "Right, are you ready? *Go now,*" Kelly shouted like he was starting a race. He opened the swinging door and pushed Evina through. The small enclosure came to life with nesting hens and new mothers protecting their startled chicks, all squawking and flying about in a clucking flurry of activity.

"Come on, sister, you can do it," Abigail yelled.

Evina was brushing away feathers, careful not to step on the circling chicks as they searched for their mothers, all the while dodging the poo to retrieve the old vegetable crate. She knew she would need a firm grip but still managed to lift it clear while turning at the same time. She did an about-face, then stepped her way back through the feathered minefield. Kelly clipped the door while Stone relieved her of the burden of weight. He made his way to a free-standing table where the odd card game of pok deng is played most afternoons and placed it down.

"Better than any bank vault, Evina. Those chickens are fierce about their territory." Kelly enjoyed the startled look on her face, as Evina unpacked and unwrapped the Himitsu-Bako with the magnificent golden casket inside, safe and sound.

Stone wandered over to where Kelly was standing. "So, Dixie has informed me, each morning he looks inside his garage, but still—there is no new 4wd?"

Kelly thought about his answer. "Each day, Tobias, my accountant named, Tiaan, reminds me I am about five hundred thousand Thai baht out of pocket after our detour to Christmas Island. The Smithsonian came good with a cheque. Where's yours—in the mail? Tiaan doesn't miss a beat. One day if you decide to take the relationship plunge, you'll know what I mean. If you ever find yourself with a woman and the words, 'where is this relationship going' pops into the conversation, swallow two aspirin, find a dark room and take some time-out until it passes." He was only half-joking.

"Arr, Jack, remember when I told you to trust me?" Stone then called out towards Till. He finished topping up the dogs and chooks water buckets and then walked over. "Till, you remember when I grabbed a shower on *Thin Lizzy* after Dixie picked me up off the coast of Kalbarri?"

Till nodded.

"I left something on that pantry top shelf, the one where you keep the fish sauce bottles. Can you go and grab it, please? Your boss is starting to whinge again."

Till looked at his boss, Kelly shrugged his shoulders as if to say, *don't look at me.* So Till made his way down the incline to the elephant lagoon, below. Kelly returned his quizzical gaze back towards, Stone. He didn't flinch. Then both men heard a loud cheer from inside the berthed yacht, soon followed by some very excited Thai language. Till came running up the stone stairs, holding something high above his head.

"Boss—Boss, look what I find. Too much and very heavy. I never see before."

Tiaan walked out, still brush-drying her hair. Her timing was impeccable. Till passed what he'd found into Kelly's open hands. Tiaan locked eyes on what Jack was holding. She knew exactly what it was and was beside him in a flash. Like a magnet, she was unable to peel her opal-coloured eyes away.

Kelly read out the stamped imprint, "Deutsche Bundesrepublik Deutschland 99.9 Fine Gold Bullion Bar 375-Troy Ounces 87823." He handed it to a delirious-looking Thai woman standing next to him before she fainted.

Tiaan was completing a mental monetary conversion. "Oh, my—this is worth over four million Thai baht." She looked over at Jack for an answer, and then she shifted her attention back towards Stone.

"Consider it payment for services rendered, courtesy of the Anomura Corporation," Stone answered her wide-eyed gaze.

Stone's mobile sprang to life. He walked towards the parked Ford *Ranger* and answered the call in private.

Tiaan was imagining herself dripping in gold. Kelly considered if he should buy another Nissan or perhaps a decent 4wd, like a Ford or a Toyota for Dixie. Stone returned while flipping shut his cell phone.

"Jack, that was, Admiral Peterson. Apparently, your MIA status has been made null and void and updated to enlisted. He wants to meet with both of us. And it wasn't a request . . ."

The End

Leaving a Review

Reviews are the life-blood of any self-publishing author. Please feel free to have your say or add any comments while placing an open and honest review on the page you purchased the book from. Any help is greatly appreciated and does make a very real difference. Copy the following universal book link into your browser: mybook.to/thebookofremedies to be taken directly to my Amazon book page. Any help is greatly appreciated and does make a very real difference. Thank you.

Other titles available from P.D. Nelson

P.N. Each book I write is a standalone story and is available in both paperback and e-book format at www.pdnelson.com. By joining my mailing list, I will send you a free copy of my debut novel: *The School of Hard Knocks*. After that I'll only e-mail you with notifications of release dates or any other worthy promotional offers.

In order of release:

The School of Hard Knocks – released Feb 2019 – free download at: www.pdnelson.com/subscribe/

Short Synopsis

When push comes to shove, there is just the family. Sometimes the bad guys do win…

In the '80s, and after two decades of calm, the slow thaw between Sydney's two ruling underworld families has just ended after nine dealers are gunned down in cold blood by one of their own. Divide and conquer, but Patrick O'Finlay still needed a fall guy, he just picked the wrong man.

After 10 toxic years in foster care, with no family, no friends and no future, Jack Kelly was the perfect patsy, and soon his life would become a disposable asset in a gang war with no rules. That was until he is handed a photo of a teenage girl being held hostage that could be a sister he has never met. Against all odds, he knew he needed to tackle this problem head-on. Out of the depths of his despair, he would challenge himself to rise above the spineless acts of others and embark on a journey to seek his retribution. This debt needed to be settled on his terms and within his chosen time-frame.

With just his street smarts and a heart already shot to pieces, can Kelly stay alive long enough to unravel an unknown past cruelly ripped away by the actions of his own mother?

In Kelly's life, there is no grey. Take your best shot—but you better not miss. Bloodlines are forever, and payback is a promise written in another man's blood.

If you enjoy backing the underdog, the first book in The Man Called Kelly Series won't disappoint. You can get stuck into it right now at www.pdnelson.com/subscribe/.

The Proposition – released October 2019.

Short Synopsis

No man can predict his future if he doesn't have a past.

After a smugglers plane encounters a tropical monsoon in the middle of the South China Sea, suddenly it disappears off the radar. As the sole survivor, Jack Kelly's life as he once knew it was about to change forever—and not for the better. With a $100,000 'kill on sight' contract still waiting to be cashed, soon he will need a new identity—and it didn't matter whose.

A desperate man will clutch at any straw, and when Travis Chivres receives the timely diagnosis of his wife's brain tumour, time was fast running out to locate his now-missing son to collect on her family estate. Then, while in Bangkok, he meets a man that could provide a possible solution.

Together, can these two complete strangers pull-off what sounds like the perfect plan? Will Kelly still end up paying the ultimate price or can he find a way to right the wrongs from a tortured and violent past he chose to leave behind?

The second book in The Man Called Kelly Series is a fast-paced life adventure about one man's journey to reconnect with his unknown family that might have you reaching for the tissues.

The Book of Remedies – released December 2019.

Acknowledgements

They say truth can be stranger than fiction. In writing fiction, an author needs to fall back on his or her own life experiences. Events that have helped shape a life. Some of my characters are based on real people. The events I write about are often true with a slice of literary licence thrown in—of course. Storytelling is as ancient as time itself, and it is a real privilege to be able to write and then have other people read that story. I can only wish our cherished relationship continues with the fourth book in the Man Called Kelly Series.

About the author

Phillip Nelson was born and raised in the Snowy Mountains on the east coast of Australia. At 16, with just his Kawasaki Z-900 he left home for the final time with a head full of bad ideas and an attitude to match. The harsh realities of gang life living on the streets of Sydney and Melbourne was a steep learning curve that ended the day some crazed meth-head bikie poked a shotgun under his chin and pulled the trigger. Saved by a dud cartridge, he needed a total re-evaluation of his life—a Plan B.

He spent time working in the hospitality industry, then as a part-time deckhand on a rock lobster boat before becoming a backup drummer in a band until he settled into delivering on-site Workplace Assessment and Training courses throughout Western Australia.

People who live in the Land Down Under are great travellers through necessity, and after continually tweaking with a fifteen-year-old idea for his first novel, Phillip Nelson jumped on a plane and headed to Europe. He now lives in a small, culturally diverse Thailand village with two very spoilt Soi dogs and a pond full of disappearing walking fish. If he hasn't got a rod in his hand, then he is normally writing, and with three books completed in 'The Man Called Kelly Series,' *The School of Hard Knocks* was his debut novel released in 2019.

Contact the author

E-mail: mailto:philnelson@pdnelson.com